FREE WOMEN IN THE PAMPAS

María Rosa Lojo. Photo by Rafael Yohai.

Free Women in the Pampas

A Novel about Victoria Ocampo

María Rosa Lojo

Edited and translated by Norman Cheadle

McGill-Queen's University Press

Montreal & Kingston · London · Chicago

English-language edition © McGill-Queen's University Press 2021

ISBN 978-0-2280-0860-6 (cloth)
ISBN 978-0-2280-0861-3 (paper)
ISBN 978-0-2280-0987-0 (ePDF)
ISBN 978-0-2280-0988-7 (ePUB)

Legal deposit fourth quarter 2021
Bibliothèque nationale du Québec

Printed in Canada on acid-free paper that is 100% ancient forest free (100%
post-consumer recycled), processed chlorine free

This book has been published with the help of a grant from the Canadian Federation for the Humanities and Social Sciences, through the Awards to Scholarly
Publications Program, using funds provided by the Social Sciences and Humanities Research Council of Canada. Work published within the framework of
"Sur" Translation Support Program of the Ministry of Foreign Affairs, International Trade and Worship of the Argentine Republic. Obra editada en el marco
del Programa "Sur" de Apoyo a las Traducciones del Ministerio de Relaciones
Exteriores, Comercio Internacional y Culto de la República Argentina.

Funded by the   Financé par le
Government   gouvernement   Canada   Canada Council   Conseil des arts
of Canada   du Canada   for the Arts   du Canada

We acknowledge the support of the Canada Council for the Arts.

Nous remercions le Conseil des arts du Canada de son soutien.

Every effort has been made to locate the copyright holders of the materials
included in this book, in some cases to no avail.

Library and Archives Canada Cataloguing in Publication

Title: Free women in the pampas : a novel about Victoria Ocampo / María Rosa Lojo ; edited
    and translated by Norman Cheadle.
Other titles: Libres del sur. English
Names: Lojo de Beuter, María Rosa, author. | Cheadle, Norman, 1953– editor, translator.
Description: English-language edition. | Translation of: Libres del sur : una novela sobre
    Victoria Ocampo. | Includes bibliographical references and index.
Identifiers: Canadiana (print) 20210248483 | Canadiana (ebook) 20210248645 | ISBN
    9780228008613 (paper) | ISBN 9780228008606 (cloth) | ISBN 9780228009870 (ePDF) | ISBN
    9780228009887 (ePUB)
Subjects: LCSH: Ocampo, Victoria, 1890–1979—Fiction. | LCSH: Authors, Argentine—20th
    century—Biography—Fiction. | LCSH: Women intellectuals—Argentina—Biography—
    Fiction. | LCSH: Feminists—Argentina—Biography—Fiction. | LCSH: Argentina—Intellectual
    life—20th century—Fiction. | LCGFT: Biographical fiction.

Classification: LCC PQ7798.22.O352 L5313 2021 | DDC 863/.64—dc23

This book was typeset by True to Type in 11/14 Minion

Contents

Acknowledgments

The support of the following organizations is gratefully acknowledged:

- The Awards to Scholarly Publications Program of the Federation for the Humanities and Social Sciences, funded by the Social Sciences and Humanities Research Council of Canada
- The Sur Translation Support Program, sponsored by the Argentine Republic's Ministry of Foreign Affairs, International Trade and Worship

In translating María Rosa Lojo's novel *Las libres del Sur*, I have benefitted immensely from the generous and unstinting collaboration of the author herself. Our continual and often far-reaching discussions by email have inspired and fostered a clearer understanding and rendering of the text.

My warm thanks go to the editorial team at MQUP, and to two editors in particular. Mark Abley launched this project before his retirement from the publishing industry. Richard Ratzlaff then took over at the helm and expertly navigated choppy waters in uncertain times to lead us safely to port.

Juan Javier Negri, director of the Fundación Sur, helped in several crucial ways to provide this book with illustrations, for which I express my sincere gratitude.

I also express my appreciation to the two anonymous readers commissioned by MQUP for their comments on the draft manuscript and their many valuable suggestions.

Very special thanks go to Jane McWhinney, who copy-edited the manuscript at an uncommonly deep critical level and offered many astute suggestions that made for significant improvements.

Note to the Reader

This edition is an annotated translation of *Las libres del Sur* (2004) (literally: Free Women of the South), a novel by María Rosa Lojo. The novel was written for general, contemporary readers interested in the historical figure of Victoria Ocampo and the role played by women in the extraordinarily brilliant cultural history of twentieth-century Argentina. The novel stands on its own. It can be read with enjoyment without consulting either the introduction or the endnotes. A glossary of Spanish terms is provided at the end of the book for the reader's convenience.

The introduction and endnotes may be perused at will. They provide contextual information about María Rosa Lojo, Victoria Ocampo, and other women and men, as well as Argentine history, politics, and culture. The notes also give supplemental information about the various international figures with whom Victoria Ocampo came in contact, along with other Argentine names and events mentioned in the novel.

Introduction

When María Rosa Lojo was awarded one of Argentina's most prestigious literary prizes in 2018, it was the crowning honour of her extraordinary dual career as a creative writer and scholarly researcher.[1] In reality, these two strands, creativity and academic investigation, have always been closely intertwined in Lojo's voluminous production. Her creative work crosses several genres – poetry, short story, novel – and often intermingles them, as observed by Marcela Crespo Buiturón, no doubt the foremost expert on María Rosa Lojo.[2] Likewise, the concerns of Lojo's academic work are never far from the themes of her narrative fiction; her scholarly research is crucial to many of her novels, which in numerous cases, such as this novel, blend fiction and the historical essay.

Three broad thematic axes may be discerned in Lojo's novelistic oeuvre: the Galician-Spanish migration to Argentina; feminism and gender relations; and Argentine history. Each of these capacious categories in turn ramifies into a cluster of related themes. Celtic-Galician culture, exile, travel, and intercultural encounters are all directly related to Lojo's Galician family background.[3] Related to feminism are women's contributions to national literature and the public sphere, as well as their experience of denial and frustration. Historical themes include both the internecine violence and the role of indigenous peoples in Argentina's emergence as a nation-state, along with the paradoxes of "civilization" and "barbarism." All three strands of thematic concerns cross-fertilize; all three inform Lojo's many novels with varying shades of emphasis, various shapes of overlap. The novel now in the reader's hands is no exception; in the case

of *Las libres del Sur* (Free Women of the South), rendered in this translation as *Free Women in the Pampas*, the Galician theme is present, but
women and history are primary.

Women and freedom, plus the quasi-mythical *Sur* or South – roughly
equivalent in the Argentine national imaginary to Canada's "idea of
North"[4] – are this novel's salient themes. However, this novel also partici-
pates in what Antonio Esteves, in discussing three of Lojo's many historically themed novels,[5] has called her abiding awareness of, and response to,
the "social demand for historical understanding" (99). Heeding that social
demand, Lojo's *La pasión de los nómades* (1994) (*Passionate Nomads* in
Brett Sanders's 2014 English translation) is a metafictional rewriting of the
Argentine classic *A Visit to the Ranquel Indians* (1870). *Passionate Nomads*
is grounded in detailed historical and geographical documentation but
reimagines a more inclusive understanding that includes the Ranquel
people's perspective on that cultural encounter. *Passionate Nomads*, one
might say, updates Mansilla's classic intercultural encounter.

A Visit to the Ranquel Indians was written by Lucio V. Mansilla. But his
older sister, Eduarda, was an equally talented writer who, though less
famous, was likely the braver and more audacious of the two, as Lucio
himself admitted (Lojo, Introduction to *Lucía Miranda*, by Eduarda
Mansilla, 14). Eduarda Mansilla is the protagonist of Lojo's *Una mujer de
fin de siglo* (1999) (*A Woman at Century's End*), a novel that imaginatively resuscitates this important writer, whose work had been temporar-
ily consigned to oblivion. Not only is it a matter of redressing a literary
injustice committed against Eduarda Mansilla and women's writing; such
erasures harm the well-being of the nation as whole by maiming its historical memory.

Free Women in the Pampas is the third of Lojo's historically based novels tackled by Esteves. Before we turn to it, however, a fourth must be
added to the series. *Todos éramos hijos* (2014) (*We Were All Sons and
Daughters*) is a unique testimonial contribution to the vast "literature of
memory" produced by Argentine writers and artists in their multi-
pronged effort to address the national trauma of the last dictatorship
(1976–1983). A work of autofiction, the novel nevertheless maintains continuity with the earlier novels by remaining faithful to that social demand
for historical understanding – the ethical imperative to serve the national
community's historical memory, this time by foregrounding more recent

events whose repercussions still shudder through contemporary Argentine society.[6]

FREE WOMEN IN THE PAMPAS:
A NOVEL ABOUT VICTORIA OCAMPO

Free *women*? Who are those women? The novel's original subtitle gives only a partial answer. It is hardly surprising that an author interested in the mentioned themes should choose to write a novel about Victoria Ocampo, that indomitable woman who, *Against the Wind and the Tide* – as Doris Meyer titled her fundamental and indispensable biography – made herself a central figure in the Argentine cultural scene for several crucial decades. Founding the literary and cultural journal *Sur* (South) in 1931, directing and financing it herself until its demise in 1970, Ocampo battled tirelessly to become a writer, translator, and cultural intervenor in the literary and artistic milieu of Argentina, a role that she played with sufficient intellectual strength and savoir-faire as to redound to her credit throughout Latin America, then Europe, and finally even in North America. Fluent since childhood in Spanish, French, and English, Ocampo felt as much at home in Paris, London, or New York as in her native Buenos Aires; her career was one of cultural translation between Europe and the Americas.[7] The journal *Sur* served as a bridge between the continents. If traffic on the bridge tended to move more in one direction than another (from Europe to South America), it is also true that the literature of Argentina and Latin America came to the attention of international literary culture – whose centre as late as the 1950s or '60s was still Paris – thanks in large part to *Sur*.[8]

Contrary to what one might expect, however, María Rosa Lojo's novelistic recreation of Victoria Ocampo's career ends precisely at the moment when her protagonist embarks on the *Sur* enterprise that was to make her famous. The novel traces instead the decisive years, from 1924 to 1931, in which Ocampo strove to achieve intellectual autonomy and become a writer. That personal struggle was to become historically significant; as Tania Diz has remarked, Ocampo's entry into the intellectual field in Argentina marks a point of inflection, defines a "before" and an "after" (327b). As late as the 1920s, women writers, if they were not attacked directly, were shoehorned by (male) critical discourse into a few stereotypes or, in Diz's analysis, into aspects of a single myth: the *poetisa*, the poetess who innocuously, irrelevantly, expresses her sentimentality in verses meant for consumption by other sentimental women. A woman aspiring to write seriously, such as the rebellious Alfonsina Storni (1892–1938), had to be contained by other cultural clichés: the poetess of love, the kindly little schoolmarm, the intelligent but ugly woman, the unloved suicide (Storni did in fact end her own life, not because she was "unloved" but because she was facing terminal cancer) (Diz, 322a). Even Storni's personal friend Roberto Giusti felt the need to explain the strength of her poetry by describing it as "virile," suggesting that it showed the "sharp definition" and "intelligence" of a man's writing; in sum, that Storni was not merely *una poetisa* but *un poeta* (qtd. by Diz, 322a) – the masculine article denoting, of course, the "real thing" rather than a mere "thing-ette." Real poets were men; a woman could at most be a poetess.[9]

Storni's attackers found such gender-bending as hers to be monstrous and threatening to the moral fibre of society.[10] Women in Argentine literature had traditionally been made to represent political or ideological ideals; the beautiful and submissive Amalia, for whom José Mármol titled his 1851 nation-building novel, is neither heroine nor even actor, but an inert symbol. Or women were cast as passive helpmeets to a masculine hero; witness the nameless *china* (woman) in the Argentine epic poem *Martín Fierro* (1872). Alternatively, they were the fallen women of *Sin rumbo* (1885) (Without Direction) by Eugenio Cambaceres, or pathetic victims such as Nacha Regules, eponymous heroine of the socially engaged novel by Manuel Gálvez published as late as 1916. In the popular imaginary, the movie *La costurerita que dio aquel mal paso* (1926) (The Little Seamstress Who Took a False Step), inspired by Evaristo Carriego's 1913 sentimental sonnet, inaugurated the stereotype, reproduced in many tangos, of the suburban working-class girl gone astray. No wonder, then, that a woman who dared to assume intellectual agency was experienced by men (and not only men) as a threat.

Victoria Ocampo (1890–1979) started out with many more social advantages than Alfonsina Storni (a single mother from a provincial, lower-middle-class background similar to that of Gabriela Mistral).[11] Ocampo was the privileged eldest daughter of one of the great landowning families in Argentina, the quasi-aristocratic *estanciero* class – the "cattle barons" in Meyer's apt translation – whose excessive wealth put them among the now-proverbial one-percent. "Riche comme un Argentin," the French used to say in the early twentieth century, at once contemptuous and envious of the moneyed Argentines who treated Paris like a "suburb of Buenos Aires," as the fictionalized Ocampo half-facetiously remarks in María Rosa Lojo's novel. But those advantages had their downside. As Victoria's friend Waldo Frank once remarked: "This fabulous creature [had] three curses upon her head – the curse of beauty, of intelligence, and of wealth" (*Memoirs*, 165). The kind of vicious attack that a woman of her gifts could and did suffer is illustrated in the novel (chapter 2) by an allusion to the pulp fiction of Juan José de Soiza Reilly, in which an upper-class mother, ostensibly emulating the example of Victoria Ocampo, neglects and heinously abuses her own children.[12]

Of course, insults from trolls were not likely to impress the proud scion of the Ocampo family. Her real antagonists, her worthy opponents, were at the high end of the spectrum of literary, artistic, and philosophical culture, both national and international. Victoria's male friends were many, the relationships often complicated. As the reader will see, her interactions with several men of stature constitute a series of stations along Ocampo's zigzagging road to becoming a writer and intellectual: the Indian poet Rabindranath Tagore (1861–1941), the Spanish philosopher José Ortega y Gasset (1883–1955), the Baltic-German cultural geographer Hermann von Keyserling (1880–1946), the bad-boy French writer Pierre Drieu La Rochelle (1893–1945). The plot of this *Bildungsroman* leads eventually to writer Waldo Frank (1889–1967), the man who enjoins her – friend to friend, equal to equal, American to fellow *americana* – to start up an America-centric literary and cultural journal. From naïve devotion and hero-worship, Victoria progresses to a hard-won intellectual autonomy and, assuming agency with Frank's moral support, embarks on the enterprise that will become the celebrated journal *Sur*.[13]

This capsule summary of Victoria Ocampo's formative years is, however, only one aspect of María Rosa Lojo's novel, as its title – free *women*, in the plural – implies. Lojo, who is also a highly accomplished scholar, sees her novelistic work as a kind of "laboratory of critique and creation." In her article "Victoria Ocampo, personaje de novela. Un laboratorio de crítica y creación," she explains how and why she wrote *Las libres del Sur*: in order to counter the extreme representations of Ocampo, both negative and uncritically positive. To do so, she invented a second, entirely fictional protagonist. This "deuteragonist" – to use Lojo's own term – is Carmen Brey, a young, educated woman who has migrated to Buenos Aires from Galicia, the northwestern province of Spain. She is part of a newly emerging middle class in Buenos Aires, composed largely of immigrants or their children, and she represents a new class of woman, the well-educated professional who can make her own living. Trained in philology, she works as a translator, but her critical intelligence makes her the harbinger of a new generation of women writers – such as María Rosa Lojo herself – who will irrupt powerfully into Argentine literature in the 1960s and beyond. It is tempting, then, to see the character Carmen Brey as a sort of fictional prosthetic device by means of which the author María Rosa Lojo can project her own consciousness into the past; Carmen's critical eye sees the problems of Argentina – political, cultural, social, economic, literary – in a way that, *grosso modo*, anticipates the views of her author. Carmen's sympathetic yet subtly critical appraisal of Victoria Ocampo's virtues and foibles is especially acute.[14] Nevertheless, Carmen protagonizes a story of her own, which is clearly not her author's autobiography. And it is a story that continues to unfold in Lojo's latest novel, *Solo queda saltar* (2018) (One Has Only to Make the Leap).

Another of the novel's free women is the writer, translator, and political activist María Rosa Oliver (1898–1977). Social peer and contemporary of Ocampo, Oliver was temperamentally very different from her friend, though by no means her intellectual inferior. Physically disabled by polio at the age of ten, María Rosa Oliver precociously developed a strong sense of social justice and injustice, and in the thirties became a Communist, an orientation that would eventually alienate her from Ocampo. However, they shared many literary and artistic interests, and their common feminism united them. In 1936, in response to a retrograde bill of law that would have set women's legal status back decades, Oliver co-founded the Union of Argentine Women; Victoria, recently returned from abroad, was elected president.[15] And a very effective president she was, until she resigned two years later, displeased by the Communists' influence in the union's affairs (Meyer, 140). The two women also collaborated on the editorial board of *Sur* – "Victoria's magazine," as Oliver came to think of it in private (*La vida cotidiana*, 275). Oliver was the more lucid regarding class structure and social injustice. If Ocampo was a fearless champion of women's independence who never deeply questioned her own class privilege, Oliver's concern for women's rights was part and parcel of larger socio-political concerns.[16]

Ocampo's admiring review-essay on Oliver's memoir *Mundo, mi casa* (World, My House) beautifully illustrates the relationship between the two women. Ocampo writes with the generosity of a loyal friend. She corroborates in detail the accuracy of Oliver's memories of their common social *habitus*, incisively analyses the problem of rendering childhood memories in writing, and then comments on a significant passage of Oliver's book. There, Oliver recalls a Christmas dinner celebrated when she was still convalescing from the polio attack. Her father had invited the whole neighbourhood to the feast, including the poor people. The memoir relates how the child María Rosa Oliver keenly observes the behaviour of all the guests and, in the story as told by her adult self, becomes disturbingly aware of poverty and social disparities. Ocampo could easily have commented on the "constructedness" of this memory – the superimposition of adult values on childhood recollections – since it was a problem she had long studied and reflected upon. Instead, she attempts to draw a parallel with her own childhood. Our Christmases had "poor kids" too, she claims, and then goes on to evoke Franky, the son of their English butler. The handsome, self-confident, blond, blue-eyed boy was the same age as she was, but refused to play with girls. Victoria not only envied the "poor" child Franky, but was also "hopelessly in love with him." His rejection "hurt and humiliated me," she writes. "It never occurred to me that I was in a privileged situation vis-à-vis this boy, but rather quite the opposite. The notion of injustice came from elsewhere, but let's not go there now" ("Recuerdos sobre recuerdos," 74–5).

The self-representation that emerges from this single paragraph in Ocampo's review-essay, written late in life, cannot be discussed here in all its complexity. Let us simply note the obvious. To confuse the "poverty" of the arrogant, well-fed son of the English butler with the grinding poverty of downtown tenement dwellers, which Oliver describes without sensationalist rhetoric, seems breathtakingly disingenuous. As does Ocampo's claim that she was unaware of her privileged situation, even though, as she openly confesses, she knew perfectly well that she could have invoked her parents' authority to force the disdainful English boy to treat her nicely. Nevertheless, what looks here like an embarrassing display of bad faith stems mainly from emotional largesse; the clumsy parallel she draws is motivated by a sincere attempt at a personal rapprochement and a wish to reaffirm the bonds of a friendship frayed by political differences. Is it supreme pride, or selfless generosity, that makes Ocampo so heedless of how much she is revealing about her own foibles? For Victoria Ocampo was quite capable of penetrating and pitiless self-analysis.

María Rosa Oliver plays only a secondary role in the novel's action, but her ethical and intellectual presence is almost as pervasive as that of Victoria Ocampo, albeit in a subtler fashion. The novel's dual epigraphs are drawn from the writings of one and the other; likewise, the two most important epigraphs to chapter 4, "1929–1931: Free Women of the South." In this sense, Oliver shares with Ocampo an "architextual" role, as Gérard Genette defined the function of epigraphs, which thematically frame this novel. Furthermore, it is highly significant that when Carmen Brey feels overwhelmed by her personal troubles she seeks emotional support not from Victoria but from María Rosa Oliver.[17] An understated but deep alliance develops between her and Carmen. And, toward the end of the novel, as Carmen vividly expresses her joy upon learning that King Alfonso XIII had abdicated, opening the way for the advent of the Second Spanish Republic, her feelings echo those of this trusted friend (Oliver, *Mi fe es el hombre*, 57–8).

Historical events in Argentina after the year 1931 – when a military coup ended the presidency of Hipóltico Yrigoyen, initiating the "Infamous Decade," and when the first issue of *Sur* came out – are beyond the temporal frame of this novel, but they cannot and are not meant to be occluded from the reader's awareness. The novel draws on many textual materials written in subsequent decades (as discussed below in the research notes). The most decisive political event to mark twentieth-century Argentine history, the presidency of Juan Domingo Perón (1946–55), is present only in germinal form in the character of a ten-year-old girl called María Eva Ibarguren, who would grow up to be Evita Perón.

Every reader who holds this book in their hands surely knows who Evita was – or rather *is*, such is the enduring quality of her myth. As one scholar has put it, if Victoria Ocampo was the second most talked-about woman in twentieth-century Argentina, María Eva Duarte de Perón (1919–1952) was the first (Greenberg, 131). The extremes of love and hatred that she inspired, to judge by their rhetorical expressions, also surpass those elicited by Ocampo. Victoria got called a lot of names (upper-class snob, the Anaconda of the Pampas, *persona non grata*, among others), but no one ever called her *la Yegua* (the Nag) or hissed between clenched teeth the epithet *esa mujer* (that woman) in allusion to Eva Perón.[18] Nor was Victoria ever called a saint, even by her admirers, in direct contrast to *Santa Evita*.[19] In the national imaginary, the two female figures stand as opposing icons on either side of *la grieta*, as Argentines call the abyssal crack that yawns between two antagonistic visions for the nation: the popular-national and the (neo)liberal-patrician. During the 1920s and beyond, families like that of Eva Ibarguren were invisible to Victoria Ocampo, not even remotely on her radar. But by the mid-1940s, that blissful ignorance was no longer possible. Doris Meyer recounts succinctly a near meeting of the "two most influential Latin American women of [the twentieth] century":

> [T]hey were antagonists, though they never exchanged a word. Surely they recognized each other that one time their paths crossed in front of an elevator in a Buenos Aires clinic … So *that* was "Evita," thought Victoria, and all she could see before her was an unscrupulously ambitious young woman who had proclaimed herself the fanatical disciple of the demagogue [President Juan Perón]. (130)

If Evita's devotion to her husband and her cause was "fanatical," Victoria's hatred of Peronism was equally so. Too visible a symbol of the oligarchy – "a thorn in the dictator's side" in Meyer's heroic version (153) – Ocampo was finally jailed for twenty-six days in 1953 (8 May–2 June). Evita had died of cancer less than a year earlier (26 July 1952), shortly after her husband was swept to his second mandate as president in the elections of November 1951, the high-water mark of the "first Peronism" (1946–55). Those two successive events – his exceedingly popular wife's death, followed by his regime's ham-handed blunder in jailing Victoria Ocampo – seemed to signal the beginning of the decline in Perón's fortunes. In 1955 a military coup sent him into exile.[20]

Victoria Ocampo and Eva Perón, two exceptional woman protagonists in Argentine history, are both paradoxical, even contradictory figures. As Janet Greenberg puts it, Ocampo was "a woman divided between allegiance to her sex and a conflicting attachment to the privileges of her class

... a self-avowed feminist who also championed the patriarchal values of the ruling class" (133).[21] Conversely, Eva Perón insisted on the conventional roles for women as self-sacrificing mothers and wives, and devoted herself with religious fervour to her husband and president, apparently affirming traditional patriarchy. But there was another key element in her mystique and sheer excess: her objective, in her own words, was "to serve Perón and the People" (qtd. by Rosano, 53) – the "people" as opposed to the oligarchy (or the one-percent, the elite, or any other analogous term, as in all populist discourse). Her devotion was not really to "The Man"; it was to the people for whom the man Perón was ultimately only the "empty signifier," to borrow Ernesto Laclau's term,[22] whose "signified," or meaning, was embodied by Evita herself. Absent his wife, and the emotional power she mobilized and parlayed into political power, Perón's days as president were numbered.

Victoria Ocampo, for her part, once she had launched the journal *Sur*, also had a sense of mission, but one diametrically opposed to Evita's cause. What Peronists called the "oligarchy," Ocampo considered to be the Argentine Nation itself. As John King observes: "For Victoria Ocampo, there was only one history in Argentina, that which had been forged by her family and friends, and which had to be defended against the mass movements of fascism and communism spawned by the late 1920s and early 1930s" (7). Her spiritual guide in this mission was Domingo Faustino Sarmiento (1811–1888), ideological father of Argentine modernity, who in his classic foundational book *Facundo, o civilización y barbarie* (1845) (Facundo, or Civilization and Barbarism) laid out the blueprint for national development. For Sarmiento, the choice was stark: either "civilization" along French, British, and Anglo-North-American lines, or "barbarism," under which he lumped indigenous peoples, the gauchos, and the medieval sclerosis of Spanish colonial culture and institutions; the former was to be promoted, the latter suppressed. Nor was Victoria's sense of mission, once she had found it, lacking in mystical fervour. As her namesake Victoria Liendo writes in an extraordinarily rich and suggestive essay: "In Sarmiento she saw a spiritual father and in his patrician lineage the call to a mission whose sign had changed; she listened to that call with the same fervour with which Joan of Arc responded to the voice of God" ("Victoria Ocampo: una esnob para el desierto," 16).[23] Moreover, Sarmiento had close personal ties to the Ocampo family (Liendo, 28; King, 7). In fairness to

Ocampo, however, it must be noted that she did not share Sarmiento's racial prejudices; she had no strong feelings about which peoples should or should not be allowed to immigrate to Argentina. There was no bigotry in Victoria Ocampo; it is rather that she zealously believed in what we would today call the "cult of excellence" – especially in the arts, literature, architecture, design. Her mission, as Horan and Meyer write, quite without irony, was "culture with a [capital] C" (*This America of Ours*, 10–11).

It is against this historico-symbolic backdrop that Carmen Brey's fictional journey to Los Toldos becomes especially significant. Geographically, the opposition between the cozy and exclusive Family Pact of aristocratic Argentina and *la Argentina popular* maps approximately onto another division, one that cleaves the nation-state's territory: on the one hand, the opulent urban centre of Buenos Aires; on the other, the "wilderness," the deep hinterland where life was largely pre-modern. In Los Toldos, Carmen meets small-minded local officials and merchants, poor *gauchos* and *indios*, and Evita Ibarguren, who one day will champion those marginalized sectors of the nation. It is thanks to the spirited little girl Evita, illegitimate daughter of an abandoned single mother and a rich landowner, that Carmen finds what she is looking for. The trip becomes a life-changing experience for the independent-minded woman from Galicia. She learns much about the other, non-urban Argentina, about her family, and about herself.

Another feature that makes this journey to the interior so significant is that Carmen Brey's travelling companions are Leopoldo Marechal and Jorge Luis Borges. Few readers will fail to recognize the name of Borges; fewer, perhaps, will even have heard of Marechal, author of the great canonical novel *Adán Buenosayres* (1948). In the mid- to late 1920s, the two poets were at the heart of the avant-garde scene and collaborating in the journal *Martín Fierro* (1924–27). Over the thirties and early forties, the two friends drifted apart and eventually became enemies. Marechal became a Catholic nationalist and later one of the few intellectuals of prestige to embrace Peronism; Borges, increasingly anti-Catholic, became fanatically anti-Peronist (the one issue on which he and Ocampo were in perfect harmony). Throughout the Peronist years and beyond, in the eyes of the embattled literary establishment that was alienated by Peronism, Marechal came to be seen as enemy Number One (Fiorucci, 184n). His ostracism from the literary community became so extreme that up-and-coming young writers in the 1960s were surprised to learn that he was still alive. After 1946 Borges refused even to speak his name, and it is difficult to find Marechal's name in Ocampo's writings.[24] In short, the dyad Marechal-Borges likewise came to signify *la grieta*, the Great Divide in the cultural, social, and political life of the nation occasioned by the upheaval whose name was *peronismo*.

María Rosa Lojo's evocation, in her fictional laboratory, of this subsequently antagonistic couple as two flawed but enthusiastic and likeable friends – a "pair of duffers" (*papamoscas*) in the fictionalized Ocampo's estimation – is a means of reaching back to a moment when everything still seemed possible, even though deep divisions – one configuration of *la grieta* or another – have dogged Argentine history since the nineteenth-century civil war between Unitarians and Federalists. More important, perhaps, it is a gesture eloquent of Lojo's refusal to submit to either Scylla or Charybdis, to succumb to the pull of powerful ideological hatreds, to either endorse or condemn in its entirety one hegemonic formation or another. One among a handful of major Argentine critics to do so, Lojo has maintained this difficult position with integrity both in her scholarly writing and in her later fiction, notably in her autofictional novel *Todos éramos hijos* (We Were All Sons and Daughters), where Marechal and Borges are both given strong intertextual presence. This does not mean adopting a posture of empty "neutrality." Lojo does not shirk her duty as an intellectual to express her views on matters of public interest in Argentina's major newspapers – *La Nación, Página 12, Clarín*.

From another point of view, it is refreshing to see two of Argentina's greatest male writers, Marechal and Borges, irreverently reduced to a pair of incidentals, their status as warring national symbols comically deflated. No male hero-worship here. Instead, the laboratory that is the novel *Free Women in the Pampas* serves one writer (Lojo) as a site to re-imagine the struggles of another from an earlier generation (Ocampo). Making it clear there was never any question of adopting Ocampo as a model, Lojo outlines what it was in the "extraordinary pages of [Ocampo's] *Autobiografía*" that attracted her:

Victoria's oscillation between the subtleties of the Orient (Tagore) and the obstinate, stentorian Occidental narcissism of Count Keyserling, her permanent need for masculine approval, the search for teachers, the intimate insecurity beneath the carapace of her money and beauty, the late flowering of her hidden potential, her definitive choice for freedom. All these matters seemed to me profoundly representative of the "*género mujer*" and the psychological vicissitudes attendant upon the historical development of the female *gender* and the *genre* of women's writing.[25] Matters which involved me and could hardly leave me indifferent. (Victoria Ocampo, "Personaje de novela," 180–1)

Victoria Ocampo's arduous road to self-invention involves re-inventing, socio-psychologically, her gender and boldly exploring, on the literary plane, the form of its expression.

RESEARCH NOTES TO
FREE WOMEN IN THE PAMPAS

An immense amount of research and erudition supports the novel *Free Women in the Pampas*. In fact, aside from the fictional Carmen Brey and her story, very little of Lojo's text is invented whole-cloth. Most of what the historical characters say and do, down to the smallest detail, reproduces what they themselves have said or done, as recorded in their writings. This does not mean, of course, that the author has literally transcribed those textual materials; most often they are condensed, glossed, or otherwise re-interpreted. What follows is a skeletal guide to the novel's intertextual construction and a sample of useful secondary literature written in English. (For full details, see the Bibliography.)

Mention has already been made of María Rosa Oliver's memoirs. Of her autobiographical trilogy – *Mundo, mi casa: recuerdos de infancia* (1965); *La vida cotidiana* (1969); and *Mi fe es el hombre* (1981) – the second book, whose content overlaps the timeframe of the action of *Free Women in the Pampas*, is the most important to the novel. As far as I know, none of Oliver's work has yet been translated into English.

Of the many books on Eva Perón consulted by the novelist, the most useful was that of Alicia Dujovne Ortiz: her *Eva Perón, la biografía* (1995) (Eva Perón, the Biography) is very good on the details of her subject's childhood (personal email, 27 February 2020). Eva Perón's autobiographical texts, largely ghost-written in the last two years of her life, are both available in English translation: *Evita: Evita Perón Tells Her Own Story* and

In My Own Words. However, they are perhaps best approached through Marysa Navarro's brief essay "Of Sparrows and Condors: The Autobiography of Eva Perón." Navarro had previously co-written, in English, a full-fledged biography of *Eva Perón* (1980).

Lojo's most important sources are probably the writings of Victoria Ocampo herself. For the newcomer to Ocampo's writing, a couple of bibliographical clarifications may help avoid some confusion. Ocampo's preferred literary mode was what she called the *testimonio*, a personal essay that is usually centred on an important cultural figure or matter of public interest.[26] The ten series of her *Testimonios* are formally distinct from the six volumes of her *Autobiografía*, even though the writing voice, style, and even the type of content are not radically different in the two bodies of work.

The *Testimonios* comprise an assortment of genres; many are articles originally published in *Sur* or elsewhere, but some are also the texts of public lectures or even letters. They are collected in ten "series" or volumes, published between 1931 and 1977.[27]

The *Autobiografías* were originally published in 1980, the year after Ocampo's death, by Editorial Sur (the journal *Sur*'s adjunct publishing enterprise since 1933). The six volumes were subtitled as follows: 1. *El archipiélago*; 2. *El imperio insular*; 3. *La rama de Salzburgo*; 4. *Viraje*; 5. *Versailles-Keyserling, Paris-Drieu*; 6. *Sur y Cía.* Then, in 2005 and 2006, the Fundación Victoria Ocampo republished the entire collection in only three volumes.[28]

Anglophone readers are fortunate that Victoria Ocampo has been the subject of a great deal of biographical and scholarly work written in English. María Rosa Lojo found two English-language biographies especially useful. Doris Meyer's *Against the Wind and the Tide* was the first biography of Ocampo to appear in any language. Written before Ocampo's death, it is extremely valuable, not only thanks to Meyer's scrupulous work but also because she had the benefit of Ocampo's active collaboration. By the same token, Ocampo's participation likely accounts for the book's shortcomings. Meyer claims in her Preface to have "pointed out Victoria's weaknesses as well as her strengths" (xi), but the young Meyer, quite understandably, was awed and deeply influenced by the powerful older woman, and her account reads like a monument to her hero. Meyer imbibes and uncritically internalizes Ocampo's extreme anti-Peronism, adopting an attitude that leads to a serious distortion in the way she represents the history of mid-twentieth-century Argentina. In fact, it is difficult to imagine how Meyer, whose intentions and scholarly integrity are beyond question, could have done otherwise, given the prevailing notion in the United States at that time, not only in the popular imagination but especially among the educated classes and the academy, that Peronism was the *criollo* version of Nazi-Fascism (Allison, 16). Fortunately, a corrective to such distorted notions is provided by the eminent Argentine-Israeli historian Raanan Rein, who demolishes the myth of the "Nazi-Fascist" Perón in the introductory pages of *Los muchachos peronistas judíos* (2015), recently translated under the title *Populism and Ethnicity: Peronism and the Jews of Argentina*. That said, a great virtue of Meyer's 1979 biography is that she provides fifteen English translations of Ocampo texts that find their echo in this novel. These include "Woman, Her Rights and Her Responsibilities," a key feminist text; "Fani" and "María de Maeztu,"[29] who show up as characters in the novel; and "Sarmiento's Gift," a short piece revealing the depth of Ocampo's personal and family ties to the great liberal ideologue.

Meyer offers further translational and editorial service when she teams up with Elizabeth Horan to collect and translate into English the complete correspondence between Gabriela Mistral (1889–1957) – the Chilean poet awarded the Nobel Prize in 1945 – and Victoria Ocampo. Gathered under the title *This America of Ours* (2003), those collected letters, along with the volume's introductory texts, provide a valuable complement to María Rosa Lojo's novel, for the thematic resonance is striking:

> Gabriela Mistral and Victoria Ocampo were freer than most Latin American women, but they still used the privacy of their letters to treasure their relatedness to one another, to authorize their own American identities, and to construct a corresponding space in which to nurture a better future for their America. (Horan and Meyer, ix)

The correspondence between Mistral and Ocampo began with distant courtesy in 1926, but their epistolary friendship gained warmth and intensity during the 1930s, after Ocampo had launched *Sur*. As documented by Horan and Meyer, the friendship between those two international Latin American female figures was significant for Ocampo's assumption of her

American identity. The two women were born only a year apart, but into very different social backgrounds (provincial, middle-class Chile *vs* aristocratic Buenos Aires). Two quite different visions of Latin America met in fruitful dialogue through the long friendship between the two correspondents, for their feminine solidarity and genuine commitment to a civil *americanismo* was proof against their considerable ideological differences. Thus any reader who longs for a "sequel" to *Free Women in the Pampas* could do worse than to proceed straight to the Preface and Introduction of *This America of Ours*.[30]

The other Victoria Ocampo biography from which María Rosa Lojo has amply drawn is by the Indian author Ketaki Kushari Dyson, *In Your Blossoming Flower-Garden: Rabindranath Tagore and Victoria Ocampo* (1988; latest reprint 2017). Ostensibly about the Tagore-Ocampo relationship (on which she is outstanding), Kushari Dyson's biography ranges over Ocampo's entire life and oeuvre, and offers a wealth of incisive observations based on archival research. She reproduces the original text, for example, of many letters between Ocampo and Tagore, and Ocampo and Leonard Elmhirst. Not least of Dyson's strong points is that her book enters into critical dialogue with Meyer's biography.[31]

Among other excellent English-language texts of relevance, in addition to Janet Greenberg's article (mentioned above), is Sylvia Molloy's "The Theatrics of Reading: Body and Book in Victoria Ocampo," which in 1991 took Ocampo studies to a new level; Molloy is especially insightful on Ocampo's frustrated theatrical vocation in relation to her voracious reading and her "obsessive preoccupation with self-representation" (60). Parts of Amy Kaminsky's *Argentina: Stories for a Nation* (2008) are especially germane as well. The first chapter, "Bartered Butterflies," is an intelligent essay on Ocampo's relationship with Virginia Woolf (absent from Lojo's novel). Chapter 5, "Victoria Ocampo and the Keyserling Effect," provides a useful complement to Lojo's novelistic version of Victoria's vexed experience with the count. Francine Masiello's *Between Civilization and Barbarism: Women, Nation, and Literary Culture in Modern Argentina* (1992) places Victoria Ocampo (among many other women writers) in historical perspective. In this sweeping essay on "the relation between women and culture in [Argentina] from the early nineteenth century, the period when a secularized postcolonial world began to take definition, through the 1930s" (4), the figure of Ocampo looms large.

María Rosa Lojo herself has devoted much scholarly attention to Victoria Ocampo in relation to her nineteenth-century literary women forebears such as Eduarda Mansilla (1834–1892). Overshadowed in the canon by her brother Lucio (author of the famous *A Visit to the Ranquel Indians* [1870]), Eduarda and her work have been brought out of the shadows by Lojo and her research team.[32] Ocampo and Mansilla have much in common: their aristocratic origins, their strong characters and intelligence, their trilingualism (Spanish-French-English), their social or family connections to both Sarmiento and Rosas. Like Victoria, Eduarda wrote first in French. Both were travellers, both were literary and cultural translators. The two women found ways to bridge the gap between the public and private, not only in life but in their writing. So compelling a figure was Eduarda Mansilla for Lojo that she wrote a novel about her, *Una mujer de fin de siglo* (1999) (A Woman at Century's End). Its epigraph, taken from Mansilla's book about her travels in the United States (*Recuerdos de viaje*), would have won the hearts of Victoria Ocampo and her friend Waldo Frank: "The American woman practises individual freedom like none other in the world, and seems to have a great deal of *self reliance*" (qtd. in Lojo, *Una mujer*, 13; the English words "self reliance" [without hyphen] are in the original). In another sense, however, Eduarda anticipates not Victoria but rather a different sort of free woman of the south, María Rosa Oliver. For, as Lojo points out, Eduarda Mansilla was the first to write about the injustice suffered by the subaltern sectors, in particular the gauchos ("Genealogías femeninas," 468); Oliver is her heir in the realm of social justice.

This same study of the "big picture" of women's writing over the life of the nation produces at least one finding that may surprise readers. Women writers such as Eduarda Mansilla and her contemporaries Juana Manuela Gorriti (1818–1892) and Juana Paula Manso (1819–1975), writes Lojo, "did not consider themselves *outsiders* in the incipient national tradition. They entered it as co-founders" ("Genealogías," 481). The first half of the twentieth century brought a setback for women in the public sphere, "a prolonged cone of shadow" for the voice of women writers (471), which lasted until the second half of the century. Victoria Ocampo, in certain respects, was born into a situation of less freedom vis-à-vis her forebears, with greater obstacles, outer and inner, to overcome. Whereas Mansilla could confidently and without inhibition critique her friend

Sarmiento, Ocampo had to strive mightily to free herself of male hero-worship and claim the right to a public voice. On the other hand, if Mansilla criticized Sarmiento's civilization/barbarism thesis to the point of writing "almost an anti-*Facundo*" (470), Ocampo accepted his basic program as gospel. She was unable to step beyond the ideological shadow cast by the patriarchs of her caste, to question those "wrathful sentences" scrawled by Sarmiento "across the manly sky" (Marechal, *Adam Buenosayres*, 10). María Rosa Lojo's deep historical perspective helps us understand the conditions of Ocampo's struggle, its degree of success and its failings.[33]

Bibliographical considerations have led us to the nineteenth century, and thus to the historical allusion (and yet another intertext) embedded in the original novel's title. In 1839 a group of major landowners in the south of Buenos Aires Province rebelled against a war tax that Juan Manuel de Rosas, governor of Buenos Aires, was attempting to impose. Ten years later Esteban Echeverría published "Insurrección del Sud," a propaganda piece set to verse portraying the episode as an idealistic insurrection by (Unitarian) "free men" against (Federalist) "tyranny."[34] Hence, the phrase *los libres del Sur*, free men of the South: a tendentious glorification of a rather inglorious, self-interested revolt against the government by powerful *estancieros*, most of whom had in fact been supporting Rosas as long as he guaranteed their interests (Gelman, 48–9). *Las libres del Sur* – free women of the South – is the obverse of that dubious honorific imposed by the eventual winners of the long struggle between Unitarians and Federalists that structured nineteenth-century Argentine politics and history. Cutting across the ideological mystifications fomented by rival gangs of males, *las libres del Sur* resignifies the phrase, leaving behind the tawdry triumphalism of the original. The freedom to which those Argentine women aspired, and continue to aspire, was never meant to be gained at the expense of another's freedom and well-being.

Moreover, the idea of South in turn undergoes a subtle transformation, as readers will appreciate when they follow Carmen Brey on her journey south from Buenos Aires in the company of Borges, author of the famous short story "Sur." The machismo and Eurocentricity adhering to the quasi-transcendental South will be gently put aside, without violence to the idea's beauty and grandeur, without angry disenchantment. A more inclusive idea of South is gradually adumbrated throughout that adventure, perhaps most clearly when Carmen, the woman from far away across the sea, finds herself greeted by a voice addressing her in the Mapuche language as *lamnguen*, sister.

The original title, *Las libres del Sur*, then, imaginatively restores an interrupted continuity from the literary women of the previous century – Mansilla, Gorriti, Manso – to the women writing in the first decades of the twentieth century who, like Victoria Ocampo, were deprived of the chance to stand on the shoulders of the female authors who had gone before them. The novel is not only about a key period in the life and times of Victoria Ocampo; it is an invitation to imagine Ocampo's career as a vital link between succeeding generations of talented women writers in the South. Ocampo's appropriation of the "idea of South" was a bold move, even if her journal *Sur* was not as "southern" as it could have been. Nevertheless, when Victoria dared to scratch her own sentences on the public slate, across Sarmiento's "manly sky," she was repeating, almost unknowingly, the gesture of her feminine forebears, helping to cleanse the slate of opprobrious masculinity, and preparing the way for an irrepressible upsurge of women's literary talent from the mid-century up to the present day.

This novel about Victoria Ocampo vividly recreates the headstrong young woman's passionate encounters with some of the best minds of her time – or at least some of the most internationally influential – as well as with their male egos. The ups and downs of the drama, at times heroic, at times comic, even farcical, are framed by the gentler story of her witness, Carmen Brey, who carries within her the seeds of that feminine upsurge. For the English-language reader, it is hard to imagine a better introduction to Victoria Ocampo and what she has meant in the history of Argentine literature and culture.

TRANSLATION, NOTES, GLOSSARY

The agile, deceptively simple style of María Rosa Lojo's prose masks the immense erudition informing the novel. The narrative is quite transparent, and the reader is encouraged to read it through without resorting to the endnotes. The notes have three basic, overlapping functions. They document the original sources of textual materials, provide contextual information, and occasionally offer supplementary commentary. Nevertheless, the text of the novel in itself is self-explanatory.

Lojo often translates from extant English-language correspondence, such as the Ocampo-Tagore and Ocampo-Elmhirst letters. In such cases,

I have simply reproduced the original text (usually provided by Kushari Dyson), with all its idiosyncrasies, rather than retranslate from the Spanish. This has been done without altering, for example, Elmhirst's idiosyncratic punctuation and spelling (such as his anglicization of the name Fani as Fanny, or his use of the ampersand for "and").

The translation's punctuation and formatting adhere in general to the protocols of the original text. Dialogue is indicated by an introductory dash (–), in the dual interest of textual fidelity and the suppression, as far as possible, of unsightly "perverted commas," as James Joyce called quotation marks. The novel makes frequent literal or near-literal quotations from a variety of texts, a procedure usually signalled by the use of italics; the source of such quotations will be found in the notes.

Certain words and usages in Spanish, such as the names of flora and fauna indigenous to South America, can be difficult to translate. For example, the *cina-cina* – a species of flowering tree often used in hedges – may be called "Jerusalem thorn" or "jelly-bean tree" or some other context-specific term such as "Mexican palo verde." Some of these names are obviously inappropriate, and none of them will mean much to most anglophone readers, so the original term *cina-cina* is retained. Such exotic terms are explained in the glossary at the end of the book. Original street names are respected. The *calle de la Magdalena*, for example, is rendered not as Magdalena Street but simply as the Calle de la Magdalena, the only concession to English usage being the upper-case "C." The reader will find the word *calle* in the glossary, however. Other examples are *estancia, estanciero,* and *quinta,* all of which in Argentina have particular inflections that would be lost in their approximate English equivalents: cattle ranch, rancher, and country estate. Part of the problem is relational: "cattle ranch" evokes western North America and cowboy culture; "country estate," the English countryside and its gentry – two very dissimilar geographical and cultural realities. The property of a typical wealthy family of the aristocratic *estanciero* class in Argentina would include an opulent *casa* (house) in the heart of Buenos Aires, a recreational *quinta* on the rural outskirts of the city, and a productive *estancia* at a further remove. The triad *casa-quinta-estancia* is quintessentially patrician-Argentine at the peak of that class's dominance in the late nineteenth and early twentieth centuries.

Victoria Ocampo *circa* 1934. Photo by Nicolás Schönfeld. Courtesy of the Fundación Sur.

María Rosa Oliver, 1935. Photo by Annemarie Heinrich.
Reproduced by permission of the Estudio Heinrich Sanguinetti.

Rabindranath Tagore with Victoria Ocampo, San Isidro (Buenos Aires), 1924. Courtesy of the Fundación Sur.

José Ortega y Gasset and Victoria Ocampo, El Escorial, Spain, 1929.
Courtesy of the Fundación Sur.

Count Hermann von Keyserling, Starnberg, Germany, 1919. Photo by Richard Wörster, from the Volgi Archive. Provided by Alamy Stock Images.

Waldo Frank, María Rosa Oliver, Victoria Ocampo, and Eduardo Mallea. Villa Victoria Ocampo, San Isidro (Buenos Aires), 1936. Courtesy of the Fundación Sur.

Founding editorial board of *Sur* at Victoria Ocampo's house in Palermo Chico (Buenos Aires), October 1931. Photo by Nicolás and Diego Forero. Courtesy of the Fundación Sur.

Top row (left to right): Francisco Romero, Eduardo Bullrich, Guillermo de Torre, Pedro Henríquez Ureña, Eduardo Mallea, Norah Borges, Victoria Ocampo. Middle row (left to right): Ernst Ansermet (to left of stairwell), Enrique Bullrich (wearing glasses), Jorge Luis Borges, Oliverio Girondo, Ramón Gómez de la Serna. Lower row: María Rosa Oliver (seated), María Carolina Padilla (standing).

Free Women in the Pampas

A Novel about Victoria Ocampo

In memory of my parents:

María Teresa Calatrava, who came from Madrid to Buenos Aires
with a suitcase full of books (among them the *Gitanjali*), then sold
her jewellery to buy a typewriter;

and

Antonio Lojo, who fought for the Spanish Republic and planted
a chestnut tree in our backyard as a reminder to me to return, in
his stead, to Barbanza and the woods of Comoxo.

It is fairly obvious that until now woman has spoken very little, directly, about herself. No doubt to compensate for this silence, men have talked about her at enormous length, but inevitably, of course, through their own nature … Men are praiseworthy for many reasons, but certainly not for any profound impartiality on this subject. Thus, until now we have listened mainly to testimony about woman from witnesses whose word would be suspect before a court of law. Woman herself has uttered scarcely a word. And it falls to woman not only to describe this unexplored continent she represents, but also to speak about man, she as a witness whose testimony will in turn be suspect.

If she succeeds in doing so, the world's literature will be incalculably the richer for it, and for me it is beyond all doubt that she will succeed.

Victoria Ocampo, *Woman and Her Expression*, 1936[1]

Aristotle set down, 2,290 years ago, two premises. The first is that man is a perfectly formed being, whereas woman is the result of imperfect procreation and constitutes a monstrosity necessary for the conservation of the species. The second is that when a man is a slave, slavery is his natural condition and therefore "it behooves him to be a slave."

Always linked to one another, tricked out in new clothing by every age, unfailingly invoked to defend privilege, these two premises continue to influence those "beautiful souls" dedicated to the maintenance of any status quo. Fortunately, history is not static, and time after time it gives them a good pounding.

María Rosa Oliver, *Sur*, September 1970–June 1971

1

1924

"... the words have not been rightly set"

Rabindranath Tagore,
Gitanjali

I

A vague shape was approaching along the little gravel path. White, floating, it seemed, as far as Carmen Brey's nearsighted eyes could make out, to be clothed in silk. It sprouted legs – eager, agile, softly dark, the ankles visible, flashes of calf, rushing ahead, almost kicking at the shoes as if wanting to leave them behind. Then arms, too, swinging to the rhythm of silk. Reddish chestnut hair beneath a small hat. A scintillating voice.

A knock at the door. The voice spoke, smiled, gave a few orders. Keys turned, releasing a gust of fresh air and perfume. The hazy figure from the path filled the space of the doorway open to the living room. A woman – young, tall, of fair complexion.

– Is that she? whispered Carmen in English.

– In the flesh, came the answer, also in English, from the young blond man standing at her side.

The lady in white (though the decisiveness of her movements was not especially lady-like) advanced without hesitation, brusquely, until she stood before them. She extended her hand to the man. Then she turned to Carmen, studying her with surprise. She spoke in English, perhaps out of courtesy to the foreign young man, who wouldn't have found it easy to follow them in Spanish.

– Are you Miss Carmen Brey? The person Bebé recommended? But, by the looks of you, you're little more than a child out of primary school!

– Don't be alarmed, I've just finished university. People are fooled by my size and my round face. And you must be Señora Ocampo de Estrada, are you not?

– Call me Victoria. Don't worry about your round face. You'll be grateful for it when you start aging, like me.

– You? Goodness, anyone should be so lucky as to age like …

The young woman named Victoria smiled, openly coquettish. She had beautiful teeth, thought Carmen, and her dark eyes sparkled as brightly as her voice.

– Will you excuse us for a moment, Mr Elmhirst? I must explain a few things to Miss Brey.

– Of course, Victoria. I'll be here, at your service. As always.

The voice was neutral, but not the smile – ironic, slightly vexed. Only Carmen glimpsed it before they left the living room. Victoria, looking straight ahead, hadn't noticed.

The house was white, too. So white that when looked at from outside, shimmering in the glare of the sun, it hurt the eyes. Inside, the semi-darkness in some of the rooms compensated for the excess of light. But there was another kind of excess here: a profusion of plants creating their own garden or bit of forest, and in the most unlikely corners, on stairway landings, on window ledges and shelves and mantelpieces apparently cleared of books or knick-knacks just to let flowers grow in their place.

Victoria opened the door of a small study. It smelled of wood freshly waxed, and a fragrant blend of honeysuckle and roses. Flowers whose immoderate size matched the vastness of the whole land, including the river with its oceanic pretensions, visible from the corridor.

– Now, tell me about yourself. Just arrived from Madrid, right?

– A week ago.

– Bebé – I mean, Señora de Elizalde – told me María de Maeztu was your mentor.

– Yes. I lived in the Residence for Young Ladies when I was studying Philology at the university.

– You have no idea how lucky you are. My parents never considered it proper that I go to university. As for living in a residence for young ladies, out of the question. Not even if Santa Teresa[2] herself were in charge. Now, let me explain why I need your services and what they entail. You probably know I've just brought the poet Tagore here to this estate. He's going to stay for a while.

– Mr Elmhirst told me. I haven't seen the gentleman yet. He's resting.

– And a good thing, too. In fact, he was on his way to Peru. But the doctors forbade him to cross the Andes and ordered total rest. So, I arranged for him to stay in this house for as long he needs. ... Goodness! I haven't offered you anything. Would you like a cold drink or a cup of tea?

– Tea, please.

Victoria pressed a buzzer on the desk. A middle-aged man appeared right away.

– José, Miss Brey is going to be lodging with us for a while. She will be dealing directly with Mr Elmhirst and Master Tagore. Should any difficulty arise in serving our guests, you and the staff can go to her for help. Be so kind as to bring us tea for two.

The valet answered in an unmistakable accent. He was a Spaniard from Galicia, like nearly all the domestic personnel she'd seen in Buenos Aires. Would she be just one more employee of the same ilk, albeit a deluxe item? She suddenly felt the same impulse she'd felt as a child at her First Communion. To just get up, walk away, leave the priest standing there, Host in hand, the predictable looks of horror, the whispering, the buzz of scandal filling the chapel. How could Señora Ocampo so easily assume she would accept the offer of a job? She hadn't even spelled out the terms and conditions. A few anecdotes Ortega had told her came to mind. And Elmhirst's recent remark about that "overbearing woman." Nevertheless, she couldn't feel anger when her impetuous employer turned to her with the candour and excitement of someone who's just offered a perfect stranger, out of pure generosity, a fabulous gift.

– I'm sure, Carmen, that you can hardly believe your good luck. Just imagine meeting Tagore out here on these pampas! And the privilege of keeping him company throughout his entire stay here! I'd change places with you with pleasure.

Perplexed, Carmen Brey scrutinized the open and luminous face of her interlocutor.

– I beg your pardon, but isn't this your house? Aren't you going to stay here?

– No, this isn't my house. It's the estate of a cousin. I'm living nearby at Villa Ocampo, my parents' place, and I don't have their permission to lodge the poet there. My cousin has lent me Miralrío for the week.[3] If Tagore needs more time, I'll pay whatever rent she asks.

– Ah, I see.

– Don't get the idea I'm awash in cash. But I do have jewellery I can sell and I'll put it to good use. Tagore is worth it. More than worth it, much more. Let me put it this way: the opportunity to host Tagore is beyond price for me.

José arrived with the tea tray. They brewed it strong here. In the thick, aromatic leaves gathered in the strainer, Carmen Brey would have liked to read, if not a map of her future destiny, then a code for deciphering the unspoken laws of the land now receiving her. Or those of the millionaires who governed that land. Could Señora Ocampo's parents really consider a Nobel Prize in Literature to be an undesirable guest? Did they take him for a starving bohemian from the Rive Gauche? Or were they trying to undermine the authority of their capricious heiress, to annoy her just as she annoyed them by courting friendships outside her class and its customs? No doubt about it; she looked fully capable of selling any jewel bequeathed by the family that clipped her wings, so as to affirm the unyielding strength of her will.

– You'll see, Carmen, neither Tagore nor Elmhirst speaks Spanish. And the household staff don't speak English. I plan to come every day, but I can't be here all the time. Just imagine how it would look. I want someone here they can have conversations with, and not just about the weather. Someone who can let me know about any discomfort or worry they may have, things they might not mention to me personally out of courtesy. I suppose you're familiar with Tagore's work.

– Yes, I've read his poetry. And I know his translator, Zenobia Camprubí.[4]

– The wife of Juan Ramón Jiménez? I must admit my reading of Tagore is thanks to Gide's translation.[5] I was educated in French, and I often feel illiterate in my own language. But I'm doing everything in my power to remedy that. Some day I'll write as fluently in Spanish as in French.

– I'm sure you'll do whatever you put your mind to.

– That's what my family says, and not exactly as an endorsement. Anyway, here's an advance for your troubles. If you find it isn't enough, call me, of course. I'll tell the chauffeur to fetch your luggage from the hotel.

They abandoned the study. In the living room, where they'd left him earlier, Leonard Elmhirst was now sitting in the armchair, staring out the window with the impotent attitude of a prisoner, even though a less jail-like setting than the Miralrío estate was hardly conceivable.

– And how is our Gurudev? asked the hostess.

– Still sound asleep. He must be getting used to the new house. Shall I wake him so you can take a look at him?

– Of course not! What do you take me for?

– Don't be angry, Victoria. It was just a joke.

– In very poor taste.

A short, stout woman, her eyes black and round, came toward them.

– Señora, your friend Adelia called. She says not to forget lunch today at Harrods, and be sure to bring Señor Elmhirst. Ah, your hat needs straightening.

– I'll fix it. Is it all right now? Would you like to join us, Carmen?

– To be perfectly frank, I'd rather stay here, get to know the house, and get settled in when my luggage arrives.

– As you wish, then. Fani, Señorita Brey is the translator I told you about. And besides, she's a countrywoman of yours.

– Really? Well I'm Asturian, from Oviedo. And you?

– I was born in Ferrol.

– So you're Galician. We're neighbours, you might say. And you, Seño-ra, don't forget to take a shawl. They said on the radio that it's going to get chilly. And change those shoes. The left one's got a stain on it. And you've got a run in your stocking.

– As you can see, Carmen, Fani treats me like a youngster. But her tyranny is useful. I protest a bit and let her have her way. Just as an indo-lent people does – the Argentine people, for example.

– Yes, yes. Go ahead, "spit at the sky," as they say! Or "nourish a viper," and … All right, come now, child, I'll show you your room. We've given you a very nice one on the upper floor.

The stairs creaked under the low heels of Carmen Brey's shoes and the flat moccasins of the Asturian woman. The creaking sound, the smell of laven-der and eucalyptus, and the ornate bannister branching out like another form of vegetation, suddenly took her back to childhood and the house of the *Indiano*, her grandfather, who might have reacted the same way as Señor Ocampo, though not for quite the same reasons, had she taken a notion to play hostess to an Indian from the Orient with a Christ-like beard and the robes of a holy man, no matter how many Nobel prizes he'd won.

Before entering her assigned bedroom, she managed to discern, through a narrow opening in the doorway to the adjoining room, a tall silhouette wrapped in ankle-length vestments and crowned by a white mane. It was the poet of flowers and evenings, leaning on his elbows as he gazed from the grand balcony out over the river.

II

Repeated knocks at the door awoke her. And a decisive voice. Fani's.

– Señorita Brey! Your luggage is here. Open up, please!

How much time had gone by? The sky was a wine-coloured sponge that looked as if it could soak up not only all the light of the setting sun but all the water of the river as well. "An ideal landscape for Tagore," thought Carmen. And indeed, from the window the poet could be seen walking slowly along the sloping riverbank: a long shadow surrounded by a sort of saintly nimbus. He looked less like a human being than a mirage. Had the window magically opened onto a chute, she would have instantly slid down to try and touch him before he vanished. But the knocking was growing louder; she had to answer to Fani and reality.

– Three suitcases and two trunks, child. Here are the suitcases. The trunks are staying downstairs, for now. What's in them? José says they weigh a ton.

– Nothing bad, Señora. Only books, pictures, a few family souvenirs.

– Well, I've got nothing against souvenirs. But the books! You're not going to tell me they're a good thing. You should see the crazy notions they put in people's heads, especially women's heads. You could've left them back in Spain, for all you'll need them here. There's no shortage of books in Señora Ocampo's houses. It's like taking oranges to Paraguay, as they say in this country.

– I'm not planning to spend my whole life with your Señora. I want to work independently and have my own house.

– Fine, woman, I mean no disrespect. Earning one's bread in another's house is no dishonour. And certainly not in this house. Doña Victorita can be stubborn as a mule, but believe you me, you won't find anyone more loyal or generous.

The advance she'd received from Victoria crossed Carmen's mind. It was more than what a university professor just starting out could earn in three months.

– I have no doubt about that. What I mean is, I'd like to do other things. I've pursued my studies so that I can teach, or translate for publishing houses. Besides, I don't think Señora Ocampo needs a secretary.

– Well, suit yourself. I'll leave you here with your luggage. If you want to eat something, let José know – here's the bell. I didn't have the heart to wake you up for lunch. But I'm warning you, don't miss supper. I can see you could stand to put on a few pounds. And as long as I'm in charge, no guest will leave this house looking anemic.

Carmen sat down at the desk by the window, suitcases unopened. She'd have to get used to living with this odd assortment of humanity – a mysterious poet, a tetchy Englishman, and two women who took it upon themselves to decide what was best for others.

She looked outside. The moving river froze into a mirror. Hovering above its arrested current was the bright memory of a distant sea narrowing into a river, the reverse figure of this proud river that broadened out to an ocean. How long had it been since she'd gazed through her window over the waters of the long inlet, the *ria de Ferrol*? The years of study in Madrid had deprived her of that enchantment. Looking out from the enormous balcony of the Indiano's mansion in Mugardos, or from the glassed-in gallery of the house in Ferrol, her child's eyes had seen, time and time again, the same captive sea. A ferocious animal that on spring afternoons became tame, and on regatta days consented to adornment by young girls tossing flowers upon its waters. On such days the mansion at Mugardos with its eight-sided roof would float dream-like in the translucid air, at the far end of the spyglass. It was the promise of imminent summer when, school finished, the motor launch would cross the inlet and deliver her into the arms of a white-maned giant: her Grandfather Brey, whose wide-set blue eyes she'd inherited, though certainly not his tall stature or his good eyesight.

She must write to "the Andalusian." Or, properly speaking, to Señora Adela Montes, the widow of her father, Antonio Brey. Her stepmother was scarcely ten years older than she was. Carmen called her by her first name, although without the affection she used with her sisters and close friends. At times she felt she was being unfair in keeping Adela at a distance, which the older woman had never imposed, quite the contrary. She opened her purse to look for her latest letter: *Be sure to tell me when you set foot on terra firma. I know I've said it before, but I just can't understand your decision to leave, and hope it's just a caprice, a passing fancy. As* she wrote those lines, where would Adela Montes have been? No doubt sitting by a window that reflected the turbulent tidal rhythm of the inlet beneath the rain-soaked light of autumn. But surely not in Mugardos, where the Andalusian had always felt strange, out of place. More likely on the Calle de la Magdalena, in the conservatory of the tall house, sheltered behind its windows among the plants hanging in their porcelain pots and, like them, a bit faded. Almost a punishment for someone who'd grown up footloose and carefree, sprouting under the hot sun like a carnation from a crack in the soft white walls of Cádiz. In Galicia the walls were built of granite, not whitewashed adobe. They didn't crumble or peel. At most they'd get split open by the roots of big trees. And even then, with their fractures smoothed over by moss, they seemed undefeated. They were only returning to their natural state – chunks of rock dislodged from quarry or mountain, parts of a forest. *I don't know what's got into young people these days, even those with education and decent prospects. What is it that makes you leave one after another, as if chased away from the land you were born in? I suffered plenty for having left my home province, not so far away as all that. But at least I left out of love for a man, your father, and not to go looking for some El Dorado or pie in the sky in some far-off country. Carmen, my dear friend, as I wish you were, since you aren't my daughter, what is it that Galicia can't offer you? Haven't you always done as you pleased? Didn't your father swallow his fears and let you go off to study in Madrid, at a time when no other girl your age went to university, and certainly not so far away from home? Why haven't you come back to Ferrol, with your education, to do something for your own people? In another two years or so, they'll have finished the renovations, and the Institute of Secondary Education will be open. Wouldn't you be happy teaching there, or in La Coruña? Or are your compatriots not as good as the* americanos? *Your grandfather didn't come back from Cuba to build his home here, only to see his descendants scattered all over the world. Maybe that's why God, in his mercy, took him early, so as to spare him the heartache.* The Andalusian liked to get melodramatic. She was sounding like a Galician matriarch; maybe she'd been coached by her husband's sisters-in-law, the Moure aunts, who after their initial shock had come round to adopting her, and who had opposed Carmen's voyage as much or more. *I just can't understand why you so insisted on going off to Buenos Aires, as if you were some poor wench without so much as a patch of dirt to stand on. All those wretched lasses and penniless lads gallivanting off in search of adventure and fortune, never mind the dashed hopes – that I can understand. But you! A señorita from a good family, a teacher and graduate of the university in Madrid. Suitors should be flocking to you! My God, Carmen, what are you thinking? Sometimes I even regret you didn't marry the professor. Though your father wasn't completely wrong in thinking he wasn't good enough for you (but what father doesn't find fault with his daughter's suitors?). He was a good man. Serious. Is it because there's someone else, some unhappy love you don't want to confide? At your age, such sorrows pass quickly. Here you could forget whatever it is you need to forget. Better here than in America.*

The Andalusian was a little too insistent. Did she really want her to go back? Or was she trying to clear herself of any responsibility in the eyes of the Brey family, who perhaps blamed her for the departure of both Antonio's children? *If it's about your brother, I don't think you should worry yourself so. He left with money and recommendations. It pains me to say this, but if he hasn't sent us word, there's no reason to chalk it up to anything but his own will. Bad news travels faster than good. If something serious had happened, we'd have known by now. And what good will it do, you going in person? From here, we're doing everything in our power to find out where he is, and we won't let up in our efforts, neither I nor your aunts. Sometimes, may God forgive him, or forgive me, I think he refuses to write us out of sheer pride. He was never refused anything. He lived like a little prince, never making an effort, never taking advantage of the opportunities he had. The biggest disappointment your poor father had before he died was when his son quit university. Maybe he's incapable of making a go of it with the capital he took with him. Maybe he just wasted it. And probably he doesn't want to show his face now and admit his failure. If that's how it is, he'll turn up one day soon. He's still young, and time will bring him round. He'll learn his lesson.* Had the Andalusian learned her lesson? Was that why, at thirty-five years old, she was sermonizing like a woman of sixty? Sermons and admonitions weren't enough for Carmen to understand her brother's silence, nor why he had left. What if he had left because of the Andalusian? They must have argued that summer, after their father died, when Carmen had refused to return to Galicia, not even to visit Mugardos. But her brother had gone back, not to Mugardos but only to Ferrol, to deal with the business of his father's will. Then, all of a sudden, he had embarked for America, without even saying goodbye, leaving her instead an incomprehensible letter. *Anyway, Carmen, don't you act the same way. Don't leave me in the dark and without news.*

The sky had turned a deeper shade of plum. You almost wanted to reach out and touch its silky texture, sink your teeth in, extract its hidden delight. The poet was no longer in sight. The outside air was suddenly chill and made her shiver. She turned on the bedside lamp and set to work on a letter to the widow of Antonio Brey. *I hope you received the telegram I sent you upon arrival. This is the first free moment I've had since then to send you a few lines. In less than a week I've seen dozens of people, delivered letters and gifts and greetings, and I've been taken to countless places in this city where everything is surprisingly outsized (starting with the River Plate, difficult to distinguish from the ocean). The degree of luxury, too, is often surprising. The millionaires live in mansions that imitate European styles. The odd one is in the Spanish style, like that of Señor Rodríguez Larreta, author of a historical novel set in Ávila at the time of Felipe II.[6] But in general, it seems to me, the preference of rich and cultivated Argentines runs to French tastes, Parisian if possible. Although in the end Argentina is a daughter of Spain, and every day contingents of Spanish immigrants arrive (most of them Galicians). I've met with Dr Avelino Gutiérrez, of the Spanish Cultural Institute, and he has promised me work. In any case, almost without realizing it, I'm already employed, thanks to the philosopher Ortega, who recommended me to a patroness of the arts here, Señora de Elizalde. Through her mediation I've been hired by Victoria Ocampo, also a friend of Ortega; my job is to serve as full-time translator for the poet Rabindranath Tagore and his secretary, an Englishman, for as long as they stay here. I'm living now in a house at the city's outskirts, well-appointed and with a view of the river. Señora Ocampo can't be any older than you. She has intellectual inclinations and has published a few things. She's very good-looking, too. But it's not only that. There are lots of pretty women. It's that one can't help but look at her, she commands attention. Her housekeeper, a bossy busy-body, reminds me a lot of my grandmother, whom you never met, and of my Aunt Elena, who not for nothing is her daughter. So, in a way, I feel right at home. I've begun to make inquiries at the Galician Centre and at the Spanish Mutual Aid Society, to see if they can locate Francisco. Don't worry about me. I'll do what I must and all will be fine.* Carmen paused, her pen suspended in the air. Did she really know what she must do?

She abandoned the letter, annoyed. She'd finish it later, tomorrow morning. She thought about writing to Aunt Elena, since she'd just called her to mind, if only for her faults. *Benquerida tía*, she began in Galician, only to erase it immediately and stop, paralyzed. She, too, felt illiterate in her own language. Everyone in Galicia spoke it but shied away from reading and writing it, despite the popularity of writers like Curros Enríquez[7] or Rosalía.[8]

She looked around her room. A small bookcase with glass doors held a few books. She promised herself she'd unpack hers as soon as possible, with or without Fani's approval. She reviewed the titles on the shelves. Authors unfamiliar to her, likely Argentine – a certain Ricardo Güiraldes,[9] for example – stood alongside others, classical or merely famous. Tagore was there, of course, in various translations, including the one in Spanish by Camprubí. What could Señora Ocampo, all passionate action spilling out into the world, have in common with those mystical meditations? Perhaps she was attracted by her opposite, as often happens. Without thinking, she opened the *Gitanjali* the way the pious (which she was not) open the Bible or *The Imitation of Christ*:[10]

The song that I came to sing remains unsung to this day.
I have spent my days in stringing and unstringing my instrument.
The time has not come true, the words have not been rightly set.[11]

III

– Miss Brey! Miss Brey! Can you see me? Over here, under the arbour.

But the long legs of Leonard Elmhirst, clad in breeches and combat boots, his figure topped by a mountaineer's peaked cap, were already striding away from a raised bed of roses and honeysuckle toward her. The Englishman doffed his cap, bowing slightly, a rose in one hand. With a smile, he placed the rose in the hands of Carmen Brey.

– Thank you, Señor Elmhirst. Very kind of you. But what's going on today? Have I got up late, or did you and the others get up early? And Master Tagore?

– Mrs Ocampo came by to take him to her own estate, after an exchange of letters by post. A necessary compensation, I understand, after the iceberg night ...

– Iceberg? My word, what a metaphor, Señor Elmhirst. Was it as bad as all that?

– Almost an hour of silence, from the hors-d'oeuvres to the dessert. Maybe you didn't notice because you were enjoying your meal so much. Or because Fani's watchful eye was making sure you didn't miss a mouthful.

– Silence between people from different cultures, persons who hardly know one another, doesn't seem that strange to me.

– But Tagore is confused; he doesn't know how to deal with Victoria.

– Why?

– Because he can't figure out what she wants from him. She sends flowers as though he were an opera singer; she attends to his every whim; she puts house, car, and servants all at his disposal; she watches over him, or has him watched, lest the slightest draught disturb him. But when they're face to face she says hardly a word, just stares at him in rapture.

– Maybe it's shyness. Or probably that her excessive admiration makes her timid.

– But what kind of admiration? Is she a snob? A flirt? Is she in love with him? All she does is devour him with her eyes. Or maybe that's the way with Spanish women. Not, of course, that I've known very many.

– Fine, thanks for counting me in. As for Señora Ocampo, she is *not* Spanish, even if her ancestors were. And I'm afraid that Argentines of her class have done all they can to differentiate themselves from us.

– Excuse me, but the truth is that I find you more like my cousins in Yorkshire than an olive-skinned, dark-haired beauty. Besides, you speak very good English, without an accent.

– Not all Spanish women are from Andalusia, nor are all Andalusians dark. My family is from the north of Spain, and I learned English as a child, with a tutor. In my city there are plenty of English people, because of the shipyards, and maybe because they've had a special respect for us ever since we turfed them out when they invaded Ferrol in the Napoleonic era.[12]

– Well, I'd forgotten about that lamentable episode. If indeed it was ever mentioned in the English history I learned at school. Here, too, they like to brag about having thrown the English out twice in a row in just a few years.[13] It must be a sort of fable invented to endow a nation with a myth because it doesn't have one yet.

– And you, Mr Elmhirst? Why do you follow Mr Tagore around on his voyages throughout the world? Out of snobbery? Or out of interest in his court of feminine admirers?

– I accompany him because I sincerely believe he's an exceptional man. I learn from him, I love India, and I hope to found a school in England like the one he founded in Santiniketan.[14] Although I wouldn't mind ending up, in the process, with one of those beautiful admirers.

– Such as Señora Ocampo, for example? You wouldn't perchance be jealous of the way she adores Tagore?

– *Miss* Brey, my one and only concern is to look after Gurudev, and shield him from upsets and anguish. And Victoria's behaviour would alarm any man. Every time I see her in action, I think of one of Gurudev's verses: *I seek what I cannot get, I get what I do not seek.*[15] She has a dangerous temperament; her passion could suddenly be hurtled at any object. If at least there were a husband in the picture, one would know what was what. But, in these circumstances, everything's too ambiguous. It's inconceivable that a woman of her tremendous energy doesn't have some lover to quench it.

– My God, Mr Elmhirst! The way you talk about Señora Ocampo, you'd think she was a meteorological catastrophe about to be unleashed, and not a person. Besides, isn't she married?

– Separated for the past two years. Since in these Catholic countries there's no divorce …

They had arrived, at a leisurely pace, almost at the riverbank. The morning tranquility was perfect. The calm expanse of the estuary, seen from up close, seemed to Carmen uselessly huge. A superfluous plain that baffled the river's egress to the open sea, vainly impeding its flow, with none of the turbulence and surprising designs of the tidal inlets in Galicia.

Elmhirst pointed to an approaching caravan of ten or twelve persons.

– Look. The devotees are arriving.

– Do you know them?

– They're most likely coming to see Tagore. Usually a small multitude gathers here. Will you please tell them Gurudev will see them this afternoon?

Carmen spoke to the two women heading up the group – two elderly ladies wearing gloves and wide-brimmed hats, old-fashioned capelines swaddled in muslin.

— Is the Master not here? When may we see him?

— Come back in the afternoon, and he'll be pleased to receive you.

One of the ladies brought a handkerchief to her eyes.

— Good Lord! I do hope I shall hold out until then.

— My friend is very ill, Señorita, and she has high hopes invested in him, whispered her companion in Carmen's ear.

The pilgrims conferred with one another, then set off walking. The capelines of the two ladies could be seen for a long while, in the distance, like a pair of tremulous corollas.

— What's the matter? Why do you look so astonished?

— You can't imagine what they just told me. One of those good women believes the Master is going to cure her illness.

— I'm not surprised. Yesterday someone showed up wanting Tagore to play the soothsayer, asking him to interpret a dream she'd had about elephants.

They laughed heartily as they turned to walk back to the house.

— Doesn't he get tired of seeing those people?

— He feels he owes it to his public, though he does complain of fatigue and ill health. It's a mix of vanity and philanthropy. Of course, many of them really do read his work and ask intelligent questions. Intelligent, at least, in Victoria's translation of them. I believe that will be your job from now on.

That afternoon Tagore came out to meet his visitors. He sat beneath a tree rising from a gentle elevation on the grounds. It wasn't hard to understand, thought Carmen, why some people believed he was a holy man with curative powers. His white head, resplendent in the light filtering through the crown of the tree; his lively gaze tinged with melancholy; the robe on his long, slender body flowing from neckline down to his feet: all in all, the very image of a saint. Tagore didn't preach a Sermon on the Mount, but he did patiently answer every query put to him, even by the Theosophists and Spiritists in attendance.

Elmhirst and Victoria weren't there. They'd gone to the city to buy books for their Gurudev and take care of some business. They were too long in returning. By the time darkness had erased all colour from the river, Fani was indignant. She ordered supper served – "dinner" in the parlance of upper-class Buenos Aires. She was not about to let any guest in her care suffer malnutrition just because some folks didn't know how to respect schedules. Carmen sat down, intimidated. She and Tagore were alone at the excessively large table.

– What are you thinking about, Miss Brey? Tired after a hard day's work, which was my fault?

– Please, you were the one who worked hard, answering even the barmiest questions with good grace.

– I'm not so sure they're barmy. God put us in this world with a terrible need for Him, and yet his secret is veiled. People can't resign themselves to it; they want to break through the inscrutability.

– And they seem to believe you are in possession of the secret.

– We poets are burdened with that bad reputation.

– It seems to me your petitioners don't see you as a poet. Maybe they take you for a relative of Jesus Christ, because you resemble the images of Christ they've seen in their prayer books.

– Who can pronounce judgment on what is the best way to draw nearer to God? If it works for them … For my part, I try not to disappoint them with my poor performance. I only hope I don't let the Lord down too badly.

They exchanged a smile.

– I didn't imagine you this way.

– How? With a sense of humour? Anyway, I didn't imagine the way this country would be. If indeed it is a country.

– I beg your pardon?

– Up to now all I've seen are the mansions of elegant persons, with their vast tracts of land, wheat, cattle. Persons who order their clothes from Paris and travel to Europe every year. But what makes a people is collective memory, what they have lived and dreamed and suffered together. A history that belongs to all, both the common people and the upper classes. And I don't find any trace of that memory. Everything seems new, everything wants to be new, as if it was made the day before yesterday. Nevertheless, there was another life here before … Have you read Hudson?

– No, who was he?

– A writer whose family was from the United States. He was raised in the River Plate region, around the mid-nineteenth century. He was an expert on birds, too. Everything I know about Argentina I learned in his books. Victoria was going to get a few more for me today.[16] But I can't see the thread linking that land he talks about with the world I find myself in now. I feel for the Argentines, especially. Sad is the destiny of peoples who choose to forget what they are.

Carmen choked on a fish-bone. She coughed, downed a glass of water, swallowed bread, while the poet himself, alarmed, patted her on the back. Then she sat up straight against the chair back, panting. Her eyes filled with tears.

– How embarrassing! I was born by the seaside, I've eaten fish my whole life, and now this happens.

– Sometimes the most familiar food is the hardest to swallow when it's served away from home, Miss Brey. Never mind, tomorrow you'll be fine, and together we'll teach a bit of Spiritism.[17]

Carmen had trouble falling asleep that night. She heard noises in Elmhirst's room on the other side of the stairway. But apparently neither he nor Victoria had come home yet. She softly opened her bedroom door, just in time to see Fani coming out of the Englishman's room. Once Fani had gone downstairs, Carmen tiptoed across the hall. Elmhirst's room had undergone a veritable police search: his belongings were strewn about, drawers emptied, books opened. A rumpled notepad must have been incomprehensible to the would-be detective. Carmen went back to bed. A while later she heard Elmhirst come up the stairs, stumbling like a drunkard or someone in great distress.

IV

Carmen Brey wouldn't know until years later what had happened that night outside the grounds of the house. Waking up the next morning, she heard Victoria and her housekeeper in the throes of a violent quarrel. Elmhirst, shut up in his room, was filling leaf after leaf of stationery with lengthy missives, none of which reached their female addressee. He crumpled them one by one into a ball, leaving them on the window ledge to be scattered by gusts of capricious spring wind. One page ended up in the river, where it quickly sank, lacking any vocation or structure to become a vessel. Others got snagged in the branches of very old trees, like incompatible sprouts, soon to be dissolved into the rough bark by the rains. Still others landed in the arbour amid the honeysuckle. Those were the ones Carmen retrieved and carefully smoothed out on a stone table, treating them like parchments from another time, in another language, in which some strange and yet human being had inscribed his longings and heartaches. *Here I am, the guest in a house which is not mine or yours or even Fanny's, & though you may be immune from rumour & gossip, already your family & others regard me with a suspicious eye.* The writing was interrupted by gaps and passages scratched out in fury or out of carelessness. *She emptied all the drawers & she had thrown the things apparently in a great hurry anyhow & anywhere. I don't care a rap for insults from your servants if you think it unavoidable, but remember that if you do keep them up late & I am with you, for them I am responsible, if meals are late for the same reason, I am blamed.*

Where one page left off, another reiterated or fortified the reproaches. *I want to be to you a real friend, as brother to sister, & I'd rather leave that impression not only with you but with others – at present in an effort to do this I only succeed in giving* everyone, *including Gurudev and Adelia, an impression that I am forever tied to you in a calflike adoration & running after you like a frantic lover – you may say this is rubbish, but unfortunately my woefully keen observation and my terrible sensitiveness tell me these things by wireless, & it is useless for you to go & ask them if it is true because no one seems to dare to tell you the truth – they're much too frightened.*

Somehow – argued another fragment – *I feel you are desperately lonely. I came asking things of our friendship, expecting – now I want nothing in return, except permission to help & be of use, to bring sympathy and affection, in silence if need be, in the realm of spirit – for your intellect is too keen for me & your temper too cruel to allow of my struggling with either.*[18]

Carmen left the pages to their volatile destiny. The south wind drove everything hither and thither, disrupted the order of things and of sentiments. What might be the deep feelings of Victoria-Circe, capable as she was of transforming Señor Elmhirst into a calf? Was she as lonely as the Englishman's presumption supposed or wished?

Carmen did not find out in the following days, but she did learn other things: that Señora Ocampo, in order to pay the two months' rent for Tagore Rabindranath's stay at the estate, had in fact sold a piece of jewellery. To wit, a crescent-shaped tiara encrusted with diamonds, which had graced salons in Rome and lit up the firmament of Parisian theatres where, newly married, she had gone to see the Ballets Russes – a spectacle still off-limits to her as an unwed woman just three months earlier. Around the same time, Prince Troubeztkoy had rendered her silhouette in

a bronze statuette wrapped in a mantle of velvet and chinchilla. Fani and
Señor Estrada, Victoria's husband, had been apprehensive, but the prince
executed his work irreproachably with the same aesthetic dedication,
unsullied by lust, that he applied to his favourite models – Siberian wolves
and hounds. Parting with the ostentatious tiara, so Victoria declared,
caused her no pain, perhaps because the nocturnal lustre of its diamonds
had dimmed since those days in Paris, darkened by a corrosive poison: her
husband's jealousy.

– If at least he'd been jealous out of genuine passion, she confided to
Carmen. But it was only proprietary jealousy. He got jealous because he
felt dishonoured, ridiculed. And the supposed dishonour came down to
such petty reasons: if I smoked in the salon, or spoke to another man
without first asking his permission. And there'd be a crisis if I happened
to say something complimentary about a man.

– Did you love him?

– I thought so when I married him. But we had met and talked so few
times. The protocols of courtship didn't allow otherwise. Had it not been
for the chance to escape my family, I would never have thrown myself into
that marriage. After only a few days of married life, I saw what he was really like, which I had maybe preferred not to see earlier: intelligent but
insensitive, handsome but cold, a ritually observant Catholic, but mean
and inflexible.

Carmen also learned (though not the whole story) that it was to this
painful failure that Victoria owed her discovery of the *Gijantali*. "Pure
happiness dulls our perception, it limits us. I would never have understood his book had I been merely happy." That discovery, Carmen found
out, had taken place when Señora Ocampo was living in her own home in
downtown Buenos Aires. A house full of objects expensive, luxurious, rare
or beautiful; or often with all those qualities at once. But the Coromandel
screens, the lacquered armoires, the set of fine China bought during the
wedding trip had become meaningless because the spouses who had
acquired them no longer shared any future, nor any world.

– I didn't want to live with my husband any more. In fact, we weren't
really living together. We occupied two different floors of the house. We
only spoke in public, at social and family gatherings. And yet I didn't dare
leave. Not because I cared about what people would say, but because anything they said would have destroyed my parents. I couldn't bear to cause

them pain and suffering. I sacrificed myself to appearances so as not to shame them. My father, especially. My love for him. I couldn't leave then, and even though I'm separated now, I still can't bring myself to make other decisions I ought to make.

– I don't know what to say, Victoria. My mother and father have both passed away.

But my father, Carmen thought, would surely have been more compassionate than yours.

– It was then that I read in the *Gitanjali*. *They come with their laws and their codes to bind me fast; but I evade them ever, for I am only waiting for love to give myself up at last into his hands.*[19]

In those verses, said Victoria, there was a God different from the one she'd been taught to fear. *Where the mind is without fear and the head held high; where knowledge is free ... Into that heaven of freedom, my Father, let my country awake.*[20] Not an angry God, thundering down from a mountain top, but one who grew silently, unexpectedly, like a delicate and complex flower from a place in the grand bourgeois mansion where a girl had opened those pages. A small cabinet covered in grey silk, a piano, and veined white marble sprang up in her memory, together with those verses, the first to tell her of the only true God, the same and different for everyone – Asians, Westerners, blacks and whites, men and women. The God who understands the acts of all his creatures and who can pardon what men condemn. Exalted and aflame as she said these things, Señora Ocampo then let her beautiful mouth fall silent, not daring to confide all, such as what other mouth had kissed or was kissing hers, reprehensibly in the opinion of the world and its gossips. What passion, what contacts had been understood and forgiven by the God of *Gitanjali*! A God her own church had denied her, and whom Tagore without knowing it had conjured up in the music room for her comfort and cheer, as though he were the magician from an extraordinary tale.

– I should have done something else in life. I should have been an actress. My destiny was the theatre. If it hadn't been for my father ...

Señor Ocampo had sworn to put a bullet through his head if ever the infamous day came when his daughter took to the stage.

– They let me take classes with Marguerite Moreno.[21] But only to round out my education. She advised me not to marry. If only I'd listened to her advice. At first my husband promised to help me. However, I saw a letter he wrote to my father, assuring him that he'd undertake to dissipate those fantasies of mine. And that once I was pregnant they'd evaporate.

– Why did you believe your father? asked Carmen. Parents always swear they'll do things like that and then they don't follow through. You should have done what you wanted, if that was really your desire. He would have come around in the end.

Antonio Brey had exerted no moral blackmail when his daughter decided to go away to Madrid, but he died without seeing her finish her studies. Before passing away he was dejected. Carmen had never wanted to ask why: whether it was because his two children had gone off to the Capital, or because his second marriage, with the Andalusian, had given him no new descendants, and perhaps no happiness either. There was no use asking Adela Montes, reluctant as she was to admit to any crack, even the slightest imperfection or decay in the image projected by the wedding photo above the bed, exactly beneath the crucifix, where another wedding photo had presided over that bed once occupied by Carmen's mother.

As the two women conversed like this, in the open secret of the riverbanks, the poet watched through his telescope from the balcony of his room. He was looking for birds, he'd told them, in the distant treetops of carobs, *tipas*, *casuarinas*, and cypresses. He was looking for those wingèd creatures of the plain that illuminated Hudson's books, to see if they had survived the oblivion of history and the disappearance of peoples. How would she and Victoria appear to him, Carmen wondered, as they floated alongside the river's flow in their pink, yellow, and white garments, like furtive blooms issuing not from nature, but not entirely from culture either. Suspended, perhaps, like other birds, in the non-human air that was proof against gravity and the force of mortals.

V

Sir Rabindrath Tagore or Thakur, or Gurudev, or Rabi Babu – depending on the occasion, the language, and the degree of familiarity of those uttering his name – was born in Calcutta, second largest city of the British Empire, as populous and variegated as the world, the same year that Manuel Silvio Cecilio Ocampo y Regueira, father of his hostess, was born in the *gran aldea*,[22] the big village of Buenos Aires, ungovernable port of a little-known republic, which years later would boast that it too was the most precious jewel in the English crown.[23] Both men were from wealthy landowning families. But while the one always knew he was from a poor and oppressed country with an ancient culture, the other grew up in a brand-new nation, confident in its fortune, where even beggars rode horseback, but where culture was something to be imported ready-made, like fine porcelain or trains. (There was nothing else for it, they thought. In that vast wilderness whose name itself was sheer fantasy,[24] there were hardly any citizens, only *gauchos* and *indios*, children of nature necessarily ignorant of the benefits of industry and intelligence.) Manuel Ocampo, a believer in Jesus Christ by tradition and in Progress by ardent conviction, earned a degree in Engineering and built bridges and roads to the Interior, the untamed hinterland. Rabindranath Tagore, to whom a God who was not Christ had been revealed in his first poetic inklings, despised formal education and especially British education. He resisted going to school, but his father instructed him in the *Upanishads* and the sacred language, his sister nourished his literary imagination, and his other older siblings trained him in painting, music, and dance. Nevertheless, as an adolescent he travelled to England, where he studied the profane English language, and read and admired Shakespeare, who seemed to him a scribe of the God of a thousand faces, because he was able to invest those barbarous words with the kind of magical power and wisdom only available to those who have lived all possible lives. The young man also proved to be exceedingly sensitive to the charms of London girls; admonished by his family, he was obliged to return home to marry a child bride and thus fulfil a contract arranged since birth, as was the tradition. Although he may have been enamoured of his sister-in-law Kadambari, who was off limits, Rabindranath respected and educated his wife, Mrinalini. When the thirteen-year-old spouse bore her first child, Mrinalini could already read the *Ramayana* in the original; later she would write an adaptation for children. She donated her jewellery in order to found, with Tagore, the school at Santiniketan, but did not see it built. She died before reaching the age of thirty and left her husband tender memories, shared dreams, and five children. Only two of them, the first-born son, Rathi, and a girl, Mira, survived their father.

By the time he came to Buenos Aires in 1924, Rabindranath Tagore had written poems and songs, novels, short stories, and plays, literary criticism, and children's books. He composed music, directed works of theatre, and was gifted with a fine tenor voice. He was also a solitary man, surprised by his fame in the West, who enjoyed and suffered two distinctions which, for a patriot of the new India, were problematic: a Nobel Prize for Literature and, especially, the title of Knight of the British Empire.[25]

In 1924 Manuel Ocampo was an Argentine gentleman whose distant hereditary title to Galician nobility had long since been erased by the law of the new republic. Still intact, however, was his pride as a founding father of Argentina, his exclusive status as one of a select club of foundational figures in a prosperous nation meant to thrive, God and good harvests so willing. Intact as well were his family and its assets. His only serious worry at the time was his eldest daughter: willful, unhappily married, she was scandal-prone both on the streets and in the papers. She insisted on driving her own car, even though she had a chauffeur. And only Victoria could write an article, for the literary supplement of the national paper, on the fifth Canto of the *Divine Comedy*, about the lovers Paolo and Francesca, condemned to the Inferno for adultery! Manuel Ocampo preferred not to think about (and fervently hoped no one in Buenos Aires would think about) what names of real, living persons might be lurking beneath the prestigious literary code.[26]

Since his arrival at the ports of Montevideo and Buenos Aires, Rabindranath Tagore, wanting only to pass through quickly on his way to Peru, felt he'd been trapped like an exotic butterfly in some collector's net. He'd been *ooh'd* and *aah*'d over like a decorative insect. Had basic good manners not held them back, people would have touched and petted and pawed him, never minding the risk posed by such abusive contact to the dust of fine gold on its wings, essential for the flight of the butterfly. Women and men had spoken of his beauty the way one speaks of sculpture or animals on display, careful not to betray scabrous motives. During the last leg of his trip, crossing the River Plate from Montevideo to Buenos Aires, he'd been accosted and interviewed as he lay ill in his berth. Thanks to a journalist from *La Nación*, all of Buenos Aires had contemplated and imaginatively beheld in advance his "dark, noble face," the perfection of its lines unmarred by wrinkles, his "noble brow," the "incredible gentleness" of his profound eyes, and the voice as musical as his poems.

In the refuge of Miralrío, he was spared the burden of that constant public gaze. The domestic personnel at the white house in San Isidro perceived no poetic aromas in his clothes; his pale orange tunics received not adoration and reverence but rather Fani's strict care – she washed and mended them personally. The down-to-earth workers didn't call him a "pilgrim of invisible worlds"; nor did it occur to any of them that "unfathomable mysteries were bathed in the soft light of his intelligence," as Señora Abella de Caprile and Señor Ruiz López had written, to the delight of other sensitive ladies and gentlemen of the reading public. Here in San Isidro, at least for goodly intervals, Rabindranath Tagore could live as an ordinary mortal. He could look, not only be looked at.

Once again he scrutinized the horizon, flat and inexhaustible as the river itself. In one direction, the two young woman in full bloom came intermittently into view, the luminous traces of their clothing – silk, linen, or muslin – appearing and disappearing as they walked along the riverbank; further off, the wake of a passing sailboat that would not stop to rescue him. In the other direction were the pillared verandah, the driveway of big rectangular flagstones, the little gravel path, finally the main gate and freedom. Freedom … ? Did such a thing exist in this world? Perhaps not, as it was understood in the egocentric West. The highest freedom was but to do one's duty. The poet walked, for the umpteenth time, from one end of the balcony to the other. If he had a duty, it was to collect donations, foster philanthropic enthusiasm for the school in Santiniketan, the Visva Bharati University, the agricultural projects in Shilaidaha, Potisar, and Surul.[27] That was his work, just as much as the poetry and novels, and even those theatrical pieces which for some mysterious reason (love of the exotic, perhaps – another form of dissatisfaction or frivolity) seemed to appeal to Europeans, as well as to the strange people of South America. Strange like those beds of cactus – all thorns outwardly, full of secret water – which his gaze stumbled against every time he contemplated making a discreet escape.

Was his health really as delicate as the doctors were insisting? Or was there some ambiguous conspiracy, a confluence of disparate interests, those of Señora Ocampo, who wanted to keep him there at all costs, and those of Leonard Elmhirst, no less desperate to attract the attention of his hostess? He let the telescope wander at random, until a golden point in the distance – Miss Brey's cropped strawberry-blond mane, fitted to her skull like a helmet – lit up a promise of relief. Might she be the neutral means of his rescue? Perhaps she could be convinced to spirit him off to the Peruvian Embassy. But what if the trip over the Andes turned out to be fatal, more than his heart could take, as the doctors warned? So, he'd have to go back to Europe and thence to India. It all got so complicated. He wasn't about to ask either the lady or the country he wanted to flee for a return passage; even less did he want to request money from his own people, in Santiniketan. It was already bad enough that he would be going home empty-handed. He'd have to wait for a Supreme Force (the Lord? Queen Victoria?) to decide matters for him.

Besides, was it not sweet, the dominion exercised by his feminine captor? Not as bad as all that to submit to her pampering. He sat down in a wicker chair he especially liked, with its high back and strong arm-rests. A sudden catch in his breath confirmed what the telescope had announced. Victoria was approaching. She'd promised to take him to see the rose garden at her father's estate, nearby in San Isidro. He breathed in the aroma, overwhelming at times, like Victoria herself, a blend of so many perfumes. If life was offering him this unexpected gift, why refuse it? What man in his right mind, unless he were a Calvinist pastor, could take issue with the constant adoration of a young, refined, beautiful woman, her attentions invariably exquisite? He'd been too long alone. Santiniketan, his children and grandchildren could wait a little longer. Even his poetic inspiration, stricken and withered by so much travel, so many setbacks, had revived in San Isidro with spring-like splendour. He repeated lines from the latest poem he'd composed for Victoria (or Vijaya, as he privately called her in Bengali):

Even in the same great voice thou hast cried to me: "I know you."
And though I know not thy tongue, Woman, I have heard it uttered
in thy music, –
"You are ever our guest on this earth, poet, the guest of love."[28]

VI

Señora Ocampo held onto her hat with one hand, while the fingers of the other hand drummed on the flap of her purse, following a beat surely she alone could hear inside her head. But anyone could recognize in that light, silent tap-dance the rhythm of happiness ... Travelling by horse and carriage through the open countryside and filling her lungs with the sea air: that, for Carmen Brey, was sufficient cause for joy. But Victoria's gaiety had additional reasons: in the carriage, seated directly opposite, travelled her Gurudev. Was Gurudev happy? If not, he at least looked pleased. Finally – he'd said to Carmen – he was going to see the pampa described by Hudson: the straw-roofed adobe huts, the marshes overflown by herons and flamingos, the people who lived off the land, with their little domestic gods (a crucifix or a plaster virgin), the horsemen who slept out on the range, in the saddle if need be, under a ringing clamour of stars.

All they had witnessed up to this point, however, was an ever closer view of a harmonious park, traced out by the precise pencil of a landscape designer, and an enormous house with the bearing of a castle. Fortunately, all things considered, Tagore and Elmhirst had their backs to that scene, and only she and Victoria, sitting opposite, could see it. Carmen admired the high walls partially covered in ivy. Some whimsical millionaire had managed to use the magic carpet of fortune to transport, almost intact, a portion of English countryside. But Gurudev didn't feel like Lord Fauntleroy entering the noble mansion of his forebears. He disembarked slowly, helped by Elmhirst. Through his telescope, he scanned left and right, finding nothing to relieve his great perplexity, only a picture-perfect tableau of turrets and cypresses.

The carriage left them some distance from the main door. "We mustn't deprive ourselves of the pleasure of a walk, especially at this time of day," said Victoria. Carmen agreed. Their feet turned up a green, rain-soaked earthen odour. The transparent silence filtered the birdcalls, the bleating and mooing of livestock being herded into stables close by but out of sight.

The interior of the house was like the exterior – impeccably British. Tagore's room, grand as a hall, was dominated by a four-poster bed enclosed by curtains of incarnadine damask. The aroma of the thickly waxed woodwork impregnated the room.

They were served tea, though it wasn't yet five in the afternoon. Victoria had taken off her bonnet and light shawl. Her bare arms and slightly copperish hair were resplendent against the wide parlour window, in light deflected from the sky for the sole purpose of touching her. Elmhirst's eyes followed the movements of those arms, the hair, her mouth with admiration and resentment.

– Well, Gurudev, there you have it. I can hardly believe we're finally here, after so much wishing for it. We can spend tomorrow touring the countryside. So, what do think of my friends' house?

Tagore looked at the Chippendale table, the Queen Anne chairs, the fine china, the lace tablecloths.

– I don't know what to say, Vijaya. Are your friends British?

– No, of course not. They are the Martínez de Hoz family, completely Argentine.

– I think, then, that this house is full of things with no meaning. Why do they copy everything?

Victoria turned red. She was furious, thought Carmen, but in front of Tagore she always held her tongue. Hours later, while strolling together in the garden, its colours washed out by the moon, Victoria unburdened herself. "He's unjust, unreasonable. I don't understand him. And he doesn't understand us. Why wouldn't they have English furniture in their home? The Martínez de Hoz family were all educated in England. What's more, the house has been decorated in the finest taste. These aren't cheap reproductions, they're genuine antiques. Every single piece has been chosen for a reason, to be placed in a particular spot. What kind of furniture does he expect us to use? Are we supposed to sit on cow-skulls, like the gauchos? Or does he think it'd be more authentic if we stayed shackled to our horrible old colonial relics, clunky as coffins, that look good only when they're in Figari's paintings?"[29]

Carmen sighed. Her grandfather, *el Indiano* Brey, too had been criticized as much as envied by the neighbours when he built the house at Mugardos; he'd had the eight-sided roof shipped over in pieces from Florida, from Yankeeland, along with the wood for new-fangled built-in closets. At times she felt for Victoria. She was neither widow, nor single, nor fully married to a husband present in person at home, at the table or in bed. At times, too, she thought Victoria was in love with Tagore. What else could one think of a woman who wrote letters like the one she'd been shown one afternoon, Victoria seeking her opinion on how well it was written, especially the spelling in English, her weak point? *Could you forget your Indian sky, even if you had no chance of seeing it again? You are to me what that sky is to you. And as the tree stretches out its branches as if trying to sink them into light, taking root in it through each bud and leaf, so is my heart and my mind extended to you. The tree can't be content to peep at the sun through a window.*[30]

Of course it was the poet himself who'd started with the equivocal metaphors, and right at the beginning of his stay. Had he not, in another letter, compared the effects of his sudden fame with what happens in a poor country when a mine is discovered and the land is subsequently razed by treasure-seekers?[31] Did he not believe he could be redeemed, like all poets since time immemorial, by the love of a woman? *My market price has risen high and my personal value has been obscured. This value I seek to realise with an aching desire which constantly pursues me. This can be had only from a woman's love and I have been hoping for a long time that I do deserve it. I feel today that this precious gift has come to me from you and that you are able to prize me for what I am and not for what I contain.*

Carmen, confidante to them both, sometimes felt like a novelist destined to bring together two ticklish and rebellious characters, mutually fascinated yet often out of touch with one another. There were moments when she found them annoying. They nearly always spoke to her in a more exalted and serious tone than normal conversation warranted, as if they were declaiming. Were they really talking to her, or to an anticipated posterity, an invisible, immeasurable public which they saw reflected in the mere transparency of her eyes?[32]

"I can't *talk* to him," Victoria would say. "When I'm with him, everything it occurs to me to say seems idiotic. The first time I saw him, in the Hotel Plaza, I went literally speechless in his presence, after having dreamed of that meeting for years. How can I convey to him how much his books mean to me?"

"Why won't she talk to me? Why is she hiding?" complained Tagore. "She squanders a fortune looking after me, she does everything within her power to assure my comfort and well-being, and then she disappears for days, except at suppertime. Maybe she doesn't want to be there because others sometimes join me at afternoon tea. She is pleasant with everyone, but distant. She isn't even present for the conversations with my invited guests. I understand, she's an aristocrat. She isn't accustomed to socializing with those outside her exclusive circle."

"My God!" Victoria, desperate, cried out to Carmen. "How does that man come up with such nonsense? Never have I been prejudiced about race or class." Carmen knew it. Victoria behaved exactly the same with everyone, seductive or imperious, and to universally devastating effect – except with Fani, who bossed Victoria around. "He and his family are more likely the ones with prejudices. Generation upon generation of Brahmins who refuse to even touch those they consider impure!"

"Maybe Elmhirst is the reason, that must be it," Tagore came back. "He looks at Vijaya with longing eyes – how did Fani put it? – like 'a lamb with its throat slit.' Picturesque, but accurate. The common people always have the best metaphors. Yes, a lamb before the slaughter. Poor boy. One doesn't win over a woman by inspiring her pity. Nevertheless, she may indeed have some sympathy for him. They spend a lot of time together, going out, gadding about town. Elmhirst is young, handsome, enterprising. I'm not selfish, Miss Brey. I've already told him: why don't you marry her and bring her to live with you at Santiniketan?"

"Can it be possible?" fumed Victoria. "He said *that*? If I spend time with Elmhirst, it's only to look for clues to help me get closer to Gurudev, understand him better. I suppose it's all a joke. Does he really think I could marry that stupid Englishman? Not even if I were a thousand times divorced!"

Carmen stopped translating Gurudev's occasional confidences. Maybe because Victoria was already upset enough by her own conversations with the master. The week spent in the countryside at Chapadmalal was turning into a small inferno of subtle misunderstandings. And the furniture, which annoyed Tagore the afternoon he arrived, continued to be a source of discord. Hadn't Tagore called Baudelaire, whom Victoria idolized, "your furniture poet" when she'd insisted on translating for him those lines that speak of the secret room set aside by lovers for their love: gleaming furniture polished by time, floral essences and amber, inset mirrors, Oriental splendour ... ?[33] "What splendour?" Tagore wanted to know. "What furniture? What Oriental luxuries? In Santiniketan we make do with a woven mat for our rest, and a veranda where we watch evening fall and enjoy the cool air. Your furniture poet sounds like a huckster at an auction house."

Nevertheless, Tagore, intentionally or not, wrote his own Baudelairean poem at Chapadmalal. It was titled "A Skeleton," as though evoking, perhaps only to refute it, Baudelaire's "Une Charogne."[34] Victoria found the poem insulting, not on account of the French bard she so admired, but to herself. "Don't you see, Carmen? Remember he translated the poem for us that same morning, not long after writing it? Just look at what he's given me now, after I asked him to copy it out for me. It's *nothing* like the original text. It's mutilated, he's ripped the heart out of it, its marrow, its essence." Carmen read the incriminating evidence, which Victoria was waving in triumph. Her observation was quite accurate, as Victoria nearly always was in her literary opinions. "It's a version adapted for idiots! Do you know what he told me when I demanded an explanation? That he'd modified a few things because he didn't think they were of 'any concern' to us Westerners."[35]

That night at the dinner table, as a gesture of peace, Tagore read them the last and definitive version of the poem. Carmen copied it by hand in a notebook. She would read it again many years later to lament the dead of an unimaginable war. Her thought then was that Gurudev had lost his wife and several children, all of them having breathed their last in his arms:

in the bosom of sufferings I have found the secret path of delight;
I have heard in my being the voice of Eternal Silence;
have seen tracks of light across the empty desert of the dark.
Death, I accept not from thee that I am a gigantic jest of God,
that I am the annihilation built with all the wealth of the infinite.[36]

But the greatest insult to the Occident, particularly in its Argentine version, was delivered not at the English mansion but after their return to Miralrío. Tagore had expressed interest in hearing some modern European music, and Victoria obliged by inviting the Castro brothers' string quartet. Arriving with viola, cello, and violins, they set themselves up in the middle of the great hall on the ground floor. The master did not come down to listen to the strange music of Borodin, Ravel, Debussy, and Manuel de Falla; he preferred that it come to search him out, discreetly, indirectly, through his bedroom door left slightly ajar. Carmen knew he was sad and upset because of a letter he'd just received from India. Victoria made excuses to the musicians, saying that Tagore had suddenly taken ill. The Castros were not at all put out, cheerful lads that they were. They thought the world of Victoria: she loved the same composers, she did what she could to help out musicians, and she was beautiful. They took for granted the extravagant behaviour of geniuses, all the more in one so exotic as Tagore. That same quality, however, provoked the barbed witticisms of Ernest Ansermet, the Swiss conductor of the Philharmonic Orchestra.[37] *I see quite well the way a prince from Bengal acts, but alas! I am not such a one,* he'd written to Victoria when she'd informed him of Tagore's disdain for Baudelaire. *Born amid cheese, sausage, wine, furniture polished by time, I must follow my path carrying all that on my back. If Baudelaire, one of our greatest, merits the label of parvenu, then – Lord above! – what must he say about us, and our entire civilization!*[38]

When, after a good supper, the guests had left, Carmen and Victoria, the latter still smarting from the affront, sat on the balcony and talked a long while. Carmen recalled a story Tagore had recounted in a book. As a boy studying in London, he was invited by an English lady to her country house to sing in memoriam for the widow of a deceased Anglo-Indian bureaucrat. The place was far away. He arrived by train, of a winter's night and, since supper was over, they offered him some lemonade and sent him off to sleep at a local hostel. Many years later, Tagore could still feel the cold in his bones. He was cold when he went to bed, cold when he got up, cold when he later climbed the stairway up to the country house and stood waiting before the closed door. Behind it the bureaucrat's widow was resting. The door did not open; he was neither received nor thanked. Someone, not even the Englishwoman whose house it was but rather a servant, told him the widow was indisposed. The servant then pointed toward the wooden rectangle and ordered: "Sing!"

VII

Leonard K. Elmhirst, son of a landed Yorkshire clergyman, educated at Repton School and Cambridge University, graduate in History and expert in agriculture, young veteran of the Great War, English gentleman and secretary *ad honorem* of Sir Rabindranath Tagore, was suffering hopelessly. Ever since Señora Ocampo had crossed their path for the first time at the suite in the Hotel Plaza, his disciplined and relatively serene life had become an unstable and turbulent web stretching between love and hate, crisscrossed by humiliations and unsatisfied desires. Mister Leonard Elmhirst had lost count of how many letters, delivered or not, he'd written to the Lady of the Castle called Miralrío, and lost track of how many names he'd called her, how many epithets, dissimilar and even contradictory, he'd penned or just thought.

He had praised her determination and audacity, and pitied her unhappiness. He'd compared her to an enraged tigress, but also to a fairy, reasoning that fairies have the wings of a bird (since otherwise they wouldn't fly), and that an English gentleman could press that rebellious, magical potency against his breast and smooth her insurgent feathers. He had made accusations: that she treated Tagore like a treasure she owned; that she demanded of him, Tagore's miserable secretary, feudal fealty. He had reproached her for being infatuated and conceited, and paid her homage as the grandest, noblest, most generous of ladies he'd ever known.

Mr Elmhirst had also painted himself, in his pathetic epistolary laments or in the intimate effusions of his diary, as the dog who licks the hand of his mistress; as the tool or utensil discarded once it has served its purpose; as the serf of the lowliest rank whom the other servants of the household permitted themselves to mock.

But his masterwork was an elaborate and intricate allegory, a document he'd never dared to show his hostess, not without good reason. There he described in exquisite detail – worthy of a medieval miniature – a great fortress (Tagore) defended by a faithful squire (Elmhirst) against the advance of an attacker (Victoria) intent upon penetrating the secret inner rooms. Sooner or later custody would be relinquished, for the fortress itself wished to surrender before the most irresistible attack: the amorous will of a woman.

For her part, Señora Ocampo had qualified Mr Elmhirst as the "stupid secretary," jealous and self-centred. And yet she had also protested her dearest friendship[39] and her gratitude for his precious collaboration, if only for his gesture of having thrown her a rope to help her scale the impregnable fortress.[40] However, the greatest insult inflicted by Victoria had not been verbal, and perhaps for that very reason Elmhirst, unable to articulate or exorcise it with words, still felt it branded upon his face in the indelible colours of ridicule.

At times he was overwhelmed by shame, at others by indignation. Wasn't it she who had led him on to commit the shameful act? Her completely inappropriate confidences about her unhappy marriage, confessed to a man almost her own age whom she hardly knew, the two of them alone in an automobile at midnight: had that not induced him to act as he did? Or was she, like a fifteen-year-old virgin, expecting him to fall to his knees – a trifle awkwardly inside an automobile – and proffer a romantic declaration? Did she think he was some clubmate of hers, her poker partner? Did she think she could behave like a man among other men? Or,

even worse, did she take him for a pansy or a eunuch, who'd be insensible
to her nocturnal confessions?

Whatever the case may have been, Leonard K. Elmhirst was moved to
compassion by the beautiful woman's story of marital failure. To attenu-
ate that failure, he had offered a healthy masculinity nourished on por-
ridge and fortified by gymnastics and hikes. But the delicate fingers of
Señora Ocampo, which he'd taken in his fingers so as then to place them
delicately upon the very centre of that British virility, had not accepted his
unconditional and exultant gift; instead they had recoiled as though from
a viscous, repulsive insect. The car door had been slammed shut with such
vengeful force that it must have been heard all the way to the house at
Miralrío. Thus had Fani considered herself authorized to search through
the satyr's belongings, justified by her unsuspecting employer's penchant
for taking strolls with him at the most untoward hours.[41]

Señor Elmhirst, treated like an oaf, had nonetheless offered his hum-
blest, most gentlemanly apologies, even though he wasn't quite certain
Señora Ocampo was a lady. Moreover, he couldn't confide his affliction to
anyone. Tagore would have openly accused him – he had already insinuated as much – of lover's pique. Little Miss Brey – being Spanish after all
– did not strike him as either fragile or much given to compassion, her
placid blue eyes and her innocent china-doll face notwithstanding.
Besides, she was a member of the tight-knit feminine cabal, the troika
whose third member was Fani, Guard-Dog-in-Chief; anything he said to
the Brey girl, he was sure, would be immediately relayed to Victoria and
used in her interests.

Being a practical man after all, he concentrated more actively on his
future life in a place where life was real, not like this strange, fantastical
country. And that possible, tangible future also had a feminine name:
Dorothy Whitney Straight, an American blessed with reasonably good
looks, calm intelligence, and the solid inheritance of her father, the New
York magnate William Whitney. Though peaceful, she wasn't exactly a
simple person. After assiduously courting her for three years, Mr Elmhirst
hadn't yet overcome her resistance; severe and cautious of character, she
was chary of falling into a second marriage (though young, Dorothy
Whitney was a widow – the best condition for women, according to certain ironists of whom Leonard disapproved). But beneath her austere
reserve, the elusive bride-to-be conserved a vulnerable heart that could

not remain indifferent to the trials and tribulations he was undergoing in an inhospitable land.

Mine is a nature that blossoms in an atmosphere of affection – he began – *and at the moment I only find myself surrounded by an infinite loneliness. I cry for bread, and though I know that bread is awaiting me, for the time being I must content myself with stones. But if I can share my feelings with you on paper, I feel the better and the happier for it. I have never felt anything but better and happier for your presence, and when all in the immediate neighbourhood seems but hard and cruel even, and tiresome and dusty, I cry out for that harmony in which the best I have is drawn from me. Am I too much a man of moods? I wanted so much to stay out of the city, and to get as near you as I could by going down to the river and watching the birds and the waving of the trees – but no! what seemed a very profitless day spent in the wretched city, failing to do all kinds of things I had set my mind on doing.*

Perhaps it is well that I came to South America after all. In some ways it could not have been a better test. I have been plunged into a world where mere physical beauty is lavished upon the women folk as rarely elsewhere, and mingled now and then with wit and even brilliance. But what a desolation inside! For mere physical beauty without charm and without charity, brilliance and satire without sense and human laughter, the perpetual striving to be witty, without the salt of human sympathy, which gives pain with the laughter and has a cutting edge instead of an enveloping kindness ... [42]

Our hostess is quite – next to the poet himself – the most difficult person I have ever come across. I feel now and then as if I was in charge of a madhouse. Some day I will tell you about her and my impressions of South America. I have seen much here that throws light upon the middle ages, the inquisition, the mentality of Spain and the power of the Church of Rome. I am the more astonished at the way in which our own island managed to rid itself of the shackles. The cruelty that was once practised in the open has now been pushed under the surface and shows itself in odd places and in quite ghastly ways. [43]

Mr Elmhirst paused. He wasn't quite satisfied with what he'd written so far, but he was out of paper. He looked everywhere, under file folders, in desk drawers, among books, and couldn't find a single sheet. He'd have to look for some in Tagore's room. The door was ajar. He was about to knock when through the crack he spied a scene that stopped him in his tracks.

Victoria had leaned over Gurudev's shoulder to read the poem he was working on. She had done this often, fascinated by the Sanskrit characters that looked to her like drawings and had the allure of the incomprehensible. But this time, the poet's arm encircled the reader's shoulders. Then his hand slipped down until it was touching her left breast. Señora Ocampo started almost imperceptibly. Then she remained still, accepting meekly, knowingly, perhaps pleasurably. Time stopped. Or rather, it plunged, along with the pride and the secret, obstinate hopes of Leonard Elmhirst, into a bottomless quaking bog.

Sir Rabindranath's secretary could never remember what he'd done with the unfinished letter, nor how he ended up at the bank of the river, whose waters he pelted with all the stones he could find and every obscenity he could bring to mind. Had he been able to endure another minute at the door, he'd have seen how the hand, slow and sure, drew gently away, perhaps because there'd been no response to its caress. The two figures returned to their habitual postures, as the river's waters resumed, unmarked after every stone, their slow, enormous flow.

VII

Christmas in Buenos Aires wasn't really Christmas, Carmen thought sadly. She didn't miss the snow (in the land of her childhood, always wet and verdant in winter, it rarely snowed). But she did miss the chill air ringing with greetings and carols, a live bell as sensitive as retractile skin to the touch of your breath. In Buenos Aires the atmosphere coagulated into a suffocating cloud, dissipated only once in a while by a breeze from the river. No chestnuts were lovingly roasted in the *lareira*, there was no sea, there were no souls coming to search out the warmth of the living on Christmas Eve, or to seek forgiveness from those they'd offended. Or, conversely, to pardon family members for assorted sins and wicked passions that had created enmity and tormented them still.

Master Tagore must not have felt much better. Carmen, equipped with Elmhirst's telescope, spied him on the riverbank. He was wearing one of the new tunics Victoria had had made, at Fani's insistence, to replace his minimal and worn-out wardrobe. Two things Tagore would never know: first, the tunics had not been cut and sewn by a simple seamstress in San Isidro (as Victoria had given him to understand) but by Madame Alice, who ran the Casa Paquin in Buenos Aires.[44] Second, thanks to those tunics, Carmen Brey caught a glimpse, brief though it was, of another side of Victoria's life, beyond Miralrío, in the city holding her past and cloaking the secrets of her present.

Madame Alice, too, had succumbed to the fascination that Tagore apparently exerted over all the women in Buenos Aires, spiritualists or otherwise. Victoria had asked that his old tunics be replicated as nearly as possible but in the best French cloth. The *couturière*, however, wanted to try out a new design on the poet. She insisted so much that one afternoon Carmen was sent with the chauffeur to fetch her.

– I hope *Madame* Ocampo feels a little more assured of my complete discretion. She was terrified thinking how people would criticize her and the master if it came out that his clothes were from the Casa Paquin. Don't you think it's all so terribly unfair? Why should a man, just because he's a great artist and almost a saint, have to go around in rags, when so many fools and scoundrels go strutting about like fashion models in suits by the best tailors? What a way to reward virtue! And tell me, *Mademoiselle*, are you French or from a French family? Because your last name …

– Yes, yes, I know. There are Breys in the south of France, but I'm from Galicia. I was born by the sea, in Ferrol.

– And you miss the sea, no? I can see it in your eyes. What can I say, since I'm from Marseilles? Anyway, I'm anxious to meet the poet. So, tell me, is he as beautiful and majestic as in the photos? He looks like God the Father, *j'oserais dire* … I'm hoping I can touch his white beard without him realizing. It'll bring me luck.

Carmen held back a smile. Tagore looked too much the part and was still a slave to *le physique du rôle*.

– He must have been splendid as a young man. He's still splendid, although too venerable. Hmm, if Madame Victoria's heart wasn't already engaged elsewhere, I wouldn't bet my life on their innocence, neither his nor hers. For goodness' sake! He must be human, after all. Even saints can sin sometimes. But what nonsense I'm talking! My word, don't pay any attention to me!

Her heart engaged elsewhere? Carmen slipped through the opening as though going down a road only too well known.

– Not to worry, Victoria trusts me, and I know all about her *affaire*. I understand it's been going on a long time, hasn't it?

– For at least ten years, I think. No woman can hide a secret from her
dressmaker or her hairdresser, even if they never say a single word out
loud. No detail escapes my notice. But don't even think about mentioning
this to anyone. In this city they're puritans, *c'est-à-dire*, big hypocrites. If
ever the rumour gains traction, they'll throw Madame Victoria to the lions
without a second thought.

To avoid getting thrown to the lions, or to the ire of her *pater familias* –
Carmen supposed – Victoria had left her male guests alone that Yuletide
day. Everything was in place and provided for; the table was beautifully set
and there were gifts for everyone. But greetings by telephone from their
hostess early in the day satisfied neither Tagore nor Elmhirst. The poet, in
a pout, ate his lunch listlessly and wanted to leave the table immediately.
His secretary, who had been awfully silent in recent days, persuaded him
to stay and leave for posterity a few reflections on the meaning of Christmas. He was careful to write everything down. It was already the second
or third notebook – Carmen observed – that he'd filled in Miralrío. Maybe
this modest participation in the Master's glory compensated for his evi-
dent sadness.

– What can I tell you, Leonard? I have no problem talking about Christmas every year in Santiniketan, where people are simple, and precisely
because they're simple they understand spiritual life very well. But here!
… *In this country the very suggestion of the infinite is, each day, smothered
by the surface quality of its enjoyment, or by its pride in wealth and by those
customs which go to make up what in the West is called civilization. The
effect is so heavy and so thick that like a stone wall one's mind feels completely
imprisoned and is prevented from finding real freedom or focus in the open
air, or access to what in India we call* amritam, *immortality*.[45]

What would Adela Montes be doing right now? Having Christmas dinner with the Moure aunts, not in Mugardos but in Ferrol, where the
Moure clan lived, too. What might be left in Mugardos now that everyone
had deserted it, either to go abroad or having crossed the river of death?[46]
Crossing the sea was like crossing over to death. Francisco and Carmen
Brey, who had sought freedom in wide open space, would now be evoked
at the dinner table like ghosts, but ghosts guilty of their own disappearance; thus, the sad and unseemly immortality that would be theirs.

It pained Carmen to think about the house of her grandfather, the Indiano; with no one to maintain it, it wouldn't last long. The wind had prob-

ably carried off a few roof tiles. The filigree of the wooden balcony would have lost its shine, ravaged by the salt air. His fishing gear would be rotting, as would the moth-eaten dresses of her dolls, stored in the same trunk where María del Carmen Moure's nightgowns and bobbin lace would be yellowing.

– A man might be born into a prison house, continued Tagore, *and so might never realise that he was living in a prison. Instead of suffering the punishment customary to prison life he might even be surrounded by every comfort, in a room provided specially for him, quite shut off from the outside world, the walls covered with pictures and the floor with rich furnishings, all of which, though they might give him some pleasure and might even flatter his pride, yet would deprive him of true happiness. What is this true happiness? The basis of it is freedom. Happiness consists in the exercise by man of his free will in an atmosphere of freedom. What is this freedom? It is man's constant and daily realisation of the infinite in so far as it lies within his power.*[47]

Victoria thought along similar lines and had written about it in *The Pond of Water-Lilies*,[48] a theatre piece inspired by the Buddha. Her hero felt he was free only after he had left the unreal perfection of the Palace of the Magus and gone into the wilderness of the world of Men, where he found ugliness, poverty, sickness, and death. But then, on the bank of the pond of lilies, as well as the gifts of effort, love, and hope, he would find the power of the Fairies who live in the human heart and have the power to cure. Perhaps Victoria did not dare leave the Palace of the Magus – her family's protection, honour, and money – completely behind. Whereas she, Carmen, had left Mugardos and Ferrol and later Madrid, and may well have forever lost her Palace. But that didn't mean she'd found or was going to find the pond of lilies.

– Who dares call himself a "Christian"? *It is one of the great ironies of fate that so many of those who call themselves disciples of Christ have become the worst sinners through their will to create divisions of race, through the building of walls of national pride and exclusiveness, and through the cultivation of a spirit of contempt, and even of hatred, for others so little different from themselves. They have even made use of the great religion of love in order to indulge in their sectarian prides ... the so-called Christian world is pursuing a career of calamity of a kind that may even result in the total destruction of man.*[49]

Tagore finished his speech seated under his favourite tree on the river-bank. The heavy heat of the day had been lightened by the flowing water, but not the stubborn harshness of his memories. Carmen thought of Adela Montes, the Andalusian: when she left Mass her face was beautiful, without affectation, like that of a terracotta Virgin. And Victoria – had she gone to mass this morning with her family? Would she have obediently covered her head in a mantilla, even though she'd chosen Tagore's God over the colonial carvings and French Virgins which, for the Ocampos and their kind, represented the golden chain of tradition, the wealth of a family line, their power over themselves and over the fatherland they had forged and would continue to lead to its inevitable, glorious destiny?

Victoria was probably just a few kilometres away from Miralrío at Villa Ocampo; the old families, always large and abundant in children, usually celebrated Christmas in their country houses. Tagore, however, who had devoted a good part of his life to children, had apparently not been judged worthy to share their feast.

Was the poet still thinking Victoria would join him at some point in Santiniketan? It was hard to imagine her dressed in a sari and teaching small children. She would be free from the Palace of the Magus she'd been born to, but captured by another Magus in a distant land, enthralled by a dream of happiness that she hadn't created for herself. He sensed that Victoria had her own dreams, nourished by a passion that lit up from within and spoke through her eyes when she entered other rooms, explored other zones such as those he inhabited.

The afternoon when Madame Alice returned to Miralrío to deliver the tunics, Carmen had gone back to the city with her and to the Casa Paquin. As they were walking in front of the Hotel Plaza, a man, still youthful, dark, and very tall, came out. He greeted Madame.

– How d'you do, Señora? I hear nothing but great things about you at my sister's house. She talks about the latest dress you've come up with as if it was a Renoir painting. I see you're in fine company. Where are you two coming from? Is the young lady a client of yours?

– Not yet, but she will be. Mademoiselle Brey is from Spain. She's working as a translator for the poet Tagore and his secretary at Miralrío, an estate you're familiar with.

– Yes, yes, I've heard about the poet. And about his secretary and the young lady. I believe Tagore and the Englishman will be leaving shortly, no?

– That's what I understand. But straight back to Europe. The doctors have forbidden him the trip to Peru.

– Very well, very well. I'm glad for him; he must be getting tired of his enforced layover here. After all, we weren't on his itinerary. And I'm rather glad the craze over the Bengali is passing. Practically every señora in Buenos Aires has fallen into mystical ecstasy a couple of times because of his poetry. You can't go anywhere in society without hearing about horse-drawn carriages, bangles, garlands, straw mats, and oil lamps. We'd just about got clear of Darío's nymphs and princesses,[50] and along comes this new lyrical epidemic. Nothing to be done about it, I suppose. Well, it's been a pleasure to see you, Madame Alice. I wish you a pleasant experience in Argentina, Señorita Brey; at least you're in good hands. You'll have nothing to complain about with Señora Ocampo. Oh, and don't think I'm mocking Tagore. He's a talented man and has done wonderful things in his country. But when deservedly famous men get turned into a fad, sometimes they become objects to be used and abused,[51] like beautiful dresses. Not to disparage dresses, of course, that's what they're there for. And so that we can admire those who wear them, isn't that so, Madame Alice?

– Did you see? That's him, whispered the couturière in Carmen's ear as the gentlemen was walking away.

– Him?

– *Mais oui!* The lover of Madame Ocampo. He jokes about everything, but underneath it all he can't stand it that the poet is spending nearly two months at Miralrío in her exclusive care. They might as well be a married couple. Ever since Señor Martínez fell in love with her, he's been with no other women. And certainly not for lack of conquests, both here and abroad. Just imagine. When he was in the diplomatic service, he was known as the *attaché de beauté.* Actually, all governments ought to have someone that handsome. With representatives like him, what lady wouldn't want to come and see Argentina?

The *attaché de beauté* could well have looked like the Tagore of fifteen or twenty years ago. Not only was he a fine-looking man but he had a lovely, open smile. Moreover, he surely had patience and intelligence. Enough to know how to wait for Victoria. Tagore couldn't wait for her. He was already far away. The white houses of Santiniketan could be glimpsed in his eyes, illuminating them from within; they were reflected, like dreams, in the inexorable current of the river.

IX

Tempt me not to load my boat with debt,
> but give me leave to go away empty handed,
lest the price of love that you recklessly pay
> should only reveal the poorness of my heart.
I can but litter your life with the torn shreds of my pain,
and keep you awake at night with the moan of my lonely dreams.
> It is better that I remain speechless
> and help you to forget me.[52]

Victoria looked up from the piece of paper she was reading, its ink barely dry. Tears ran down her cheeks.

– Do you think these words are going to be a comfort to me, Gurudev? Do you really believe so? They're beautiful, but beauty too can hurt if it is true. What will my life be like without you?

– Weren't you living your life before I came along? I won't forget you, either, Vijaya. Never. And I hope you'll pay me a visit in return, come and see me at Santiniketan. But we'll both go our separate ways, each in our own time and place, richer than we were before our time together. We must continue to live. You, above all.

– Me? Why me above all?

– Because there is much to do here, and that responsibility falls to you. This country, your country, has not yet seen its face in the mirror. Look how they educate children. Only with books. Foreign books. They prefer to send them to Europe or England rather than have them travel in their own land. Not like the Incas, who had no books or even written language, who never crossed the sea, and yet what wonders they wrought in science, in agriculture, in arts, and in architecture as well. You have to learn to look to yourselves rather than looking always to Europe.

– But we *are* Europeans. Transplanted Europeans.

– Well, transplants to other climes always produce fruits and species with distinct peculiarities. And don't include yourself in that plural form, my dear Vijaya. Fortunately, you are not *only* European. Or rather, you are *not* a European. If you were, I wouldn't find you nearly so interesting.

Tagore approached and kissed Victoria on the brow, as was his custom when greeting her or taking his leave.

– Now I must pack and write some letters. Don't worry. You'll come to understand what I'm telling you. Rest assured that the children of your social class would be much happier if, instead of being kept in expensive cages with unnatural food, they were taught to live in what used to be called here the *Tierra Adentro*, the hinterland, one year in each of the major regions of the country. Their parents would economize a great deal by maintaining them almost in the wild, primitive like Robinson Crusoe, rather than paying for residences at European colleges and universities, where it is impossible to learn to be truly Argentine.[53]

The Master sat down at his desk in front of the window.

Victoria left the room. She took a seat beside Carmen on the balcony and began drying her tears of heartbreak, anarchically mixed with tears of fury.

– He'll never quite understand me. I mean, he'll *never* understand me.

– Do you understand him?

– No one could understand him more profoundly, I believe. I've lived in his poems and for his poetry. I've recited them like prayers. They may even have made me a little better, I owe them that.

– But in literature there's always something more than what we read in it. Maybe we see only the part that fits with or corresponds to our own existence. And besides, he is more than his words. He is also outside them, in the world and in a life that goes beyond them.

– You may be right, Carmen, but I find it hard to accept. While he was living here, if I wasn't sleeping outside his door like a domestic animal, it was only because our habits and norms don't permit it; everyone would have thought it improper.

Sir Rabindranath Tagore and Leonard K. Elmhirst, BA, left Buenos Aires on the third of January, 1925 on board the *Giulio Cesare*. Victoria Ocampo, efficient to the end, had obtained free passage for them, thanks to a family friendship with the president of the shipping line. The poet's state-room had a sleeping berth and a small writing room. Victoria had insisted that he take as a gift his favourite wicker chair, in which he had spent so much time gazing at the river. Since it wouldn't pass through the state-room's narrow entrance, Señora Ocampo ordered the door removed. She was obeyed. Later, Tagore would write to her that he could no longer do without the wicker chair, attributing such an odd dependence to a form of delayed revenge by Vijaya and her Baudelaire. He used the chair constantly in India until his dying day.

Leonard Elmhirst married his fiancée, Dorothy Whitney Straight, a few months later, ending his time as Tagore's secretary. Dorothy, besides her inheritance, would give him two children and would be his partner in founding Dartington Hall, a school later to become famous in England and further afield.[54] Thirty-five years later, Victoria Ocampo would dedicate her book on Tagore to Leonard K. Elmhirst;[55] despite everything the two had said and written to and against one another, she called him *amigo*. The prudent Dorothy received her courteously at Dartington Hall, but never dropped the reserve with which she treated both the lady from South America and the poet from Santiniketan, although she was always generous in her philanthropic donations to Tagore's school.

Victoria Ocampo was never to set foot on Indian soil, neither while Tagore was alive nor after his death, although the poet never stopped sending letters inviting her to visit. Only there, she thought, only on that land and beneath those skies would those who loved him come to know him as he really was. They would, however, see each other again in Paris, where Victoria organized an exhibition of his painting. They bid each other adieu in London in 1930, unaware that never again would they touch or listen to one another.

The English community in Buenos Aires published in *The Standard* a eulogistic farewell to the Knight of the Empire. Indians such as Tagore, cultivated and princely, demonstrated that liberty was not incompatible with British rule. Other Indians, rather, were to be pitied – the wretched and degraded indigenes of the South American republics. Unlike the now down-at-heel Lion of Spain and her sickly cubs, noble Albion knew how to civilize natives.[56]

The day he left, Carmen fainted at the pier. She tried to put it down to the heat, complaining of sunstroke and crying as though the sun were inflicting pain; she wept all those tears not shed when she left Mugardos, and later, Spain. *Madame* Ocampo had to drag her, almost carry her, to the waiting car. As they drove away, while Carmen dozed with a handkerchief moistened with eau de cologne on her forehead, Victoria decided that she, at least, would never weep again. Not for the sun, not for Tagore, not for the lover who awaited her return with wise obduracy. She smiled, at once offended and flattered, thinking about Tagore's last words: "From this stage-set of a country, where nothing is what it seems, I take away only the memory of two living beings, extraordinarily real: this river and you, Vijaya."[57]

1928

"I have been an Argentine in imagination."

José Ortega y Gasset
Impressions of a Traveller, 1916[1]

He has imagined these lands as we have imagined Europe. He has inhabited them in dreams. He has settled them. He has loved them. For me there is no other form of knowledge.

Victoria Ocampo
My Debt to Ortega, 1957[2]

I

Don Peregrino Loureiro was peering at her through his spectacles. His round eyes, almost blue, echoed the roundness and diluted colour of the oceans on the terrestrial, or rather aquatic, globe which, perched on the bookshelf behind him, looked ready to start spinning above his head.

– What a pleasure to see you, young comrade. What d'you say? Where are we off to today? Rome or Moscow?

– Neither Rome nor Moscow. Isn't that the federation's motto?

– Only for the time being. You'll see, when we socialists win the elections, I'll invite you to the steppes, and we'll ride a troika and watch the snow fall.

– Too cold, Don Peregrino. We're better off staying here on these urban pampas. Do you have any news? You sent me a message yesterday.

– I do have something, dear girl, though I don't think you'll like it much.

Carmen took a slow breath, as if trying to contain an earthquake. Inside her gloves her palms began to sweat.

– Really? At this stage of the game, anything is better than nothing. I'd settle for news that he's alive.

Don Peregrino gave her another look, but said nothing. He took some papers out of a drawer.

– This is the report from our branch in Chivilcoy, Province of Buenos Aires. A certain Francisco Brey bought land in the area in 1922 ...

– Do you have the precise address? Do you know how to get there?

– ... and then he sold it at the beginning of 1924.

– Is that all?

– No, it's not all. Can you not be a little bit patient?

– I've been more than patient for nearly four years. Waiting and waiting, and no sign of him ... Excuse me. I suppose for that very reason I can wait a little longer. What else is there?

– A letter from Bahía Blanca. I'll read the relevant passage: *I believe I've met the man you're looking for; it was at a horse market. He was about thirty years old, medium height, skin white but gone leathery, grey eyes. He also had a long scar, probably a knife wound, running from his left eye almost to his jawbone. The scar was striking: a single long, clean line. I could tell from his accent he was Galician, like me, and I tried to engage him in conversation. But talkative he was not; you might even call him rude. Later, I heard his name from a neighbour of mine; the man had sold my neighbour a stud horse and two young mares, and he'd signed as Francisco Brey Moure. He had an Indian with him, one Pedro Coliqueo, who seemed more like a business partner than a hired hand or underling.*

Carmen looked up, her short-sighted gaze seeking the round map of planet Earth. At that distance, Spain was barely distinguishable, never mind the peninsula of the Peninsula: Galicia, always on the edge, pure outbound impetus from the interior to the coast. At any moment its rock hinges might snap; voluntarily unmoored, it would head out to sea like a ship. It would anchor, all of a piece, in another, luckier land, and no longer would Galicians be separated from Galicians, those at home from those abroad, their bones condemned to moulder anywhere on the planet, their souls entwined – deep, vegetal, imperceptible – in the dark foliage of the *castiñeiras*, the chestnut trees.

– I find that hard to believe, Don Peregrino. The names coincide, but that person can't be my brother. He wasn't a rude or uneducated man, and he certainly had no such scar. How could he have turned into such a vulgar roughneck? Nor can I picture him having anything at all to do with Indians.

– Well, if he's in the business of raising horses, it's quite natural, seems to me. Nobody knows horses like they do. They are, after all, the real lords and masters of the pampa.

– You're not exactly a partisan of the Sword and the Cross, Don Peregrino.

– May God, if he exists, deliver me from that tribe. Unfortunately, they've been thriving, now that Ramiro de Maeztu[3] is the Spanish ambassador here. Of course, there's more intelligence in a single page of his than in all the pamphlets those sacristy heroes are churning out. But intentionally or not, he provides grist for their mill. Sorry if I offend you. I know you're a good friend of his sister.

– More a pupil than a friend. I owe her a lot. But don't put them in the same basket. María is one thing, he's another.

– Let's hope so. For his part, he serves as ambassador for Primo de Rivera's dictatorship. He might have applied his talents to a better cause. I'm just waiting for the day when our "primo" tyrant finally falls, along with his "bobo" king.[4] We'll have the republic yet, my dear. It's a shame your father won't see it; he was a good liberal. Will you join me for a coffee?

– Thanks, but I don't have time. I'm expected at the Cultural Institute[5] and also at Friends of the Arts.[6] We're getting ready for Ortega's visit.

– You don't say! So the ladies' philosopher is coming back? After his first triumphal tour, I'm surprised it's taken him so long to return. I remember him well in the Hotel España, awash in a sea of fan mail and scented calling-cards begging his precious autograph. Rudolph Valentino couldn't hold a candle!

– How naughty you are. Do you have to find fault with everything? Besides, it's not all true what you say. From what I've heard, the cards and letters weren't all from ladies; nor did they all smell of French perfume. There were many gentlemen who went to hear him speak, from the president of the Republic to university professors and students.

– Well, they say he was rather smitten by the blushing pink ears of a certain attractive *señora* whom you hold in high regard. He does have one great merit, *that* I'll admit: at least he's a republican and doesn't go around wafting incense at infidels and believers, like some other hangers-on. It makes my blood boil that they can't just let a person go to hell in peace, at his own risk and taking his own responsibility.

– Tell me, Don Peregrino, assuming he's the man mentioned in the letter, how can I track down my brother? Isn't there any more information? Where were they headed after the sale?

– Not in the letter. But give me some time. We'll try asking at our other branches in Buenos Aires Province. Don't worry, I'll keep you posted. But tell me something, Carmen. Hasn't it occurred to you that a person who voluntarily disappears may not want to be found?

– All the time. But I too want something. I want to know why he disappeared and why he doesn't want to be found.

– Good questions. But what if the answers are more than you can bear?

Leaving behind the Federation of Galician Societies,[7] Carmen ducked around the corner and took refuge in a dairy bar. She ordered hot chocolate and downed it breathlessly, like an anxious child trying to assuage her pain and anger with the thick liquid. Don Peregrino charged for his intelligence services by dishing out warnings and advice nobody asked him for. Like parents do, she said to herself, just to remind us they've been in the world much longer than we have, and that we owe them the strange and dubious privilege of life. But Don Peregrino wasn't her father, perhaps wasn't even trying to be. Maybe he already knew those terrible answers and didn't have the heart to tell her. Or he was preparing her, slowly, to hear the worst, the way considerate doctors do with the loved ones of a dying patient.

By the time Carmen turned her steps homeward, the movement and sounds of the Avenida de Mayo had changed in direction and tone. Late afternoon was sweeping people out of the offices and into the cafés. She passed in front of the palatial, seven-storey building where *Crítica* fabricated the sensational stories of the moment; the tabloid had a siren that would suddenly announce the day's Great Events. Today the siren hadn't wailed, so there was apparently nothing earthshaking to report. The four statues of the façade watched her walk by, their blind eyes returning no reflection. She was just one more, she thought. One more among thousands of passers-by who left no visible trace on the world's surface, as anonymous as this day among days.[8]

At her apartment she found an envelope slipped under the door. Her name was scrawled over the linen paper in sharp, slanting letters, rushing forward. Recognizing the hand instantly, she sank into an easy chair to read. The note was in French – a sure sign that Victoria had written in a flush of excitement. She never wrote in Spanish unless she had the time to translate and correct herself. She was still lamenting that she hadn't yet turned her mother tongue, homely as a tarnished old pot, into a set of Sèvres porcelain in which the lowliest fruits of the earth would elicit a gasp of admiration.

Ma chère, chère Carmen – she began effusively – *I know you've spent the afternoon with our friend Ortega's "legitimate wives." I've resigned myself to the rank of humble concubine, if I'm still allowed even that. I see that Bebé and all the "Sansinenas"*[9] *will take ownership of him and won't want to share him. I can't ask too much of Ortega, however. I've dug my own grave with my interminable stubbornness. Call me please, tell me all, come quickly, I expect you as soon as you have a free moment. I'm dying for some news, it's absolutely* unbearable. *Why don't you come out to Villa Ocampo this weekend? Let me know and I'll send the chauffeur. Don't ignore your old friend. Je vous embrasse tendrement. V.*

II

Carmen Brey looked herself over in the mirror. The little felt hat with its muslin tuft, the smooth tailored suit, her round cheeks and short stature all made her look like a schoolgirl on holiday. A touch of rouge, a bit of Arlette powder on her nose were not enough to alter that impression. She found herself somewhat similar (though slimmer and younger) to a fashionable poetess: Alfonsina Storni.[10] "I'll never grow up," she accused herself, annoyed at her own ineptitude, as though her diminutive stature were a grammatical error, a habitual solecism that could be corrected with concerted effort. "I'm going to look like a little shepherd girl, a Bohemian-glass knick-knack, for my whole life. Until I get old and fat. Then I'll look like a vase full of wilting tulips."

She adjusted her velour coat, picked up her suitcase and the *nécessaire* packed for two days out of town, and went down to the vestibule. The chauffeur, ultra-punctual, was there waiting. The new doorman, this one Polish rather than Galician, gave her a look of mock perplexity. He surely found it passing strange that Señorita Brey, the very antitype of the vamp or the luxury *cocotte*, was continually being fetched at the door by shiny new automobiles, whose chauffeurs – either Victoria's or Bebé Sansinena's – hopped out to open the door for her, cap in hand.

It was a cold, clear day. Buenos Aires fairly danced in the transparent air; the sunshine stirred up life in abandoned nooks and crannies, and lit up dark corners. The city was wide open, everything and everyone resplendent, airing out like stale furniture, coming back to life like sleepy human faces after a night of mourning or heavy partying. As they got closer to San Isidro, the river became greener, the trees shimmered in its waters.

In the garden at Villa Ocampo, seemingly waiting for her, stood Fani, immovable and concentrated as if she'd grown roots. It was Carmen who went to meet her upon getting out of the car.

– Aren't you a sight for sore eyes! I thought you didn't care about us any more, now that you're working for the competition ...

– But Fani, how could I ever stop caring about you? Of course not. Besides, any talk of "the competition" strikes me as a bit rich. As far as I know, Victoria and Señora de Elizalde haven't stopped being friends.

– Friends they may be, but that doesn't mean they're not competing. She acts modest, but the Sansinena woman is jealous of Señora Victoria. Every chance she gets, she sidelines her. And with all the favours Doña Victoria has done her! She's had to swallow her share of bitter pills, thanks to that woman, with all her dainty airs. Butter wouldn't melt in her mouth, but she's sneaky. And you? Still slogging away at this and that? How come? Didn't I hear you'd married a doctor?

– No, woman. That was Adela, my father's widow; she married a doctor. He's a good man, widowed as well, from Ferrol. I've known him since I was a little girl. I'm happy for her; she was very lonely. But I'm still single, and I'd keep on working even I were married. I wouldn't want to be kept by my husband so he could then subtly remind me of it and rule over me.

– Well, that sounds fine to me. One's better off under self-rule, like we have in this house. But get married anyway; pretty soon you're going to be an old maid.

– Look who's talking! Why don't you get married?

– It isn't for lack of propositions ...

– "Pro-po-sals," Fani. I've told you a hundred times.

The correction came from Victoria, standing behind the Asturian woman in a vicuña-wool shawl, on her wrist a bracelet of old silver, flat finish. Nothing could suit her better, thought Carmen, than such down-to-earth attire, at once dignified and simple.

– Well, you talk however you please, and let me speak as I see fit, since I can make myself understood anyway.

Offended, Fani had got in the last word. She left them at the door and stomped off to see to lunch.

Carmen and Victoria hugged, the latter fragrant, as always, with the scent of fresh-cut flowers and brimming with enthusiasm. Like a bright morning in mid-winter, she beamed, her radiance dispelling the darkness.

– Carmen, my dear. It's been so long since we've seen you here! The last time was two years ago when you came with María de Maeztu, wasn't it? We don't see enough of each another in the Capital. I've so many things to tell you! I've made some extraordinary discoveries.

Carmen looked at her. In a way, Victoria had never quite grown up either, though in her case it wasn't a question of her stature. Her chestnut eyes, with hints of green, looked beyond the ordinariness of daily objects. Like that of a child, her gaze could turn a barber's basin into the storied helmet of Mambrino,[11] and no doubt more than one frog into a prince. She clung to the arm of this kind sorceress, always ready to brave danger, whether it was called for or not.

– I've received a letter from Tagore. I'll show it to you in a moment. He remembers you kindly and sends his regards. To me, he sent a poem. But tell me, have you read Keyserling?

– The German from the School of Wisdom? No, not yet.

– Well, you can't live *another minute* without reading him. *This very day* I'm going to lend you his *Travel Diary*.[12] Do you know what he *means* to me, Carmen? I'm *in* those books, I *am* those books. That man knows me. He says all the things I don't know how to express on my own … I write him practically every day. I'll show you his letters. I've asked María if she can arrange to have Morente translate him into Spanish. I'm afraid she doesn't care much for Keyserling, but his work is simply grand. Come in, sit down! They'll bring us a nice cup of tea … Now let's talk about Ortega.

They'd reached Victoria's study. The table was nearly covered in little stacks of letters that contained the second life, profuse, lush, branching out toward invisible distances, of a woman who did not yet dare write her own books.

– I suppose Bebé already has his entire itinerary planned out.

– Bebé and the Spanish Cultural Institute, don't forget. But of course there will be idle moments when he'll be able to see his friends.

– Friends, certainly ... I *was* one, of course. Now, though, I won't be at ease until I actually see him in person. You don't know my story with Ortega.

Carmen blinked in surprise.

– No, not *that* kind of story. Or maybe it is that kind, but not the one he would have liked.

The story had begun twelve years earlier, in 1916, without authorization from either of its protagonists, and would last, in all likelihood, for the rest of their lives, or even longer through the renewed turbulence of the written word.

Victoria hadn't been the least bit interested. "I didn't attend a single lecture of his, Carmen, even though all my women friends were going, and despite the hall packed with students and professors, and the running commentary in the newspapers. Spain meant nothing to me at that time. Or rather, it meant everything I couldn't stand: the pompous Spanish language, so stilted and solemn; medieval relics and old-fashioned furniture; a cruel bullfight where I'd seen a horse disembowelled. I had no interest in what a Spanish philosopher had to say. In fact, the very notion of a 'Spanish philosopher' sounded absurd, impossible. A fantastic creature like a mythological animal, a flying horse."

When had Victoria Ocampo begun to *see* José Ortega y Gasset, the professor of Metaphysics in Madrid, classified in his passport as short, hair brown, eyes brown, no distinguishing marks? Victoria had *seen* Ortega only when he decided to speak in her presence – a lady in a straw hat who looked like a timid girl, withdrawn into herself, in the salon of Julia del Carril. Ortega had really *seen* Victoria when, in evening dress in the library of her house downtown, she decided to remain silent and look at him. Perhaps because at that moment she was offering him the most coveted gift a philosopher can hope for from a woman: to feel himself wholly and perfectly interpreted by a delicate intuition, beyond the laborious mediation of words. At that point, the ecstatic woman who persisted in contemplating him ceased to be a mortal individual and became a suprahuman mirror. Explanation, dialogue, response: all became superfluous. Do the eyes of statues respond, or the eyes in paintings? Do they speak? They are just there, eternally open, omnipresent, saying all without uttering a word. Especially the eyes of women, whose nature – Ortega had said – does not develop through the effort of doing, but rather in the serene irradiation of pure being. Thus, as the philosopher acquired reality and credibility, not as a horse with wings but as a genuine man of wisdom, Spanish though he was, it was Victoria who was undergoing transformation into a myth.

– Can you believe that in his letters he calls me the "Giaconda of the Pampas"? *This Gioconda has understood me forever and to my very roots. Never will she confuse me with anyone else. She has discovered that, for me, to Live is a question of style ... and she could all of a sudden draw in the air with her* finger *the movement of* my *style* ...[13] He wrote to me several times, more or less in the same tone, once he'd returned to Madrid. I didn't answer his letters. I stayed silent for years, even when he published my first essay in the *Editorial de Occidente*, without my even asking him. It was "From Francesca to Beatrice."[14]

– Maybe it's good that you didn't answer his letters. Your silence must have made you even more enigmatic, more like the *Mona Lisa* than ever.

– But I needed to speak out. I don't want to be a goddess or a famous painting. Who can deal with that? Besides, I don't understand him nearly as well as he imagines. Or I do understand all too well and don't agree. I felt like arguing against the Epilogue he wrote for my "Francesca" book. I don't like the role he assigns to women in history, no matter how flattering he thinks it is. Keeping quiet so as to enchant and attract men with our splendour, like a stand-up lamp or a house-plant! What a frightful bore!

– Why didn't you want to write him, then?

– Because of a man. Or more accurately, because of my pride for a man I love. Ortega found out about him through a friend of mine, and I still don't know how she knew, because I never spoke to anyone about that relationship. He let me know I was wasting my time with a lover who was inferior to me. Or with a lover inferior to him ...? But I can't fall in love with talent alone. The body makes no mistake about this; it knows much more about the soul than mere intelligence can.

Carmen smiled. She could just imagine Ortega's irritation with the injustices of fate and the irrational whims of a woman's heart. What could Victoria, his Gioconda of the Pampas, possibly see in that despicable ladies' man with the affected grace, poise, and charm of a movie star? Could it be that she didn't appreciate the supreme value of intangible reason, that most virile attribute of men? The philosopher had said, and held it to be a general rule, that women are imaginatively handicapped, their capacity for fantasy limited and minimal; that they abhor genius and seek out mediocre men who can guarantee what they most value: the routine security of daily existence. But not even Victoria, supreme exemplar of femininity, seemed to perceive the irresistible eroticism of concentrated masculine intelligence – testosterone prodigiously distilled into syllogisms – whose appeal could transfigure even the most insipid or unattractive body.

Carmen had several times crossed paths with the *attaché de beauté* since that meeting with Madame Alice. She'd even seen him in Victoria's apartment on the Calle Montevideo. He was still deserving of his nickname and definitely gave the lie to the sophism that associates stupidity and beauty. What's more, he could sing; with his fine tenor he gave moving renditions of whole arias from Bizet and Massenet. Recalling her former professor of Metaphysics back in Spain, Carmen felt that Victoria had made her choice with irrefutable accuracy. Ortega's genuine seductiveness was surely limited to his books.

– If only I'd understood from the beginning the source of his fits of spite, his jealousy, I'd have forgiven him at once and wouldn't have stubbornly, stupidly ignored him. Or maybe …

– Might you have felt you were being unfaithful to your love by cultivating an intense friendship with another man, even if it was purely intellectual?

– Probably. But it isn't enough for me anymore to devote myself to passion alone. I need Ortega.

– What for?

– If only I knew exactly … There's something in me that I myself don't yet know, something I still can't clearly see.

– And you think the philosopher holds the key to the mystery? Oh, my! Now it's you who want to turn *him* into a Gioconda.

– Not to worry. The role doesn't suit him. He's too ugly to be a Gioconda and too averse to obscurity and mysticism to be a prophet or a soothsayer. But he knows something I don't: what needs to be done in the times we live in.

Victoria lit a cigarette and offered one to Carmen. They smoked for the pleasure of the aroma, and because they enjoyed watching the rings of smoke waft skyward, little clouds replicating the texture of their thoughts.

III

When José Ortega y Gasset arrived in Argentina for the first time on the twenty-second of July, 1916, on a ship fatefully named the *Queen Victoria*, there was no man more ready than he to find a Gioconda or, if none were at hand, to invent her. Invention turned out to be unnecessary. A young Argentine woman, a talented but frustrated actress, was ready to take on the great role of "Our Lady of Discontent," as he had a few years earlier dubbed the virtual lady of Leonardo Da Vinci (the real lady, Lisa di Zanobi del Giocondo, being a mere pretext, a pale anecdote).

Their paths first crossed at a bland social function, their memorable encounter a meeting of two complementary dissatisfactions. Spain, for Ortega, was a landscape in ruins repeating yesterday's gestures, where the voice of the future thudded against dead walls, without echo. Argentina, for Victoria, was a long family saga in which her destiny was already written in indelible characters.

Ortega, Junior – so called because his father, the writer Don José Ortega Munilla, was along on the trip – made his first moves in Buenos Aires with the stern pomposity of a German professor, which the local press found off-putting. While Ortega, Senior, a veteran journalist and gallant guest, quickly soothed the city's anxiety by doling out compliments with boyish enthusiasm, his son preferred to strike the pose of mature reflection, reserving judgment, as he said, until he might find a modicum of time in which to "coordinate impressions." From his first lecture at the University of Buenos Aires, he made it clear he had not come to lavish compliments, much less to get distracted by superficial opulence; no, he came in search of intimate depths.

His warning was not altogether inappropriate. Argentina had been falsely named the land of silver by Don Martín del Barco Centenera – mediocre poet and pious ne'er-do-well – inspired by the genuine but very distant treasures of the Andes.[15] Likewise, Ortega would more than once have to wend his way through brilliant labyrinths, forged as if from precious metals. From the day of their arrival, the Ortegas were swept up in a whirlwind, colourful and flattering but obligatory – society celebrations and academic dinners, evenings of concerts and theatre, banquets, suppers, afternoon tea, *cinq à sept*, aperitifs, and cocktail parties. They attended honorary galas and horse-races, heard speeches by chancellors and presidents, ministers, and diplomats. They were received by the Argentine Academy of the Spanish Language and the Association of Critical Thought; fêted by the Centre for Students of Philosophy and Letters, the Arts and Sciences Association, the Club Español, the Jockey Club, and the Progress Club.[16] Two literary reviews, *Nosotros* and *Myriam*,[17] jointly organized a homage attended exclusively by gentlemen of letters, while in the salons of private homes the admiration of the ladies added one more perfume to those exuding from garments of silk, tulle, satin crêpe, and the creamy texture of bare arms. In the cities of the interior – Tucumán, Córdoba, Mendoza, La Plata, Rosario – there were more beautiful women, and more festivities, smaller in scale than the lavish affairs in the Capital but even more enthusiastic.

While Don José Ortega Munilla pleased everyone with his gifts for courtesy and a good story, José Ortega y Gasset irritated and dazzled with sparkling metaphors. His provocative intelligence divided Buenos Aires into two camps. Against his attackers, his defenders praised him for bringing a different philosophy; even if he'd studied at German universities, he was making it new in the old tongue of Spain – a language many considered apt only for theology, anathema, or pompous rhetoric. But now the idiom of Castile was filling the university's lecture halls, its lisped *ces* and *zetas* emphatic enough to banish the mummified Spencer[18] in favour of a subtler and more introspective approach, less concerned with chasing down facts than with revealing to naïve men the fine-meshed net of space-time where facts are sketched, caught quivering and silver-sheened.

Ortega junior not only gave classes on philosophical systems. He also spoke like an oracle on domestic problems that needed settling; he gave his listeners a looking-glass into their secret perplexities. At first he claimed for himself the rights the ancient Greeks accorded the stranger, whom they considered quasi-divine for his ability to examine, god-like, an entire people with the wisdom afforded by difference and distance, untouched by their tragedies and joys, their triumphs and defeats. The stranger's truth, Ortega told them, lies in his error, for peoples and individuals are not only what they are or believe themselves to be; they are also that which they seem to be to others.

Thus the Argentines, he thought, were incubating an extraordinary novelty: a nation not to be defined in the usual way by past, language, religion, or customs. Argentina, made up of potent diversities, was like an avant-garde metaphor combining heterogeneous elements in a brand-new figure. And it was achieving the miraculous cohabitation of those diverse elements within the compact edifice of a common state. Argentina, for the traveller from Castile, was pure futurity: the attempt to live in a way never before tried, outside the mold of established concepts, which cracked and exploded, powerless to contain the new. There were risks involved. One was that the machine of state, required for the task of conciliating nearly irreconcilable interests, might end up trampling individual initiative. Another: that a society such as this, assembled out of so much diversity, might come apart under the pressures of as many disparate impulses. Or yet another: if it turned out that getting rich, amassing fortunes, was the sole collective desire, thus repeating the same old colonial ambition that had dragged the Vice-Royalty through a history of corruption, extortion, and embezzlement. But the grandeur of the challenge was worth the risks, and the intellectuals of Argentina were apparently prepared to deal with them, albeit with incoherent strategies. Don Ricardo Rojas, professor and poet in cape and top hat, had written a book that enthused about the indigenous myths from his distant province of Tucumán, all jungle.[19] Another poet, Leopoldo Lugones, was publishing his lecture series on *Martín Fierro*, an austere canto about local destitution and misery, alleging its family resemblance to Homeric epic and making it a living cornerstone of the Argentine nation.[20] Ortega found it hard to understand this passion for retrospect, imitative of the methods and nationalist manias of Europe. "Are you trying to invent your own fictitious Middle Ages with those poems about gauchos and caudillos? Do you seek your epic in the poems of yesteryear? If so, then what's the point of America?" There in the lecture hall of the Faculty of Arts, he was practically rebuking them.

America was not to be found in the nostalgia of those mustachio'd gentlemen, paladins of a lost cause. America's heartbeat, still unknown to itself, was in the deep eyes of its women, who did not make its laws but did make its men, and one day they'd forge men equal to their desires. America was in those fine ornamental ladies taking up the front rows at all his lectures, to the chagrin of students indignant at not getting into the room. America was within those mannequin women who would eventually stop playing the happy housewife, socialite, and frequenter of charity functions. No longer would they seek at the confessional box a word of advice for their absurd lives. Without pious abnegation or good manners, they would strive for the right to their own happiness. And that happiness would place new and exquisite demands upon men who thought only about raising Dutch cattle, racing pure-bred horses, and harvesting grain.

Later, back in Spain, Ortega would still be writing for those women in the pages of *El Espectador*, with its mission to look equally at both sides of the Atlantic, or in *El Sol* and the *Revista de Occidente*. He wrote explicitly addressing Bebé de Sansinena. But he wrote to Victoria as the nameless woman of *harmonious and divine countenance* and *iridescent soul*. Interpreting poems by Tagore, his public writing perhaps extended what he'd said in private letters that had gone unanswered by their female addressee and were tucked away in a *secrétaire* in Buenos Aires. He wrote evoking the luminous outline traced, one foreign evening, in the twilight by a female body. In relation to that memory, all thought amounted to a mere footnote, *un excursus*, a marginal comment that could neither absorb nor obliterate its mystery: *It seemed as though your posture was the topic of conversation, and what we said merely fervent commentary on the line drawn by your body in the half-light. It shouldn't surprise you, then, that I imagine you with neck arched forward, elbow on knee, hand on chin and the tip of your index finger sunk into your cheek. Your gaze has wandered so far off, it seems to have gone around the world and returned to peer at what is behind its own eyes.*

For love of the dreams created in him by that woman, by those women who transformed their own bodies into an eloquent question, Ortega had ceased to be a "divine stranger": *This winter my soul has for an hour danced in fantasy with the Argentine soul. I have been intimately concerned with your vicissitudes and have been an Argentine in imagination.*[21] Perhaps, during the last months in Buenos Aires in 1916, it was his life in Spain that had come to be a dream. The concentric wheels of the Cibeles fountain, the Arco de Cuchilleros, appeared in his mind as sepia-coloured photos or ancient postcards. Madrid, with its narrow streets, and Castilian villages were reduced to nothing, crushed beneath the wheels of the train that for nearly a day and a night carried him over the inexhaustible pampas to

Tucumán, the smallest province of the Republic.[22] In the provincial capital, not only the university lecture halls but also the theatres – the Odeon, the Opera – hosted lectures in packed rooms, as though the audience were there not to hear Ortega's invisible verbal arabesques but to see with their own eyes the décor and props of a Spanish *zarzuela*.

Still in Argentina in December, he spent New Year's Eve on an island in the Tigre estuary. A few new friends – Doctor Torrontegui, the Marquis of Belpuig, Mercedes Duchamps – had organized a farewell dinner. His father was not present at the festive board; Don José Ortega Munilla had already left for Spain on the second of December, as per their original plan. His son had stayed on, obliged by success and his engagements to speak in Rosario and Montevideo. Under the light of the streetlamps, mirrored in the tremulous river waters, he saw reflected back to him the image of someone else. In his white Garvinet tuxedo jacket and linen vest, both garments tailored in Buenos Aires, he glimpsed another possible life: as an Argentine, a son not of dessicate Spain but of a young and carefree people, new-born, *full of desires, free of envy*, where the burden of existence dissolved in enjoyment, light as a bubble of champagne.

He turned back to the table. Soon he would have to face the other Ortega – the professor of Metaphysics, with his simple life divided between a Madrid apartment and El Escorial, town under a shadow of stone.[23] He was married to a discreet, domestic woman whose name was a common flower[24] and who never attended his lectures, just as the wives of bullfighters prefer to stay away from the *plaza de toros*. A beautiful and tranquil woman who by the light of a small lamp read French poetry – which, unlike the Gioconda of the Pampas, she would never recite in public – she had given him three children, the last (another José) born during his father's absence.

On the second of January, Ortega y Gasset switched queens and boarded the *Isabel de Borbón*, bound for the port of Cádiz. Before his departure, the students and professors of the Faculty of Philosophy and Letters had gifted him with an effigy of Kant. His fourteen pieces of luggage included boxes of books and trunks full of brand-new, Argentine-made clothing. Plus a *tatú carreta* (an armadillo) and an embalmed *yacaré* (alligator). His children would fit out the yacaré with horse's reins and use it to play Cowboys-and-Indians in the imaginary jungles of America.

IV

To Carmen's relief, Ortega had arrived at last. She'd been overwhelmed by Victoria and her ceaseless questions, her need to know every scrap of news immediately without the humiliation of getting it second-hand from Bebé. And Bebé, too, had been quite trying. Zealously controlling every detail, she wanted this second apotheosis to outdo the first, for the glory of both Ortega and her own reputation as patroness of the arts.

What will Argentina be? The Río de la Plata, the Paraná, the Chaco, Tucumán, the Pampa, Buenos Aires! Above all the Pampa ... What will the Pampa be? I already know more or less what the Pampa is geographically, but what will it be sentimentally? At thirty years of age, the heart of a melancholy man loses interest in geography and, if he is honest with himself, he recognizes that his foremost concern is with things as sentimental entities. La Pampa, Buenos Aires! From the bottom of one's soul arise flocks of confused hopes that fly straight to the infinite horizon, piercing it like these dark airplanes that seem nailed into the azure. The life of a Spaniard of polished sensibility is so harsh, sordid, miserable that in it there lives almost nothing but hopes, hopes that have no place to find nourishment, vague and errant hopes, desperate hopes. And when at the periphery of his soul a pore opens, letting in a bit of light, those poor hopes rush there avidly to slake their thirst in the ray of clarity. What will the Pampa be when seen from the sensitive summit of my heart?

These thoughts Ortega had jotted down just before his first trip to the River Plate, trying to anticipate in toponyms exotic places and unheard-of pleasures. On his return to Spain, he published them in a piece on Azorín, that subtle poet of Spain's invincible past, still so persistent in its present.[25] He dedicated the article to Bebé, in the gallant and ornate style of a courtier: *To Señora Elena Sansinena de Elizalde, Argentine Lady of exquisite and exceedingly noble soul, honour of a people capable of bringing forth such virtues.* In the same text he'd inserted an extensive paragraph, in French, from a letter written by Victoria. Not mentioning her by name, he spoke of a wise reader and unripened writer, an effigy of Diana who wanders the world *swift and svelt, urging on the hounds of her sentiments.*

Bebé, corsetted by Ortega's courtesy, mummified into a venerable public monument, had no choice but to observe silence and be grateful for his *respectful admiration.* Victoria could secretly take solace in meriting more

audacious praise, so much more personal, addressed not to her respectabil-
ity and moral qualities but to her passion and intelligence. Both women,
the "legitimate" and the "concubine," were awaiting the new Ortega, eager
perhaps to hear him say how much they had (not) changed, and to put a
precise name to desires and aspirations not yet fully conscious.

The man who now trod Argentine soil again was no longer the thirty-
two-year-old of 1916, when the exotic place names, endowed with visions,
smells, and flavours, had inspired errant hope. Back in Madrid, he had
moved to an upper-floor apartment at Calle Serrano 47, where he practised short-range peripatetic philosophy, insatiably walking up and down
the long hallway, then heaping file-cards crammed with notes upon the
great oaken table in the dining-room. Politically, he wanted to move
house into a new and different Spain. Along with Gregorio Marañón,
Pérez de Ayala,[26] and other intellectuals, he was embarked on the grand
adventure of the Second Republic. When he was received at dockside in
Buenos Aires by Ramiro de Maeztu and the honorary committee, Ortega's
greeting was cold and officious. He saw in Maeztu the ambassador of a
nation of belltowers and cemeteries and rusty old swords, the Spain that
Ortega wanted consigned to a family album, like so many photos of forebears or ancient manuscript illustrations. He preferred not to remember
him as the brother of María de Maeztu, or even as his own inseparable
companion when they were both very young. Refusing to stay at the embassy, he went straight to the rooms reserved for him at the Hotel Plaza.
There, following the initial round of honours, he met with Carmen to be
briefed on the details of his first public lecture.

Carmen found her old professor of Metaphysics noticeably more
wrinkled, balder, skinnier. Up close and *tête à tête*, this impression
was accentuated.

– Have you been able to rest?

– Hardly at all. If this keeps up, I'll have to write my lectures in letters
several inches high and then read them half-asleep. Something has to be
done. Since you're in charge of public relations, I'll thank you to reduce
contact with the press to a minimum. And social gatherings as well.

– May I remind you that Victoria wishes to receive you at her home?

– Nothing to worry about there, smiled Ortega. Some appointments are
impossible to forget. All in good time.

– How do you find the city?

– Sprouted up like mushrooms after rainfall. More theatres, more schools, more monuments, more institutes, more immigrants, more avenues, more parks, wider streets, skyscrapers. I'm overwhelmed. But the quality of all this remains to be seen. The mere reign of quantity is dubious. And you? Do you plan to stay on here?

– Actually, I've been staying on longer and longer without realizing it. I work in the Spanish Cultural Institute with Bebé, teach literature classes in a high school, and work as a translator. Time goes by, or passes *me* by, and I hardly notice. And the most important issue is still unresolved.

– What issue is so important?

– I thought it was a family problem, but now I'm not so sure.

– Señorita Brey, there's a whole ocean between you and your family. I don't think you should worry about them so much. Spanish women should learn to be more themselves and less concerned with family. Deep within every woman is a gazelle who wishes to run free as the wind. Go ahead and run.

Professor Ortega, now up to fifty or sixty smokes a day, lowered his cigarette-holder and exhaled two or three elegant columns of smoke. Carmen followed the smoke's lazy spiralling. How much of a gazelle remained in the graceful Señora de Ortega, surrounded as she was by children in the confined space of a Madrid apartment, while the philosopher was in far-off lands speaking to other gazelles who, between forest and Louis XIV tapestries, had not yet been domesticated?

– Speaking of ladies, can you please do me a favour? Take this letter to Victoria and deliver it in person.

The conversation with Ortega had been draining. Her professor, as often happens with disorganized men afraid of losing their way in the chaos of reality, wanted to know everything in precise detail: venues, audiences, MCs, even the intensity of the lighting that would fall on his hand-written lecture notes. Before heading to Victoria's place, Carmen dropped into Harrods department store.[27] New spring fashions were on display: a white satin evening gown with hand-embroidered flowers, a dance outfit in *crêpe de Chine* with painted flowers, and for afternoon wear a two-piece suit in silk muslin. She decided to come back for the suit as soon as she received her bonus for Ortega's visit. Otherwise, she'd have to use the money she'd been saving for a gramophone.

She ordered tea at the *confitería* and leafed through issues of *Mundo Argentino*.[28] She skipped over an article about monkey-gland grafts which, according to Professor Voronoff – another sage visiting Argentina – were supposed to restore to patients their lost faculties. She read a heart-rending plea on behalf of teachers whose salaries from the Municipality of Buenos Aires were several months in arrears ("What, are we teaching in a country out of some comic opera?"). Then came a screed lambasting English women writers: "female factory workers," according to the author, who churned out industrial quantities of novelettes for housemaids and typists. Only a few were spared – the equivalent of "*haute couture* designers" – such as Rose Macaulay, Dora Russell, and Charlotte Haldane, who should properly be considered not female scribblers but masculine writers. *It's surely no accident that the surname of each of these three is coupled to a glorious male antecedent*, concluded the article's author.[29] The outlook for River Plate fiction was equally lacking in promise. *Tragic Innocence*, by Soiza Reilly, told the tale of a rich and beautiful young woman – widowed or separated – on a voyage to Europe with her two little girls and their nanny. Alas, the young beauty was a wicked, conceited monster. She spent her days preening on deck, reading books by Keyserling, Ortega, and Tagore. At times she was merely indifferent to her daughters' weeping; at others her annoyance was so great that she locked the children up in the cabin and beat them to her heart's content. Finally, the elder girl, terrified by the beatings and reprimands, threw her little sister overboard so her cries would no longer provoke their mother's ire.[30]

If Victoria had children, thought Carmen, Señor Soiza Reilly would be quite capable of calling on the courts to lynch her. In Spain, the occupations available to women, as Concepción Arenal had put it, were two: kiosk-owner or queen.[31] But in Argentina the choice seemed even narrower: you were a mother or a mother. There were other stories, all of them abridged, all variations on the same theme. Only one article stood out against this dreadful moralizing: "What Good Is a Housewife? Reflections of a Philosopher." *The housewife, as she is known throughout the civilized world, is a stupid product that serves no purpose in the life and needs of an intelligent man*, summed up the unknown thinker, one José Lorenzo. "One simply must meet that saintly man," said Carmen to herself.

It was nearly suppertime when she arrived at the apartment on the Calle Montevideo. Victoria was expecting the Castros and two or three other members of the Association of Professional Musicians.

– I've resigned as official patroness of the association, Carmen. I can't go on after that moron the secretary of culture decided to fire Maestro Ansermet and replace him with a mediocrity, just when a municipal grant has finally been arranged so that musicians can be paid honorariums. But I have to let them know just why I'm doing this. In any case I'm still going to help them, only not through the APM.[32] As for Ansermet, he doesn't need us. A conductor of his genius will be snapped up in no time by New York or Paris. Thanks to people like the secretary, the only damage done is to Argentina. So, tell me, my dear, have you seen Ortega? He's been friendly with me, but rather distant; he still hasn't answered the letters I sent him at the Plaza …

– As a matter of fact, he's just sent this one for you.

Victoria tore open the envelope in one quick gesture. When she'd finished reading, she was flushed red and shedding tears of fury, but also of laughter.

– What's the matter? What does he say?

– He's indulging in revenge through vitriolic flattery. He says he's dumbfounded by the favour of so many unexpected missives. That only the sisters and brothers of Napoleon could receive a kingdom at the break-fast table and remain unflustered, having been without food only the day before. But he needs time to accustom himself to such marvellous gifts as I've deigned to bestow upon him. He asks me to have patience until he has discharged his "masculine" obligations.

– And how will you answer him?

– I won't. Or at most I'll send a note telling him I'm assuming my "feminine" obligation: to wait for an illustrious man to get over his fit of pique.

v

The philosopher's success at Friends of the Arts surpassed all expectations. *My only reproach to the public* – Victoria had written to María de Maeztu – *is that they already agree with Ortega beforehand.* Thanks to him, Carmen Brey enjoyed a few moments of transient glory. Bebé Sansinena credited her with Ortega's good humour and was sure that everything had gone so swimmingly thanks to Carmen's management skills. To anyone who would listen, she presented Carmen as "her" discovery, received from Ortega in 1924 as a personal gift wrapped in the tissue paper of his prestigious recommendation. (Bebé preferred to forget that Victoria had been Carmen's first employer.) *Of course Bebé plays the proprietress; Ortega belongs to her, he's here for her and thanks to her* – the letter concluded, furious at the injustice. But the victim himself wasn't complaining about the abusive appropriation.

For her part, Carmen was sure the rising star of Friends of the Arts was not due solely to Ortega's visit, as Victoria maintained, but to Bebé Sansinena, her iron will to make things happen dissimulated beneath her charming smile and gracious, bird-like gestures. The lecture, concert, and exhibition halls were always full of people from the general public as well as artists, writers, and bohemians young and old. Carmen had become friendly with a few writers from the new generation. A poet with curly hair and a French surname (Marechal) had startled her with his verse; his poetry took the basic things of the wornout, work-a-day world and recombined them in a new light. A handsome fellow dressed in black, with an unpronounceable Prussian name (Arlt), called himself an inventor, although his friends swore that his presumed inventions had ruined his family, and that his inventiveness was all in his stories and vignettes of city life. Both men wrote for the daily newspaper *El Mundo* and were fond of mysteries and investigative inquiry. Carmen had put them on the trail of her brother, Francisco, and Marechal, familiar since childhood with the rural south of the Province of Buenos Aires, had promised to bring news.

Ortega's first public lecture had been interrupted by a "sudden indisposition" – a fainting fit the doctors diagnosed as nicotine poisoning. The subsequent talks brought in ever greater audiences, perhaps in hopes of receiving the benefit of the philosopher's wisdom before he swooned again. Carmen took notes for Bebé's archive; it was hard to resist the desire to linger over certain sentences, as if over a newly revealed landscape, whose forms might vanish with a change in the light. While note-taking, she'd felt pressed by an insistent gaze. Its source was a pair of dark eyes belonging to a young woman, about her own age but about the height of a child. Carmen had seen her on other occasions but had not approached, lest her interest be misinterpreted as morbid curiosity or compassion. The girl came and went accompanied by a caregiver, sometimes in a wheel chair, at other times on crutches, dragging her completely immobile legs. That night, after the lecture, while Ortega was being congratulated by unknowns and illustrious alike, she wheeled over and addressed Carmen.

– I'm María Rosa Oliver, she smiled. A friend of Bebé. I want to ask you a big favour. I'd very much appreciate having a copy of this lecture. This one in particular. Don't think they're all the same to me. Would you be able to do that for me?

A few days later, Carmen knocked at the door of a two-storey mansion around the corner from the Hotel Plaza. The doorman led her up a marble staircase, down the entire length of a very long hallway, and left her in a vestibule where she stood, amazed, in front of an enormous fireplace built of green stone. Above the mantel was a gold-framed mirror proportionate in size to the fireplace. It was hung so high, however, that Carmen reckoned she wouldn't see the top of her head reflected even from the top of a stepladder. In the absence of any ceiling, the distant roof looked like a ponderous firmament crossed by heavy beams. Her journey continued, now guided by the caregiver, through another series of vestibules, stairways, glass doors, and skylights, until they reached a vast library. María Rosa Oliver was waiting for her there.

– Señorita Brey! What a pleasure to see you. I know what you're probably thinking: that this is a house of giants, like the one in "Jack and the Beanstalk." Not at all true. We're all short, almost dwarves. I believe my grandfather Romero was indulging in a compensatory fantasy when he had it built. You should have seen the upholstered sofa we got rid of – it was as big as a room all on its own.

Carmen laughed.

– Good, I'm glad to hear it. I won't feel so overwhelmed. Especially if there are no ogres.

– Ogres come in all shapes and sizes. Even our admired philosopher can be one, for all his gallantry.

– Do you think so?

– Of course. If it were up to him, we women would be kept stored away along with the magic harp and we'd sing only when the giant wound us up, so as to inspire the hen who laid the golden eggs. That's about where he's going with his talk of the "diffuse influence" of women, and when he says we're private and passive, whereas men are public and active.

– Well, in my case, he recommended I run like a gazelle. Like the gazelle every woman carries inside.

– Naturally. Because running means running away. It's for the pleasure of the hunter who chases you. Didn't he compare courtship to the hunt? ... Besides, he's a "little rich kid." He's only comfortable when surrounded by bourgeois luxury. You should have seen him here, in this very library, not long after his arrival. He flopped down in that armchair with palpable relief, as if he'd finally taken off a pair of tight-fitting shoes ...

– Couldn't it have just been fatigue? And excuse me, but if he's a little rich kid, then what are you?

– A little rich kid who isn't resigned to being one. I'm perfectly aware of our prejudices and privileges, and I don't like them one bit. I'm not saying he can't see it. Still, those select minorities he talks about so much ... he seeks them among the upper classes more than among the teachers and writers of the middle class who are his real colleagues.

Carmen went over to the chair used by the philosopher, sat down, and untied her shoes.

– I'm guessing he was attracted by the comfort of this chair. He probably felt like having a nap. Just as I would right now if I weren't here on a visit. Anyway, why do you go to hear him speak, and why did you invite him here if you judge him so harshly?

– Because he's the first man to treat Argentine women like intelligent beings. At least he believes that women can think, even if he does see us as wrapt in the hazy mystery of our inner world because it's our nature, and refuses us the right to create outstanding works of genius like men do. But just because he gives us the right to think, I'm not going to join the chorus of those ladies who at the drop of a hat start simpering: "Well, as Ortega says ..."

– Ha ha! Yes, I've heard that sing-song before. It's on the lips of all the Sansinenas.

– The Sansinenas? That's a good one! It's true, quite a few of them seem like Bebé's courtly retinue, all singing from the same hymnbook. Who calls them that? Don't worry, I won't tell anybody.

– Okay, it's something Victoria says.

– Which Victoria?

– Victoria Ocampo.

– I'm not surprised, she's very witty. I've heard her recite at Friends of the Arts and we've known each other since we were girls. Or rather, I know her, but I don't think she's noticed me. Our families always went to mass at the convent of the Catalinas. I still remember seeing her in Paris, at the Hotel Majestic. She was a lovely girl, tall, with a moiré ribbon in her hair.

– And with a grotesque fool of a suitor.

A señora of doll-like stature and form, with startlingly blue eyes, had appeared behind the wheelchair.

– I'm María Rosa's mother, María Rita. But people call me Beba. I'm glad of your visit. My daughter has told me about you. Quite an act of deference. Usually I'm not even aware she's receiving guests.

Carmen kissed the lady's soft cheek, redolent of baby soap. Mother of eight children, as María Rosa would later tell her new friend, perhaps she couldn't get used to any other scent.

– You should have seen the suitor. A hideous young man! Bleach-blond hair and a checked suit as tight as a dancer's leotard.

– Mamá, he was the son of Rostand, the poet.

– Rostand's son or not, he looked like a … one of *those*, you know what I mean. A beauty like her wasting her time with that mannequin! Well, Victoria had her whims. *Has*, I should say. I'll have tea and sandwiches brought to you. And don't pay any attention to the nonsense this one tells you. (She nodded toward María Rosa.) She's good and generous, but stubborn as a mule. Sometimes as prickly as a porcupine.

Would María Rita, alias Beba, be listening behind the wall? She was clearly more concerned about her eldest daughter than all her other offspring.

María Rosa shrugged her shoulders as soon as Beba left.

– My mother is always afraid I'll say something scandalous and frighten people off.

– I don't think that will ever happen with me.

– That's good. So tell me, did you bring the lecture?

– Yes, indeed. Here it is.

Her dark eyes raced up and down over the typewritten lines, finally fixing on a particular passage. She looked up, smiling.

– He's an ogre, but capable of saying extraordinary things: *Our true and deep personality is constituted by a number of endeavours, longings, and desires. These are the vital springs that give tension and shape to our soul. The true being of each of us lies in the profile of our desires. Our worthiness is in equal proportion to our desire. The quality of our aspirations determines the rank of our soul.*[33]

Carmen looked down at María Rosa's legs covered by a dark velvet skirt. They'd been imprisoned for years in straps of leather and iron, like the unfortunate son of a king in that novel by Dumas, whose sin was to be born a few seconds later than his twin brother.[34] In that prison, hadn't the normal aspirations of life been suffocated? When Carmen glanced up, María Rosa was looking at her with dark eyes, serene, almost condescending.[35]

– I hope you're not thinking I don't have desires. Maybe not the same desires as other women, but they're worth just as much to me as anyone else's.

When Carmen Brey left, María Rosa Oliver wheeled her chair over to the curved balustrade overlooking the ground floor. She called to mind that week in 1918, before the end of the Great War, when supporters of the Allies were still pitted against those of the Germans, both in Argentina as a nation and within the family. But just then, a joyous revolution of a different sort took place: the invasion of an army of servants, upholsterers, polishers, electricians, porters, and plumbers. The entire house resounded, boomed, shook, creaked, like a huge instrument, from basement to rooftop, brimming over with voices, grunts, music of various kinds, the swish of cloth against cloth, the thud of shoes, clashes and strange alliances of scents, tobaccos, and perfumes. Even the pianos hopped from one floor to another, and enormous flower pots glided as though on swift wheels.

Those days of feverish activity were to culminate in a single night, when the second daughter of the Oliver-Romero family made her début in society. That night, María Rosa Oliver, in her party dress, had sat in this same spot, as if the balustrade enclosed a theatre box and the figures drawn by the feet and bodies down below were a distant spectacle or the silent and absurdly moving images of the cinema. Beside her sat the third sister, not yet authorized to attend the ball. Nearer, and more tempting, there arose the thick aroma of food delivered from the Confitería del Gas or the Confitería del Águila,[36] or prepared in the house's own kitchen. Listening to the orchestra play waltzes and tangos, the sounds of laughter and conversation, María Rosa Oliver did not consider it cruel on the part of destiny, or her parents, that she was excluded because she had not legs for dancing, just as her younger sister had not enough years of age. She simply watched it all like a movie, let herself be entertained as the diminutive figures danced the night away, until finally the pink dawn light filtered through the skylights. *There was no one to blame for my misfortune,* she would write many years later. *And since no one could be held to account for it, the best thing was to pay it no heed, as far as possible.*[37]

VI

It is my destiny, Victoria, to sail toward you when you are possessed. In 1916 I don't know what it was that possessed you, but you were a "possessed woman." Now I find you colonized by dreams of Germany and Hindu memories. Carmen had miraculously rescued those lines of Ortega's just as Victoria, after reading them, was about to crumple and toss the note in the wastepaper basket. And it got worse, despite an apparent change in the feminine object of his mockery.

— Have you seen the stupidities that famous wise man puts to paper? A waste of good stationery, isn't it? Not to mention time. The time he needs for his worthy "masculine obligations." Why tell me all about yesterday's social event hosted by the ex-mayor? He was surrounded by mermaids, "sirens" he calls them, who when introduced went bouncing off him like Basque *pelotas* off a *frontón!*[38]

— Calm down, Carmen had said. Stop writing to him for a few days, and then show up impromptu, just when he's getting seriously worried. He won't want to lose a friendship he so recently recovered.

— What friendship? All he does is laugh at me and skewer me with barbs. Colonized, he has the nerve to call me. But who does he think he is? How dare he?

— Well, frankly, I too am a bit alarmed about your obsession with Keyserling. Have you taken a good look at who you're getting involved with? Have you seen his photographs? He looks like an albino orangutan!

— Carmen, how childish of you! I'm not going to let myself be swayed by a person's appearance. That's an attitude from the last century, when they used to believe blindly in everything phrenologists said. Besides, our correspondence is on another plane. Strictly intellectual. Spiritual.

— Are you sure? What you're thinking when you write to him doesn't necessarily coincide with what he reads into it.

— Fine. In any case I'll soon have the chance to find out for myself. I'm going to Europe. Soon. The sooner the better. It's been ages since I last

went. Besides, I can't stand this situation any longer. Ortega and the Sansinenas, or the *Sansirenas*, or whatever he's pleased to call those ridiculous
women – they aren't even pretty – who line up to kiss his hand.

What about the *attaché de beauté*? What was to happen, what was
already happening with him, in the double whirlwind of Ortega and Keyserling, and between the life Victoria was leading and the life, barely
glimpsed, that she aspired to? She had never spoken clearly about that tall,
beautiful man, who was gently aging and whom she introduced as a friend
at tea parties and dinners. Carmen knew that Julián Martínez had spent
two months at the Corbusier-style house Victoria had had built in Mar del
Plata, to the horror of both neighbours and visitors, to the point that it
became a sort of circus phenomenon, a must-see for visiting tourists.
Their relationship was the closest thing to a marriage they'd been able to
manage. Maybe neither of the two desired marriage any longer, even if
Victoria were to break free of hers.

– Are you going to Europe alone? Carmen dared to ask.

– I don't want to go alone. That's why I'm having trouble deciding to
leave. I'm trying to convince a certain person, *that* person, to accompany
me. Even if at first we have to travel separately.

Indeed, Victoria's urgency to be off was being dampened by her own
indecision and Julián's. Ortega's letters may have been another factor. Mol-
lified by the personal and epistolary attentions of the formerly disdainful
beauty, he had condescended to a stylized and oblique courtship. Buenos
Aires for him, he wrote, now satisfied nothing more than the vague need
to be in love, the empty form of a love without object that moved him to
shoot arrows into the wind, like the hunter who vainly lets fly at an unat-
tainable prey.

What sentiment, what requirement – Carmen wondered – did Buenos
Aires fulfil for her? There were afternoons at the Tortoni or the Richmond[39] when, at the end of a work day or after another interminable
conversation about letters not meant for her, she would be struck by a
sadness as ineluctable as the taste of the coffee she'd just ordered. Why
was she in America? What for, Carmen Brey Moure? Victoria longed for
Europe, to return to a continent where she had no one, no long-standing
affective ties, no deep and real connections. Except for her penpals, of
course, among them a German count she didn't even know in person,
whose luminous aura, his saintly halo, was conferred by the magical

words of his books. Carmen, in contrast, had left everything behind – her childhood, the bones of Antonio Brey, the *ria* at dawn, the green roofs of Mugardos, the trunk containing María del Carmen Moure's clothes, the damp whispers of enchanted forests where the roots of memory grew, where her father and mother had dreamed the shape of her soul long before she was born. She, Carmen Brey, fugitive without a cause, was not planning to return. What, or whom, was she waiting for? Her brother? He had decided to erase the page of time inscribed with his face and those of his ancestors, and to block out the blinding glare of the sea's light reflected from the distant balconies of Ferrol, fearsome mirrors. Was she really waiting for him?

If a girl with María Rosa's disability was capable of ennobling desires that exalted the map of her life, what desires did *she* have – she who walked freely on her two sound legs? Was she like the sick child in that poem by Tagore, the little boy who waited day after day for a letter from the king, until it arrived the very day he died, along with the doctor who could no longer save him? Was she waiting for a great love, the love she'd heard other women talk about, in Spain and Argentina, a love that seemed to depend more on the lover's capacity for fantasy than on the beloved subject? And how long did they last, those great loves, for those who experienced them? Would Victoria's great love endure, protected up until now within its own clandestine glow? Wasn't she always on the point of dropping it for another, greater desire, one whose very excess made it less definable? Every move Victoria made was intense, each gesture of adulation or scorn more emphatic than necessary, every act designed to be seen from afar, as though her life were the performance of fabulous script written by a demanding playwright, which she acted out to her utmost strength.

Carmen preferred to stay behind the scenes, near the prompter who knew the entire libretto, perhaps to catch an up-close glimpse of the real skin behind the makeup. To take a peek at the holes in a stocking, or a garment's stain no longer disguised by distance, or the glass beads beginning to show through the worn sheen of false pearls. She thought about her loves and saw them as stupid – old playthings, flimsy and falling apart. Her adult self could no longer remember the secret of their former charm.

The first had been a boy of dark complexion, son of a rich Indiano, the finest lad in all of Ferrol, Mugardos, O Seixo, Fene, or any of the surrounding towns. The best dressed and the nicest. Little Carmen Brey had pined over him, unnoticed, for two years. Until a summer romance, between high school and university, turned her into the most envied girl in the city and environs. But when she came back from university the following summer, her boyfriend had a new car, imported from the United States, and in that car sat a gorgeous woman with an egret-feather boa, who paraded her beauty and average talent on stage at the theatres of Santiago and La Coruña. Antonio Brey heaved a sigh of relief; reality had quickly confirmed his warnings and advice. Disillusioned by physical attraction and easy money, Carmen then sought gravitas and wisdom; for a time she thought she'd found them in her professor of English Philology, Doctor Swinburne, son of a Gibraltarian and an Andalusian. Despite his surname (he was a distant relative of Algernon Charles),[40] Swinburne had very little of the Pre-Raphaelite poet about him. He looked more like Mr Casaubon, the arid and laborious theologian imagined by George Eliot.[41] Tall and grave, he was a man of few words, but courteous with the young ladies. He lived alone in Madrid and spent vacations with his widowed mother in Almería. At times, Carmen imagined how marriage to the professor might have turned out. There'd have been a child, perhaps two – Mrs Swinburne was anxious for a grandchild from her only son, already getting on in years – but no more than two, so as not to disturb the studious silence of long days spent reading, and to avoid burdensome expenses. Carmen, who had never learned to cook properly, would have hired kitchen help and a nanny from the village; and she'd have compensated for her meagre domestic virtues with her self-sacrificing labour as her husband's secretary, having demonstrated her abilities for the role when she was the best student in his class. They'd have spent two summers in Almería for every one in Mugardos (Swinburne was a devotee of London, yet he could not abide the rain and fog of Galicia), and one day they would have visited England to acquaint the children with the land of their paternal forebears and let them hear genuine English spoken, unsullied by vowels too pure or by importunate *jotas*.[42] At the Sociedad Inglesa in Madrid, Carmen would have applauded her husband's lectures from the front row, suitably attired in fur coat and pearl necklace. She herself would have helped him prepare those erudite talks, diligently researching archives and filing cabinets. Such an active role would have thrilled her at the age of twenty; most professors' wives were lace-draped ladies who never set foot outdoors, let alone work as research assistants. Why, Doctor Swinburne even supported the suffragette movement; he had read, approvingly, John Stuart Mill and Mary Wollstonecraft!

Why had she left that potentially perfect husband, shortly before graduation, when his formal proposal was already made and sealed by a star sapphire encrusted in an engagement ring? The most important decisions, she thought, are sometimes provoked by the tritest of incidents. The insight had come in a wave of negative inspiration from the fillets of salt-cod that were soaking for a dinner she was preparing her fiancé and her future mother-in-law, hoping that for once her codfish would turn out not too salty and not too bland. Then, just as she was draining the flat colourless slabs of fish, the long pale face of Ricardo Swinburne appeared among them. Instantly, the memory of her aunt Elena's voice was in her ear: "My dear child, are you really going to marry that man? Have you taken a good look at him? He may be as learned as you like, but he looks dry as a bone and colder than a codfish." At the time, the comparison made her angry and indignant. Now, however, it suddenly hit home. Everything came clear in a flash. It wasn't that she was marrying a man called Ricardo whom she loved; she was contracting marriage with a professor and with a life that she hoped would be her ticket out of the monotonous, pretentious, common round of bourgeois Ferrol. She also sensed that her decision to marry an older man was in some way a challenge to her father. Antonio Brey had replaced her mother, María del Carmen Moure, with a woman not much older than her, his daughter Carmen. The following week she returned the sapphire ring to Doctor Swinburne, who received it not quite as disconsolately as one might expect, but rather with a hint of unspoken relief. Later, in Argentina, she found out through María de Maeztu that, after his mother died, the professor married a childless widow from Almería who had inherited money.

Argentina had given her neither adventures nor love affairs. Carmen Brey, a formal young woman not quite twenty-seven years old, was still a virgin. A flapper of the Roaring Twenties would have been ashamed of such a condition, but in that southern redoubt of *machismo latino* it was tantamount to a feminine victory. Señorita Brey was not inclined to join some gallery of conquered virgins collected by one of those braggarts abounding in Hispanic lands on both sides of the Atlantic. Nor did she fancy selling herself on the matrimonial market, despite several appreciable offers from successful doctors, entrepreneurs, and businessmen who frequented the Spanish Cultural Association or the Club Español or the Federación Gallega – candidates whose marital aspirations would have been more than satisfied by the acquisition of a comely and cultivated young woman, a university graduate from Madrid with an authentic Peninsular pedigree. *I've heard from Don Peregrino Loureiro that you have a string of admirers. Carmen, for the love of God, the years are passing. Who has hurt you so badly that you cannot see a decent husband in any man? Do you not want children? Don't you realize that a woman is practically old when she turns thirty?* The letters from Adela Montes, now Señora de Núñez, came every month or so, overwhelming her with admonitions and anxious affection. Carmen had framed the photo of the Andalusian's wedding. She kept it on the corner table of the living room, and sometimes, when night was dousing the colours of the city and the only sounds were lonely echoes from a deserted stage, she would run her fingertips over the glass protecting Adela's image. Gone now was the bitterness she had once felt for her, caused by loss and also childish caprice. Adela just wanted Carmen Brey to live, to know the happiness and sadness of having her own children, an experience Adela had been denied. Adela loved her. She kept photos of Carmen in her new home, the house of Doctor Núñez, the apartment of Carmen's father now being rented out. They probably talked about her at Sunday dinner. Her stepmother had married discreetly: her impeccable violet silk dress, the little hat with black speckled veil and the bouquet of forget-me-nots held between gloved fingers all showed a respectful delicacy in the young widow – young but not happy. Had Adela Montes found a great love? Or were Antonio Brey, and now Doctor Núñez, safe and trustworthy substitutes for the father who had died when she was still too young?

Would Carmen Brey be lucky enough to find love with a man who wasn't merely a replacement father, a love that was more than a silly, tedious game? Someone who would commit heart and soul, who would burst open the round of identical days? She didn't believe in knights in shining armour or matinée idols. Nor, unlike Victoria, did she have any faith in the clairvoyant wise man who could reveal the true face of her inmost being, or the enduring track of her destiny beneath the shifting sands of daily life. Nonetheless, in the clear eyes of Señorita Brey, too wide open and too ironic, there stirred, for one who knew how to look, a touch of green, a freshness of untapped sentimental illusion.

VII

Each of Ortega's visits had coincided with a change in president. Both times, thanks to the Argentine penchant for repetition, the same candidate was returned to office: the grave and elusive Don Hipólito Yrigoyen. Devotee of Karl Krause,[43] Yrigoyen had twice gone to hear the Spanish philosopher speak, in part because of the Kantianism he professed, but also to fulfil what at the time was considered a duty of the head of state – head in more than one sense of the word. Thus, on opening nights at the Teatro Colón, the president was there to say a few inaugural words. On those evenings, as in 1916, high society would again stay away, their theatre boxes deserted, just to avoid applauding their top state official. But many of the new young writers, weary of former president Marcelo de Alvear and his *belle époque* top hat, supported the *criollo* Yrigoyen, popular and mysterious as a myth.[44] Don Hipólito's most fervent promoter had been Marechal's friend Jorge Luis Borges, robust and near-sighted, founder and president of the Committee of Young Intellectuals for Yrigoyen, with Marechal himself as vice-president. They won over for The Cause the brothers González Tuñón, Nicolás Olivari, Ulyses Petit de Murat, Francisco López Merino, Francisco Luis Bernárdez, Sixto Pondal Ríos, and Roberto Arlt, among others.[45] Carmen used to see Marechal and Borges at the Confitería Richmond, where the avant-garde poets liked to gather. A somewhat disreputable crew, they were. Not only because they insolently pilloried politicians and literary figures, but also for their dubious wanderings in the *arrabales*, where they allegedly downed *aguardiente* and *milongas* straight-up, and hung out with bad-ass *malevos* and *compadritos*, revering them like gurus.

Victoria had finally calmed down. The philosopher had returned from silence and irony with his admiration intact, auguring their future transoceanic verbal alliance. The cold sting of the formal *usted* form of address given way to the friendly, informal *tuteo*. *I owe you an enormous debt of gratitude* – he had written from Mendoza in the Argentine interior – *as great as these Andean mountains that I can see before me at this moment and which I feel like reaching out to give a pat on the back as one does with an elephant at the zoo. This gigantic debt is you yourself, your magnificent being, the mere fact that you take the trouble to exist. This old debt I've been carrying around so long is one I'll never be able to repay you.*[46]

Professor Ortega was leaving, not *sin pena ni gloria*, but loaded with both heartache and glory,[47] and in the mood for controversy. The idyllic light of the first impact had dimmed. Victoria Ocampo had become dense, heavy, real. In spite of his ideas about the eternal feminine – being-as-such, the ontic *par excellence*, inchoate individuality that never quite emerges or gels[48] – the Gioconda of the Pampas *was* becoming an individual; her tennis-shoed foot was stepping out of the laced boot, off the pedestal, and into the combat sport of life. Argentina, too, had become real. No longer an imaginary land for Ortega, the scene for an alternative destiny, it had begun to fade into a vague nostalgia, a might-have-been nipped in the bud.

Carmen, commissioned by Bebé, had helped him to expedite formalities, classify paperwork, and even gather his luggage, this time lighter and less extravagant – no more alligators or armadillos.

– You can leave content, Professor. You've been a success.

– Best not say that word, girl. It's almost immoral among intellectuals. Nowadays intellectuals cannot and must not be too successful. If they are, they immediately become suspect.[49] They must be betraying something, doing something bad to make the masses adore them like sports or show-business celebrities. Those are the real idols.

– You take a dim view of the masses.

– I neither love nor scorn them. They've always been there. Mass is the condition of all societies, and democracies in particular. But another condition is that the masses choose minorities to govern them, on the basis of aptitude and excellence. These days the masses no longer accept them and insist on governing themselves.

– Maybe because their needs weren't being met by the minorities in power.

– Maybe. It's true the elites have abandoned their duties. But the masses believe they have unlimited rights, simply by virtue of having been born. Rights have to be earned. The masses don't create anything, they only desire. They aspire to enjoy goods and innovations they wouldn't know how to produce.

– Do they not produce them materially with their work?

– That doesn't qualify them to impose direction on society. And since societies do not drift aimlessly forever, leaders will arise who know how to implement the reason of violence, the only "reason" the masses believe in. In fact, they've already appeared. Take Mussolini, for example.[50]

– Fine, but here we are a long way from Mussolini.

– I don't know for how long. And even if that's true, it's no reason for celebration. America has its own problems. Especially Argentina. Have you seen the Pampa?

– Of course.

– Well, I've seen it again with fresh eyes, on the way to Mendoza. There is something extraordinary, disconcerting about it. Something that may set it apart from all other landscapes on earth. Have you noticed that it *has* no limit but rather *is* its own limit? That it crushes, as irrelevant, all objects and beings that show up in it? One's gaze can rest nowhere, but rather flees, straight ahead toward the vastness, as though devoured by the attraction of the horizon. Toward what the vastness promises. It's a tempting and poetic experience, and it captivates one's will like a spell. But it is also extremely dangerous.

– Why?

– Because that spell is baleful. Under the effect of the attraction toward the limit, to a misty yonder, no one lives in himself but rather outside himself, running ahead of himself, chasing illusions that perpetually recede like mirages, which everyone thinks they've made real merely by dreaming them. Until they discover, too late to remedy the situation, that life has evaporated, slipped away between their fingers before they knew it. The curse of the Pampa is the greatest risk Argentina runs today.

– What risk do you mean exactly?

– Of dissolving in vain hopes of greatness, in pure dreams. Of being no more than a great unfulfilled promise.

In his latest letter to Victoria, written while gazing at the Andes and sent from Mendoza, Ortega issued a challenge: *I've written, all in one go, an article for* La Nación *titled "The Pampa ... Promises."*[51] *It will have the virtue of supremely arousing your ire.* The letter also bore a chivalric declaration of submission. Perennially fond of the medieval metaphors of the hunt and of war, the philosopher promised to resign himself even to being ignored by the lady of the castle who had done without him for so many years, who had kept and would always keep him at a prudent distance from the centre of the castle, outside the doors of her intimacy, outside her secret citadel.

When they said farewell at the pier, Ortega didn't know he would be back in the Land of Promise in 1939, when the reality of his own nation had been laid waste. Nor did he know that the Pampa, provider of so much future for others, would hold none for him; he would end up seeking refuge in the harsh, restrictive horizons of old Europe. Exiled first in Lisbon, he would spend the last years of his life in Madrid, ful-filling his own bitter sentence: *One only returns to Spain to run aground, like an old boat.*

Ortega's departure left the leading ladies of Friends of the Arts relaxing in a quiet eddy of mutual congratulation and the pleasurable exchange of anecdotes. One afternoon, as Carmen was leaving the office a little earlier than usual, she heard someone calling at her back. Only because she rec-ognized the voice did she heed the anonymous, ethnic appellative:

– Hey, don't run away on me. Wait a sec, *Galleguita!*

She didn't respond, but did wait while the man of the agitated voice ran to catch up, stopping short a few steps away. It was Roberto Arlt.

– Don't look at me like that! Okay, I know what your name is, but don't get mad. Anyway, it's a compliment. There are no women more womanly than you *Galleguitas.*

Carmen smiled a sceptical half-smile. She was not at all sure that the word "woman" for Arlt connoted anything very praiseworthy.

– So, what is it? Why are you in such a hurry?

– The teacher sends you this. It explains what he managed to dig up about your brother.

Carmen took the envelope and thanked him. The "teacher" meant Leopoldo Marechal, who was indeed a primary-school teacher.

– He didn't come personally because he's down with the flu. So long, Señorita Brey. I'm expected at the newspaper.[52] Maybe another day you'll let me buy you a coffee.

Carmen walked slowly, in a bid to gain time; she was afraid to open the envelope and wanted put it off as long as possible. Finally she came to El Molino[53] and sat down with tea and pastries. *My good Carmen* – she deci-phered the tiny, vertical, separate letters of a handwriting so similar to Borges's, she sometimes went straight to the signature to know who was writing – *I've been asking relatives, friends, and acquaintances in the province, to see if anyone could put me on the trail of your brother. Borges, too, has been investigating, and with a will. But no one knows where he is. The search may go better if you start with Pedro Coliqueo, an Indian who they say was going around with your brother. The Coliqueo clan is part of a community in the town of El Toldos. It's not far from Chivilcoy, which is where your brother, apparently, owned some land at one point. It may be a good idea for you to go there in person. You can count on us if you want company for the trip. Your friend as always, Leopoldo.* Señorita Brey smiled. She was flattered by the offer, but had no intention of accepting it. Those two were likely to end up in some rural watering-hole in front of a bottle of gin, getting mixed up in brawls with drunken peasants. Instead of finding her brother, she'd end up taking them to the hospital.

She left the café. Outside, the moon was rising against the curve of the sky. It looked so close, almost within arm's reach, a moon you could talk to intimately. "Moon Across the Way," like the one in the poem by Borges she liked to recite in silent, secret confession.

Poor in love I was.
Nevertheless, the streets and the moon are yet by my side.
Water is still sweet in my mouth and verses deny me not their grace.
I feel the dread of beauty: Who will dare condemn me if this grand
    moon of my solitude forgives me?[54]

3

1928–1929

The Most Fantastic Woman, Dreams of the Plain

... in the orbit of the most fantastic woman I've ever met in my life.

Hermann von Keyserling,
Journey Through Time II, 1951[1]

... and all these things were fortuitous, like dreams of the plain.

Jorge Luis Borges,
"The South," *Ficciones*, 1944

I

The automobile of Victoria Ocampo, but without Victoria, was slowly leaving the port area, cutting through clouds of steam rising from the asphalt, thick and turbid, like exhalations from the muddy river. Carmen Brey reclined in the back seat. Beside her, Angélica Ocampo watched the docks in silence, the comings-and-goings of departing travellers and those having just seen the departees off, their goodbyes tinged with sadness or disguised relief, but nearly always with the secret longing to be the one who goes away, perchance to a new life, released from the daily grind and the same old face staring back from the mirror.

It was just as hot as four years ago when they'd come to see Tagore off, thought Carmen. She remembered how she had got back to the car dizzy and faint from the heat and the glare – or was it because someone else was going home and not her? Now she almost felt sorry for Victoria; she had cried all the way to the port, and then throughout the farewells on deck. Julián was not there among the friends and relatives. Was that why she wept so, because she could not say goodbye to him, too? Fani, who was accompanying her on the trip, consoled her with reprimands. "Well, I don't see what need there is to go gallivanting off on this blasted trip, if you find the going-away so hard. If it were up to me, we'd stay in this land for all eternity. To think how we went hungry in Spain ... I can't see what Europe has to offer that we don't have right here on our doorstep." But neither Señora Ocampo, nor Fanny, nor José, who was also going with them, would be suffering any privation in Europe. Manuel Ocampo had given his eldest daughter ten thousand pesos for the trip, the equivalent of a hundred thousand French francs – a sum that would buy every comfort and convenience in an old world in liquidation.

What fears, then, what heartaches could perturb their carefree and lavish ocean-crossing? Carmen Brey turned to Angélica, who at times looked like a replica of her elder sister, but slightly faded and blurred, with no sharp edges, like a song that, muted by distance, loses some of its seductive intensity.

– It isn't normal for her to get like that. She's only going for a few months. It's as if she's afraid. What does she think she'll find in Paris? A dragon?

– It's been many years since she last left Argentina, Carmen. The last time was her wedding trip, and she didn't exactly come back happy. Maybe she has forebodings this time, too. And too many expectations.

Victoria had certainly encountered a dragon in that last trip. Or discovered one – a "monster" as she'd once said to Carmen – in the man she married. And she had also found the prince who could save her when she met Julián Martínez one afternoon in Rome. Now it seemed she was going in search of another prince, beautified by the light of the written word, without suspecting that beneath such glitter might lurk a dragon in camouflage.

– I don't like that count she's continually writing to and plans to bring back to Buenos Aires. Can't you do something?

– I don't like him, either. But just try telling anything to Victoria. I have no doubt at all about her affection for me. If someone were to hurt me, she'd suffer more than getting hurt herself. But I've never managed to make her listen, once she's made up her mind. When we were girls, she protected me to the point of tyranny. She has always done whatever she pleases, and it's still inconceivable to her that I could ever stand in her way.

Angélica finished her speech with a tranquil smile. Then she turned away. Would she always be like this, accepting everything as a fait accompli, with ostensible resignation? Scarcely a year younger than Victoria, she was still single at the age of thirty-eight, because her parents had disapproved of the man she wanted to marry. She came and went from Villa Ocampo, always equable and tolerant, ready to help out with her sister's latest enthusiasm or scheme. Was she really living a subsidiary life – the cool, quiet shadow of Victoria's life? Or did she prefer this evasive form of existence so as to avoid being bothered, so that her feelings and perceptions could flow protected, like a river underground, and come to light only when the atmosphere was propitious? At times, Carmen compared herself with Angélica. Maybe it was because they sensed their similarity that they avoided looking at one another: in order to forestall an overflow at the wrong moment of the secret torrent coursing within them both, underneath the cold, bright surface.

Victoria, in contrast to their self-containment, was always brimming over, bursting her banks. She had been dreaming fervently for months about the city where she could see places in their original version, not the stilted, watered-down imitations abounding in America, or at least in Buenos Aires. Rue de Rivoli, Place de la Concorde, les Champs Elyseés – she imagined them, though they had inspired Baudelaire's spleen, as the locus of the real, where true life was finally possible. In that space, lit by the noonday light of revelation, she was to behold in the flesh Hermann von Keyserling, creator of the School of Wisdom. The name was apt, thought Victoria. Keyserling's wisdom was invaluable, beyond measure. He was worth the trip, many trips.

The philosopher had apparently found what is denied to the great majority of mortals: the meaning of life in the diversity of peoples and creeds and cultures, millenarian or newborn. Why humans had lived in the past, and for what. Why and to what end they were living in the present and would live in the future. Until then she had blindly let the years go by, almost always in the same place, stunned by impressions and desires, limited by conventions and proprieties, tied to her sympathies. But Keyserling, philosopher of geography, had wandered over nearly the entire face of the planet. He had learned about the customs at the antipodes. From Ceylon to the Grand Canyon in Colorado. From Agra and Benares to Burma and the Himalayas. From Shanghai and Macao to Yellowstone and Salt Lake

City. He had frequented palaces in Kyoto, Buddhist sanctuaries, Mormon churches. He had been in the House of Serpents in Anuradhapura and the pagoda of Dagon and the monastery of Koya-San. He had admired the dances of Tanjore, the theatre of Udaipur, the bonsai gardens in Japan. He had spoken with holy men and yogis and fakirs and mystics and Chinese sketch artists armed with pencils. He had been a Liliputian alongside the vertical walls of Yosemite Valley and the gigantic trees of the Mariposa Grove. Fascinated and possessed, he had stared for hours at the creation of the world in the entrails of the crater at Kilauea. He had seen the strangest fish in the aquarium at Honolulu – dark blue fish of velvet sheen and bird-like beaks, or moon-shaped with fins flying like banners. In the Bay of Waikiki, he thought he'd found the mold of the first men, who swam like amphibians, were as beautiful and irresponsible as gods, tender as a lament, wild in their orgies, and cruel in war. There was hardly a corner of the whole wide world where Hermann von Keyserling had not brought to bear his microscopic vision and telescopic eyes so as to produce a comparative report. Except South America.[2]

The man who had written the *Travel Diary of a Philosopher* in two volumes had never set foot on the banks of the river wide as a sea, never lost the dimension of things silhouetted against the infinitely receding horizon of the plain. Victoria would come as the emissary of that remote place, still resistant to interpretation and profound intellection because the polyhedral gaze of Keyserling, multifaceted as the eyes of an insect, had not been present to illuminate it. Victoria would bring Keyserling back with her, as she had brought home beautiful objects before – her Coromandel screens or Léger tapestries – but this time not for the merely selfish purpose of decorating her own home. No, it was for the sake of all Argentina: the nation would undergo inspection by the geologist-philosopher, so that he might discover its veins of diamond.

Some afternoons, stretched out on a chaise-longue on the ship's deck, she closed her eyes and, with no one to interrupt her, thought about that fundamental encounter, when *chela* meets *guru*, neophyte meets initiatic wise man. Her hitherto erratic steps would then be guided in the adventure of learning. "Each person aims for something that is beyond individuality," had said the Count. Everyone therefore had a "mission" to carry out (the word didn't entirely please her, it inevitably brought to mind convents and catechizing nuns). But whether it was a mission or a destiny transcending the immediate and ephemeral, the fact was that hers was still out there somewhere, waiting for her to find it. At such moments she would also remember her lover, with passionate anxiety. Would Julián follow her on this path? Would he accompany her on pilgrimages to the sanctuaries of writers, philosophers, musicians – to those places where, if not the final destiny of humankind, at least the elusive meaning of human existence was decided, for better or worse? There were moments when her sole, clandestine love affair, which had lasted as long as many marriages and to which she was exclusively and zealously faithful, felt like a millstone around her neck. But the love was still there. Perhaps it always would be. The mere idea that Julián might die before she did was enough to make her whole body hurt, just as it pained her to think about the death of her sisters or parents – flesh of her flesh, inscribed in the marrow of her bones by the oldest memories of infancy and bloodline, beyond all reason and deliberative will. Julián had promised to join her in February. With two months between their respective voyages, they were unlikely to be suspected of connivance. For twelve years they had been taking similar precautions. Sometimes she worried that even this forbidden relationship, still hidden and still dangerous, had become another form of routine.

Paris was cold, piercing, crystalline. It cleared away nostalgia and uncertainty. She met with Ansermet again. Snubbed by Buenos Aires, he was conducting the première of a concerto in the Salle Pleyel. The theatres and art galleries did not disappoint; it seemed the passage of time had only made everything better. But it wasn't just that. The air outside, not just the invisible refuge of her mind, was filled at last with French. The words she'd first learned to read. The words of prayer, song, and recitation; of love, surrender, and courtship – *Je me tordrais le coeur pour te plaire*, Julián had whispered to her in a furtive telephone conversation – were now common currency, available to everyone, no longer a class marker or a symptom of ostentation which to others (including foreigners themselves) looked like ridiculous snobbery. Thanks to Ortega and efforts of her own, Victoria Ocampo had managed to go beyond the hundred-odd terms in the Spanish vocabulary of the upper classes – that minimal lexicon for objects and basic necessities that Argentine ladies, when back home, used with the servants (not even with pets: they were trained in English or German). She had left what in Argentina felt like the prison-house of French, and yet she continued to feel like an exile in the language of her forbears. It consoled her to think of that displacement, that foreignness in one's own territory, as the imprimatur of Hispanic America (or only of its masters?); in any case, it was irrefutably a mark of their paradoxical belonging.

Keyserling was arriving from Schönhausen, the castle of Bismarck (the home of his parents-in-law) on the fourth of January. He had first asked that Victoria travel to Germany, but she refused to meet him face to face in *terra incognita*. The protective circle of Paris would neutralize to a more tolerable level the powerful force exerted by "the Baltic giant," as she called him seriously and in every sense of the term. His physical and philosophical stature notwithstanding, Keyserling had sent her a list of childish demands, enumerated in good Germanic order, which at the time struck her as charming, or at least forgivable – the peculiar whims of a genius. They included details regarding his lodging, Victoria's conduct, and the life-style she was to provide for her guest while he was in Paris. The Count wished to stay at the Hôtel des Réservoirs in Versailles, a very old and exquisite place surrounded by gardens evocative of the splendours of deposed royalty. He would have an apartment with living room, bedroom, and bathroom; he was to be supplied with envelopes, blotting paper, red ink, and a spool of twine (Victoria, on her own initiative, would include discretionary flowers, various soaps, and eau de cologne). With respect to the pleasures, attentions, and personal services his hostess was to provide, *Madame* Ocampo had to visit him regularly during the month of his stay, avoiding worldly social events and all that might distract her from their philosophical conversations, but it was also up to her to arrange at least one formal dinner, in Paris, with distinguished Argentines (the women in *soirée* attire and the men in tuxedos), the menu of which would include oysters and champagne.

Victoria did not suspect what fits of anger and arbitrary injustices lurked behind that punctilious list of conditions. She resolved simply to fulfil them. And, to the required oblations, she decided to add the beauty of her own person, after an appointment at the Maison Chanel. On the eve of the Transcendental Day, she laid out on the bed the garments she would wear – a blue, pink, and brown pullover and a navy blue suit. She tried on the felt cloche hat from Reboux over her sleek hair cut short. The philosopher, apparently as fond of sensorial delights as he was of intellectual pleasures, deserved such a reception on the part of his disciple.

At midnight, just back from the Ballets Russes and the image of the beautiful Serge Lifar lingering on her retina, she wrote Keyserling a final missive that cost her an effort. Her handwriting slanted anarchically and she struggled to keep her hand from trembling. *At this hour tomorrow, what will you think and what will I think? I am very emotional. Do not make fun of me … May God keep you. I almost feel like I'm saying goodbye on this bit of paper. Goodbye to the person you were for me and who will cease to be so within a few hours, in Versailles. How will I get along without that Keyserling of mine, invented by me?*[3]

II

Marechal was waiting for her at the Once train station,[4] under the big clock, as planned. No sooner had his pipe and broad-brimmed hat come into view than Carmen Brey's feet nearly turned back the way she came, her eyes darting around in search of Elena Sansinena's automobile, which had brought her. But it was too late to change her mind. Marechal had spotted her blue felt hat and was waving a hand.

She sighed in resignation and went to meet him. Up until the last minute she had been doubting whether to go with them, still thinking that proverbs tend to be infallible.[5] Of course, she was not sure, either, that the two friends were really such bad company.

– Hello, how are you? Is Borges not here yet?

– He is. But he went looking for a telephone to tell his mother he arrived safely.

– Heavens! Isn't he a bit old for that?

– It depends how you look at it. As you *gallegos* say, *el pobre no ve tres en un burro*; the poor fellow's blind as a bat.[6] Doña Leonor worries about him constantly, afraid he'll barge into something and one day be brought home injured. Of course he would never get lost here. He often comes to La Perla;[7] this is where he and a few friends meet the great Macedonio, expert metaphysician. Sometimes I go, too.

Carmen refrained from any comment. The "great Macedonio" wasn't exactly a compatriot of Alexander the Great, but rather Macedonio Fernández del Mazo, Doctor of Philosophy. According to the gossip at Friends of the Arts, he was a lawyer of good lineage who apparently lost his wits after his wife died. His children had been left in the care of affectionate relatives, while he – barely able to fend for himself – lived on a small part of the family fortune in miserable boarding houses, and held philosophical *tertulias* in several of the city's cafés with the young avant-garde set. Every once in a while he moved to another boarding house, leaving behind a pile of illegible papers, rough drafts – so his disciples claimed – of master works that never got published.[8]

Borges soon turned up. He was happy. Excessively happy, in Carmen's judgment.

– My good man, what's got into you? You look a boy on his way to the circus.

– I always get like this when I leave Buenos Aires.

– Why is that? I thought you were a city animal.

– Animal I may be, but not entirely an urban one. What I love most about the city is what remains of the pampa in it.

– But haven't you said that you're a *pueblero*? A "barrio man"? A "man of the street"?

– Señorita Brey! Is it possible that you've read *Luna de enfrente*.[9]

– Certainly I have. Or do you think I'm unworthy to be your reader?

– Not at all. It's just that whenever I discover a reader, I'm astonished and filled with gratitude. If I could, and it weren't so ridiculous, I'd send every one of my readers a medal.

– Ridiculous, all right, but it wouldn't cost you much. For the number of readers we have! remarked Marechal. We could round up the whole bunch of them, and they still wouldn't fill the hall of a neighbourhood club.

Carmen smiled. Writers were always complaining. If the public was reading their books, they whinged about the critics not taking notice. If they had critical attention, they grumbled about the lack of readers. And if they had both, their numbers were never enough. If ever I get married, she thought, it won't be to one of those insecure narcissists – their narcissism no doubt due to their insecurities.

They boarded a train waiting on the last platform and got settled in an almost empty car. They had very little baggage, though Borges had stuffed the pockets of his jacket with books.

– You look like a walking library.

– I carry the burden others don't wish to bear. You'll come running to me asking for reading material.

– It depends on what it is.

– *The Arabian Nights*, for example. I've got an edition by Weil that I picked up in a used bookstore.

– See? It wouldn't do me much good. I don't read German. So, you're fond of wondrous events and evil genies?

– Why not? Isn't reality always full of wonders? Moreover, the world is full of evil genies. Just take a look around: there's a lot more evidence of evil than good.

– But not because of genies. It's us, with our free will.

– Well said, Carmen. Let's not blame God for original sin.

– I wouldn't blame Eve, either. You have to admit, Marechal, that both of them sinned, except that Eve did it with more personal style and initiative. Adam lets himself be comfortably led by the nose. And when facing God, he was a coward and blamed it all on Eve. Like a child who snitches at school.[10]

– This isn't the time to be arguing over mythology, interrupted Borges. Silence, some decorum, please. Behold: there lies the homeland, the *patria*!

The patria was ancient, modest, almost empty. At times it was in a state of nature, or barely modified by the creation and destruction of men. They left behind Morón and Castelar.[11] The country estates, the summer residences, and the last little houses were ranged in concentric arcs, their curves ever more distant from the city, like the diminishing foothills of a great mountain range. Then they reached open country, and everything – shacks, cisterns, little schoolhouses, men on horseback – looked pitiful and precarious, unstable and fugitive, like thistledown or thornbushes or sisal that for a few moments came to rest in one spot. But only briefly, then off again they went with the wind, free of weight and form, only to take another shape elsewhere, resplendent objects in a process of perpetual transfiguration.

Before the invaders crossed the Mare Oceanus,[12] before they brought cattle and horses, the peoples scattered across the plain used to walk in search of fruits of the earth, animals to hunt, and salt. They too were swept along by the wind, like seed that would abruptly flourish in odd places. Suddenly, at the foot of a mountain or in saltpetre pampas, tiny human heads would be born and cry out, like tremulous apparitions at risk of vanishing.

– La patria no sabe su nombre todavía. The patria does not yet know its name,[13] said Marechal. Every morning it rises early to surprise us and surprise itself, like a curious young girl who looks in the mirror and laughs at seeing herself, that's all.[14]

– The patria has known too many names, said Borges. The names of those who bled to death here.

He was thinking, as he would later say, about an old memory made of bones buried and sedimented like geological strata. Goths and criollos,[15] Unitarians and Federalists,[16] Indians and Christians. His grandfather Francisco Borges, killed at La Verde, speared by Catriel's men.[17] "Now they are together, at least," Marechal would comment. "So what?" Borges would rejoin. "Even in their graves they've probably been fighting, like those two gauchos bound together by mutual hatred for their entire lives; when they were taken prisoner during the civil wars, just as their throats were being slit, they asked to run a race to see who could take the winning step before falling dead."[18]

For now, however, the travellers spoke little and read even less. The flatlands bewitched eyes and sealed lips, their emptiness a powerful force of suction. The flatness of the land, but above it all the great plain of the sky, where enormous clouds scudded along, faster than the train, like the *ñandúes*, ostriches of fabulous plumage that could outrun horses' hooves and evade *boleadoras*.

At nightfall they pulled into the station at Los Toldos, one more town of the Humid Pampa,[19] whose name came from the *tolderías* of the Mapuches, their encampments of tents. Most of the indigenous families, however, lived some distance from town in a place called Tapera de Díaz, where once there really had been traditional *toldos*, floating houses made from leather and wooden beams by the first Vorogano Mapuches.[20] The new Los Toldos had been founded by a criollo from Tucumán, Don Electo Urquizo, merchant-owner of the place's first *pulpería*. The town was built around the main square. It had a parish church, schools, post office, banks, cemetery, stage-coach company, civil registry, police station, and even local newspapers. The *gringos* actually outnumbered the *indios*: there was a Spanish Society of Mutual Aid and a French Society; and there were many poor immigrants looking for a parcel of land, which went cheaper in Los Toldos than in towns like Bragado, Chivilcoy, or Nueve de Julio. There were thriving general stores, owned by those who

in frontier times had been mere *pulperos* at the mercy of attacks by Ranquel Indians and militiamen. There were small shops, the odd *confitería*,
auction houses, pharmacies.

When they got off the train, Carmen took the lead and dragged her
companions straight to the Hotel Español, across from the station.

– But what are you doing? Borges wanted to know.

– What do you mean? I'm making sure we have a place to sleep tonight.
It doesn't look as if there's an abundant choice of hotels around here.

– We won't find out anything that way. It's obvious your brother doesn't
deal with Spanish merchants. If he hangs around with indios and gauchos, we have go looking elsewhere.

– Listen, Borges, we've done enough for today. We're not going to start
playing detective now. We'll begin the search tomorrow.

What Borges said was true enough. The hotel owner, a Basque called
Arzuaga, had never heard of Francisco Brey Moure, although he did think
that once or twice he had seen a man matching his description, always in
the company of a couple of indios.

They took two rooms, one for Carmen and the other for the two poets.
Then the author of *Luna de enfrente*, emboldened by his good guess,
insisted they go out to eat at a country-style *almacén*, a general-store-
cum-restaurant. That, he swore, was the irreplaceable fount of information about persons considered less than "decent" by the town burghers.

After some careful scouting around, based more on smell and hearing
than on his deficient eyesight, he found a place to his liking out past the
edge of town, beyond the last paving-stone. It was an adobe-brick building; its front door a quilt curtain. Carmen felt desperately absurd and vulnerable in her blue silk suit and her little cream-coloured Mary Janes,[21]
now greyish-brown after their walk through streets muddied by an afternoon rain squall.

Passing among the horses tied to the stockade outside, they went in and
sat down at a table beside a narrow window. The other customers were
gauchos – ranch-hands in rope sandals or muleteers in rustic boots – who
seemed more interested in drinking than eating. The grated window gave
a view of shacks dotting the edge of town and straggling over the pampa,
fading in the darkness and barely marked by a candle or oil lamp. They
were served by an apathetic lad who could tell them nothing new, only
that they should wait for his boss, a Galician from Logroño who probably

knew all the Spaniards in the area. He brought bread and wine, a Spanish tortilla, roasted meat, and sardines.

They ate undisturbed. The sounds of the countryside – dogs barking, owls hooting, horses whinnying at some slight noise or shadow – were occasionally punctuated by the laughter of the three gauchos. As their hilarity got louder and louder, Borges, not to be outdone by his neighbours, ordered gin. Carmen peered anxiously into the night outside, as the two poets applied themselves to the bottle, assiduously proposing toasts prefaced by a full-throated *Yapaí!* Only later would she learn they were emulating the libations to Mother Earth offered by the Ranquel Indians and shared by Lucio V. Mansilla, author of a book written when he visited them in 1870 and which both Borges and Marechal had read.[22] She didn't dare leave them alone, and yet it was getting riskier by the minute to stay. By now it was clear the gauchos' merriment had a definite target: the poets' "townie" clothes, the broad-brimmed hat sitting on a chair, her silk outfit, and the Mary Janes she was doing her best to hide behind a table leg and under the overhang of the grimy checkered tablecloth. The countryman from Logroño was nowhere to be seen, although in view of the threatening aspect of his clientèle, the boss could not necessarily be counted on to save them. Pretty soon, a little nugget of bread, accompanied by hoarse guffaws, landed on the table beside Borges's glass. He turned around and gave them a mean stare. For a second or two, all seemed frozen in a gesture of defiance. But then there was another peal of laughter. A second nugget of bread, well aimed, struck the porteño poet on the forehead. Carmen reached out to grab the lapels of his jacket, but Borges was already up and walking like a sleepwalker in a suicidal trance toward the other table, where awaited him three faces carved by old knife wounds and three huge knives that to Señorita Brey looked like Moorish scimitars.

– Somethin' I can do ya for, Rosy? Speak up, *che*, I can't hear you.

Those words, incredible from Borges's mouth, were directed at the most fearsome of the three, who in height and weight was twice the size of the myopic bard of the *arrabal*, no small man himself.[23]

There wasn't a moment to lose. No help was forthcoming from Marechal; whether stunned or pleased by the demented behaviour of his colleague, he just sat there. She would have to assume they were what they seemed: a pair of morons with no common sense, useless for anything but spinning philosophies and scribbling verse. Almost in a single bound, she was in front of Borges, bravely covering for him.

– Señor, I beg you please to pay no attention to what my brother says or does. He is not well in the head, he's half mad, do you understand?

Standing on tiptoe, as high as she could stretch, she was whispering to the giant, trying not suffocate from his alcoholic breath.

– In fact, with this friend of ours (she pointed at Marechal) … he's a doctor … we're on our way to Buenos Aires to put my brother in an asylum. My mother is beside herself with heartbreak, you can just imagine. And I'm taking care of him. What am I going to tell our poor dear mother if something happens to her unfortunate boy?

Borges, furious, was about to pipe up, but missed his chance. Carmen had stomped on his foot and her sharp elbow to the gut had left him speechless.

– *Madre hay una sola.* Motherhood is sacred. Say no more, my dear. With all due respect to you and your sainted mum. But if that's how things are, you'd better keep him safe indoors. And don't be takin' him out in the night air where he's liable to get 'isself moonstruck. He wouldn't be a werewolf, now, would he?

Another outburst of laughter, louder than ever. Carmen, grateful for the reprieve, was quick to press her advantage. She and Marechal, who seemed to have come to his senses, took Borges in tow and shot out the door, running as though chased by the devil or the recently evoked werewolf. They slowed down only when they were within spitting distance of the Hotel Español. For all its flaking walls and modest height, it looked to her more marvellous than any edifice in *The Arabian Nights*, not excluding the extravagant palace of Aladdin.

III

Count Hermann von Keyserling got up and took a few strides to stretch his legs. Even as the coach's sole occupant, and travelling in first-class comfort, he felt a bit out of sorts on the train. He found all human spaces too confining, and not only because of his considerable volume and stature. He lit a cigar, drew the velvet curtains all the way back, and peered out the little window. Definitely, thought the Count, I shall never quite get used to all the small spaces the great majority of men squirm around in. In some corner of his memory he would always be longing for the lost forests of Lönno and Rayküll, where he lived as a child, as happy as some philosophers believe the savages once lived. Not that the child Keyserling, male heir of landowning aristocrats, had ever suffered the material penury of the primitives; instead, he had enjoyed a freedom unknown to city-raised boys. Until the age of five or six, when he made his first trip to the nearby town, he had lived in another dimension of time and space. Passenger trains seemed to him no bigger than toy trains. Streets were like narrow corrals, where people instead of cattle bustled with an unseemly haste that cows would never be guilty of.

But that was in time past. The son of Nature, who had fed untamed falcons from his hand and whose world was trees, wild animals, and ancestors like unto gods, was no longer lord and master of Rayküll or Lönno. As always, History – this time in the guise of the Bolsheviks – had cruelly irrupted into Paradise, then tossed him into the German city of Darmstadt, manipulable as an architect's model, well ordered and polished as an eighteenth-century garden. After marrying Gudela von Bismarck Schönhausen, granddaughter of Chancellor Otto von Bismarck, he was obliged to accept the patronage of the Grand Duke of Hesse and take up residence in a house that once belonged to the Preacher of the Court, where instead of sermonizing he would create what he considered to be a sanctuary of the Free Spirit: the School of Wisdom.

He took a deep drag on the cigar, annoyed by the ironies lurking in the school's name and destiny. If there was one thing that could not be taught, it was Wisdom. At most, one could incite or provoke it, so that eventually the creative Logos might inseminate souls waiting in feminine expectancy. As for freedom, his pupils might have it, but not he. He had always felt like a caged elephant among those methodical and routine-loving Germans, who valued above all else order and the security of repetition. German by birth and by tongue, and seen as such by the Finns, Russians, and Latvians of his native Baltic land, Hermann von Keyserling also bore in his veins the secret dynamite of Slavic and Mongol blood; and he saw himself as an exile behind the bars of the utilitarian Germanic prison where the wicked witch of History had put him, painfully cut off from the "realm of Nature."

Withal, for a temperament convinced that life is a mighty, abundant adventure, there were always solutions. Keyserling found relief from the

Teutonic grid in the spirals, arabesques, and diagonals of travel. Thankfully, the School of Wisdom and the prestigious guests he received there had made him famous. The income from the ancestral lands of yesteryear was no more, but his fame brought him invitations to give lectures and assured him of princely treatment, which he was pleased to demand. Of course, the conditions weren't always his to impose.

He reached into the inside pocket of his jacket and looked again at the signed portrait of the South American woman who was waiting in Paris. For nearly two years, that strange female had been writing him letters that bordered on sublime mystical exaltation or pagan idolatry. No doubt she was an intelligent woman, since she was so enthused by his work. And so passionate she was that she had declared she could not wait *a single minute longer* to meet and know him. And so wealthy, she was building a house in the most aristocratic zone of Buenos Aires in order to lodge him there when he finally weighed anchor in the Río de la Plata. Not to mention that she was footing the bill for his stay at Versailles, including all the requirements merited by his dual condition of accomplished philosopher and nobleman. On top of it all, she was beautiful: her Latin face, so carnal, its features slightly asymmetrical, stared at him from the satin paper in a kind of defiant supplication.

The beautiful unknown woman, however, had obstinately refused to join him in Germany. From the Schönhausen castle, his mother-in-law's property (the nearest thing to a replacement for Rayküll and Lönno), the Count had been obliged to take the toy train to Paris, interrupting work on his book about the United States.[24] Although Paris, he had to admit, was a golden imposition. Keyserling felt himself rejuvenate like an old oak in springtime every time he went to the city of his youth and first great love. The city where he'd arrived with a useless degree in Geology in hand, and where he'd learned the refinements of art, thought, and eroticism. There, for the first time, he had felt completely free. Since no Parisian knew him as a Keyserling, a German nobleman from the Baltic, he needed answer to no one regarding his conduct. He would eat in any old student bistro in the Quartier Latin and lodge in an obscure little hotel on the rue de la Seine, which as an adult he revisited once in a while to recall the glory days of anonymity and dreams. Afternoons, he used to visit the Jardin des Plantes as one might return to the woods. After inhaling the moist vegetal effluvia for a couple of hours, his body would feel lithe as a tree branch and his brain porous as a sponge. Next, he would submerge himself in the morgue for a spiritual cold shower, acknowledging the inexorable decadence that follows upon all organic ferment, sensing thus the profound kinship between humans, stones, and fossils. Finally, he would hear Vespers at Notre Dame and let the Spirit bathe him, neutralize his crepuscular experiences in that liturgical beauty, a poignant commingling of the mineral, the vegetal, and the carnal. After night had fallen, with body and soul well integrated, the microcosm felicitously attuned to the macrocosm, Count Hermann von Keyserling was ready to make an appearance in the *grand monde*, dressed in tails, accompanying the Countess of Wolkenstein, ambassador of Austria; the sparks of divine inspiration gleaned during the afternoon's spiritual exercises would then be applied to dancing and good conversation.

The Count closed his eyes – small, slanted, pale-blue – and let the cigar smoke envelope him. The Paris of those years was populated by Massenet and Debussy, by Henri de Régnier, by Rodin (in his view a crude artisan who thought magnificently with his rough hands and only with his hands), and by André Gide, an exquisite and puritanical artist who pursued a sort of platonic ideal of beauty in homosexual love by going out every night to applaud some handsome actor, the way ascetics practise ritual self-mortification, testing whether he might be aroused to a sublime passion. Perhaps, after this trip, his personal Paris would be further enriched with a strange, new, precious human memory, and henceforth become, as well, the Paris of Victoria Ocampo.

Although, when it came to women, of course, one could never be sure. Western women especially, whose caprice was their only law, could sometimes destroy a man's happiness by acting unpredictably. His own mother, for instance, after decades of irreproachable behaviour. (A chill invariably ran down his back – a contradictory shiver of hatred and remorse – whenever he thought of the Baroness Johanna Pilar von Pilchau.) Nevertheless, women were undeniably the most suitable, the finest instruments for educating males. They were the civilizers – and in this he entirely agreed with his friend Ortega – who had made knights and gentlemen out of brutes whose chief entertainment consisted in cracking open each other's skulls with a mace. Women were weavers of men; they selected the textures, threads, and designs for the species with the same patience and creativity they applied to weaving tapestries. His Germanic compatriots, by the way, poorly understood that pedagogy of love which had flourished with so much grace in France and Italy. All they knew was vice (of the grossest sort) and marriage.

Count Keyserling, who had witnessed feminine perfection incarnate in the *geishas* of Japan, impersonal and delicate as flowers,[25] drew a subtler division in the world of women. On the one hand, there were the ordinary prostitutes, modest workers for masculine pleasure. On the other were the dutiful wives, guarantors of one's paternity, who maintained the hierarchy of the home and ensured the moral elevation of the scions. But there was a third type: the *Grande Dame*, descendant of the *hetairai* of Athens. This supreme model of womanhood, evading the domestic corral, was created to reign supreme in the salons of high society. Sibyl, Muse, prodigal in love, exempt from commitments, liberated from matrimonial subjection and the duty to reproduce, she was consecrated to the function of inspiring the philosopher and the artist.[26] Keyserling couldn't complain about his lot. He had an exemplary wife, Frau Gudela, who sustained the virtues of their noble stock and knew her place as the happy mother of two sons. That had not prevented him from visiting brothels during his long travels, the same red-light establishments frequented by his hosts or sponsors (government ministers, bankers, ambassadors), even though – excepting the case of the geishas – they satisfied only the base rudiments of the erotic entertainment needed by a cultivated man. He still felt tender nostalgia for the sisterly whores of his adolescence. Hermann von Keyserling had never been what the French call *un homme à femmes*. Withdrawn and violent, arrogant as a prince but timid as a peasant, he had been innocent of virile malice until rather late in his development. So it was that, back then in his youth, only the tranquil prostitutes in Pernau and Geneva could make him forget his ungainly arms and legs, the brusque clumsiness of his movements, the overwhelming sense of his ugliness. Later, the fame of his school and his books had begun to enhance his persona, until now it enveloped him like a magnetic force field; fame was like another feature of his sexuality, more notorious than an Adam's apple or a thick beard.

Thanks to those books, women from all over the planet – intelligent women, passionate, wealthy, beautiful – wrote him missives like this one, its handwriting slanted and perfumed, which he kept next to her photo and which produced in him a deliciously aphrodisiac effect: *Sunshine of your letters! Let me drift off to sleep in them, be suspended in them. And*

afterwards I shall flower because of them. Ah! How good it feels, how sweet.
How I love them! I wouldn't know how to speak to you reasonably tonight.
No need for philosophical reason or the good sense of mediocrity, not in
the woman who could compose such lines, where the soul's passion exu-
berantly overflowed into the senses, as with Teresa de Ávila or Mariana
Alcoforado.[27] *I feel I've been filled so full of what you are, that at the slight-*
est movement I'll emanate a precious aroma. And if you were present, I
wouldn't raise my eyes to your eyes, for fear of losing that you who is beneath
my zealously shut eyelids.

The metaphor transfigured Count Keyserling; he became like a censer
burning a concentrate of oriental fragrances, inhaling the incense of the
letter as though smelling himself. Such was the ecstasy induced by the
adoration of the lady from Argentina. Intoxicating was the power he
exerted over his distant correspondent, for whom his letters from Darmstadt were like a drug necessary for breath itself. *When your letters arrive,*
it always seems to me that just a moment before I was suffocating, and I
understand this better thanks to the oxygen you provide me. I read you with
my lungs. He almost felt like someone in a fairy tale, living a kind of love
that was of this world and at the same time beyond it, and whose light
transformed reality into the most perfect poetic fantasy.

The train was about to arrive at the end of a long trip that had been
monotonously beautiful – rivers and trees, chocolate castles, and distant
cities of sugarplum houses. What would the landscapes of South America
look like, where Victoria Ocampo wanted to take and present him like
a god or a prophet? He wouldn't be seeing her at the station. He had
expressly asked her not to meet him. The Count wanted to prepare for
their first meeting, scheduled for the next day. Waiting for him in Victoria's stead was a short man (a trustworthy servant, she'd said), who pronounced his full name and title in a heavy Spanish accent.

Night was falling by the time they got to the Hôtel des Réservoirs. The
rooms looked as comfortable as one might expect from a French hotel.
Everything he'd requested was there, including paper, envelopes, and red
ink. Once bathed and perfumed, he had supper brought to his room,
with a bottle of chilled champagne. The bed, built to Latin proportions,
was barely long enough. Uneasy and apprehensive, he decided to leave
the night-light on, as he used to do in case of nightmares when he was
a child.

IV

– Just as well he hasn't come down for breakfast. I don't much feel like seeing his face, said Carmen Brey as she dipped a croissant in her café con
leche. Marechal was slowly munching on his, apparently at a loss for
words. Finally he managed to say something:
    – Don't be angry with him, Carmen. It's his *criollo* sense of honour.
    – Honour, my foot! What does he think? That we're living in the Siglo
de Oro? Don't you Argentines boast about how modern you are? Are you
not men of letters? What does honour have to do with a brute stinking of
rot-gut alcohol? And Borges was hardly in better shape, either. With the
amount of gin he'd poured down his gullet, he was a walking fire hazard;
if someone had lit a match, there'd've been an explosion. That's why he
hasn't come down yet. It isn't embarrassment, it's the splitting headache
he must have.
    – But he is a fine intellectual, a sensitive poet …
    – That's precisely why his stupid behaviour is so upsetting. Thanks
to him, we might all three of us have ended up with our throats slit.
No wonder his poor mother lives on tenterhooks. He acts a like a child
in kindergarten.
    – But don't tell him that. You don't know how much he respects you. In
fact, I believe it may be more than respect he feels for you. Of course, he's
shy. More than likely he hasn't dared declare himself.
    – Well, he can keep his delicate sentiments to himself. Wrap them in tis-
sue paper like a bouquet of violets and give them to someone else.
    – So, what's on the agenda for today?
    – After yesterday's disaster, we'd better proceed separately. I'm going to
do some investigating. If no trace of my brother turns up in town, I'll ask
about the Coliqueo family, where to find them, and how to get out there.
You'd best stay here till your friend gets up. Since he hasn't an ounce of
sense, he clearly can't be left on his own. Although you don't have much
more yourself!
    With barely a goodbye, Carmen walked out and straight toward the cen-
tral square. She must have looked like a model out of *Para Ti*[28] or *El Hogar*[29]
– not only for her style but also for her size, she thought ironically. Piqué
and silk, hat and gloves, all in cream and antique rose, her little leather
shoes now scrupulously clean, her outfit had been calculated specifically

for an interview with the town worthies. Doors swing open gladly, she said
to herself, before quality clothes, good manners, and fine shoes.

She sat down on a bench in the square and perused the list Señor Arzuaga had given her: the police commissioner, two doctors, two accountants
(in charge of loans at the Banco de la Nación and the Banco de la Provin-
cia), the owner of the general store where the folks of Tapera de Díaz
stocked up on provisions. She heaved a sigh. She'd start by seeing the police
commissioner and hearing the worst. (Hadn't Don Peregrino Loueriro
been informed that her supposed brother had a scar across his face? Might
he not have run afoul of the authorities?) She looked around. The plaza
was like any other, with the inevitable statues of eminent men and the
nation's founding fathers, whom Argentines seemed to love so much. But
there was something fresh and charming about this square, so neatly rectangular and abundant in trees. One decorative feature made it worthy of
a larger town. It was an artificial cavern, with waterfalls, hiding-places,
small pools of quiet water where goldfish swam.

Curious, she approached. She began to follow the flashing motions of a
particular fish as it disappeared into a tunnel and reappeared in a cup-like
hollow in the fake rock. When she looked up, she saw a young girl in front
of her. She was thin, petite, her chestnut hair cropped short, and she was
staring fixedly at Carmen.

– Hi, the child said smiling, but her eyes still serious. Do you like the little fishes?

– Very much. I was born in a seaport. These are different, they're aquarium fish with almost no room to move. But fish all the same.

– At least here everybody can admire them. In the sea, nobody would
see them.

– Do you think it's important to be seen?

– Of course. I want to be a movie actress. I have a collection of photos
of movie stars. Want to see them?

– I would, but not right at this moment. Are you from around here?

– Yes, I live a little further out, on the Calle Francia. You're from Buenos
Aires, right? What lovely clothes you have! You look like an actress. Where
do you buy them? At Harrods?

– Sometimes. This suit was a gift from a friend. It was made to measure.

It was a design by Paquin, cut by Madame Alice, a birthday gift on
which Victoria had insisted.

– How nice! My older sisters know how to sew. And my mum. But she doesn't have much time to make fancy dresses. People always order work clothes. The prettiest thing I ever got was a Fairy of the Night costume. All made of blue cotton, with stars on the head and a half moon on the magic wand. I wore it for Carnival. My sister Elena made it for me. Now I'm learning how to sew.

The girl looked at her again. She seemed to want to say something more, but was hesitating.

– Tell me, she finally said. Are you the one who has a crazy brother?

– Goodness! News does travel fast in this town. How did you know? Who told you that?

– We live around the corner from the *Gallego's* place. And Estanislao is one of Mama's customers. She makes *bombachas* for the ranch hands.

– Who is Estanislao?

– He's a great big guy. Two heads taller than everybody else. You must've seen him yesterday. He said your brother wanted to knife him, just because they were horsing around and threw a few breadcrumbs at him.

– So he thought my brother was going to knife him? Well, isn't that something. Tell me, dear. This Estanislao, is he the owner of a ranch in these parts?

– No, no way. He's the foreman at *La Blanqueada* ranch. It's close to La Tapera, where the Indians live. They sometimes get clothes from my mum, too.

– Really? So your mother has dealings with them and knows how to get there?

– Sure she knows. We often go there to see Juana Guaiquil. She's the Indians' doctor, and she looks after us when Dr Bargas isn't in town. Juana delivered me when I was born.

– Listen, do you think I could have a chat with your mother? There's something I'd like to ask her. Would she mind?

– No, why would she mind? I'll take you to our place, and you can ask her. At the same time you can see my photo album. And my Fairy of the Night costume. And my garden and wooden piano and a circus my brother helped us build out back. We also made some little houses to play house in.

– I can see your family is very resourceful and full of ideas. Fine, let's go, then. You show me the way.

The girl took her by the hand. She was wearing rope-soled sandals, and her dress was somewhat faded but freshly ironed.

– How many children are you in the family?

– Five. La Blanca is away studying to be a teacher, and we hardly ever see her. Now she's home for the summer holidays. Elisa works at the post office, and Juan helps out at the school. Erminda and I are the youngest. We're in elementary school.

– And what's your name?

– Eva, but they call me Evita.[30] Or Chola. But my full name is María Eva, you know? On account of original sin.

Carmen smiled. Typical of small-town priests and their catechisms. The poor old mother of humankind has to be neutralized and upstaged by the Mother of God.

– Don't you worry about sin. You are innocent. Evita will do just fine. And your father, what does he do?

– He died in an accident three years ago. A long time ago, when I was little, we had some land and he used to take me in the *sulky*.

– I'm so sorry for your loss, child. But your mother, from what you tell me, knows how to fend for herself.

They walked several blocks until they arrived at a brick house, too small for a family of six. But the yard was large, as if to compensate. It was separated from the street by a hedge of *cina-cina* with yellow flowers. The house was surrounded on all sides by trees: weeping willows, *paraísos*, fruit trees, fig trees, poplars.

– Mummy, the señorita from Buenos Aires wants to talk to you. She wants to know about La Tapera and the Coliqueos.

– Please excuse me for not getting up. It's my varicose veins. It was hard enough for me to get to this chair.

– Of course, please don't trouble yourself, Señora. My name is Carmen Brey, she said as she went to shake the woman's hand.

The woman was large, beautiful even. She smelled of soap, talcum powder, and cologne, as if she had just come from the bath.

– Juana Ibarguren, widow of Duarte, at your service. Evita, child, bring her a chair. Will you join me for a few rounds of *mate*?

Beside the Singer sewing machine, on a low table, there was a porcelain *mate*.

Carmen had never got used to the bitterness of the herbal tea, even with sugar. But she accepted lest she offend her hostess. Her apprehensions were assuaged by the cleanliness of the house and everything in it.

– Señora, I have a brother who left our home in Spain several years ago. He came to Argentina, but we've lost track of him. The only concrete information I've been able to find is that he was apparently selling horses in partnership with some Indians called Coliqueo. At the Hotel Español, where I'm staying, they've never heard of him. Señor Arzuaga gave me a list of people I could ask, but I suspect they'll all say the same thing.

The woman smiled.

– I imagine Arzuaga didn't put me on that list, am I right? But in fact I do know the Indians, and quite well. If you want to get straight to business, the best thing will be just to go out there. Look, I'll give you a few names …

The imminent revelation was interrupted by a knock at the door.

– May I, Doña Juana?

– Come on in.

Carmen turned to see a man coming into the house, ducking to avoid bumping his head against the doorframe. She tried to shrink away and hide her face … in vain. Her city clothes flagrantly gave her away. The man looked her up and down, no less surprised than she was.

– Afternoon, ma'am, he said, hat between his hands. How is your little brother doing? Calmed down some after last night, I hope? I thought he was gonna let me have it, all because of a silly joke. You know, you might wanna think about changing doctors. The doc you got now don't look up to much.

– Do you know what? I was thinking the same thing myself. But we already have an agreement, and there's nothing for it but to go on to Buenos Aires with him. When we finally get my brother committed, I'll rest easier.

– God willing. Listen, Doña Juana, I just came to let you know I'll be by here tomorrow for the *bombachas* and shirts, so you've got time to finish up. Anyways, I won't be leaving for the estancia till after lunch.

– That's fine, Estanislao, tomorrow's better. They'll be ready for sure.

The man took his leave with perfect urbanity, having first given the girl a sweet. The malodorous beast of the night before had been transformed into an ordinary countryman, decently dressed in a clean shirt and a gaudy belt studded with gold and silver coins.

– But do you mean to tell me, then, you have two brothers, the crazy one plus another living with the Indians?

– No, Señora. The one from last night isn't really my brother, and he isn't crazy either, Carmen said, although not quite convinced of the latter. And the doctor isn't a doctor. They're two friends who came with me to look for my real brother; their intentions are good, but they have a tendency to get into trouble. My friend took offence with Señor Estanislao because they were making fun of him, and he wanted to challenge him to a duel. I got scared by the look of Estanislao and his friends. They were all armed, so I invented that story, hoping they'd take pity on my reckless friend. Between the other friend and myself, we hauled him out of there.

Doña Juana guffawed.

– You needn't have gone to so much trouble. The dog that barks doesn't bite. Estanislao is a good man, so are his people. Don't fret, they wouldn't have done any harm. They all have families to look after and none of them needs problems with the law. They come to town now again and get a bit happy. But that's as far as it goes. Knives are for out in the country, for butchering cattle, not for disembowelling Christians. All of them are poor, like me – she sighed – and work from dawn till dusk. Look, what you should do, actually, is get Estanislao to take you back to La Blanqueada tomorrow. From there it's not far to where the Indians live. Either him or one of the ranch hands can take you in the sulky. Anyways, since tomorrow is Sunday, they'll have the afternoon off, and somebody or other will want to go for a ride. Once you get to La Tapera, go to Juana Guaiquil's place. She tends to the sick and assists at births, so she knows everyone. If your brother really is with the Coliqueo clan, she'll know about it for sure.

Carmen nodded her assent. Both to Doña Juana and Evita, who was tugging at her sleeve. She held up a sort of folder made out of flattened sheets of parcel paper.

– Don't you want to look at my photo album? And then I'll show you the piano, the circus, and the little houses.

Doña Juan made a disapproving gesture.

– Sometimes I just don't know what to do with this one. She's a good girl, but she's got a head full of dreams. With a couple of sticks of wood and some old cloth she can make a world. So much imagination isn't good for poor folks like us.

– Well, if she doesn't dream now, when will she ever? She's the right age. With imagination poverty is more bearable. And she may even end up leaving poverty behind.

That day, Carmen admired Evita's photos of luminaries. There were movie idols from Argentina and abroad, opera divas, and show-business celebrities. From Carlos Gardel to Rudolph Valentino, Olinda Bozán to Raquel Meller, Tita Merello to Gloria Swanson, George Bancroft and Loretta Young to Enrique Muiño and Angelina Pagano.[31] But the girl reserved her most devout worship for Norma Shearer, whose photo she had framed by hand in flowers and gold foil. "See? One day I'm going to be as pretty as her. With curls and blond hair. I'll have a white telephone and a bedroom lined in satin, like a chocolate box or a jewelry box, and I'll be a queen. They'll cut off my head in a movie, and the whole world will cry for me."

Carmen also saw an enormous porcelain doll with eyes of mauve-coloured glass and a long dress covering her missing leg. Apparently, Doña Juana was as given to fantasy as her youngest daughter: she had told the little one that the doll had fallen off the camel when the Three Wise Men were delivering it. (Thanks to that mutilation, the good woman had been able to buy the beautiful doll for next to nothing.) Eva had set the doll up on a cardboard throne upholstered with scraps of velvet.

Then she saw the circus – two painted lengths of pipe teetering on sawhorses, plus a trapeze dangling from the paraíso trees. She looked at the piano made out of a cardboard box, sheet metal, and barrel hoops. She examined the little houses fashioned from odd chunks of wooden boards and covered by a roof of branches, and she took a seat in one of them to take flower-petal tea, which Eva served in a battered old gilt-rimmed cup.

She listened as Eva sang the tango "Mi dolor,"[32] her voice sweet, slightly hoarse and out-of-tune. Finally, the girl told her favourite story, "Aladdin and the Magic Lamp," with a few variations of local colour. The palace magically summoned up by the genie was in Buenos Aires, not China; its balconies of veined pink marble gave onto the Plaza San Martín, like the Oliver mansion. Aladdin and Brudulbudhura were married not in a mosque or even a cathedral, but in the Teatro Colón, where a full house gave them a standing ovation. The new prince's first act of government was to declare a school holiday and distribute toys to all the children in the realm. He also wanted to bring back to life all the fathers who had ever died so there would be no more orphans. But God, who is greater than a genie from a lamp, hadn't allowed him to.

God was bent on accumulating powers and secrets that He didn't share with anyone, thought Carmen, just as the rich go on piling up millions in hidden bank accounts. And she began to nod off to sleep on ragged old pillowcases, in the doll's house, the child's head nestled on her lap.

v

The Count looked in the mirror, then out the sitting-room window at the park, frozen and diminished by winter. The cold outside contrasted with the heat of the room and the temperature of his body and spirit, both pleasantly warmed by anticipation.

At five o'clock sharp in the afternoon, as in the poem not yet written by an Andalusian poet whom Keyserling had not read, the Event would come to pass. And, as in Lorca's poem, it would be fatal, though not as bloody as the death of Ignacio Sánchez Mejías.[33] The Event was going to change, in two divergent ways, the lives and self-understanding of its two protagonists.

At five o'clock sharp, indeed, Victoria Ocampo, the Lady-from-Afar Annunciate, appeared at the door of his suite at the Hôtel des Réservoirs. The Count was expecting exotic beauty, and exotic beauty he saw, but amplified to the cosmic proportions of a deity. Her magnificent form, worthy of Cleopatra's tunic of translucent linen and royal headdress, was covered instead by a ridiculous tailored suit, made for speedy *businesswomen*, telephone operators, school-marms or secretaries jittering like Chaplinesque marionettes in these disenchanted modern times; a mean scrap of cloth, an unworthy patch, her garb was a desecration. His fecund imagination racing, the Count stripped her naked and then reclothed her: first as Cleopatra, then with an Indian sari of ochre and gold, yet again in the ponderous attire of a Byzantine empress. Finally, he restored her to the nude, but garlanded in jewels. Dazzled by the splendours of his own creation, he had to close his eyes and restrain himself from falling to his knees before her – a gesture

befitting an empress or goddess but susceptible to misinterpretation in
the frivolous ambience of a French hotel. A moment passed. Then he
lunged forward to take the hand extended towards him and, unable
to contain himself, took as well that egregiously voluptuous body in
an embrace.

At five o'clock sharp in the afternoon, Victoria Ocampo, the Devout
Disciple, at last saw before her, in all his length and breadth, the Baltic
philosopher, Master-Teacher of the School of Wisdom, hitherto venerated
only from a distance in the reflected light and echoes of books and epis-
tles. Arranging those letters and books like pieces of a jigsaw puzzle that
fell together perfectly, she had composed the image of a charming gentleman. Tall and subtle like Tagore, but younger; expert in the intense but
selective, slow, and deliberate *dégustation* of the world; vigorous but delicate; sagely humorous and above the fray, evading the seduction of objects
and the treacherous sting of passion. She saw, instead, a giant with the
oblique eyes and moustache and pointed beard of a Mongol warrior. She
too undressed him, not to leave him in the nude (the very idea made her
shudder), but to superimpose on his well-cut suit the clothing of Genghis
Khan, who might have been his immediate forefather. The barbarian
proffered, first, a greeting in syntactically correct French, gutturalized by
a heavy German accent, then a paw proportionate to his physical size. Terrified, Victoria closed her eyes, expecting her hand to be squashed. Hardly had she recovered from her fright than the monster wrapped her in
both arms and crushed her to his chest, where a heart was beating fast and
furious, like a tattoo of horses galloping over the pampa in a *malón* or an
invasion of Tartars from the steppe.

Extricating herself from the embrace, she took a deep breath, not only
to replenish her emptied lungs, but also to overcome her repugnance and
fear and the wild impulse to flee, right now, from the Hôtel des Réservoirs.
The Count was now looking at her with the beady eyes of a bird of prey,
smart and ferocious. And gaping at her with his enormous mouth – the
brutal mouth of an ogre, she thought, with thick red lips that looked like
raw meat, ready to gobble up the entire world, starting with her.

For his part, the Count, speechless with ecstasy, scarcely able to believe
his good fortune, was inwardly celebrating the most extraordinary meeting of his life. This divine woman, who had sighed upon leaving his arms,
who was now breathing heavily, so overcome she was by the same strong

emotion he was feeling, was his Muse. *His* Muse, *his* Grande Dame, *his* Sibyl. She was the exact missing piece, the third type of the feminine triad whose other two vertices were the understanding Wife and the obliging Prostitute. A jewel of the highest order, comparable on the higher plane of Life-as-Art (that work of art which was his life) to the Cullinan diamond, from whose rough form were cut the brilliants now encrusted in the Scep-tre with Cross and in the Imperial State Crown of Great Britain. Likewise, from the rough diamond of this feminine matter, he would carve out his most outstanding philosophical gems ever.

Such a union, physical and metaphysical, would in their ephemeral lives re-enact the conciliation of the eternal Yin and Yang, the Coincidence of Opposites. Their copulation would be as sacred as the *maithuna*, the lov-ing couple whose joyous union produces the cosmos and the music of the spheres. Although the Count felt like consummating *ipso facto* that anthro-pocosmic rite which would redound both in the satisfaction of the partic-ipating subjects and in the renewed harmony of Creation, he thought it prudent to pay tribute to the customs and conventions of society (for all that one of his letters had strongly recommended to his feminine disciple to shun "conventionality"). Moreover, his eager desire for pleasure and knowledge (or pleasurable knowledge) inclined him to delay, if only for a few days, the consummation of the supreme act which was to link, pro-foundly and intimately, Hermann von Keyserling, Nordic heir to European Tradition, representative of the Spirit, with Victoria Ocampo, Southern Female of Indian refinement but constituted from passionate telluric vibrations. The Masculine Logos of Europe (H.K.), potent and solar, would penetrate the moist, florid, light-and-shadowed Feminine Land of Ameri-ca (V.O.), Conquistador and Conquistada thus jointly figuring the human condition in its totality.

Having thought out this plan of action, the Count found himself oblig-ed to engage in trivial conversation with the Devout Disciple, now pro-moted to the category of Muse. They discussed matters of secondary importance, such as the orphaned condition of Argentina and Latin America, the state of philosophy in America, and even trifles such as the family of Victoria and her clandestine lover, whom she insisted on men-tioning with annoying frequency. Her tactlessness in this regard was as inopportune as it would have been for him to obsessively mention Gudela von Bismarck, rather than keep her situated at a more than prudent distance, belonging as she did to an utterly distinct plane of existence. He held Frau Gudela in the highest esteem and was very grateful to her for assuring the noble descent of the Keyserlings, but that family bond, along with the domestic sexual commerce he courteously practised with her, was not to be confused with the symbolic and metaphysical transcendence of his relations with the Muse. Quite out of place, then, was Victoria's obscure lover, who had never written so much as two pages of a book and to whom Victoria didn't even owe any children – much less a surname. That quidam of no consequence was not to be dragged into her conversations with him, the man who was going to guide her to the summit of her carnal, philosophical, mythological efflorescence.

As always when annoyed by human stupidity and the quotidian pettiness of life, the Count thought about food. And drink. He had another supper brought to the room (lest Victoria be exposed to contamination by the curious looks of others) and, without a dent to his loquacity, applied himself with a will to one of the activities that partially calmed his insatiable Primordial Hunger and distracted him from the aridity of existence – an arid condition which he abundantly irrigated with champagne. Between one bottle and another came a succession of courses: a platter of hors d'oeuvres, another of oysters, ham *gratiné* with cherry sauce, partridges cooked in batter, and for dessert a floating island. He hadn't failed to notice, between mastication and monologue, that during the meal the Muse had hardly eaten or drunk, much less spoken. Astonished, transported, she just stared as though in disbelief. He was moved to tenderness. No doubt the Devout Disciple, still subsisting in the Muse, was overwhelmed at witnessing his humanity. In her letters she had adored him as a god, and when one's god becomes a table mate sharing this-worldly food, within arm's reach, then her cup runneth over.

That night Victoria Ocampo went back to her apartment on the rue d'Artois and frantically went through the philosopher's books and letters, rereading her marginal notes and underlined passages. Then, lying in bed and staring at the ceiling, she made an effort to reconcile the recent image of the Mongol warrior (Genghis Khan or Tamerlane ensconced in the dainty rooms of the Hôtel des Réservoirs) with the images she'd dreamed when reading him. A case of Dr Jekyll and Mr Hyde, apparently. Was it really possible to identify the aesthete who bought delicate porcelain in Japanese antique stores, who attended tea ceremonies within the fragile paper walls of translucent geisha houses, with the giant of Homeric laughter who drank like Bacchus, ate like Pantagruel, and looked at her with the lustful eyes of Silenus the Satyr? True, the Greeks attributed to Silenus, despite his constant inebriation (or maybe thanks to that condition), the gift of wisdom. She wondered if Keyserling, impatient with the tiny exquisite morsels served by the geishas, might not have devoured one of *them* as an appetizer. When it came to cardinal sins, he was probably guiltier of gluttony than of lust.

"But have you taken a good look at his photos? He looks like an albino orangutan." The words of Carmen Brey, specialist in puncturing balloons of illusion, had been archived deep in Victoria's memory, but – alas! – had gone unheeded at the time. Just as she had ignored her sister Angélica, always perceptive and sensible. And María de Maeztu and Ortega; both of them knew her and knew Keyserling's character. The only person who hadn't said anything was Julián. Had he been afraid of losing her by appearing to interfere and restrict her freedom? Or was it that he had already grown distant, and thus indifferent to her decisions?

What to do now about Keyserling? The Argentine-German Institute, Friends of the Arts, the Faculty of Philosophy and Letters: she had got all of them enthusiastic, and all now expected her to organize a lecture tour in Argentina. The Count, moreover, was going to give her letters of introduction to poets and intellectuals living in Paris (although, under the circumstances, she wasn't so sure anymore whether it was wise to go from books to their authors). And besides, did it matter that she was repelled by the philosopher's physical proximity? Did his repulsiveness wipe out, just like that, the truths of his writing? She decided to keep on going to Versailles every day, as she had agreed to do, even if it meant witnessing – not sharing – his Pantagruelian supper. She would try, slowly but surely, to dissuade him from his erotic fixation.

By the end of his stay in Versailles, however, the Master from Darmstadt was dissatisfied. He had managed almost to finish the book he was working on (*America Set Free*), but the Muse had balked at the complete assumption of her role. The Devout Disciple continued listening to his monologues. She said little, as behooved her "pristine" and "telluric" feminine nature; she was polite, delicate, even obedient. Except in one regard. Although the Count's explanations were crystal clear; despite the iron-clad syllogisms he deployed (sacrificing for the sake of comprehension his intuitive and torrential philosophical *style*) in order to demonstrate the urgent necessity that the spiritual fusion between the Feminine and the Masculine be translated to and enacted on the carnal plane, thus to overcome the medieval sundering of body and soul and the bourgeois prejudices of Victorian society; still, the Southern Female remained enigmatically silent and reticent, she persisted in devious evasions, neither offering a convincing reason for her refusal nor taking the decisive step.

Could it be that certain atavisms of her Hispanic Catholic upbringing were at play? This didn't seem very logical in a woman who was not only an adult but an adulteress. Or did she consider that lover of hers, given his merits and antecedents in the role, as another husband to whom she owed fidelity? Even less logical. If she hadn't kept the first husband, all the less reason to keep the other one, to whom she was bound by no sacrament or papers.

There were times when the Count felt like an utter imbecile, and he contemplated resorting to extreme measures. After all, did there not lurk in the dark chthonic mysteries of feminine nature the secret desire to be raped? Maybe that was Victoria's case. Maybe, after a healthy enforced penetration at the right moment, their relationship would get on track and follow the normal channels. However, several significant objections occurred to him: 1) his lack of experience (at almost fifty years of age, truth be told, Count Keyserling had never raped anyone); 2) the scandal that might be provoked by: a) a botched attempt, due to inadequate procedures and security measures; or b) an incomplete or even totally false diagnosis of the problem. Due to that falseness, the rape – even in the case that it were carried out with irreproachable perfection – could become an act which, rather than curative, might be interpreted as aberrant by the recipient and by the rest of the world. He was paralysed by visions of his picture in the newspapers beneath grotesque headlines screeching "The Wicked Baltic Count!" or "The Satyr of the School of Wisdom!" The dishonour to his person, to his family, and to German-language philosophy would be irreparable. Not to mention that he would be the laughing-stock of all France, due to his obvious ineptitude in the arts of gallantry and seduction – that preserve of the hunt and courtly intrigue in which the French had always been insufferable braggarts.

Thankfully, the month at Versailles was coming to an end. He was having trouble controlling his anger and resentment. He would suddenly berate the waiter over a serving of mashed potatoes that wasn't just so. When in reality, all he wanted was to take Victoria in his two hands and shake the truth out of her: make her confess, coherently, her real reasons for holding out on him.

He had one last hope – Buenos Aires. Perhaps there, in the land where she was born and raised, he would better understand that telluric psychology. And, just maybe, the familiar surroundings would render her more amenable to receiving in a full, unqualified embrace the Planetary Traveller from the North.

V

The sulky bounced along the country road, heading for La Tapera de Díaz and the house of Doña Juana Rawson de Guaiquil. Fortunately, thought Carmen, the pampa was utterly flat. Lucky, too, that Evita and Carmen needed only one seat between them, for the third traveller took up the space of two.

Estanislao, friend and protector of the youngest daughter of the Duarte family, had in the end offered to take them to the fields of La Tapera on his free afternoon. The girl was in her Sunday best, showing off her lace-edged stockings and her patent leather shoes, blacked and shined to hide the wear and tear of being passed down from one sister to the next till they ended up new on Evita's feet. Carmen looked at her out of the corner of her eye. She wasn't especially pretty, and perhaps not all that intelligent either. But something set her apart from the regular run of children. She seemed to live at a greater speed, moved by her fervent will to anticipate events, as though her dreams, desires, and earnest efforts had already reached fulfilment in those dark eyes of hers, more intense than those of other children. The weak – thought Carmen – could sometimes find powerful resources to endure grief and humiliation.

Arzuaga had smiled knowingly when she told him of her visit to the house on the Calle Francia. So had the police commissioner, the two bank employees, the doctors, and the general store owner. Doña Juana Ibarguren was not a widow of the proper sort. She was a "fallen woman" who for years had been the concubine of Juan Duarte, a married man, a conservative *caudillo* from Chivilcoy; when his legitimate spouse died, he had not taken Juana as his wife. (The spouse had been a señora from a good family, whereas Juana, of peasant stock, had been mere kitchen help.) Nevertheless, Duarte had recognized the children, at least the first four, and had provided for the family until his sudden death. But Eva – they said – had been registered with only her maternal surname, as she was cruelly reminded by a message scrawled, in handwriting not entirely child-like, on the school blackboard.

As for the current virtue of "that Ibarguren woman," there were different opinions. Some thought she was being kept by the owner of the little brick house she lived in, a certain Rosset, who didn't charge her rent. Other people mentioned other names. Still others swore the family supported itself on its own, working like slaves at the sewing machine. And finally there were those who said it didn't matter: a mother who did whatever it took to look after her children was doing right by them. In any case, reasoned Carmen, if there were indeed any lovers, they spent precious little on the supposedly kept woman, clearly no more than enough for minimal subsistence. And besides, it was Juana who had put her on the trail to La Tapera de Díaz with a basket of fried bread[34] to enjoy along the way, and not those respectable citizens she'd consulted, who knew nothing of Francisco Brey Moure and preferred to keep no record of any dealings with Indians.

The medicine woman of La Tapera lived in a decent house. With its wrought-iron gate and humble flower bed, it almost looked like a town house deposited out there on the pampa. Doña Rawson de Guaiquil received them in a little room where there hung a crucifix. On a side table was a Virgin of Luján[35] with a lighted candle and jasmine flowers. Their fragrance filled the room and continually refocused the visitors' attention on the holy image. With the Virgin's protection, and her gringo maiden name, the Guaiquil woman was perhaps trying to forestall any suspicion of witchcraft or quackery, as the Mapuches' therapeutic and liturgical practices were considered by the authorities. The display of Christian icons may also have been calculated to erase an obscure episode from her past. Back then, it was rumoured, she had been a disciple of "Santa María," a *machi* (witch or shaman) who, though baptized with the Christian and criollo name María Hortensia Roca, was the granddaughter of Chief Calfucurá. Santa María – Estanislao Hernández[36] told Carmen – had presided over the last great *ngillatún* or prayer ceremony of the old cult. That act had been considered unacceptable by Chief Simón Coliqueo (an intelli-

gent and progressive man, according to some; a traitor to their blood and
traditions, according to others), because it broke with the commitment
that the people of Los Toldos – during his father Ignacio Coliqueo's tenure
as chief – had made to Civilization.[37] The devout insurrectionists who
attacked him had left him badly wounded. Santa María had done time in
jail, but she was still living somewhere in the Province of Buenos Aires.[38]

Had Doña Juana Rawson, despite her surname, been among those last
rebels? She didn't look the part; her clear blue eyes were as peaceful and
neutral as those of a doll. Accustomed to listening, she asked them to
speak. Carmen told all. Much more than she was planning to say. Not just
facts, dates, a missing man: out there on the pampa, she told her story to
a little girl and an old woman she didn't know. She talked about the voyage to Buenos Aires, about Mugardos, her grandfather Brey, her dead
mother, the sea creeping inland like a wild animal half-tamed, her childhood, the wind in the chestnut groves, her father left alone, Adela Montes,
her jealousy and eventual forgiveness for a harm never inflicted, or at least
never intended. She spoke of Francisco Brey, brilliant, solid, so promising,
but who had done nothing for anyone, not even for himself. And yet, if he
ran off the way he did, someone must have done something that drove
him away, and she needed to know, she needed to find Francisco Brey, her
only blood relation, the only link she had to her earthly origins.

She finished talking. For a moment she hoped, absurdly, that Doña
Juana Guaiquil would have nothing to tell her about her lost brother. That
the Brey family history, now narrated, would end there in an open-ended
question. Maybe then Carmen Brey, having made every possible effort,
could be free of unsettled business and finally turn the page, begin living
a story that was hers and hers alone.

Juana Guaiquil, however, did have news. She did in fact know a young
white man, blue-eyed, who went by the name of Pancho.[39] He was married or living with one of the Coliqueo women. The long scar on his face
was so noticeable because it had poorly healed, something that would
never have happened had she treated the wound. This same Pancho lived
on the land of Pedro Coliqueo. She herself had delivered his two sons, now
five and seven years old, both of them healthy. The boys' mother, Sara Coliqueo, was also in good health – a hard-working woman of good character. In fact, she was sweeter in temperament than her husband, a dour fellow who shunned company outside his immediate family; but he was

known as a fine horse-breeder and he knew something about the law. Which was why the Coliqueos always listened to his counsel in the constant struggle to keep their ancestral lands against the encroachment of politicians and big landowners who coveted the fertile fields of La Tapera. Too fertile – they said – to be wasted on a bunch of Indians who didn't make it produce the way it should, and who could get along just as well anywhere else.

This information imparted, Juana called over one of her grandsons so he could show them to Pedro Coliqueo's place. Then she saw them to the door. Estanislao Hernández was waiting for them in the sulky. Before they boarded, Juana took Carmen by the arm and spoke softly in her ear.

– You seem like a good woman. Be a wise woman, as well. Don't ask too many questions. And don't think that where you come from, over there, is better than here.

During the short trip, Eva stole astonished glances at Carmen. She had been fascinated by the scenography of foreign names and distant landscapes brought to life by Carmen's story. Estanislao Hernández and the midwife's grandson (a skinny twelve-year-old) talked about the upcoming session of cattle-branding at La Blanqueada and competing in the *carreras de sortija*.[40]

The Coliqueo house was a big, ramshackle place with many rooms. Near the entrance, in a kind of gallery-space, a woman was working at a loom. Hernández lifted Carmen and the child out of the sulky and set them down as delicately as a pair of bone china figurines. Carmen leaned for a few seconds on the foreman's arm, dizzy from the emotion and seized by a cowardice she felt ashamed of. Hernández, though she'd told him almost nothing, seemed nonetheless to understand the situation, for it was he who went and knocked on the front door, asked for Francisco Brey, then led out toward the sulky a robust man of weathered face. In whom Carmen gradually recognized, as the distance between them shortened, and as though she were lifting away the surface layers of a palimpsest, the features of her brother.

Hernández led the children away and left the two of them alone.

Francisco Brey, however, made no move to come any closer. A sense of indignation slowly displaced in Carmen all other feelings. She had come all the way from Madrid to Buenos Aires, spent more than four years in this country searching, with never a word from him, not so much as a single letter – and this was the welcome she got?

Only when she saw the tremor in Francisco's right cheek, a sign of extreme emotion she remembered from way back, which only someone who knew him well could recognize, did her bitterness suddenly vanish and it was she who ran to give him a hug.

Carmen told him so much less than what she'd planned to say. She kept to the bare facts, ticking off the objective events of her life, the basic itinerary, expecting that any meaningful story would no doubt come from him. Francisco Brey talked about his false illusions, his pitiful adventure in America, stumbles and setbacks, dissipation and neglect, gambling debts and the criollo duel that had scarred his face. He spoke of his friendship with the Coliqueos, how he'd salvaged his remaining money by partnering with them and investing in horses. He talked about his life here, not luxurious, but enough to satisfy their basic needs, his two sons, the clear mornings with frost on the ground, the blankets that Sara wove to cover their four bodies.

Carmen, however, felt he'd told her nothing. Nothing had been explained or even suggested between the lines. She forgot about the advice of Peregrino Loureiro and Doña Juana Guaiquil, and anxiously started asking questions.

– But how could you just up and leave Spain like that? Without finishing your studies? Practically without saying goodbye? Did you think that letter you sent was enough for me?

– Saying goodbye in person would have been worse. I didn't want to go back on the decision I'd made.

– Because you weren't sure it was the right decision. There, you did well, all right. Because if all you came for is this …

– And what is it about "this" that's so bad, in your opinion? That I lost a big chunk of my capital, or that I live in the countryside and have children by an Indian woman? Is that what bothers you?

– You don't know me at all if you suppose that's how I think. What I mean is, you had no need to go off to America to make a good life for yourself. You could have finished your studies and had a career in Spain, instead of getting mixed up in a business you knew nothing about.

– That's easy to say in hindsight. Before we try something, we all believe things will turn out well.

– Not in your case.

– Oh no? Why not?

– Because you liked studying law. Because you believed in what you were doing. Coming to America wasn't an adventure, the wild idea of young man. You were running away.

When her brother's right cheek began to quiver again, Carmen Brey should have stopped. But she was not wise – she thought later – and maybe it was better that way.

– What were you running away from? Or from whom? Are you going to tell me?

– Why don't you shut up, woman! So, did she tell you everything, and now you're coming to rub it in my face? Don't you think I've suffered enough remorse all these years? That I've been punished enough? I cut myself off from everything and everyone. I lived like a pariah, without language, without country, without memory, without a past. I fled from everything that reminded me of who I had been. Until God took pity on me, or I took pity on myself, and now I have another home and another country.

A violent retrospective film passed before her mind's eye, an indiscreet collage of forgotten looks, words, gestures, letters, silences: all that had gone unnoticed before and was now surfacing in obscene exposure. Still she clung to the hope he would deny it.

– Who are you talking about? Who is "she"?

– Adela. Who else would it be? I was in love. Crazy in love for years.

– That's not a reason to go away … Or did you sleep with her? Were you actually capable of sleeping with Adela?

– Once. And not because she wanted to. Do you think that after that I could look her in the eye as if nothing had happened? Or look at you? Don't you think that's reason enough to run away?

Carmen bowed her head. Beneath the arch of her shoe an orderly multitude of ants was filing by and around the corner of the hitching rail a metre or two away, surely in search of a better world in the shelter of some rock.

– Your inquisitional tribunal has been a success. Are you satisfied now? Be off with you then, if that's what you want, and we'll each live our own lives, like before. There's no reason you have to tell anybody you've seen me.

Carmen looked at him again.

– I won't say anything to anyone, if that's what you wish. But I'm not leaving. I want you to introduce me to your wife and to my nephews.

Slowly, without speaking or touching, they walked toward the house. Sara Coliqueo – the woman at the loom – and Esteban Hernández were waiting for them. Carmen opened her arms to Sara, and they kissed each other on both cheeks.

That afternoon the Brey siblings, the Coliqueos, Estanislao Hernández, Eva, young Prudencio Guaiquil, and Francisco's two sons shared *mate*, bannock, cow cheese and goat cheese, and bread fresh out of the oven. Francisco's children had soft, dark skin. Luis, the younger one, had inherited the intense blue eyes of Carmen and grandfather Brey. Both of them knew the names of plants, flowers, and animals. The elder son, Antonio, was already riding horseback.[41]

Sara Coliqueo took Carmen aside into another room and offered her the gift of a small woven carpet.

– Carmen, *lamnguen*, I'm glad you are my sister. When you got off the sulky, I thought you were another wife that Pancho had left back in his native land, and you were coming to get him.

– This is my brother's land now, answered Carmen.

At nightfall, after leaving Prudencio at his grandmother's house, they set out for Los Toldos. Carmen had promised to write, promised to come back. She thought about the midwife's advice. She had ignored it and now she was paying the price of knowing the truth – grief inexhaustible. She became dimly aware of the risk of ignoring the other piece of advice: "Don't think that where you come from, over there, is better than here." But was it fair that her nephews, the grandsons of Antonio Brey and María del Carmen Moure, would grow up among the conquered and defeated, out on the edge of the world? That the ladies and gentlemen in town would look down on them because of their mother's native tongue, even if that language could name hopes and fears, beauty or evil in the creatures of the earth, just as effectively? That they would always come last, because their hair was thick and black and coarse and shiny? Because their terracotta skin better withstood the sun of America? Fury and sorrow burned red-hot within her breast. For that very reason – so as not to be last in everything – the Galicians had had to leave Spain, for generations, carrying their language with them. *Prados, ríos, arboredas, pinares que move o vento.* "Meadows, rivers, copses, pine trees swept by the wind."[42] All this they left and continued to leave behind, along with mothers, sons, wives (*e nais que non teñen fillos, e*

fillos que non tén pais. Viudas de vivos e mortos que ninguén consolará).[43]
They headed for Havana or Buenos Aires, with cardboard suitcases, with
papers in order or without, legitimate third-class passengers or stow-
aways huddled in the ship's hold. Caravans of farmers and fishermen
sick and tired of misery, hand-outs, contempt. People who had risked
everything so that no one ever again would look at them askance
beneath God's sky. But in breaking away they were broken up. Parasitic
plants on rotting tree bark, vines without a wall, floating, their roots
exposed to the air and rubbed raw. Vulnerable as the retractile eyes of
snails, reactive to the slightest brush of a fingertip. Would their nephews
have to go to the city, to high schools and universities, be catechized by
priests or scientists? Would they have to abandon the horses, wheat
fields, insects, fish, and birds that country people knew better than
botanists and zoologists? Yes, like it or not, they would have to pay that
price to earn the right of return. In order to have a place, deeded and
unquestionable, in their own land.

Estanislao Hernández, methodically chewing tobacco, paused to spit off
to one side before commenting gravely:

– No offence intended, but to tell the truth, this brother of yours, I
like'm better than that other one. He knows a lot about the land. And he's
no puffed-up swell.

– Well, I won't say you're wrong about that. But everyone has their
good side.

Eva had drifted off to sleep on her lap. A bump on the path suddenly
woke her up.

– Your cousins are nice, eh? she said. The mother invited me to go
horseback riding with them, whenever I want. There were lots of queens
rode horses in the olden days, wearing a crown with feathers and other
pretty things. Do you think I could play Joan of Arc?

– As long your story ends better than hers, fine. Make up a happy ending. It doesn't always have to be tears and regrets.

– I like stories that make you cry, said Evita, giving Carmen's hand a
squeeze. And you? Are you glad you came? Are you happy?

– Yes, I'm glad, and I'm grateful that you came with me. But I can't say
I'm happy. This story, too, was the kind that makes you cry.

The scattered lights of Los Toldos began to appear against the black
pampa. Eva's eyes reflected them, and her face of transparent skin floated

white as a plaster mask, swaying with the lurch of the sulky like a small errant moon in the darkness.

VII

The train finally left the station, noisily, wearily. Carmen leaned far out the window, arm upstretched, waving a kerchief. On the platform beside her sister Blanca stood Evita, her thin bare arm waving another kerchief, a red one.

– I'll be darned! said Marechal. Apparently for lack of old friends you've made new ones. And better, too, since all we did was cause you headaches …

– No, no, that's not right. It was very generous of you both to keep me company on this trip, even if we didn't exactly get off on the right foot.

– Who would have thought that help would end up coming from a bully gaucho in a pulpería? added Borges.

"You were the one who played the bully," thought Carmen, but kept it to herself.

– I like this town, said Marechal. It may not be the real South, but it *is* the pampa.

– Old-time gauchos like the ones from the South are no more, lamented Borges. Except on the other shore, on the *Banda Oriental*.[44] Here it's full of gringos[45] who only believe in progress and making their fortune in America. Pretty soon, even the Indians will be dreaming of electric lights.

– Well, let them dream, if that helps them live better.

– In any case, Carmen, this pampa isn't old, it is forever young. "I announce to you a land where each morning will give birth to a different god."[46]

– And poets will be the midwives of mornings, I suppose, just as Socrates was the midwife of philosophers.

– You said it, Carmen. Something like that.

– Of course, modesty is not a virtue of poets.

– But is modesty a virtue?

– In this instance, I guess not. Go ahead, keep on helping mornings be born, burn your hands with the new sun, dare to see the face of the different god. The earth will thank you for it.

– Well, for now, I think I'll go smoke, if you'll excuse me. I'll be back soon.

Borges looked at Carmen with cautious affection.

– I hope you won't bear me a grudge for all the trouble.

– Not at all.

– You know, it's a curious thing, your brother's story. A European who comes to America and becomes enamoured of the wild, and even evades his own family. But it isn't the first time. Leaving aside the many stories of the Spanish Conquest, among us here in Argentina, Sarmiento talked about a Major Navarro, a gentleman and apparently quite a dandy, who married the daughter of a chief and drank blood "at the slaughterhouse for horses." Mansilla relates other similar episodes. My own grandmother, an Englishwoman, came close to meeting someone like that. They were in Junín with my grandfather Borges, who was chief officer at the frontier, and one afternoon a blond woman dressed in Indian clothing came into town. She came to stock up on "the vices" (yerba mate, sugar, *aguardiente*) and brought furs, weavings, and ostrich feathers for barter in the pulperías. My grandmother asked to speak with her, and she told her story in rusty English. She was an Englishwoman taken captive in a *malón* when she was a girl. She wouldn't dream of going back to the Christians, even though my grandmother offered her all kinds of guarantees, both for her and the children she'd had by the chief. Some time later, she ran into her again. They were in a low-lying marshy area, cutting a sheep's throat. The Indian Englishwoman rode over, threw herself on the ground, and drank the hot blood ...[47] Just imagine! So why wouldn't your brother ...

– Good Lord, Borges! Why are you telling me these stories? All that must have happened fifty or sixty years ago. Now the Indians of Los Toldos live the same way as other country folk. Or like any Galician farmer. The only difference is that in the north of Spain the houses are made of stone and here they're adobe. But they're all poor; in that sense they're alike. Why don't you write a story using those memories, strange and beautiful as a legend?

– I'm not quite ready to tackle narrative fiction, and ...

Borges stopped talking, embarrassed and a little frightened. He had never known how to deal with a woman's tears, especially if they were falling in perfect silence, while the woman's breast was heaving convulsively, without a sob, as in a silent film. He put his arm around Carmen's shoulders.

– There, there. Please, don't be upset. I didn't mean to imply that your brother's gone native. And even if he had, who's to say those we call savages aren't happier than we are. No doubt he's just fine where he's decided to live. The soul has its secret urges, and they ...

– Borges, listen to me. My brother went to live with Indians, lost his money, tried to lose his memory, but not because he fell in love with barbarism. He ran away from Spain like a madman because he slept with my father's wife, forced her in fact. He didn't want anyone's forgiveness because he couldn't forgive himself.

Borges spoke in a soft, neutral voice that Carmen found consoling.

– The Bible is full of things like that. And life too, of course.

He sighed, passing her a carefully folded handkerchief slightly scented with cologne. Had Doña Leonor ironed it for him, as Doña Juana Ibarguren ironed Eva's dresses? She suddenly imagined Borges, at his adult size, stuffed into a child's school uniform and drinking his milk in the kitchen. She laughed between her tears, feeling tenderness for that big kid, and a loyalty that would endure – and she dried her eyes.

When Marechal came back, they were talking about English poetry. About Swinburne, it so happened. The name no longer triggered irksome memories in Carmen. They gradually fell silent and the two porteño men nodded off, rocked to sleep by the dull clack of wheels on iron rails. Carmen Brey recalled her last moments with Eva. The child had made a gift of her prize possession: the photo of her adored Norma Shearer, gold-foil frame and hand-drawn flowers included. Carmen wanted to reciprocate properly. She gave Eva her rouge, eyeshadow, and face powder for her dress-up games; a pair of earrings and some perfume for her mother; and that same Monday, before the train left, she bought her the only copy in town of *Famous Women in History*. "I'm going to write to you," she'd told her, "and I hope you'll write me back." Eva swore she would, despite her bad handwriting.

It was hard to go back. Buenos Aires, that illusory little nation within a greater, unknown Argentina, would never again be the same. The whole city looked to her now like a fairy-tale palace, grown up overnight, foundation-less, a mirage in the unchanging wilderness. But that wilderness was inhabited, beyond the architectural caprices bounded by the city.

Who would she talk to about the women, children, and men ignored and forgotten, as though they were mute, because their voices did not cross the enchanted line of demarcation between City and Chaos?

Victoria was too far away and too preoccupied with her own magical city, the City of Lights, where not even the urban voices of Buenos Aires could be heard, for in Paris porteños were just as remote as the other denizens of the Argentine wilderness. If consulted, Elena Sansinena, open-handed and quick to help, would likely launch a rescue operation for Carmen's nephews, as if they were prisoners of war in a foreign territory, just as Borges's grandmother had offered – in vain – to redeem the sons of the Indian Englishwoman. But she didn't need or want that kind of help. Then she recalled a pair of dark eyes, unique among the women "friends of the arts"; dark eyes that had learned to look above and beneath the dazzling surface, that knew how to see both grandeur and indigence in the wilderness, even from within her palatial house in the golden city. She would go to visit María Rosa Oliver and tell her the whole story. A feeling of trust and confidence calmed her. Her eyelids gravely lowered, with relief and gratitude, like curtains falling to the stage after an extraordinary drama.

4

1929–1931

Free Women of the South

When I arrived in Buenos Aires I was received by a person I no longer knew. Nothing was left of the *donna umile*, of that *fervente admiratrice*, of that being for whom my mind had meant everything.

Hermann von Keyserling
Journey Through Time II, 1951

... he looked at me for a few seconds, and then said:
– You are most patent case of *amor fati* I've ever seen.
– ... *Amor fati*...?
– That's how Goethe called love for one's own destiny.

María Rosa Oliver
La vida cotidiana, 1969[1]

Women, vis-à-vis men, have had against them, and still do, the "handicap" that children of the proletariat have vis-à-vis children of the privileged classes. And they have had it for centuries. Nothing today can justify that state of affairs, even admitting there might ever have been reasons for it to exist. Neither in the one case or the other.

What men do not seem to understand, apart from a minority whom I bless, is that we are not at all interested in taking their place, but rather in taking our own place completely, which until now has not happened ... I think the great role women have played in history – until now in a subterranean fashion – is today beginning to rise to the surface.

Victoria Ocampo
Woman, Her Rights, and Her Responsibilities, 1936[2]

I

In the apartment of the Duchess of Dato on the avenue de la Bourdon-nais, the walls were high and white, impeccably bare. Against that sheer white background, Victoria could marvel at the unorthodox beauty of several innovative artworks: two by Miró, a Dalí, and one Drieu. The Drieu was actually alive: art object and author were bundled together in a single body, long, hard, and lean. The strong arms were regularly exercised by swimming and rowing. The hands had fingers thick and gnarled at the knuckles like blind eyes on tree roots; they had killed with rifle and pistol; they also wrote, in a neat, dry script, brilliant fictions that were almost a form of confession. But Madame Ocampo knew nothing of that yet. For the two or three hours she spent beside him at table, she saw a literary playboy, a dandy who flaunted his blue shirt, cuff-links, and impeccably creased trousers with the same aplomb as his cynical commentary on local politics – matters incomprehensible to her. He also flaunted, as a noncha-lant complement to his natty attire, an angular masculine head whose irregular construction combined heavily-lidded blue eyes, an excessively high forehead, slicked-back blond hair, and fleshy lips – cigarette dangling rakish – expressly designed for mockery.

"Drieu" – the signature of that insolent painting – was the first surname of Pierre Drieu La Rochelle, great-grandson of one Jacques Drieu, who had won the heroic sobriquet of his second surname at bayonette point, fighting in all the campaigns of the Revolution and the Empire.[3] His father, however, was nothing like that warrior. In the eyes of young Pierre, he was a seductive charlatan, a failure when it came to creation, combat, making money, or any other productive or destructive activity requiring human ingenuity. Pierre Drieu hated him. And hated his deceased moth-er even more for having obstinately remained (out of love, not resigna-tion), like a useful piece of furniture or a faithful pet, by the side of that man whose ineptitude caused his firstborn son everlasting shame.

Pierre Drieu La Rochelle considered himself also, in some ways, to be *un raté*, a fiasco. For eleven years he had been the only grandchild of two Nor-mand families and the darling of two affectionate grandmothers. A solitary child given to reading, he held out the promise of genius. Through his soli-tary readings, he developed an unconditional cult of a few heroes (later he would say he knew about Napoleon before God, before France, before himself). But, by the same token, he became painfully aware of his own flaws and failings. Although attending a school for rich kids, he was the impoverished *petit bourgeois* thanks to his father's lack of business acumen. Or he was a mere dreamer, ungainly among his athletic schoolmates, who ruled the world with their muscles and prestige. At the age of fourteen, Nietzsche's *Zarathustra* and *Un Homme libre* by Maurice Barrès[4] were his bedside reading material, and he could not see how to raise his insignificant life to the lofty heights of either of them. He thought the way forward might be in the budding genius that not only his grandmothers but also his teachers perceived in him. Soon he became the most outstanding pupil of the School of Political Science. But then disaster struck. In the final exams before graduation, against all expectation, his performance was not only less than brilliant but earned him an outright failure. For the second time in his life, he seriously considered suicide (the first having been when he contracted a venereal disease from his first visit to a brothel). Nevertheless, the Great War would redeem him from these indignities. Not so much because of the heroic wounds suffered at Charleroi and Verdun, but because in battle he felt he had at last found the measure of his own strength. In the fizzy glitter of life in Paris, however, that strength was muffled, semi-mollified, a useless secret he did not know how to put to use. His dormant potency only emerged, impure and deviant, in the verbal skirmishes and quarrels that drained his days. By the time Victoria Ocampo saw him in the apartment on the avenue de la Bourdonnais, exhibited there like another painted canvas, Drieu had published books of poetry, an ironic autobiography, collections of short stories, two novels, and several political essays about the bourgeois century's withered beauty, or about the old Europe caught between the inexorable pincers of New York and Moscow. Though he worked with ink, Drieu as the "Young European"[5] aspired to blood. On the field of battle – brutal, measureless, gratuitous effusion – he had had the only mystical and communitarian experience of his life. There he had shaken off the pitiful remora of his individuality, his complex, inconclusive identity.

Meanwhile, in his Parisian exile, he found distraction in love affairs, if only to pour those caprices into a book. He had written *Un homme couvert de femmes*[6] and did not contradict those who saw his self-portrait in Gilles, the novel's protagonist: a Don Juan bored with the transparent, futile mechanisms of feminine desire. Far away from sports and war,

chained to a desk by passion and pride (or proudly refusing to resemble
his father), Drieu indulged in his favourite game: he drove the *belles dames*
of Paris crazy, first by flattering them with his interest, then by disconcerting them with humiliations until their plumage began to pale, their
magic to wilt, the myriad eyes of their peacock tails to blink in bewilder-
ment before the aggressive indifference now being inflicted by their erst-
while paramour.

Had he found in the *dame Argentine* a new partner with whom to play
this game? Or had it perhaps irritated him that *she* seemed to view *him*
as an amusing object? Her carefully painted mouth had not twisted in
displeasure at his brutal remarks, her lips sketched no scandalized gri-
mace. She merely smiled, faintly amused by the antics of an insolent boy,
un enfant terrible. Her fingernails, painted with similar care, had with
ostensible indifference leafed through two of his books (*Blèche*[7] and
Genève ou Moscou[8]) displayed on the mantelpiece above Isabel Dato's
marble fireplace. *Madame Ocampo*, unlike the other rich and beautiful
women who had elected to admire him insatiably, between the sheets and
outside them, was apparently permitting herself the liberty of not taking
him seriously.

Two days after that meeting, Drieu left one of his books and a card at
Victoria Ocampo's apartment. The book was signed, barely; the card
invited her for cocktails at a bar on the Champs Elysées. Victoria made no
comment on the book, but accepted the invitation, though at a different
venue. She preferred to take tea *chez* Rumpelmayer, rue de Rivoli, for she
never drank cocktails.[9]

Drieu decided to bowl her over from the get-go with ferocious sincerity.

– That silk dress you were wearing the other day looked good on you.
What made you decide to put on that porter's sweater today?

– I wanted to make sure the Maison Chanel continues to prosper,
thanks to us Argentine parvenus, and to give you the pleasure of trying to
impress me with your vulgarity.

Drieu smiled. Despite the cigarette that never left his lips, the whiteness of his teeth was almost exaggerated, unstained by nicotine. Likewise, his fingers and nails were smooth, clean, polished. Everything
about him evoked baths, soaps, brushes. Victoria moved as close to him
as was possible without provoking misinterpretations, just for the smell
of him. A whiff of Atkinson's cologne, a moss-like aroma, gratified her

expectation. To some degree, the Frenchman was a blond version, lighter and younger, of Julián. And he was probably also a healthy anti-dote to the "Keyserling effect."

– Nevertheless, my vulgarity, as you call it, is a gesture of good will that you ought to thank me for, Madame. I'm only trying to make sure you don't fall in love with me. First and foremost, you should know I have the soul of a pimp. I've ruined the lives and fortunes of two young, beautiful heiresses whom I had no other choice but to marry, so insistent were they.

– So, are you a bigamist? Or a Mussulman?

– Neither one nor the other. I married twice successively, both times in accord with French law. But I squandered the dowry from my first wife, and now I'm working my way through the second one, until I get a divorce. It's a shame women are so stupid, there's just no dissuading them.

– Not to worry, I've no intention of falling in love with you. And even if that were to happen, it wouldn't do you any good. My wealth would remain outside your grasp. I'm legally married, and our laws don't allow for divorce.

– What a shame.

– That I'm married?

– That you can't divorce. Must be unbearable. For my part, I've never been able to stay interested in a friendship or a love affair for more than six months. One can always resort to running away, of course. Isn't that what you're doing?

– I don't intend to discuss my private life with you.

– *Tant pis.* The only persons one can confide in are complete strangers. You'd be better off confessing to me than to a priest in Buenos Aires. Who would find out from me about your intimate affairs?

– All of Paris, of course.

– And what's Paris to you? It's as far away as another planet.

– Don't you believe it. Paris is a suburb of Argentine polite society.

– Conversation with you is a real delight. Almost as amusing as with a man. An intelligent man, of course. With oafs it's worse even than chat-chit with women, absent the compensatory pleasure of sleeping with them afterwards. But, to return to the subject at hand, I don't think "polite soci-ety" means much to you.

– About as little as oafish men and ugly women mean to you. But that is the society of my parents, and they *are* important to me.

Drieu later walked her home. She did not invite him in. Julián was in
Paris. Perhaps at the apartment even now, waiting for her. Or they might
cross paths in the vestibule or on the stairs. It came to her that she was
afraid of seeing the two men together; she wanted to avoid any comparisons. Was it because she was in danger of making Drieu her lover? Because
she was reluctant to replace one lover with another? But Julián was not
replaceable. That grand passion, now in its vertiginous death throes, would
never be repeated. She felt, however, on the verge of another passion that
had to do with her alone, not with a man. And certainly never with a man
like Pierre Drieu.

That afternoon was the first in a long series of encounters for tea and
walks with the French dandy. Julián, as though he were being thrown out
or some emergency were calling him from the other side of the ocean,
soon decided to leave the city. Did he feel superfluous in the world they
once shared? Had he tired of entering Victoria's life through the back
door? In Buenos Aires, would they be able to discuss those absences and
mutual silences that precede a sad ending? When Julián left Paris, Victoria found herself definitively free. She did not forget him, but he was no
longer in the new design of her life coming to light in the friendship with
Drieu. She enjoyed him in the way many men enjoy women. The charm
of his physical proximity; the textures and colours of his clothing;
the precisely elegant lines of his bones, gestures, steps, movements; the
blended scent of moss and tobacco: all this configured the "Drieu
ambiance" and confirmed the stunning effect of his body against the
white walls at Isabel Dato's place, alongside the two Miró's and the Dalí.
However, Drieu the beautiful object, pleasant to smell, look at, even to
caress, clashed scandalously with Drieu the intellectual. Relentlessly
provocative, his ideas were diametrically opposed to hers. On the upside,
at least he had no pretensions to be her Hero or Teacher. With him, there
was no need to wait for reality to destroy idle dreams about some ideal
woman because the real woman no longer cared to be his disciple. On the
contrary, he made sure to ferociously destroy any hint of a compliment
concerning either his moral qualities or his artistic will and talent. Victoria began to suspect there was something behind such savagery. Drieu,
the lazy dilettante who bragged that he only wrote books to keep suicidal
boredom at bay, was in reality a patient artisan who hand-wrote up to
five or six versions of every page he produced. The result of so much

effort was brilliant, turbulent, and casual, giving the impression of having been carelessly dashed off. Drieu, the immoralist and supposed gigolo of aristocratic millionairesses, who claimed the worst villains in his stories were self-portraits, in fact despised himself furiously for never having persevered in a relationship long enough to make a woman pregnant and have a child. Drieu, who preached death to the nations and extolled the era of a European alliance ruled by a dictator, was at heart an anachronistic survivor of the France of Saint Louis[10] or Joan of Arc, and preferred to see the old France dissolved or annihilated, rather than languish in a lay realm of vulgar bourgeois happiness.

Drieu, above all, did not stubbornly insist that she love him. At most, he blamed himself for his own inadequacy, his incapacity to be for her a necessary lover. (Years later, he would write to her: *You are my friend, my greatest woman friend, my friend. I shall regret all my life not having been able to be your lover. All my life. It would have been profoundly magnificent.*)

Victoria laughed at his verbal roughhousing. She collected his absurd compliments, surreal phrases of malignant praise: *I love your distraction, like that of a beautiful beast.* Or another: *I like talking with you, arguing with you, telling you: "Merde, belle vache." You chew on the cud of all philosophies and produce good milk. Homer had no more beautiful metaphor than: "She was a heifer."*[11] Other sentences, which no Teacher would have dedicated to her, she appreciated deeply and silently: *I need you, I like fighting with you, making peace after every battle. We do not see the world the same way, but each of those two visions exists and I rejoice in the fact that you are Victoria, victorious in your realm, if not in mine.*[12] Drieu, the presumed apologist of force, who despised the abject weakness of modern times, nevertheless conceded her the right to her own world, as well as full liberty to dissent (perhaps because Victoria was strong?). Pierre, she would think later, had obstinately and pathetically admired defects he did not have; he had lived defending the irrationality of power with refined intellectual arguments.

The strangeness of their unexpected fraternal relationship comforted and reassured her about herself. For that reason, perhaps, she preferred Drieu's company over that of the idols of her youth, whom she was now frequenting in Paris. She had lunch with Paul Valéry, Jules Supervielle, or Madame de Noailles; she visited the home of Ravel. But with Drieu she went out for tea, for walks, visits to the Louvre and the cinema (their vice), or attended the Comédie Française. Drieu too preferred her to any other person. He had fled his wife, as well as his old house on the rue Saint-Louis-en-l'Île. He shut himself up in hotels to write, leaving those anonymous rooms, full of random objects, only to spend time with Victoria.

Later, they met for a few days in London. Victoria was there shopping for furnishings for the new house she was having built in Buenos Aires by the architect Bustillo[13] (a plain, rectangular house with interior walls as white as those of Isabel Dato; there, too, Drieu would have been a commendable choice as a painting). Before leaving France, she agreed to go with him to Normandy where he had been born. They took two rooms in Deauville at a seaside hotel. That night, insomniac both, stalled at a bend in the road of their time together, not yet ready to make the leap to another place where nothing would protect them (neither passion nor marriage nor prudent scorn), they kept one another company sleeping in the same bed, attempting no greater intimacy than a hug. That was as close as they would ever come, thought Victoria. She would never allow Drieu, the man practically *couvert de femmes* like the character in his novel, to cover himself with her body, use it as a shield to fend off his uncertainties and the reflection of his own contempt.

When she departed from the Gare d'Orsay for Spain, Madame Ocampo was without a lover: Julián was in the past, Drieu in a hypothetical future. She had only herself to count on, her destiny like a blank cheque she dared not fill out. And still pending, like a bitter debt from a former life, was the confrontation with Keyserling in Buenos Aires.

II

Carmen Brey finished her fourth cup of tea. For almost three hours she had been listening, fascinated, to the tale of Victoria and the Count – an imbroglio of misunderstandings from start to finish. An inverted fairy-tale, she thought, where the prince ends up turning into a toad. At moments she suffered fits of indignation born of feminine solidarity. Other times she felt like laughing out loud, not only at the Count but also at his imprudent and capricious woman friend, who had turned a deaf ear to all warnings.

– You can see what a disagreeable mess I've landed in. If it were up to me, I'd run away and avoid seeing him at all. But the Count refuses to give lectures unless I'm involved, and I've already promised Bebé, the press, the university, everyone. Carmen, dearest, I need your help; I need you to be an intermediary. More and more I appreciate down-to-earth intelligence – she added with a sideward glance of humble recognition – ; I think you and Angélica together will do a superb job of handling my public relations with the, uhmm, individual. The thing is to distract him, entertain him, so that my contact with him can be minimal.

Carmen smiled.

– As long as you're not offering us to the Minotaur as propitiatory victims ... What if that satyr takes a fancy to one of us?

– In that case, all diplomatic considerations are off, and the three of us take him down.

– With Fani's help. She would be invaluable, if it comes to that.

– Don't even mention it to her. She suspects something, but if she finds out what happened with Keyserling, she'll really let me have it; there'll be no end to the reproaches, both direct and indirect. The only consolation she'll offer will be: it serves you right for being so stupid. And as usual, she won't be entirely wrong ... But anyway, what about you? Here I've been yakking about myself for hours on end. What have you been up to these last months? You look different, maybe a bit sad. Has something bad happened?

– Yes and no. It's a long story, and I don't think this is the right moment. We'll talk about it another time. I'm fine, don't worry. It'll be a good distraction to take on the Count.

Carmen went out into the placid autumnal afternoon, its light burnishing the clean, dry lines of Victoria's new house. It was a plain, austere house that clashed with the complicated mansions surrounding it. The neighbours had all expressed their disapproval; even the architect had built it against the grain of his own aesthetic sense. Contrariwise, the house would soon earn the praise of Le Corbusier. Carmen was inclined to agree with Bustillo. There were too many openings, too many blank spaces mercilessly exposed to the light. She still loved alcoves, nooks and crannies, cozy little corners that offer refuge to modesty and the secret inner development of human lives. And rooms destined never to be opened, and stories impossible to erase because without them we would not be what we are, nor become what awaits us in the future. But Victoria apparently needed to make a violent break, change houses as one might change bodies in order to be born again.

Soon the Count arrived. Regally lodged by his resigned Maecenas at the Hotel Plaza, he was swarmed and flattered on his arrival there by photographers, journalists, and readers. The following morning, at the headquarters of Friends of the Arts, the receptionist handed Carmen a little card.

– It's from a foreigner, on behalf of Count Keyserling. He says he's the Count's secretary and would like to see you.

Señorita Brey remembered no personal secretary among the crowd when the Count disembarked, but it seemed credible that he would have one. She studied the card: *Herr Doktor Ulrich Werner von Phorner Jaeger.* She would need an exercise-session in phonetics if she was ever going to pronounce correctly that onomastic mouthful of partial rhymes. She mentally steeled herself for a laborious conversation in English or French with a Prussian who would likely pass her a list of requirements and recommendations.

– Tell him to come in.

She got up to receive the visitor, but what she saw before her was no stereotypical Prussian. A young man of regular height and build quickly stepped forward and bowed to kiss her outstretched hand, lightly clicking his heels.

– I am Von Phorner, Señorita Brey. It is a pleasure to meet you, he said in correct Spanish in a rather harsh accent. Please do not struggle with the name on my card. I suppose that we have not the right to mortify South American ears with such names. Fortunately, we like short forms. My name is Ulrich, and my friends, among whom I hope to count you, if you will do me the honour, call me Utz. Please, you may do the same.

Señorita Brey looked the secretary up and down with frank interest. Was it by virtue of some mysterious law of compensation that the ogre from the Baltic had found himself, as a sort of antidote, a secretary of pleasing presence and charming manners? Doctor von Phorner returned her look with even greater interest. Carmen Brey tried, unsuccessfully, to define the colour of the eyes behind a pair of rimless glasses. It changed according to the light – a strange blend of honey-inflected green? In any case, they radiated a silken peacefulness. As silken as the light-chestnut hair, a mass of unruly curls. It was all she could do to stop her hand from taking a plunge into that gleaming tangle to feel its texture and consistency.

– I'm not South American, I'm Spanish. As you see, I too am working away from home. As for rights and obligations, there's no reason why you should have to know our language, which you speak very well, by the way. Where did you learn it?

– I did my doctoral degree in Spanish History and spent some time in Seville, researching documents from the Indies. I lived in Madrid, too.

Doctor von Phorner, or Utz, smiled and shrugged his shoulders, as though trying to explain his own inexcusable folly to an understanding listener.

– I suppose that after so much delving into stories of Germans and Spaniards seeking the Fountain of Youth or the palaces of El Dorado, I ended up as misled as they were and started to believe it's possible to seek and find Wisdom. I enrolled at the School in Darmstadt and ended up staying on. I find travel interesting, and the Count travels a lot. I usually go with him.

Many times in the course of Keyserling's stay, Carmen Brey would be thankful that Ulrich von Phorner had accompanied the philosopher on the trip to South America. Before long, relations between the philosopher and Victoria had deteriorated to the point of exploding. The scraps of organic material left by the explosion quickly decomposed, corrupted by rancour, and the air around them became pestilential. But through it all, Utz handled the Count (who several times needed emergency treatment for violent bouts of irregular heartbeat) with a patience as angelic as it was ironic. Behind his glasses, his eyes of indefinable colour glinted with suppressed laughter. Carmen knew the look well. "My God, this young man could be Galician. If Grandfather Brey had ever laid eyes on the Count, his eyes would have lit up with exactly the same expression."

– Oh well, good thing he doesn't have high blood pressure. If he were to have a stroke, we'd have to take him back to Germany in a wheelchair. In that case, *Madame* Ocampo would have to hire three male nurses just to lug his bulk around. You should tell her to thank her lucky stars.

From the very first day, the Count and Victoria annoyed and upset each other. The new house in Palermo Chico had been the scene of a welcome reception, including crates of champagne (for the philosopher's near-exclusive use), renowned writers and professors, the cream of porteño society, and well-known beauties. With this scenography and cast of bit players at his disposal, the Count mounted an unforgettable one-man show. For months and years to come, the inebriated giant would be remembered as a philosophical Rasputin who kept nodding off, having consumed enough alcohol to fell ten normal men. Who could have failed to notice, at one point during his spirituous talk, that his great paw, as though grasping the polished handle of cane, came to rest on the bald head of Alfonso Reyes, the eminent man of letters and diminutive ambassador of Mexico?[14] No one, probably. And certainly not the hostess and owner of the house, who had not brought the founder of the School of Wisdom across the Atlantic Ocean so that he could make a vaudeville spectacle of himself, a circus act.

Two persons in attendance, however, were quite unconcerned about Keyserling. One of them (Doctor von Phorner), because he knew him all too well. The other (Carmen Brey), because she couldn't care less about knowing him. Moreover, the two of them were putting their time and energy to better use – getting acquainted.

Von Phorner thought about the paradoxes of fate. He, who had travelled as far as China, had lived in Seville and knew Madrid, but had never set foot in the foggy north of Spain, the birthplace of this woman as tiny and luminous as the fairies that appear after rainfall in a child's garden. Despite her fay aspect and alarmingly translucent skin, white over a network of little blue veins, Señorita Brey was fortunately not incorporeal. Doctor Phorner began to dream about her soft, round cheek, where a delightful dimple seemed designed for the sole purpose of receiving a kiss from his lips.

In Señorita Brey's view, Ulrich or Utz may have been disappointed in his search for wisdom under Keyserling's mentorship, but he had nonetheless acquired a certain nomadic sagacity, whose most notable attribute was his keen sense of humour. Whereas Doctor Swinburne's knowledge had drained his vitality, the gay science of the German professor had not at all affected his earthy solidity or his robust, sanguine health. A slab of dried cod he was not.

Between lectures, when he wasn't busy babysitting the philosopher, Doctor Phorner was getting to know and love a city and a woman. Carmen introduced him to María Rosa Oliver; to Borges, inventor of the *arrabal*; to Marechal, vatic midwife of Southern mornings; and, through the two poets, to the great Macedonio Fernández. As a result, he would go from beers at Aue's Keller to tertulias of coffee and croissants (plus the odd late-night gin) in La Perla del Once, where the talk was of Nietzsche and Schopenhauer, and where Doctor Phorner, only moderately sober, was prevailed upon by a not-very-respectable public to belt out Goliard songs for dessert. But nothing could compare with the afternoons spent with Carmen at the pictures. The moving images on the big screen were the least of their interests. For the first time in all the years he had been running after the Count's luggage and bad temper, Ulrich von Phorner felt he was the hero and star of his own private movie. What was Hollywood love to him? Let John Gilbert and Rudolph Valentino perform their slow, languid seductions on Mona Maris or Greta Garbo, up there on the two-dimensional screen. He, in the flesh, was kissing for the first time the single dimple on the cheek of the sole woman made to the exact measure of his desire. Carmen Brey, too, was indifferent to the celluloid *femmes fatales* and horsemen of the Apocalypse and desert sheikhs, when Utz's curls were within reach of fingers that, over and over again, tugged at them, smoothed and re-wound them – fingers dimly aware that beneath the starched shirt (and also in other places, subterranean and unmentionable) lurked other curls, crinklier, but just as deserving of caresses.

But the best was yet to come, when they would come out of the cinema and walk without tiring all the way to the gardens of Palermo. Then, in the Botanical Garden, submerged in vegetal aromas as though in their own protective little forest, they told each other about their past lives, which now seemed like a curious adventure novel, moving, but somehow a bit distant. For the real life of each of them was yet to commence.

Señorita Brey was pleased to find out that Doctor Phorner, like her, was interested in the mystery of faith, but decidedly anticlerical and for even better reasons than hers. His mother was born to a wealthy Lutheran family of the bourgeoisie, his father was a Catholic from the lesser nobility. His mother's family had had in mind for her a quite different marriage, with a Protestant much richer than the indigent Papist nobleman. When she married against their wishes, they disinherited her. Growing up poor as a church mouse by comparison with some of his ancestors, Ulrich von Phorner witnessed first hand the way religious institutions of all stripes generally served to prohibit or spoil earthly joys, or to aggravate the contradictions of human discord. God, if he existed, must have been sick and tired of those zealous domestic quarrels among factions vying to monopolize the right-of-usufruct of Divine Truth, as if it were a vacant lot in a residential neighbourhood or the private beach of an exclusive resort.

In any case, with good fortune and ill, Utz had become a traveller. He had it in the blood, he explained to Carmen. In reality, his coming to the Indies, or rather to South America, was a kind of return. A century earlier, another von Phorner had set out for Argentina, armed with his Engineering degree and seduced by the hidden splendour of the silver mines that Bernardino Rivadavia,[15] then president in Buenos Aires, claimed he would exploit in the province of La Rioja. That first von Phorner, his great-grandfather, never did become a miner, because a local caudillo, one Juan Facundo Quiroga,[16] had refused to cede the silver mines of Famatina to the porteño leader. But he did not return to Germany. He stayed on in those arid, mountainous lands with hidden valleys because he had fallen in love with a beautiful foreigner (something else Ulrich had in the blood). It was an uphill struggle. He was considered a heretic, even though he was not a Protestant, as the locals of La Rioja falsely believed, but a Bavarian Catholic. He suffered prejudice in this land of brown-skinned people for having ridiculously blue eyes, which the fiancée's father compared to those of a Quitilipe horse.[17] His prospective father-in-law repudiated him, despite his two titles (one from the university, the other from the nobility), because he was not a major landowner and knew nothing about cattle. Then, after being despoiled of what little he had to help finance General Quiroga's wars; after showing up at the general's finca in Malanzán to challenge him to a duel, and instead receiving recognition and credit from that outlaw general, who appreciated gestures of wild courage; after all that and more, great-grandfather Karl von Phorner, no doubt an admirable lover but also, and especially, more stubborn than a team of mules, had married the beautiful criolla woman.[18]

But nothing lasts forever. When the new family sent their firstborn son to study in Germany, he never returned to La Rioja. Years later, the eldest son became estranged from his brothers over messy questions of inheritance rights. There were mutual reproaches. The upshot was that all affective ties between Bavaria and the ranchlands of La Rioja were cut. Not, however, to the end of time. Thanks to the wheel of fortune and its ceaseless turning, here he was, Ulrich von Phorner, great-grandson of a Bavarian man and a Riojan woman, back in the lands of America. And this time (but he dared not say this yet, not out loud), neither wars, nor religious heresies, nor colour of skin or eyes were going to come between him and the woman he loved.

Carmen listened to these tales with as much pleasure as if the two of them were children turning the pages of a book with big, colourful illustrations. To their double book, they went on adding stories about school and university, hopes and experiments, failed relationships, childhood landscapes, broken families. The parents of Utz, like hers, were deceased, and he had two younger brothers in Germany. Carmen told him about Francisco Brey, his sin or disgrace or misfortune. She had written Adela about their meeting, leaving out certain details, enhancing others, not revealing what she knew. Did Adela Montes deserve to be wounded by those recollections? By now, she understood her brother, at some distance, as one understands the behaviour of characters in a novel, although she did not know whether to believe him altogether. Even less did she know how guilty he was, and whether or not to forgive him. In any case, no one had asked for her forgiveness.

For the rest, Buenos Aires was one enormous dance floor, and their four feet went sliding over it with marvellous ease. Thanks to the Count's jealous distrust of his patroness, Utz usually had to stay behind in Buenos Aires to keep an eye on her while Keyserling was travelling to towns and cities of the interior or to neighbouring countries. Utz was not in the least put out. He had his own plans, and they included eventual visits to those places and others, with all the time in the world, and in much better company.

Meanwhile, Victoria Ocampo was ticking the days off the calendar, like a prisoner awaiting release. The Count was out of control, unstoppable, no matter how many secretaries they put in his way; he invaded every space of her life and tormented her in every possible way. Had he not showed up at her house in Palermo Chico shouting and threatening José, as if the dignified Asturian butler were one of those *mujiks* who cowered and cringed on bended knee every time a nobleman came near? The Count had no idea who he was dealing with. With great difficulty Victoria managed to restrain Fani from calling the police or "shooing off that maniac with her broom." Her chauffeur, too, suffered verbal violence if, due to rush-hour traffic, he arrived a few minutes late at the door of the Hotel Plaza. Meals were an obligatory and ongoing tribulation, for the Count never missed a one. If they took place in other people's homes,

Victoria made sure to be seated as far away as possible from the glutto-
nous philosopher. If she was hosting the banquet, she seated the illustrious guest at the opposite end of the table, never mind the breach of pro-
tocol. Viewed from that distance, the spectacle of the Teacher devouring,
chomping, licking his fingers, as he talked and drank with nary a pause
to wipe away the greasy, bubbly-flecked aureole smeared round his lips,
seemed almost amusing, the antics of a clownish villain in a Charlie
Chaplin movie.

While the Count, inconsiderate barbarian that he was, stuffed his face
with the finest cuts of meat produced in the pampas, Victoria was forced
to swallow a daily brew of the blackest disparagement. Every member of
the golden circle of the Jockey Club and Friends of the Arts knew the
Count had called her "the squaw who shot him with poisoned arrows";
he'd made the comment to the president of the Argentine-German Cultural Society, then continually repeated it in a stentorian voice at banquets. To the same gentleman he said that, were he back on his feudal
lands in Estonia, he'd have ordered his valets to give the insufferable flirt
a good whipping. And hadn't he insinuated to the doctor treating his heart
condition at the Hotel Plaza that she'd carried on a Versaillesque romance
with him, only to drop him like a capriciously cruel *donna mobile*, without a word of explanation? On top of it all, she had been forced to visit
him when he was bed-ridden and decked out in indescribably hideous
pajamas that made him look like a phosphorescent whale.

At night, bathed and fragrant with Floris essences, about to go to bed,
Victoria would suddenly recall certain Brylcreemed society gentlemen,
feel their gaze creeping over her skin like a centipede, slow and viscous, as
they imagined her (fantasies about her being the only recourse available
to them) obscenely copulating with the loathsome body of the Count.

III

Hermann von Keyserling couldn't sleep. He was peeved, depressed, furious. It wasn't that he could complain about his reception by the citizens
of Buenos Aires. They were flocking to his lectures, they celebrated his wit,
they wined and dined, flattered, and entertained him. They would arrive
with photos of him to be personally autographed, along with his books.
They invited him to the Hippodrome, to the theatre, to their opulent

estancias on the pampa. They took him sailing on their yachts and horse-back riding, and showered him with so many birthday presents, he was going to need an extra suitcase to take them all home.

In that unanimous chorus of admirers, there was only one dissonant voice. And that voice – deep, cavernous, like a basso continuo beneath a bevy of trilling sopranos – was so clever, hypocritical, insidious, indeed *reptilian*, that no one, but no one, except him, could perceive it. No *objective* argument (if there was truly such a thing as objectively existing facts) could be made against Victoria Ocampo's comportment. The rooms she paid for at the Hotel Plaza were spacious, comfortable, sumptuous, worthy of any minister of state or high-ranking dignitary. His meals were varied and abundant enough to satisfy any appetite, limitless or fussy though it might be. His envelopes and letter paper were of the exact colour and texture he'd requested. Madame Ocampo's chauffeur, albeit unpunctual and lazy like any good South American, was always at his beck and call. But she, Victoria, was nowhere to be seen.

That impassioned woman who used to read him *with her lungs*, who needed the oxygen of his letters to continue living, was now a distant, all-powerful queen who communicated with him through servants and mediators. When she should have been there in body and soul to hear his impressions or requests, he would receive instead a terse note delivered by her sister Angélica, or by his secretary Ulrich via little Fräulein Brey, right-hand woman of Bebé Sansinena and, it would seem, of Victoria as well. Not even the deplorable state of his health softened her. When notified by Doctor Moner about his tachycardia, *la belle dame sans merci* did at least announce that she would visit his rooms – no doubt for appearances' sake only, lest she be accused of heartless indifference. The Count had awaited her arrival, carefully combed, perfumed, and dressed in his most attractive pajamas of salmon-coloured silk. And what had his painstaking toilette earned him? Had she even deigned to draw near his bedside? And forget about her taking his hand, or pressing a cologne-soaked handkerchief to his fevered brow! No, on the contrary, Madame Ocampo had not even removed, in his well-heated suite, the furs covering her from head to foot; she sat down on a little chair as far away from the bed as she possibly could without overstepping the limit of elemental decency.

Sometimes he thought Victoria must be dissatisfied with the worthy role of Grand Dame he'd assigned her; perhaps she yearned for the honour of being the Spouse. That would explain why, at the banquets in her house in Palermo Chico, she seated him at the opposite end of the table, as if he were husband and not her guest of honour. It wasn't logical, of course, because even if the Count had wished to divorce his loyal Gudela (which he certainly did not), Victoria could not break off that irksome Catholic marriage of hers. But it was no use looking for rational, virile logic in a woman's behaviour. Especially not in a South American woman, whose little serpent-like head could barely rise above the thick, primordial magma. The Count gave a start, struck by a sudden insight. That had been his mistake all along: his obstinate attempts to understand Victoria's behaviour in terms of the spiritual norms of Europe. No. It was a different supreme principle that informed the will of the inhabitants of these immature, primitive, turbulent territories of America. And that principle was GANA. Argentines, every last one of them, were arbitrary, fanciful, whimsical entities. Remember that urchin at the golf course? The youngest Ocampo sister offered him a generous tip to carry her golf clubs, and he obstinately refused. Why? *Porque no le daba la gana*, he just didn't feel like it. Likewise with Victoria. She stopped adoring him *just because*. No reason or sense to it, just blind, indomitable impulse. It was the distinctive mark, the irrational law of the American soul that lived, dreamed, more or less "thought" in the telluric feminine register.[19]

He wondered sometimes if he would emerge alive from this devastating southern experience. The tachycardia he suffered in Buenos Aires was followed by more attacks in the Puna, along with shortness of breath, delirium, fevers. The Earth, hyperbolic, monumental, overwhelming, had unleashed her demons to hound him, buffetting and throttling him as if he were a helpless child and not a big man over six feet tall. A child. That was it. Men were mere defenceless children when Earth and Women took control over them.

The Count tossed between the sheets. He tried to stretch his legs, to no avail. Not even the Hotel Plaza had beds that could accommodate a human specimen of his size. Anyway, he preferred this uncomfortable wakefulness. If he managed to fall asleep, it would be worse. Invariably, his mother showed up in his dreams; the Countess Johanna Pilar von Pilchau seemed to have been summoned by this land of America, apparently sharing an affinity with it. Her severe face with knitted brow and admonitory mien had migrated to the body of Kali, and the goddess's multiple arms brandished equally countless knives or scimitars. None actually wounded him, but the look in her eyes, at once sardonic and pitying, infinitely reproachful, was more penetrating than the knives, and he would awake sticky and sweaty, the blankets clinging to him like a chill shroud. Resigned to sleeplessness, he got up. He downed two glasses of water, splashed his head and face, changed his pajamas, put on a kimono, and settled down in an armchair. He had to clear his head, dissipate his remorse by thinking through his absurd regrets.

His mother had died refusing to speak to him. But was it his fault, her atrocious repudiation? She was the one who transgressed the boundaries of class and caste, which by and large correspond to genuine gradations in the ontological hierarchy. She was the one who had trampled underfoot his father's memory, the family honour, and his pride as firstborn son. Who was the more cruel and unjust, he or she? As long as his father, the Count Leo von Keyserling, was alive, Frau Johanna's behaviour had been faultless. Her authoritarian character had been stifled at her parents' home, where her mother had ruled with an iron first. Installed at her husband's property, she found a splendid opportunity to unfurl her will to govern and dominate. Like all the Keyserling males, Count Leo was intellectually inclined and temperamentally melancholic; he took no interest in vulgar administrative matters, and Countess Johanna took them into her own hands from the outset, and with admirable results. She knew what to do under every circumstance: she dictated, ordered, invigilated, and executed all the affairs of the domestic economy. Her husband, introverted, dreamy, susceptible to migraines, had put himself in her hands like another of the children, his infantile trust reciprocated by her absolute dedication. Everything was going fine, would have continued so indefinitely, except that suddenly, still young and vigorous, he fell victim to a fatal thrombosis.

One catastrophe brought another. For the first two months of widowhood, Johanna was inconsolable, nearly mad with grief. But then she underwent an unbelievable transformation. First, she made her own children's art teacher her intimate advisor and consort. The fellow was a Russian pleb, several years her junior, with the soul of a lackey and the intellect of a village schoolmaster. Then, in a fit of moral panic, she decided to legalize their relationship – far less shameful as long as it remained clandestine – by marrying the miserable whelp. Hermann von Keyserling would always remember the fateful night when his mother informed the fifteen-year-old boy, who at that time dared not talk back to her, about her plan to marry. Would it have changed anything if he had said something?

No, talk was not the cure. The young Keyserling could have, should have, shot the vile usurper the very next morning – shot him down like a dog. His father, the gentlest man on the planet, had once told him: "If any teacher dares lay a hand on you, shoot him." Out of laziness, fear, guilt, he had remained passive. On the other hand, the ghost of Leo von Keyserling demanded no vengeance. He too used to appear in Hermann's dreams. He was always in good humour, wearing his hunting jacket, smiling as though suggesting a walk in the woods. A happy, ambitionless vagabond, he invited his son to a toast with a stein of frothy beer.

Maybe that was why Hermann, the heir, accepted it so meekly when the Countess moved to France, taking everyone with her. She broke off relations with her own family because they had reproved her for the ridiculous wedding *ab initio*. Only when he reached legal manhood did he openly side with his aunts and uncles. Then it was his mother who turned rancorous and implacable, violently repudiating him, scorning him as a renegade and a traitor. Could this really be his mother, this new person who changed allegiances, beliefs, values, attitudes? Perhaps this was who she truly was all along, and only the rigid corset of nobility had contained her within the habitual molds. When Johanna Pilar von Pilchau decided to abjure her nobility, she became a fervent egalitarian, championing every cause from women's emancipation to the social advancement of the proletariat. Her astonished son wondered if one day she wouldn't show up in Moscow to lend a hand to the very Bolsheviks who had confiscated their lands in Estonia. And even there, Hermann von Keyserling could not come out and accuse his mother of wrong-doing, haunted as he was by the distant echo of evangelical precepts. It was for good reason that, when his mother died, hundreds of indigents joined the funeral cortege and accompanied her to the cemetery, while her own son, incapable of humiliating himself before the widower, had only watched the swaying coffin go by from inside a rented car.

Johanna Pilar had always done whatever she felt like – *lo que le daba la gana*. She lived according to her own laws. Ah, that tremendous, unstoppable power of the Mother, the omnipotent creator from whom her children gradually detach themselves, even while remaining her creatures,

incomplete fragments who will maintain, willy-nilly, a link with that enigmatic goddess their whole life through ... Not by chance did Johanna
choose to torment him in the country of GANA, in the emotional swamp
at the South End of the world – in the realm of Victoria. The Count
trudged slowly back to bed and did something unheard of, completely
outside his adult habits. He recited an Ave Maria and fell asleep immediately, as if he'd taken a narcotic.

The following evening, none the worse for his insomniac vigil, he was
brimming over with joviality at the Mexican Embassy, tossing off monologues and guffaws left and right. The food and drink were up to his
standards, and he was happy. Also worthy were the young women who
adorned his table like an ikebana, diminutive and pretty as geishas. The
Count, enthusiastic and gallant, encouraged them to come closer. All he
wanted was delicately to breathe in their floral aroma, but the young
beauties slipped away skittish and tittering.

As always at the end of a soirée, he sat down to improvise something at
the piano. The public gathered round on chairs and cushions to listen.
Nearly everybody was there, except those who really should have been.
Victoria Ocampo was no longer granting them the grace of her presence.
His secretary, though of course he was not a valet but an academic assis-
tant, was neglecting to pay the attention due to his person, as had been
happening more frequently of late. He sighed. The boy was lucky. The
petite and exquisite Señorita Brey was apparently giving him all the affection that Victoria implacably denied the Count. Their two heads of hair –
his chestnut curls and her lank ginger locks – harmonized in a dimly lit
corner of the room. He'd have to have a word with von Phorner and
remind him of his obligations, but not too harshly. After all, he was a gentleman, a PhD, and a favourite disciple at the School of Darmstadt.

The Count's hands came down on the keyboard and played a minor
chord. First, he extemporized a homage to the Spirit of the Pampa. Then,
irresistibly, he fell back into his own memories. He heard the howling
wind of ancient forests, the call of the horn at the elk hunt, the horses'
hooves crunching the dry sticks beneath the snow. He sang with gypsy
violins, Cossack horsemen, Yuletide bells, and Greek choirs gravely inton-
ing funeral masses. He wept a lament to his dead father, recalling the
horse-drawn hearse sledding toward the church at Reval, verst upon verst,
past estate after estate, saluted by the neighbours, threading its way

between two rows of torches that kept the wolves at bay and banished the spell of darkness. He sang praise to the myths of his childhood and the great wild animals lurking among tall trees whose trunks could not be embraced by human arms. Back then, the Count did not hear the Spirit. He was one among the creatures of the Earth and, like all other cubs or pups, he sought his mother's lap on stormy nights. Thunderclaps – mere carnival masks, feckless scarecrows – hurtled past the cupolas of Rayküll without touching them, and Johanna's fingers gently smoothed his fine hair as he dropped off into slumber amid the scent of lavender wafting from her breasts. Safe, invulnerable, reconciled with the turning world.

IV

Carmen Brey wrinkled her nose. Something soft, dry, warm, feathery, was tickling the bridge of her nose and moving slowly down her left cheek. She opened her eyes. A ray of sunshine. She opened the curtains, too. Someone had carefully closed them to protect her sleep. Down in the street, hats and heads were coloured dominos, moving in a game of chance and adventure played by the onset of springtime. She would gladly have joined the game if the morning light weren't thumping so, beating her head like a drum, hammering out a tattoo on a network of taut nerves incapacitated for thought.

She threw herself face down on the untidy bed. Her first clear memory was of drinking an umpteenth toast, at the Mexican Embassy, the Count playing the piano in the background. The Teacher from the Baltic, truth be told, seemed to her a better musician than a philosopher. She and Utz had approached the piano and placed their hands on the beautiful dark wood to feel its vibrations. Keyserling's singing was unintelligible – likely a cocktail of German, Russian, and Finnish – but the melodies and chords reproduced the storm preceding the creation of the cosmos, the ecstasy and tragedy of mortal lives to be devoured, all of them, by silence.

Tears rolled down the ogre's cheeks, and not solely from drunkenness, which by this time was shared by the better part of the guests. Carmen wept with him, and Utz slowly led her away, first to the garden, then out on the street. Why so sad? he'd asked her. And she couldn't say a thing in response. At some point Carmen washed her hands and face – a paste of face powder and eye shadow – at a little fountain on the Calle Arroyo, a secret little place like a garden, and Utz had used his large handkerchief to dry, then kiss, her eyelids. Not a good cure for tears, it turned out: Carmen cried even more, overwhelmed by tenderness, and Utz got all weepy too, and they went tumbling lachrymose down a slope of consoling endearments in German and Galician. They re-emerged like two small figures in a romantic postcard beneath the English Clock Tower,[20] where they kissed passionately and had to flee the indiscreet lamp of a night watchman. Then the images got all mixed up, indiscernible, lost down a dark well.

What had happened between that embrace suspended in time under the English clock and her arrival at the apartment on the Avenida de Mayo? It must have been Utz who'd brought her back, opened the door with her keys, taken her shoes off, undressed her, got her into bed and pulled the sheets up to her chin. A wave of panic cut her breath short, and the painful thumping in her temples spread to her shoulders and spine. What else had Utz done with her? Doctor von Phorner was a disciple of the satyr from Darmstadt, wasn't he? How could she have let herself go like that? Laboriously, she sat up. She examined herself, feeling around for traces of intimate contact. She was still in her slip and all her undergarments, down to her stockings and garters. There was no evidence of abuse. Or consent. Maybe, she thought scornfully, she ought instead to be wondering what outrages *she* had perpetrated with poor Utz, in her pathetic state of alcoholic weepiness. In any case, the worst thing about whatever did or didn't happen was how obviously insignificant it had been, given that she could remember nothing.

But she need not have worried. The professor had postponed full carnal commerce for a future moment of happy lucidity. He had also hung up her party dress and made sure to leave a pair of slippers beside the bed. She put them on now to rummage in the bathroom for a painkiller. Looking for a glass, she noticed a letter on the kitchen table, its corner slipped under a vase. The syntax was acceptable, the spelling horrendous. Her beloved had doggedly tried to write in Spanish, producing bizarre orthographic innovations like *kerida* (for *querida*, "dear") and *atmirrable* (for *admirable*).

She made herself a strong coffee and sat down to read his missive. As her head began to clear, she remembered Utz was leaving for Chile with Keyserling that very midday. Of course, he would be back in a week's time. And, before he left definitively for Germany, he wanted to know if

Carmen's feelings were as serious as his. He was nearly *nel mezzo del cammin* – at the age of big changes, Copernican revolutions, the time of major decisions. The age Dante was when he saw Hell, but also Paradise. Would Carmen like to be that paradise? For if the homeland of every man was his childhood, as Rilke had said, his paradise was quite simply the woman he loved. No one had to be perfect or angelic for this. After all, the etymological root of "paradise" – he added, unable to resist showing off his Germanic erudition, but to good purpose – was a Greek word meaning "garden." And if human happiness was at all possible – as Voltaire's poor old Candide had discovered for himself – it could come about only by cultivating one's own garden in good company. Nothing could replace such happiness – not glory (a tall tale always told poorly and too late), nor money (something he did not have, by the by), nor travel (which he was sick and tired of, especially with the Count). *Kerida Carmen* – concluded Utz – *why dont we cultivate together our garten? Who knows that which we will harvest, but I am anyways sure we will always laugh about the same things.* That, too, was love, thought Carmen. Sharing a joyful complicity. Utz closed the letter in his own language. His simple statement, common and personal, the way children speak, was well within reach of Carmen's rudimentary German. *Ich liebe dich sehr!*

Carmen decided to run herself a deep bath. She needed to reflect. The headache was lessening but her anxiety was on the rise. What's the fuss? she sighed as she tested the bathwater with her big toe. Why so much fretting? Had she turned into a pernickety old maid? What Utz had written with admirable precision and persuasion, in spite of the late hour and all the champagne – was it not what she was hoping and expecting him to say? She eased herself into the bath until the water was up to her chin. Hadn't she fallen crazy in love with that curly-headed German? He wasn't full of himself or empty-headed or a slab of dried cod, like her other boyfriends. Were they not both single and without commitments? She threw a handful of bath salts into the water and inhaled the aroma as though trying to expel the last alcoholic vapours from her system. Life was strange. With so many men in Ferrol and La Coruña and Madrid and especially in Buenos Aires, why did Providence or chance determine that the right guy, the other half of her Platonic sphere, should turn out to be someone from the other side of the world, dropped from the sky like a shooting star, the unlikely guardian angel of a philosopher who looked like a bear? Suddenly she knew she never wanted to leave Buenos Aires for anywhere else. Not Madrid, or Ferrol, or even Mugardos, and certainly not exotic Darmstadt, where the bear would become her employer and daily company.

She closed her eyes and floated with her head back. Why all the anxiety? Had Ulrich said he wanted to go back to Darmstadt? Hadn't his letter said he'd had enough of travels with the Count? You're drowning, Carmen Brey. Not in the bathwater – in a glass of water.[21] Maybe her real problem was just plain fear. The fear of falling into the invisible depths of love as one falls into a void. The fear of giving herself over so entirely to a stranger, yet a stranger who was closer to her, whose being was more intimately attuned to hers, than anyone she'd ever met in her life. Because if Utz, despite his misgivings, couldn't stay in Buenos Aires, she was going – she knew she would go – all the way to Darmstadt to be with him. Maybe she would finally get used to the Count, at least at those times when he sincerely let go at the piano.

She rubbed the soap between her hands until she'd reduced it to a foamy paste. Stupid. She had exactly as much power over Utz as he had over her. Both had freely decided to be in the other and with the other. The matter of establishing *where* was going to be a peaceable and fair process of weighing their options.

Late that afternoon, after a light meal and a nap, Carmen dressed to go out. She had to meet María Rosa Oliver at a lecture at Friends of the Arts being given by a famous new visitor to Buenos Aires – Waldo Frank. As she crossed the foyer to go out the front door, the Polish concierge detained her.

– May I have a few words with you, Señorita? You'll think me rather forward, but what I'm going to say is what I'd say to my sister. You actually look like her and you're probably the same age.

– I'm listening.

– Look, you did the right thing coming to Argentina. What's left in Europe nowadays? You've got to follow the money when you're young and still have time. Here money flows like water, and you are … very well connected.

– What do you mean by that?

– Nothing bad, Señorita. Anybody can tell by the clothes you wear. I'm not reprimanding you or anything. Quite the opposite. I just want to give you a bit of free advice, so your efforts get you somewhere. It's about that friend of yours who left the building here at six this morning. Is he Polish?

– No, Señor, he's German.

– Amounts to the same thing. Guys like that are all the same.

– Like what?

– Those academic types. The old universities keep on churning them out. Turn them upside down, give them a shake, and you won't get a single *kopeck* out of 'em. Don't waste your time on him. I know, I know. You're both young. Have fun, but don't get serious about him. Keep your powder dry for the big guy.

– The big guy?

– The tall fellow, with the fur collar. The boss man. He must be a Russian bigshot. You'll say the Russian nobility has been ruined since the Bolsheviks took over. But they all escaped with the family diamonds and pearls sewn in their coat linings or trouser cuffs. They drink like fish, and if you're patient enough to wait for him to get drunk, he won't bother you. Not only that, he'll give you the shirt off his back. Look, with the diamond ring he gives you, you'll have enough to buy another apartment like this one and rent it out. Try and tell me that's not a good investment. You work three or four guys like that, you got it made. You could even marry one of those little academics, if that's what you like. But I wouldn't recommend them as husbands. They're basically useless, all the time with their nose in a book. Better you find yourself a good solid businessman. You could team up with him and start earning dividends on your capital.

– Señor Sovotnik. Frankly, I'm not sure what you're doing here working as a concierge. Why aren't you managing one of those houses of … good-time girls?

The Pole shook his head.

– Ah, no. I don't have the character for it. Just imagine. Here am I advising you, all for free. I'd end up working for the women instead of them working for me. Maybe in my next incarnation I'll have more luck.

– You don't say.

– If I got to be reborn and had my choice, I'd be a woman. A pretty woman, of course, so I could aim higher. I'd have a good time and get rich at the same time. You can't imagine how incredibly dumb men are. Press the right buttons and you got whatever you want out of them.

– Is this something you know from personal experience?

– Sure is. I was no Russian bigshot, but I did inherit a good business in Poland. Why do you think I'm a concierge now? I'd already blown half my inheritance when I left Warsaw; they finished fleecing me in Paris. That's why I'm here cleaning houses and minding doors, I got no education or skills. Thank goodness I'm not bad at picking up languages. But I'm not bitter or mean. When I see a pretty woman working on her own, I try to give her some advice so she won't let the best capital she has go to waste. Smooth skin and an hourglass figure don't last forever, mademoiselle. Take care of what you've got.

– Well, thank you for your concern, Señor Sovotnik. I hope God in his heaven will repay you severalfold, and that if you are reborn you'll be the most successful whore in all Buenos Aires. Provided the money is still flowing, of course.

The concierge shrugged his shoulders, disconcerted, as the furious heels of Señorita Brey stomped out through the door. She says she ain't Argentinian, but she sure acted like it. All these *demi-mondaines* and *cocottes* around here pretend they're nuns.[22]

Carmen Brey stormed into Friends of the Arts red-faced and upset. She wasn't the only one to arrive late. At the door she ran into Arlt.

– Hi, what brings you here?

– You know I'm a press rat and a slave to celebrities.

– So am I. It's my job.

– At least you don't have to write about them afterwards.

– You don't either, my good man. At your paper you write about whatever you please.

– I won't deny it. But I need time to get on with my novel. I can never get round to finishing it.

– Does it have a title yet?

– *Los siete locos.* The Seven Madmen.[23]

– Hey, very appropriate.

– Some personal allusion?

– No, no, there's no reason why a book's characters have to reflect their author; a novel's value doesn't lie in that direction.

– Señorita, you're pretty hard on me. Borges and Marechal are just as crazy as me, and you treat them like friends.

– Señor Arlt, it isn't a question of who's crazy and who isn't. Could I be your friend, if I tried to be? It seems to me you aren't interested in women as friends but as *minas*, as you Argentine men say.

Arlt laughed.

– Why aren't there more women like you in Buenos Aires? If there were, I'd probably have some women friends. One of these days I'll do an *aguafuerte* in the paper about you. A sketch of you and all Galician women … Okay, I gotta join the guys from the paper. Hey, look over there. That brunette, she's trying to catch your eye.

It was María Rosa Oliver. Carmen sat down beside her. She caught sight of Victoria at the other end of the lecture hall, and they waved to each other.

There was an abrupt silence. A short, robust man with a round face and grey eyes was coming on stage. Waldo Frank, author of several works of fiction not yet translated, was better known for his essays *Our America*, *Salvos*, and *Virgin Spain*.[24] Unlike most of his compatriots, he refused to appropriate the exclusive right to the term "American," claimed as well by the *americanos* in the south. Some Argentines called him the *norteamericano*; others, more familiarly and with a hint of scorn, the Yankee.

V

Bacon and eggs tasted as good in Vicente López (suburb of Buenos Aires) as they did in Cape Cod, or Maine, or New York. Maybe even better, because the cook prepared them with special care for the distinguished guest, and because the breakfast venue was unusual. Still, Waldo Frank had to remind himself now and then that he was in the outskirts of the vastest and most populous city in Argentina, and that this placid green area treed by eucalyptus, casuarinas and paraísos was a makeshift simulation imposing homey suburbia upon the immense pampa. Moreover, there was nothing typically Argentinian about this villa, designed for modern comfort; it belonged to an English businessman who rented it out during his lengthy absences. Judging by its architecture and interior décor, it could have been a cottage in Surrey or a chalet in Switzerland. Plus, of course, the domestic service and chauffeur-driven limousine. But all in all, something in it resisted easy comparisons.[25] The pampa insidiously dissolved everything – humans and their works, architectural pastiches and the simulacra of civil coexistence. Formlessness embraced all forms and submerged them in a hazy irreality. Under the pampa's influence, Spanish rectitude, its vertical profundity, had been rendered fluid and fertile, disseminated infinitely toward the horizon. The Argentines had that labile quality, scintillating and ungraspable, of an aqueous mirage.[26] It made them – for Frank, at least – as unconquerable and difficult to define as the great plain they inhabited without understanding it.

He looked through the morning papers – *La Prensa*, *La Nación*, and *Crítica* (its style so reminiscent of William Randolph Hearst's publishing empire). None mentioned him in their headlines. He was less displeased by the omission than by his own annoyance at it. In spite of all his reformist mystique – every individual, preached Frank, must realize that they are a tiny part of a Whole – he himself sometimes got caught up in the most trivial vanity. Nevertheless, from the time of his arrival in Montevideo, the local press had constantly followed and flattered him. *La Nación* published summaries of his lectures in two columns; *La Prensa* was angling to take him on as a permanent collaborator; and *Crítica* featured him in front-page articles, as if he were a Hollywood star. Even Hipólito Yrigoyen, the president of the Republic, with his serene, faded-blue eyes and manners of an old-school country gentleman, had agreed to give him a lengthy interview – interrupted though it was by endless civil servants pestering him to sign mountains of papers. The old president, even if annoyed, would finally deign to sign them with his ancient fountain pen, then continue discussing with his guest the vicissitudes of politics, as if they were in the parlour of a country house and not in a presidential office crammed with files.

This time, however, there was something more important than Waldo Frank's lectures and their reception in Buenos Aires. *La Nación* reported with alarm that Wall Street, the emblematic Power Principle presiding over North America, was collapsing. Frank shrugged his shoulders. The catastrophe could well turn out to be meaningless. It wasn't logical to suppose that share values could keep on rising forever, nor that, due to a momentary dip, his compatriots would stop thinking, first and foremost, about making money. Money: the Prime Mover, the Great Motor of the civilization they were so proud of.

Of course, it wouldn't do either to demonize money. Notwithstanding his admiration for Tolstoy, the monastic vegetarian of Yasnaya Polyana, he was rather fond of dollars – or any hard currency – as well as red meat (beef or goat kid, both outstanding in Argentina) and the perfumed flesh of women, as well as cello music, modern literature, and bourgeois life in general. In reality, he thought, there would be nothing wrong in those goods and pleasures if they were more fairly distributed, and if human beings didn't sell their souls to the Devil of Quantity for the sole purpose of grasping them. Waldo Frank had never gone wanting for those good things. He had been raised in a multi-storey house between the Hudson River and Central Park: a harmonious realm of well-being, magnani-mously governed by two monarchs, Father and Mother, and divided into three classes – adults, children, and servants. It was filled with music (his mother, a soprano whose aspiration to a professional career had been thwarted, daily regaled them with Schubert lieder and operatic arias) and the smell of good cooking. The youngest of four brothers, Waldo had been a bit despotic, something of a child prodigy and arrogant genius. After travels and education in Europe, then graduation from Yale, he decided to put into practice a pact he had struck, at the age of fifteen, with no less a personage than God. He would be a writer, one who renounced all the material rewards to which writers, certainly those of North America, nor-mally aspire – fame, fortune, followers, glory; as long as God, for his part, as He had done with Solomon, opened for him the path of Truth.

Waldo Frank wasn't sure what the Lord might be thinking of him right now, as the breeze sighing in the eucalyptus trees come to caress him and the smell of toast to ravish him, while he leafed through the papers secret-ly hoping to find a photo of himself. Nor was he sure to what God he had made that promise, even supposing He had actually accepted the deal. Was it the ancient God of his forebears, the Jealous Lover, the Yahweh of the Torah, the Prohibited Name of the burning bush, who struck down those who were unfaithful to him? Such a deity had never received sanctuary in the comfortable mansion on West Street. His cultivated and cosmopolitan Jewish family had replaced the Thundering Voice of Mount Sinai with the respectable lay rigour of those Moral Norms espoused by the New York Society for Ethical Culture (of which his father, Mr Frank, senior, was a trustee). Felix Adler, the society's founder, preached Kantian ideas as fer-vently as a Catholic priest or a Protestant pastor; and sermonized to chil-dren from the pulpit of a Sunday school which Waldo, as a child, refused to attend. Without Kant, Jehovah, or Synagogue, the boy Frank had nonetheless spoken to a God. That God, dimly perceived at the time, may have been – he later surmised – the God of the Spanish mystics, unread by him as yet, or the Great Hidden Splendour in the web of appearances: the Shekhinah of the Cabbalists, whose tradition was still unknown to him.

By the age of forty, Waldo Frank believed in the music of the spheres, in the secret concord of the Totality: the harmony that humans outraged with their horribly dissonant words and deeds, starting with himself, perjurer and sinner. *All men, like me, love beauty, bespeak the good; yet their history like my own deed[s] is shame and violence. If devotion to what I call truth has not transfigured me, it has not transfigured the world. Like me, mankind professes peace and loves war, despises Power and dies to gain it ... All the study of my conscious hours has not prevailed against the chaos in me. All the scriptures of Wisdom, I conclude, will not prevail against the chaos of the world – this chaos of which America is archetype and product,* he had just written in his latest book.[27]

America, model for the world, tomb of Europe, junkyard of a broken order, needed other remedies. The conduct of its people had to change in such a way that men and women would not be inert nouns, but rather verbs capable of modifying reality. Through their practice and example, a different cosmos was to be engendered out of those chaotic ruins. From North to South, whether in the empire of machines moved by greed for power and ruled by the brutal law of efficiency, or in the mestizo lands of Hispanic America, where beauty and courage had not yet bodied forth their ideal forms, many solitary individuals were emerging to design the figure of a new America. They would form groups, then multitudes perhaps. For now they were still invisible; but like God, invisible as well, they were just as real. Waldo Frank, successor to the old prophets, sometimes believed the Unknown God had charged him with a similar mission. Was he not proclaiming a better society, built through the work of all for all, and without feeling shame, as Marx had (despite his biblical beard), for the genuinely religious utopia latent in the promise of a classless society? Although he had renounced followers in his old pact with the Supreme Maker, Waldo Frank now recognized they were necessary, not for mere narcissistic reasons but for the good of his Cause. In any case, he had not sought them; they had come on their own.

Eduardo Mallea, for example. The swarthy young journalist, silent and enthusiastic, had offered to translate his public talks, and his meticulous work went beyond the call of duty. After work sessions, they would converse while walking around the garden or rambling the little suburban streets like the peripatetic philosophers of yore. They spoke of the cosmic canticle, the immeasurable spaces open to the adventure of creation, from South to North, from Sarmiento to Whitman. They talked about how life needs order and order needs life. Their conversation ranged across a panoply of themes: the pioneers and Puritans who had made North America great but mean, because they alienated the soul from the body and sacrificed earthly pleasures; the primal jungle as opposed to the machine jungle, mechanical Nature, chaos of iron, where the new savages barely survived, dominated and lost; the First Nations, the red-skinned lords of the forests, whom the white man in his pride refused to accept as the foundation stone of his own memory; the Blacks, the Irish, Italians, Jews, and all the immigrants who, both in the United States of the North and in Argentina, must compose, not a formless melting-pot, but a great symphonic nation.[28]

They talked about the rebel artists (Edgar Lee Masters, Theodore Dreiser, Sherwood Anderson, Frederick Booth) who abjured the religion of success and preferred to exalt the saintliness of apparent failure. From time to time Frank indulged in the vanity of rhyming off his various renunciations. First, his "escape" to Kansas, beyond the literary cenacles and cocktail parties that ensued from the success of *Our America*, where he participated in the militant National Farmers' Alliance. Then, his refusal of Samuel Goldwyn's invitation to write screenplays for Hollywood, as well as those of W.R. Hearst to work on one of his dailies or go with him as a special guest to his castle in San Simeon, California. Only a literary type, at once prophet and emulator of Don Quixote, could afford such liberties. The young Argentine listened to him, ecstatic. Frank appreciated his rapt attention, but above all his intelligence, recognizing that mere bovine devotion would have been useless. The boy was writing for a major paper, *La Nación*, and had written a book of short stories; its title was too long, but the tales were remarkably intense.[29]

The most extraordinary human specimens in South America were not men, however, but women. An emerging world, thought Frank, always speaks through its women, just as a culminating world generally speaks through its men. Was it because the women, once they managed to put the men to work, could then rest? Or because men contrived to capitalize on the results of female energy and then displaced them from centre-stage? Whatever the case, Argentina, like a millionairess who insouciantly dons her diamond necklace without a thought for its worth, exhibited an array of magnificent women who were brimming over with energy. It was a torrential energy, disoriented but clairvoyant, which they themselves did not yet know how to put to use. The case of Victoria Ocampo seemed to him a superlative example.

Victoria had heard his lecture on Chaplin and invited him to her house in Palermo Chico. Frank walked in and inhaled avidly, as though filling his lungs with oxygen after passing through airless spaces. Amid mansions copied from the Faubourg Saint Germain, the Bois de Boulogne, or Castile, which shut the pampa out, Victoria's house alone was open to its sightlines, joyously making that simple clarity a seal of belonging. Through windows invading entire walls, the open skies of the great plain flooded the white rooms and were mirrored in them; the whole house gave the impression of being a transparent portal to the pampa. The spirits of Le Corbusier and Gropius were there, certainly; but also, and above all, the light of America. That the house was so exposed as to be not quite habitable, Frank understood, was a challenge to its immediate cultural context, a defiant gesture which, moreover, he sensed was too impetuous to be contained by those four walls. How curious, he thought: Victoria, beautiful, generous, refreshing as summer rain, was fond of cactus plants. He saw one at the foot of the staircase, boxed in by mirrors catching and refracting light from the sky. And another, a smaller one, in an earthen vase on an antique mahogany table. Three more sat in glass vases on the marble mantelpiece. Victoria had surely chosen the cactus as her own emblem, a substitute for her ancestors' useless coat-of-arms. An emblem of resistance, willing to survive amid rocks, steep mountainsides, arid wastes, unscathed by the sun's ire and relentless winds, its perfect flower sheltered within spines.[30]

Another example of resistance, astonishing and moving, was María Rosa Oliver.[31] Frank had been to her house too, or rather her family's majestic and ornate mansion, the antithesis of Victoria's house. María Rosa overcame the immobility of her legs with the incessant mobility of her hands and eyes. Over the iron fence limiting her physical locomotion her imagination flew free. He had lunched with María Rosa, Carmen Brey, Alfonso Reyes, and Pedro Henríquez Ureña.[32] Though he didn't remember at first, he'd already met Miss Brey, very briefly, at the Residence for Young Ladies in Madrid, five years earlier, when he was staying at the apartment of her friend Victoria Kent (another disciple of María de Maeztu) and falling madly in love with Spain – a love that would last forever and was now extending to Spanish America. There was nonetheless something unique about Spain, he told Carmen Brey. A certain force, a sharpness of definition, a resolute manner of understanding life, with the natural vigour and music of a pine tree. An excess of being (perhaps proper to the authentic human condition, before it gets domesticated and mutilated) which was lacking in Spanish Americans, whose charm and risk was in their refined, elusive softness. And was lacking in other Europeans too, of course. Other Europeans? Was Spain really European? No, Spain was not Europe. It didn't fit within the wrought-iron fences of French gardens, or the symmetrical towns of Germany, or the clubs and tea rooms of Britain. Nor was it Africa. It was Spain and Spain alone, barbarous and exquisite, singular and inimitable, irreducible to Europe. Unamuno was right, and not Ortega, who wanted Spain to file off its rough edges and integrate, with no grinding of gears, into the continental body of Europe.

Wealthy and cultivated Argentines, it seemed to him, were too self-satisfied. They displayed their extensive worldly knowledge and acquired languages like accoutrements to go with their Parisian salons and their English country houses in "estancias" the size of counties. Even the most lucid and honest among them – Mallea, María Rosa, Victoria herself – repeated sacramental phrases out of the catechism taught in school to the middle and upper classes, although a few dissidents, such as Ricardo Rojas[33] (he was to Argentina what Unamuno was to Spain) had seriously tried to emend that rosary of comfortable clichés. At how many lunches, suppers, afternoon teas had he heard them recited like self-evident truths? That Argentina was a white, European country. That its wealth would keep on growing indefinitely, thanks to Argentina's mission to be "the world's granary." That the Republic was invulnerable even to bad government, since any wrong was made right by a good harvest. That Argentina was "essentially" different from the rest of Spanish America, not only for its ethnic composition and high standard of living, but also for its civilized political structure, immune to the coups d'état and military revolts that plagued her supposedly sister nations.

Nevertheless, if Argentines were so sure of themselves, why were they constantly badgering foreign visitors to their country to tell them about their identity and destiny, as if the travellers were sphinxes or soothsayers? Maybe they wanted to hear confirmed what they already thought of themselves, for when that consoling self-image wasn't endorsed, as with Ortega's analysis and prognosis, they got angry.

In reality, the supposed whiteness of Argentina was given the lie by the many mestizo faces among them. He had seen them not only in the big city but in Salta, Jujuy, Tucumán, Santiago del Estero, where he had heard the Quechua language spoken and lived, and where many natives, ignorant of their basic rights, worked in the sugar harvest. Men, women, and children would work in a group of five or six, then get paid the minimum wage for one person only. Crammed into barracks, stripped of everything, they were far away from the splendour of Buenos Aires, as though in another galaxy. Argentina's greatest wealth was not in its cattle or wheatfields, but in those dark faces, humble, beautiful, still incredibly docile, whose bodies the masters of the land used and reaped as they did other crops, only to toss their desiccated husks into a heap to be burned. Did his civilized hosts really believe, moreover, that those feudal lords would allow legally elected governments to rule if the latter happened to stop serving the interests of the former?

He didn't believe so. Nor did the other guests, Spanish Americans. He'd noticed the dissident irony in the eyes of Alfonso Reyes and Henríquez Ureña, too diplomatic or merciful to snatch away the illusions of their Argentine friends. Those truths were difficult to accept unless experienced personally. Frank knew something about that. Years ago, he'd lived as a Negro in South Carolina, helped by his dark complexion, in the company of poet Jean Toomer.[34] He had travelled in dirty, dilapidated buses with those people who, like the workers in the sugarcane plantations, were citizens in theory only. He'd sat on the hard benches in the Negro section. Watched movies from the most distant rows, reserved for people of colour. Learned there were restaurants where he could serve but not be served. Many a morning he awoke in a panic, looked at himself in the mirror, touched and smelled his clothes, checked out his photo and biographical sketch on the cover of a book, just to verify that he had not irreversibly become a Negro, that he was still Waldo Frank, Yale graduate, son of a white, bourgeois, enlightened family from West Street, New York.

Victoria, María Rosa, Mallea had none of them gone through such a test. Nor was it necessary or fair to require that they see and understand everything, when they already understood much and would come to understand more. Their mission was a different one, and in the long run it would affect everything else. The mission, that is, which Frank had in mind for these individuals who did not yet know one another.

VI

Count Keyserling, sunk deep in a deck chair creaking under his weight, had not spoken a word for hours. He was ruminating over the cruellest letter he'd ever received in his life. Were it not for the poison secreted by those handwritten words, he would probably be returning to Darmstadt more or less content, thanks to his social and intellectual success, as well as the pocketful of hard currency that would keep him in oysters and champagne for a good while. What was it about the miserable human condition that made him read, over and over again, those mortiferous lines? *What happened in Versailles is horribly unforgettable for me. All of the devotion, the admiration, the pure fervour I had for you was poisoned by your attitude. My greatest guilt is that I did not tell you brutally, immediately, that the physical repulsion you inspired in me was as intense as the spiritual enthusiasm that had attracted me to you. Instead of taking that path (short and cruel), I felt forced to dissimulate my reaction out of love for your talent, your work. I put myself to one side. In a sense I sacrificed myself.* He wasn't even furious. He felt depressed, devastated, annihilated. Victoria had endured his presence, in Paris and in Buenos Aires, as one swallows a loathsome dose of castor oil. *For my refusal to meet with you in any way except spiritually, I have given you reasons that were not the only ones I could have invoked. Because one of the reasons, profound and sufficient in itself, was that* I did not love you *(I'm talking about the love that can arise between a man and a woman). When I have loved a man, I have given myself to him.*[35]

The Count cleared his throat, unwilling to surrender to the shame of tears. Was he truly so repulsive? Did he not wash and dress like a gentleman? Was he not well mannered? Was he not well bred, raised by a mother who – her disastrous second marriage notwithstanding – came from the noblest stock? He'd had a love life before marriage, affairs with beautiful, cultivated women from Ireland, Italy, and Paris. And Gudela, grand-daughter of Bismark, had chosen him as her husband. So, what was it Victoria found so off-putting about him? His size, his jovial self-assurance, his robust appetite, his fondness for the bubbly and for affable, worldly-wise conversation? He was no mannequin, no stiff and conceited milksop afraid to raise his voice a notch higher than was considered elegant, like so many Argentine men he'd come across. Hypocrites, cold fish, all of them. And the Argentine women were worse, with their slippery verbal feints and their camouflaged reptilian sexuality. Victoria, malignantly fascinating as a cobra, would probably prefer some wilting fop she could manipulate at a snap of her fingers. Herr von Wuthenau, for instance, the cultural attaché in his own embassy – blond, pretty, gleaming like a tinsel angel. No doubt she had him under her spell with her lying charms. On her instructions, he had returned all the letters the Count had sent her, silently staring at him in baleful disapproval.

My intelligence cannot hold a grudge against you because you are – I repeat – deaf to others. But my heart cannot do otherwise than bleed and forget. Goodbye. Deaf to others! As if he didn't love devotedly his wife and children. Or his faithful friends. Why, he even worried about that nincompoop of a secretary of his, over there gazing out to sea with that placid, mindless expression that all men get when they're in love. He'll see, he'll eventually find out what's what. Who was this Señorita Brey, anyway? Certainly no reliable German *Hausfrau*. A Spanish woman with a suspicious-sounding name, like a Gypsy cigarette-girl.[36] Besides, after all these years of close contact with the country of GANA, she'd probably gone half-native, Indian, and could turn on him in an instant, dump him as easily as someone tosses a pair of shoes gone out of style.

He had one final thought about *Madame* Ocampo. "I should have raped her," he said to himself before sinking into an unquiet, painful stupor.

"I shouldn't have wasted five minutes of my life on that man," Victoria scolded herself, having resolved to put the Keyserling case firmly behind her and to start, that very day, to work toward the fulfilment of Waldo Frank's request.

What Frank wanted from her was truly unusual. No man had ever made her a proposition or suggestion or demand like this one. He did not want to look upon her as a statue or admire her like some beautiful object. He was not interested in making her his Muse, or his Mother, or his Lover –

much less his Wife (he was happily married for the second time). He was
seeking neither a secretary, nor a housekeeper, nor a feminine soulmate,
nor an exotic pen pal.

It had all happened one spring afternoon, not long before he left
Argentina, as they were strolling through Palermo.

– You can't go on wasting your talent and energies in this life of idleness.

– My life isn't idle. I read a lot. I take singing lessons. Sometimes I recite
poetry in public. I listen to music and go to the theatre. I write articles.

– And you think that's enough? It's fine for your personal growth and
satisfaction, but it's rather selfish.

– I also help bring artists and intellectuals to Argentina, in spite of the
trouble it costs me at times.

– That's all fine, sure, but if it isn't done for a purpose, as part of a plan,
that kind of thing has no more significance than any other social diversion.

– I don't know what you expect me to do. I don't have a university
degree or a profession. Only my love of the arts, and a few skills.

– You don't need a degree for what I'm going to tell you.

– It would be distasteful to boast, but I also make donations and help
people in need, though not through the Church. Priests and I don't get
along all that well.

– I've noticed. You don't need the Church. Even less to become a lady
of charity going to benefit teas and handing out images of saints, as your
grandmother must have done, and which a few old maids and matrons
still do, from what I've seen around here. You can go on collaborating
with whoever your conscience tells you to. But what I'm asking is something else.

– For goodness sake, Waldo, what are you talking about? Out with it! As
long as you're not asking me to run afoul of the law.

– It's no crime or misdemeanour, even if you do gain a few enemies to
keep you amused. I'm asking you to found a journal.

– A what?

– An absolutely necessary journal. A bridge between the two Americas.
A journal that reveals our common destiny, and also our differences vis-
à-vis Europe.

– That's obvious already. We're in need of everything they already have
in Europe.

– It's more that we're in need of what we have yet to produce ourselves, and that's very good.

– Do you think so?

– Of course. They are *complete*. Even though the order sustaining Europe as a unified cosmos is fractured and dead, they feel complete. They double down on their achievements, their great works, their museum of quotations. Our great works have yet to be forged, according to our own rules, in response to our own needs, which aren't the same as theirs. Our condition of lack is also creative dissatisfaction.

– I've always thought we were transplanted Europeans who got damaged by the transplant.

– That's what we used to be. We are no longer Europeans but Americans. The transplant didn't occur in a vacuum. America already existed, and it has transformed us. And now we, who have more future, are the ones who will transform Europe. It's our turn. The journal will be the ambassador of American appeal, the link between worlds.

Victoria laughed.

– A modest little undertaking, what? Tailor-made for your penchant for prophecy.

– No need to put ourselves down before others do it for us.

– That's true. But why me? I have no experience producing journals. Why don't you do it? Weren't you the managing editor of *Seven Arts*?[37]

– I certainly was. I've already paid tribute at that altar. It was a stage in my life, it's in the past. Now I'm writing books. This journal is a task for you.

– My God. I'm not going to do it alone.

– Put a team together. Just around the corner, you have a whole raft of excellent candidates. Invite Samuel Glusberg, he's already a publisher. And my secretary, Eduardo Mallea; I've been meaning to introduce you two. And Miss Brey, the Spanish woman. And María Rosa Oliver.

Not long afterward, Victoria picked up the phone to call María Rosa. They met at the white house in Palermo Chico and spoke together for the first time. Their paths had crossed at mass, at theatres, at banquets, but they had never really met. Victoria had completely forgotten that María Rosa, ten years younger than her, had seen her at the turn of the century in the vestibule of the Parisian hotel where both families were staying, dressed in a long skirt and wearing a moiré bow in her hair.

They hit it off immediately, as did the others – Angélica Ocampo, María Rosa, Mallea, and Carmen Brey – when they met and began to plan the journal which, though still without a name, was already ramifying into potential projects and designs, like a garden of forking paths.[38] The Glusberg connection, however, went wrong from the start. He and Victoria didn't like the same authors, and they didn't see eye to eye about the future of Spanish America.

One afternoon, Victoria asked Carmen over to her house in Palermo.

– My word! Either I'm here very early, or our punctual friends are late today. Where is María Rosa?

– It isn't about the journal, Carmen, it's about you and me.

– How do you mean?

– I want to know why I've not been worthy of your trust.

– Victoria, I've never said any such thing.

– Of course not. You are too well bred to tell me so. That's why I'm saying it myself, and I'll try to answer my own question. I know you well enough to know that you don't do anything without good reason. I feel like I've been living for several months in a whirlwind of silly mistakes, looking after people who didn't deserve it, and I've forgotten about the friends in front of my nose. So, when I ran off to Versailles to meet the Genius, it turns out you went off looking for your brother with a pair of duffers[39] who should never have accompanied you as far as the corner. I know the whole story, thanks to María Rosa. And now that the cobwebs have fallen from my eyes, and I'm back in my right mind, I just want you to know you can count on me.

Carmen said nothing. She was thinking about herself when she first came to Argentina, and about Victoria, who had looked like a patch of white silk against the gravel path at Miralrío, and then offered her the job as interpreter for Tagore with the enthusiastic candour of a little girl offering a precious gift. A girl who had now grown up and was her friend. She got up and hugged her and kissed her on both cheeks, all without a word.

In January, Victoria left again for Europe, this time with no intention of seeing Julián there. She again saw Drieu to appreciate him, get annoyed with him, visit Berlin together, where she met her admired Walter Gropius. And, inevitably, she and Drieu argued.

– Why Berlin? Victoria had asked him. Why all this interest in people who tried and failed to kill you?

– Maybe to find out why they failed. They must know the secret of my good luck … Or of my vital force.

– You could stand to theorize a bit less about the vital force and instead get to work putting it to use.

– Are you looking down your nose at my eleven books? Are they not proof of my praiseworthy vitality?

– Vitality is never praiseworthy. It just *is*. It surges, it flows spontaneously. Otherwise, it wouldn't be vitality. And of course I don't look down my nose at your books. Just at some of the things you write in them. For instance: *Woman, always imbued with a powerful realistic sense, can only love a man for his strength and his prestige …*

– And is that not how it is, my dear?

– Maybe *your* women, but not woman in general. You choose women to suit your theories.

– Could be. That's why they leave me. As soon as they realize I don't have strength and my prestige is an illusion.

– They leave you when they get fed up with your living in hotels, and when they understand you despise being cared for as if it were a humiliation.

The train trip to Berlin sweetened the bitterness between them. Victoria became absorbed in her orange pudding; Drieu, in his travel guides, spread out in a fan over a table in the dining car. He studied entrances and exits, avenues and museums as though pouring over the map of a city to be conquered.

They took two hotel rooms near the *Tiergarten*. At night they could hear the distant sounds of the zoo animals, unrhythmically snorting, roaring, growling against the deaf, indifferent light of the moon. Drieu also snorted, in his way, in the next room. Neither he nor the animals, thought Victoria, were where they should have been. They had lost their place in the concert (or, as Drieu might have said, in the army?) of the multiform planet. But unlike the caged beasts, Pierre Drieu did not know where exactly it was, that illusory place.

What Victoria appreciated in Berlin was the music and the clean lines of the Bauhaus School. They went to the cinema and the theatre, mainly to enjoy the actors' movements and gestures, not the lines they declaimed in German.

– I don't know why you admire them so much if you can't even understand what they say, she said to provoke him.

– Words are tiresome noise, most of the time. Body language suffices.

– The bodies of German women? I don't think they correspond to your virile ideal. They look as soft and comfortable as mattresses.

– It isn't about seeing bodies to sleep with. There are superior activities.

– Such as military parades? I'm not going to join you.

– Nor do I plan to invite you to any. You would ruin it all with your ironic comments.

– But I'm not ironic. Quite the contrary, alas. I have the unfortunate tendency to see genuine Greek gods where there are only bad plaster copies of them. I leave irony exclusively to you. Although I'm not sure that's what it is. Childishness, maybe. The Countess of Noailles thinks you're a little dog that likes to pee on the flowers.

– *La vache!*

– Her or me? I'll take the compliment, don't worry about it. But, after all, her poetry may be replete with fountains, corollas, and birds, but poor Anna has surely never seen a pasture in her life. We peasants from the River Plate are more knowledgeable about such things.

– I can't believe how spiteful you are, that you should listen to such slander. Did I ever pee on your lovely person?

– I never gave you a chance to play the little dog. Anyway, do you think I belong to the "flower genus"?

The argument continued in restaurants, Victoria praising the desserts, Drieu the beer. But it was not confined to matters gastronomical.

– There's Conrad Veidt, at that table across from us, said Drieu nudging her with his elbow. Why don't you go over and introduce yourself? Aren't you a great admirer of his?

– Right. I'm not going to fling myself at him. If it's in the cards that we meet, the right occasion will come along, and someone will introduce us properly.

– I didn't think you were so conventional and prejudiced.

– I'm not prejudiced, but others are. Wasn't it you who said there are two kinds of women, pretentious snobs and flirts? And lamentably, that's what the majority of men think. I'm not going to run the risk that Veidt include me in one category or the other.[40]

– Well, I don't include you in either one. Quite the contrary. What annoys me is your dignity. Or rather, your English-governess morality.

– If there was one thing my English governess complained about, it was having failed to make me a lady. And if I were like her, I would never befriend a man who brags about scorning every single virtue attributable to gentlemen.

– So you are my friend? Sometimes I think you prefer being my warden or my moral censor.

– How can you think such a thing? If you reformed yourself, I'd lose one of my favourite sources of amusement.

Surprisingly, Drieu tired of Berlin before Victoria did. When she got back to Paris, alone now, others were there waiting. Tagore, for example. He had a new secretary and he wanted to take her to Oxford and then to India. But she declined: she had promised to meet Waldo Frank (and the dream of the journal not yet born) in New York. She tarried in her favourite city longer than planned, however. She had some new friends. She wrote to Angélica and Carmen about Jacques Lacan, a medical student of shocking intelligence, insufferable character, enormous energy, and Napoleonic dreams of power. They quarrelled even by telephone, and she came to the conclusion that Lacan affected her the same way as Drieu, though in other respects the two men were polar opposites.[41] She saw Cocteau, the Countess of Noailles, Ortega, Valentine Hugo, Isabel Dato, Ansermet, Miró, Léon Fargue, Ramón Fernández, Leo Ferrero, Guy de Poralès, the Atucha sisters,[42] both married to Spanish noblemen, as well as various Surrealist poets and painters. It was springtime when she finally decided to cross the pond, and Waldo was waiting for her in May sunshine. She rented an apartment overlooking Central Park. There, in the centre of the city of skyscrapers, she found another zoo, another redoubt of wildness that civilization seemed to need as though to keep in view its ancient memories, carefully contained behind the line of bars marking off the uncertain abyss between it and them. With the windows open at night, she heard the lions' roar mingling with the sounds of traffic in the mechanical jungle. She discovered American Negros, elegant as cats, capable of infinite plasticity; she danced with them and Waldo in the dancehalls of Harlem. She heard Negro spirituals sung in the street and in churches. The sermon of a black Methodist minister struck her as the most superb show she'd ever seen, as well as the most moving profession of faith. She had an argument with Waldo when he accused her of letting the lights of New York seduce her, instead of paying attention to plans for the journal. He also accused her of dwelling on the obstacles rather than on potential resources. How could she tell him that, in a country as rich as Argentina, with so many millionaires, none would come forward to finance the project, once they'd heard her talk it up? It was only later, when she tried to raise money to engage Sergei Eisenstein, that Waldo came round to believing her; the Russian cinéaste was leaving Hollywood and was ready to cooperate in establishing a film industry in the pampas: no one in her social class was interested.[43]

The return trip to Buenos Aires unexpectedly put a disturbing mirror before her. As her ship passed through the Panama Canal, she suddenly witnessed a painful dichotomy: two spaces and two temporalities in contrast. On one side of the canal were the clean, modern neighbourhoods of Balboa and Ancón made up of symmetrical bungalows, freshly painted, with picture-postcard lawns – the abodes of North American employees. On the other side, a hodge-podge of motley shacks, the primitive, miserable dwellings of Latin America – no more indigent, however, than the poorer barrios of Argentina. Nevertheless, on that side, amid the people badly dressed and often barefoot who thronged the plazas, there was something in the air, glimmers of a treasure distinct from the ordered paradise of white refrigerators and doll-house-perfect bungalows. It was the low rumble, the warm, profound murmur of the mother tongue. *My* mother tongue, Victoria felt. After six months abroad in foreign lands, never had it felt so much hers. While the passengers aboard the *Santa Clara*, curious and slightly scandalized, passed comment on the local colour and Hispanic chaos, Victoria knew she was at the beginning of the sure road home, southward bound.[44] The sense of belonging was reinforced in Lima, where a visit to the museum holding the remnants of the Inca civilization made her doubt the degree of civilization of Spaniards capable of reducing that world to rubble. And it brought back the memory of the first Ocampos in America; they had gone south, departing from Cuzco, the sacred Navel of the World, the centre of Tahuantinsuyo.

In Antofagasta, on the north coast of Chile, the mirage of an exotic flower was resolved into a familiar aroma. It was an angel's trumpet, like those in the garden at San Isidro with their lush velvet bells the colour of ivory. Back on the ship, to fight off the vertigo she was suffering,[45] Victoria put on the phonograph and bathed her head in the music of

Debussy by way of therapy. *Debussy=Oxygen=Europe*, she wrote to Ortega in a letter sent from the *Santa Clara*.[46] And yet, many years later, her
sole memory of that sere desert landscape was of the homey perfume of
that rich flower.

VII

Victoria arrived home just in time to witness the strange "September 6th
Revolution," as they called the coup that toppled the presidency of the
elderly Hipólito Yrigoyen, perhaps by then readier to discuss history than
to deal with the day-to-day business of governance. That same gentleman
had put his old airplane and a pilot at Waldo Frank's disposal so that he
could see Argentina from the air. No gauchos or Indians participated in
that 1930 upheaval, as they had when the English invaded in 1806 and 1807,
or a few years later during the Wars of Independence. The militants in this
putsch were cadets trained at the Military College and the School of Com-
munications. The daily paper *Crítica* had fostered it. The people, unhappy with Yrigoyen, celebrated the coup in the streets, though they had not
instigated it. They would all soon regret the turn of events.[47] Ricardo
Rojas – the author from Tucumán, rector of the University of Buenos
Aires, historian of Argentine literature (judged by more than a few to be
non-existent)[48] – saw in those uniformed boys in spit-and-polish boots
the beginning of ominous times. "The folks of Buenos Aires are the same
gullible snobs as ever," he said to anyone who'd listen. "This has nothing
to do with nationalism or anything like it. Since Fascism has now become
trendy in Europe, they want to bring it over here, just as they would
import a set of French porcelain or a British tweed jacket. They've opened
a Pandora's box. They have no idea what they've got themselves into, and
we are all going to pay for it."[49] Intransigently opposed to the new order,
or disorder, he would pay for his outspoken dissidence with three months
in Ushuaia, in the southernmost prison on the planet.

On the day of the coup, María Rosa Oliver was trying on a dress. She
rushed out on the balcony as fast as she could on her crutches, in time to
see a silver airplane circling above the dispersed multitude. One of her
maternal uncles – an old bachelor, night owl, and skirt-chaser – leapt out
of the bath wrapped in a towel, but quickly lost his impetus to ally himself with the heroes. He would, however, join in the celebrations later in

the day, along with all those season-ticket holders of the Colón Theatre who'd been staying away from gala events out of distaste for the official presence of Yrigoyen, that champion of little employees, small farmers, and small-business owners. Nearly all the balconies of the houses and palatial mansions surrounding the Plaza San Martín were sporting bouquets of flowers and patriotic ribbons. In their living rooms, coffee, liqueurs, and pastries were being served. The men smoked cigars, speculating about who would get the vacant positions in state ministries and the especially coveted postings in European embassies. The owners of those houses could finally breathe easy. Natural law had now come back into force, thanks to the opportune intervention of General José Félix Uriburu. Now the Nation, restored to the purity of its origins and brought back into line by virile discipline, would again have its proper leaders, qualified by birth, education, and class, and a populace that would be content to follow, their heads no longer full of delirious nonsense.

There was no celebration at the house in Palermo Chico.

– I don't like the look of this at all, said Victoria. Too many army boots, too many priests' robes. No cause for happiness.

They would soon be happy, however, for other reasons. The journal was making rapid progress, its first issue almost ready for publication. But it still lacked a name. They could not agree on one, and their arguments were going in circles. Victoria decided to call Ortega and ask him to act as referee.

– Is that a good idea? He isn't American. It's as if we're betraying the agreement with Waldo, objected María Rosa Oliver.

– Yes, he is American in a way, responded Victoria. Didn't he say he was an Argentine in imagination? Life in imagination is so often worth more than real life.

The philosopher in Madrid pronounced his verdict over an atrociously buzzing telephone line. "*Sur!*" he shouted above the interference. "*Sur*, I said!" He was adamant in his choice, even before Victoria had finished reading their list of possible names.

The journal was as sober in design as the house in Palermo Chico. But the dimensions were generous (7½ by 9½ inches), and it was put together from the finest materials – the paper, the printing, the contributing writers. On the white, glazed-paper cover were printed only three letters, the numeral "one," and a green arrow. The arrow of the South, which had pinned the lives of migrants to the map of Argentina.[50] It featured pieces by the Argentine writers Borges, Ricardo Güiraldes, deceased since 1927, and Victoria. The foreign contributions were by Ansermet, Waldo Frank, Drieu, Alfonso Reyes, Jules Supervielle, and Walter Gropius. It wasn't all text, either. There were photographs of Argentine and American landscapes – the pampas, the Andes, the Iguazú Falls, and Tierra del Fuego. There were images of two *palo borracho* trees with their convex trunks in the shape of a vase, and of Brazilian buttes and palm trees. There were reproductions of artworks by Norah Borges, Spilimbergo, and Basaldúa placed cheek-by-jowl with two portraits of women by Picasso; two women on a colonial street of Buenos Aires by Holland; and a cubic and Cubist woman in lilac by Pettoruti.[51] A few photos documented the inscriptions on wagons used on the banks of the Río de la Plata and discussed in Borges's article. Another photo reproduced the portrait of Colonel Santa Coloma, the enemy of Hilario Ascasubi who also inspired his work. Past and future, nature and culture, both popular and avantgarde art were interwoven into the singular vector of the southwardpointing arrow.

The staff of *Sur* indulged the temptation of photographic immortality. Carmen Brey, refusing to pose herself, took two photos, one on the staircase and the other in the living room of Victoria's house. Included were Jorge Luis Borges and his sister Norah Borges, the Spaniard Guillermo de Torre (Norah's husband), Eduardo Bullrich, Eduardo Mallea, and Oliverio Girondo (an avant-garde colleague of Borges), all permanent members of the Editorial Board.[52] Representing the Foreign Advisory Committee were Pedro Henríquez Ureña and Ernest Ansermet. María Rosa Oliver was there in a little white collar, diminutive and girlish, as were María Carolina Padilla, the journal's translator (Carmen was the other translator), Ramón Gómez de la Serna, and the philosopher Francisco Romero. And Victoria too, of course, was in both photos, standing alert, wrapped in a silk scarf. Carmen thought she would keep a copy for her family photo album. In that house, with those people, she had built a part of her life.

The arrow of *Sur*, repeated on the covers of four thousand copies, penetrated the bookstores not only of Buenos Aires but also Madrid and Paris. Its commercial success was accompanied by a bittersweet mix of critical reviews by insiders and outsiders. Among the outsiders, there was one who had almost been one of their own: Samuel Glusberg, whom

Frank had chosen as one of the founders, was not resigned to his exclusion and incompatibility. As director of the journal *Vida Literaria*, he criticized *Sur* for its lack of *americanismo* because it included an article on Picasso. He likened *Sur* to the Parisian journal *Commerce*.[53] The literary demi-monde of Buenos Aires, for its part, wrapped itself in a protective blanket of lukewarm condescension. In distress, Victoria wrote to Ortega: *Here it has been received as if every week such journals came out; they say I can easily afford to pay for this luxury. Every one of them has made snitty little remarks conveying that impression.*

Nosotros and *La Nación* both published commentaries, more interested in praising the quality of the paper, the excellent printing, and the number of pages than in pointing out the innovative features of its content. *Nosotros* did not miss the chance to wax ironic, particularly regarding Drieu La Rochelle's "Letter to unknown persons," in which he affirmed that he knew nothing about Argentina, except that it was the country of the *whites of the southern world*, located at the same latitude as South Africa; or about the Argentines themselves, apart from their habits of spending money like water and buying women in the cabarets of Montmartre. But the worst came a little later. An anonymous insert in *La Nación* satirized the delicate sentimentality of another letter, signed by the editor-in-chief, Victoria Ocampo, and addressed to Waldo Frank, and which had opened that first issue of *Sur*. In the letter she recalled her contrition toward the friend who had reprimanded her for getting distracted in New York from the journal project: *You saw my eyes filling with tears (tears that fell on the pease on my plate). I was annoyed and moved at the same time. Annoyed by my own tenderness and moved by your brusque friendliness.* The anonymous journalist in *La Nación* wrote: The culinary flavour of Doña Victoria Ocampo's tears is a going concern among the numerous Brillat-Savarin of Buenos Aires who keep themselves up-to-date on gastronomic trends. Consequently, we shall soon see announced the latest *plat du jour* in our local restaurants – "Pease à la Victoria Ocampo." The rudimentary Spanish of Victoria's childhood had tripped her up, and the sarcastic critic took full advantage.[54]

Some commentaries faulted *Sur* for all the photographs. Even the insider Borges objected:

– What's the point of so many photos? If we keep on in that vein, the journal is going to look like a Baedeker or some travel agency's commercial propaganda.

– Well, if they show something of the rest of our country to those intellectuals who never leave the Province of Buenos Aires, they'll have served their purpose.

Victoria's answer to Borges was a mocking rebuke for his taste exclusively for the pampa and the environs of Buenos Aires.

– Anyway, you haven't complained about the photos documenting your articles, have you? If we follow your logic, by including those wagon-inscription photos,[55] I risk being taken for a shareholder of a transport company.

Ortega, once he was assured that the journal wasn't going to be a venue for the latest literature from the United States, gave his verbal and moral support but contributed no texts. After his decisive intervention in naming the journal, he endlessly put off sending an article he thought would "suit" the new publication. Alfred Métraux, an expert on indigenous cultures, predicted an ephemeral existence for the journal; he saw it as a greenhouse phenomenon, a weak sprout produced by an exquisite minority in an artificial climate, deprived of the genuine sap running in the roots of the native soil. Victoria took a good look at herself in the mirror, then at the faces surrounding her: Borges, Mallea, Oliverio Girondo, María Rosa Oliver. Like her, they were Argentines each and every one, willy-nilly, Americans by the fate of birth, and now by choice. Even foreigners like Guillermo de Torre or Carmen Brey – had they not been Argentinized? In the end, she smiled. Métraux knew little about botany and gardens; his metaphors were poorly chosen. Even in greenhouses, the soil was of the same land where plants must live their precarious lives. And something of that native soil inexorably impregnated and modified them.

She sought refuge in the ever-consoling letters of Waldo Frank. *I forgot to mention (due to fatigue) my first, most profound impression of Sur: its absolute americanismo. I regret my failure to say so earlier because then it would not be necessary to tell you now that I radically disagree with Glusberg (if indeed it was him) and what he says about Sur. One's Americanism has nothing to do with generations; it is in the soul. Glusberg is no less American for being the son of immigrants, just as you are no less American for being the daughter – the illustrious daughter – of the Conquistadors. Undoubtedly there are other daughters of Conquistadors in whom the soul of a new world does not live. It is in acts, not in talking about and proclaiming America, that the authentic stuff shows through. You, my dear, were an American without knowing it!*[56]

His confirmation of her identity may have been badly needed for other reasons as well. She was left fatherless when Manuel Ocampo died on the eighteenth of January, 1931, almost at the same time as the journal was coming out. Señor Ocampo had not been especially sanguine about the future of this publishing venture. His eldest daughter, his favourite, the brightest among the brilliant Ocampo sisters, still showed no signs of having any common sense. Resigned to her extravagant character, he uttered a laconic prognosis for her latest project: "You'll go broke." At least he hadn't been as caustic as when he first saw the house in Palermo Chico, with its array of cacti and a fish skeleton displayed under a glass bell on the mantel. "You should tell Count Keyserling to donate his skeleton and set it up beside the front door. You'd flatter his vanity, and it would go well with the rest of the décor."

Nevertheless, if there was one thing Victoria could cling to with blind certainty, it was her father's love. A strict and jealous love, inseparable from the family's pride and honour, of which she was apparently the principal custodian. "My one consolation," she said to Carmen and María Rosa, "is that now my life can no longer hurt him."

Carmen looked at her in silence. She thought about Julián Martínez, lover turned virtual husband, whom the little forty-year-old girl had hidden away for fourteen years so as not to offend Manuel Ocampo with her shameful, serially repeated naughtiness. She thought about the silences, about what Victoria had given up, about the child she had not allowed herself to have. "Who was it that hurt whom?" thought Carmen.

VIII

That same summer, Ulrich von Phorner came back to stay. He'd sold the empty family house in the city of Straubing, and brought along his share of the inheritance, plus the wedding ring that had belonged to his great-grandmother from Rioja. The Count had decided to demonstrate his magnanimity and human sensibility by giving his secretary and Fräulein

Brey an incredible cheque. He'd also sent an article, relatively moderate in tone, for the second issue of *Sur*. In private, however, he never stopped badmouthing the Cobra, the Anaconda of the River Plate, who would soon reappear in his much less affable *South American Meditations*, where she figured as a monstrous Sphinx.

Carmen's wedding was a quick formality in a Buenos Aires office, a toast at Friends of the Arts, and an intimate dinner at the house in Palermo. It was also, however, a church ceremony in Los Toldos, with different guests, complete with rice, silk wedding dress, veil, and bouquet of jasmine; Carmen had planned this piece of theatre with her Galician family in mind, the photos her aunts and the Andalusian would be expecting, but also so that her nephews and her little friend Eva could have some fun. But she couldn't find Eva. After an initial exchange of letters, there had been no more contact. When asked about her whereabouts, the Basque Arzuaga shrugged his shoulders. "I heard tell they up and ran off to Junín one night, leaving a raft of unpaid bills. There's no cure for people of that ilk."

The newlyweds decided to set up house in Chivilcoy. Carmen didn't want to be too far away from family, and that rural town, peaceful and prosperous, was a good place to found a specialized school and a Language Institute. Despite the jackboots, the Wall Street crash, and a sudden drop in the price of grain, the muddy Río de la Plata still looked to many migrants like the best route to the Silver Mountain. Or, in the case of Ulrich von Phorner, an excellent place to cultivate one's garden.

Their honeymoon trip was to Malanzán so they could see the historic site where Karl von Phorner had challenged General Quiroga to a duel. In Rioja they came across a few von Phorners, whose surname had been criollized by faulty pronunciation and worse spelling at the local registry office to become "Hornos" – quite appropriate, given that the Bavarian forebear, a mining engineer, had been nicknamed the *gringo del horno*, the Blast-Furnace Gringo. In spite of the traduced name, the family resemblance was unmistakable; quite a few had the great-grandfather's blue eyes, once scorned as those of a Quitilipe horse, and some had his curly hair.

Carmen settled into marriage as comfortably as she did into their new house. Goethe was right, she thought; there were elective affinities between apparently quite different human beings. Utz, although he dreamed in German and his eyes carried another past and other landscapes, was as transparent to her as the mountain streams where she had played as a child. Wherever he was, her home would be.

Only when she thought about her childhood in the Indiano's house did the glorious vault of the pampa sky seem to turn grey and bear down upon her like a great bell-glass, plastering her to the ground. She couldn't avoid it. Her former paradise had lost its shine, was grubby, dirty. A pollution insidious as an oil slick had snuck up to the stone walls, slid under the double-leaved oak door, invaded the interior walls like a film of black mould, a stain of rot never to be erased. *It* must have happened there, in Mugardos, while her father was quietly drifting from sickness to death in a bed in Ferrol. That was why the Andalusian didn't want to go back, had never gone back, never mind that the wind tore tiles from the roof, that the humid salt air was swelling the wood of armoires and window frames, warping the floor boards. That was why Carmen Brey, too, had no desire to go back. That was why neither she nor her brother would ever go back.

She had brought with her from Buenos Aires the photo of the Andalusian's second marriage, with Doctor Núñez. It sat among the other framed photos on the corner table. She resisted the occasional impulse to turn its face to the wall. She did not want to do the obvious thing, what had always been done: blame the wicked stepmother, or blame the bodies of women for the violence they had suffered. Moreover, her brother had never said a word against Adela. Had he not taken the entire burden of guilt upon himself? Nevertheless, she found it hard to believe that Francisco Brey could have used sex as a weapon for power, revenge, spite, or humiliation. She felt it more likely that, in spite of himself and Adela Montes, he was responding. Responding to desires that words obstinately deny, but which bodies express anyway, with no need for words and often against them. Human beings knew or wanted to know very little about themselves – almost nothing, only what reason told them. Reason: a clumsy funambulist, balancing a heavy pole and swaying on a slack high-wire, who at any second could plunge into the void, pulled down by the passion of the public, the only reality, howling and milling around far below on the stage of life.

But maybe Adela did know herself a little better. Or maybe she intuited that Francisco knew what she dared not say, even to herself. Perhaps it was for that reason, and not out of fond feelings for her stepdaughter, that she tried to dissuade Carmen from her voyage by every means possible. That would be why her reaction to Francisco's reappearance was so measured and wise. Or cautious. She had not made a fuss, she hadn't deplored the promising future he'd squandered on a few acres in Los Toldos. She neither insisted that Carmen demand an explanation from her brother, nor exhorted her to get him away from there. She had merely expressed the opinion, with serene detachment, that sometimes what seems the strangest destiny is really the right one, the one that suits us; and if Francisco was satisfied with his decision, then no one should bother him about it.

One afternoon, while working on the card catalogue for the future institute, Carmen found the framed wedding picture particularly offensive. She finally did turn it against the wall. Utz was just coming in with stack of papers in his arms. Bumping against the table, he noticed the change.

– What happened? Has Señora Adela been misbehaving, like the village saints? Or has someone died?

Carmen looked daggers at him, almost as angry at him as at the photo.

– Yes, someone died. My father.

Utz put the papers down. Then he hugged her, stroking her hair.

– Your father didn't die because of that.

– They helped him along, sobbed Carmen hoarsely.

– Don't judge what you don't know. You don't want to start looking like a pious old sour-puss or one of those priests doling out Hail Marys by the bushel as a safety precaution.

Carmen looked at him furiously through her tears.

– And you'll end up like one of those Oriental holy men who live in the streets, all blissed out, beard down to their feet, getting shat on by the pigeons. Sure, they forgive everything – because nothing matters to them.

Utz kissed the dimple in her cheek.

– No way. I like living under a good roof, in this house, and especially in our bed, my favourite place. I shave every day and can't stand pigeon shit. It's true, though, that after ten years of putting up with Count Keyserling, I can forgive anybody just about anything.

Utz always knew how to make her laugh, thought Carmen. And that wasn't his only or best virtue. She stood on tiptoe to kiss him on the mouth, feeling lightened, almost free of her anger and pity for Adela Montes, for her brother, for herself, and also – dimly – for her father, maybe because he'd married the wrong woman and because he hadn't seen what he didn't want to see, or because he'd let happen what should never have happened.

Such moments of melancholy aside, the future, insistent, as demanding as a spoiled child who has to be the sole centre of the real world, left her little time for looking back. Every fortnight she travelled to Buenos Aires, visited Bebé and Victoria, who continued giving her translation work for the journal, and bought books and materials for the Language Institute, for it had been up and running since March. Utz, for his part, was continually putting people straight when they supposed the institute and school were to be a subsidiary of the Keyserling school in Darmstadt. "All I'm going to teach, on my own terms, is the German language, History, and the History of Ideas. If ever I hear that one of my pupils has attained Wisdom, I'll send them a card of congratulation. But it probably won't be my fault." So he said, while in his spare time he went on cultivating, literally, a small garden.

That year, when it was autumn in Buenos Aires and springtime in Spain, the Republicans and Socialists won the elections for the Cortes Constituyentes, the Spanish Parliament. Spain would become a Republic. The "Bobo King" would henceforth be just one more portrait in the halls of museums. The news took Carmen by surprise. She happened to be in the capital, sitting at a little table in the Café Tortoni, an order of *café con leche y medialunas* before her. Leaving a half-eaten croissant behind, she rushed off, newspaper under one arm, a bottle of sherry in the other hand, to see Don Peregrino Loureiro. Together they would drink a series of toasts: one for the Republic, another for the new Constitution, and one more for Antonio Brey, who hadn't lived to see it.

Don Peregrino was no longer at the headquarters on the Calle Salta. When the Spanish nationalists won the Federation's internal elections in 1929, the socialists packed up and left, along with their twenty-odd associations. These formed a dissident Federation of Galician Societies; its new headquarters opened in May on the Calle Mitre. A little balder, a little older, a little more tender and vulnerable, Don Peregrino was blowing his nose and drying tears of joy in front of the same newspaper Carmen was waving as she burst into the office singing the Internationale, as though they were on a secular pilgrimage.[57] They embraced, unable to say a word. Over the shoulder of her friend, short like her, she again saw the globe – Don Peregrino's personal possession – sitting on a shelf identical to its former perch.

The painted ocean, faded, was still in its place. So was Galicia, hanging off the end of Europe, where Cape Finisterre rises as the last watchtower before the abyss, the last bastion against the Unknown Sea for the ancients. Galicia: always on the edge, peninsula of a peninsula, pure outward impulse from the interior countryside toward the coast. In her mind's eye, Galicia had broken free of its rocky matrix, crossed the sea, and come to anchor in another land. The same Galicia, all of her: those within and those without would no longer be separated. Her deep soul, vegetal and imperceptible, would grow like another plant in the soil of the ombú, with the strength and music of a pinetree, with the dark passion of the *castiñeiras*.

Glossary

almacén – modern usage: department store, supermarket. In nineteenth-century Argentina, a general store that could also serve food and drink (cf. *pulpería*).

andaluz, -a – Andalusian, native of Andalucía (province in southern Spain).

arrabal – suburb.

boleadoras – bolas; a missile consisting of two or more stones connected together by strong cord; these are swung round the head and discharged at the animal to be captured, so as to wind around and entangle it. Invented by the indigenous peoples of the pampas, later adopted by the gauchos.

bombachas – baggy trousers, tied in at the ankles, worn by gaucho horsemen.

café con leche y medialunas – literally, coffee with milk and croissants. However, in Argentina the *medialunas* bear scant resemblance to French croissants.

castiñeira (Galician) – a grove of *castiñeiros*, i.e., chestnut trees.

casuarina – an evergreen tree, grey-green in colour, that grows as high as 35 metres.

caudillo – chieftain, strong-man, de facto leader.

che – interjection, similar to the English "hey," but also used at the end of an exclamation.

cina-cina (also, *cina cina* or *cinacina*) – a species of flowering tree (*parkinsonia aculeta*) with fragrant red-and-yellow flowers. Often used in hedges because of its spiny branches. Variously known in English as Jerusalem Thorn or Mexican Palo Verde.

compadrito (dim. of *compadre*) – well-dressed tough-guy, dude

confitería – cake shop and tea room. In Buenos Aires, the confitería resembles an elegant café.

estancia – cattle ranch.

estanciero – rancher; cattle baron.

gallego, -a – Galician, of or pertaining to Galicia, a province in the northwest corner of the Iberian peninsula (not to be confused with the former kingdom of Galicia, located between Poland, Ukraine, and Hungary). In Argentine popular usage, due to massive Galician immigration, *gallego* came to mean any immigrant from Spain. The diminutive, *galleguito* or *galleguita*, may express affection or condescension, depending on the speaker's attitude.

gaucho – originally a term designating the mixed-race or mestizo inhabitants of the pampa, the men famous for their semi-nomadic lifestyle and horsemanship. Often compared to the North American cowboy. By the twentieth century, the quasi-mythical nomadic gauchos had been reduced to a class of poor ranch-hands.

indiano, -a – a person who goes to the "Indies" (the Spanish colonies in America), makes money, and returns home to Spain.

indio, -a – cognate to the correct and incorrect senses of "Indian" in English. Correctly, a native of India; incorrectly, an indigenous person of the Americas.

lamnguen (Mapuche) – sister (see Figueiras, 89).

lareira (Galician) – fire, hearth, fireplace.

malevo (abbrev. of *malevolente*, "malevolent") – bad guy, bully, tough-guy

malón – an attack by "Indians" (indigenous warriors).

mate (< Quechua *mati*, "little gourd") – the gourd in which the tea-like infusion yerba mate is prepared and then drunk; the beverage itself.

mina (argot) – woman, in *lunfardo* (underworld slang of Buenos Aires).

ñandú (Guaraní) – bird native to the pampas, similar to the ostrich, five to six feet tall, that runs very quickly.

ombú – a tree native to northeastern Argentina, Uruguay, and Brazil. On the pampa it can serve as both shade tree and territory marker.

palo borracho – a tree of the Ceiba genus, whose trunk bulges in the shape of a barrel. Sometimes called in English "bottle tree."

paraíso ("paradise") – bead tree.

patria – homeland, fatherland. More literally: "parent-land" (Latin *patrius* = parental) and often figured as a mother: *la madre patria* (the mother homeland, the motherland).

porteño, -a – native of, or proper to the port city of Buenos Aires.

pulpería – general store in nineteenth-century rural Argentina, owned and managed by a *pulpero*.

Puna (Quechua, "high point") – a high bleak plateau in the southern Andes; altitude sickness, mountain sickness.

quinta – recreational country estate.

ria (Galician) – a large inlet indented into the rugged coast of Galicia, sometimes likened to the fjords of Norway.

Siglo de Oro – the Spanish Golden Age, dated usually from 1492 to the mid-seventeenth century. A period of Spanish imperial might and a corresponding flourishing in the arts and literature. The "honour" theme was prevalent in the plays of Calderón de la Barca (1600–1681), the last of the Golden Age playwrights.

sulky – a light two-wheeled, horse-drawn carriage or chaise. "So called because it admits only one person" (OED). But pictures of Argentine sulkies often show two or three riders.

tatú carreta – giant armadillo (*tatú*, Guaraní, "armadillo").

tertulia – a gathering, usually weekly, for intellectual conversation, sometimes centred on a respected writer or philosopher (e.g., *la tertulia de Ortega y Gasset*). The OED's definition, "an evening party in Spain," is misleading: a tertulia may be held in a private home (like the literary salon) or a café or other public space, anywhere in the Hispanic world.

tipa (*tipuana tipu*) – a beautiful shade tree that blooms in late summer with bright yellow flowers. Also known as *palo rosa* or, in English, rosewood.

toldería – a group of *toldos* or tents. Unlike the terms "wigwam" and "tipi," *toldo* derives not from an indigenous language of the Americas, but from the Old French *tialz* (modern French *taud* or *taude*, "tent").

yacaré (Guaraní) – cayman, alligator.

zarzuela – a genre of musical theatre originating in the dramaturgy of the Spanish Golden Age (the sixteenth and seventeenth centuries).

Notes

Abbreviations frequently used in these notes: VO (Victoria Ocampo); MRL (María Rosa Lojo).

Unless otherwise indicated, all translations are mine.

INTRODUCTION

1 El Gran Premio de Honor de la Sociedad de Escritores Argentinos (the Grand Prize of Honour of the Society of Argentine Writers), first awarded in 1944 to Jorge Luis Borges. Among many other national and international prizes, MRL received in June 2020 the Homer European Medal of Poetry and Art. In November 2020 the Fundación Argentina para la Poesía awarded her another Grand Prize of Honour: https://www.facebook.com/fundacionargentinaparalapoesia /videos/4765766986796604/.

2 See María Rosa Lojo's webpage http://www.mariarosalojo.com.ar/; and the bibliography in Marcela Crespo Buiturón, ed. *Diálogo de voces* (2018).

3 In December 2019 MRL was named an Honorary Member of the Real Academia Galega (the Royal Galician Academy).

4 Glenn Gould's landmark documentary, *The Idea of North*, first aired on CBC Radio on 18 December 1967.

5 Significantly, MRL has been contracted by Penguin Random House Spain to teach a ten-week online course entitled "The Historical Novel: Theory and Practice" (April–June, 2021).

6 *Todos éramos hijos* is unique in foregrounding Liberation Theology as it swept through Argentine Catholicism during the 1960s and '70s; the novel's very original testimony opens onto a meditation on the relations between the political and the religious. Religion (in the broadest sense), though understated in *Free Women in the Pampas*, is a fourth thematic axis in the creative work of María Rosa Lojo.

7 "[T]he entire world is my domain and I feel as at home in New York as in London. I need the whole earth," wrote VO in an unpublished letter to José Bianco
(qtd. by Sarlo, *La máquina cultural*, 137). Ocampo's first literary language, however, was French; Paris, her cultural polestar.

8 For example, Roger Caillois, long a collaborator with *Sur*, introduced contemporary Latin American writers to France through Gallimard's series La Croix du
Sud in the 1950s; among them was Jorge Luis Borges, soon thereafter catapulted
to international renown and awarded, jointly with Samuel Beckett, the Formen-
tor Prize in 1961.

9 Alfonsina Storni was also active politically. In 1919 she was involved in founding
the Asociación Pro-Derechos de la Mujer (Association for Women's Rights)
(Gallo, *Las mujeres en el radicalismo argentino*, 17, 60). She collaborated in the
early 1920s in the journal *Nuestra Causa* (Our Cause), organ of the Unión Feminista Nacional (National Feminist Union) founded in 1918 by the socialist Dr
Alicia Moreau de Justo (Gallo, *Nuestra Causa*, 17).

10 Diz cites Norberto Lavagnino's misogynist article "Literatas" (Female Literary
Types): "A *literata* is a woman who ignores the duties proper to her sex in the
kitchen and home in order to scribble in notebooks, believing herself to be the
very materialization of the Word … women who in our country apply themselves to literature [cause] misfortune to their family and relatives. Rats, the
poor rats of suburban sewers, they seem to us. Rats conscious of their mission
as propagators of pestilential literature that is sometimes vulgar and tacky, at
others obscene and pornographic" (qtd. by Diz, 320a; original: *Claridad* 199, 25
January 1930).

11 On Storni and Mistral, see Claudia Cabello Hutt, "Working to Pay for a Room
of One's Own: Modern Women Writers in Latin America."

12 The same Soiza Reilly, in the early twenties, wrote an article ("Hay doscientas
mujeres de talento que escriben en nuestro país" [Diz, 316]), celebrating the
number of women "expressing their sentiments" as a sign of the nation's
progress. Here the intent was still to contain women writers in the mold of
harmless cultural adornments, quantifiable luxury goods, whose dainty scrib-
blings were not to be confused with important literature, written by men. By the
late twenties, however, Soiza Reilly was expressing – perhaps cynically exploiting
– the same moral panic channelled by Norberto Lavagnino, when he implicitly
portrayed VO as a dangerous, immoral monster (cf. chapter "1928," n30).

13 Tagore, Ortega, Keyserling, and Waldo Frank are the four names that most often
come up in the scholarly literature on Argentina's "cultural visitors" – a long list
of foreign intellectuals and artists who travelled there to give public lectures
and/or university courses in the early decades of the twentieth century. One
recent book, *Visitas culturales en la Argentina 1898-1936* (Paula Bruno, ed.),

devotes chapters to a broad spectrum of examples: from French statesmen to Italian anarchist poets, from German scientists (Einstein) to modernist architects (Le Corbusier). The four mentioned above are there as well, but for one conspicuous absence underlined by a single passing reference: "the ridiculous [*irrisorio*] Count Keyserling" (Bruno, 262). Nevertheless, like Ortega and Frank, Keyserling had a considerable impact on Argentine literature (Lojo, "Los viajeros intelectuales" [cf. n208] and "Ernesto Sabato y Hermann von Keyserling"). Tagore, for his part, was a kind of outlier, since his visit to Buenos Aires was accidental and he gave no public lectures there.

Most of those visitors wrote about Argentina. Such has been their impact, especially during the 1920s and '30s, that volume 6 of the *Historia crítica de la literatura argentina* dedicates a chapter to the "Viajeros culturales en la Argentina (1928–1942)." Authors Aguilar and Siskind propose a chronological typology: 1) in the mid-twenties, visitors of the artistic avant-garde (e.g., Marinetti or Swiss conductor Ernest Ansermet); 2) in the late twenties and early thirties, thinkers concerned with Argentine identity – Ortega, Keyserling, and Frank – who influence the so-called essay of national identity by such writers as Eduardo Mallea or Ezequiel Martínez Estrada; 3) in the mid-thirties, national and international tensions shift the emphasis from *who are we?* to *what is to be done?* (370), the point of inflexion being 1936 and the polarizing visit of Jacques Maritain (among others). Considered against this scheme, VO's increasing protagonism in the nation's cultural life becomes clearer. In the early to mid-twenties, she cultivated a close friendship with Ansermet but was otherwise indifferent to the avant-garde scene. In the late twenties she was involved in bringing Ortega and Keyserling, but not Waldo Frank. Once *Sur* was launched, her protagonism expands and consolidates. When Maritain was attacked in Buenos Aires in 1936 by right-wing Catholic nationalists, he and his supporters were practically driven to take refuge in *Sur* (Zanca, 293). Maritain and his wife, Raïsa, became good friends with both Ocampo and María Rosa Oliver.

14 Novelist Luisa Valenzuela appreciates the narrative wisdom of deploying the mediating perspective of Carmen Brey, "made to measure. Carmen is the eye of the enlightened sector of Galicia, come to take a close look at Victoria Ocampo … with her sweet personality, at once firm and respectful, wearing like a halo her quite Celtic sense of humour, perfect for understanding the Frenchified criollo lady educated English-style" (Valenzuela, 212).

15 In that role, VO wrote and delivered a powerful address by radio in August 1936 entitled "Woman and Her Expression" (cf. 192n1).

16 Oliver was also keen observer of character. Her memoirs are peppered with incisive insights into the famous artists and writers whose company she frequented. On Jorge Luis Borges, for example: "His indifference [*desapego*], which

translated into an ability to make fun of those who surely considered him a friend, did not inhibit me, but subconsciously it led me to avoid, when conversing with him, any subject having to do with either feelings or ethics. In a strange way, in the extremely intelligent author of the essay on Argentine character, I sensed a secret and obsessive admiration for the bully or tough guy [*malevo*]" (*La vida cotidiana*, 303).

17 Lojo herself makes this point in "Escritoras y secretarias" (23).

18 "Esa mujer" is the title of a famous short story in *Los oficios terrestres* (1965) by Rodolfo Walsh, a writer and activist assassinated by the military dictatorship exactly a year and a day after the coup of 24 March 1976.

19 *Santa Evita* (1995; English translation 1996) is a brilliant novel by Tomás Eloy Martínez.

20 The distance between the "two Argentinas" is illustrated by the two-year correspondence (5 March 1971–3 May 1973) between VO and the nationalist intellectual Arturo Jauretche (1901–1974), of much humbler social origins than VO (Galasso, *Dos Argentinas*, 125–67).

21 The most dramatic illustration of VO's contradictions may be the position she took on women's suffrage. In 1936 she was passionately in favour of it. In 1944–45 she helped mount a campaign *against* women's right to vote, because she knew it would work to Perón's advantage (see Meyer, 144–8). Her class loyalty handily trumped her commitment to women's rights.

22 Laclau, *On Populist Reason*. My use here of the "empty signifier" simplifies Laclau's theoretical elaboration of the term.

23 VO wrote to Ortega: "Just as Joan heard voices, I see more and more clearly what the journal [*Sur*] will be or could become" (qtd. in Liendo, 45n122).

24 María Rosa Oliver, however, recalls that in the early years of *Sur* several assiduous visitors would spend time at the editorial office; she remembers only three names: Eduardo González Lanuza, Francisco Luis Bernárdez, and Leopoldo Marechal, "so reserved that from his mouth came more pipe-tobacco smoke than words" (*La vida cotidiana*, 334). Marechal in fact published in *Sur* as late as 1939, but soon afterward fell afoul of the whole group for political reasons (cf. n219).

25 My translation here attempts to unpack the dual meaning of *género mujer*. The more elegant original reads: "Todas éstas me parecieron cuestiones profundamente representativas del 'género mujer', en su desarrollo histórico y sus condicionamientos psicológicos."

26 Francine Masiello observes that "Victoria Ocampo integrated an awareness of the *res publica* with a representation of her private life to form the basis of her memoirs" (14).

27 Eduardo Paz Leston has compiled two collections of selected *Testimonios*, the original ten series being by then out of print: *Testimonios, primera a quinta series* (1999) and *Testimonios, sexta a décima series* (2000). Paz Leston provides some bibliographical and contextual information about the original texts. However, the two volumes carry only a small sample of the totality of VO's *Testimonios*.

28 In the new edition by the Fundación Victoria Ocampo, nothing has been lost. The original six volumes have simply been repackaged in three volumes as follows: I. *El archipiélago, El imperio insular*; II. *La rama de Salzburgo, Viraje*; III. *Versailles-Keyserling, Paris-Drieu, Sur y Cía.*

29 María de Maeztu y Whitney (1881–1948). Spanish feminist author and educator who was famous for directing, from 1915 to 1936, the Residencia de Señoritas in Madrid, attended by the novel's Carmen Brey. That institute served not only as a residence for young ladies – Meyer justly translates it as the College for Women – where young women of seventeen or older could live while pursuing higher education; it was also a community with goals shared by the Instituto Internacional de Madrid, an American-run cultural and pedagogical institute. At the Residencia, Maeztu taught courses in pedagogy and philosophy.

30 "Mistral's emotional defense of indigenous America [and the poor in general] seemed excessive to Ocampo, and Ocampo's predilection for European culture struck Mistral as misguided" (Horan and Meyer, viii). MRL and Marina Guidotti have just embarked on a new research project into women's collaboration in the journal *Sur*, with particular focus on Latin American women such as Gabriela Mistral (email from MRL, 24 September 2020).

31 Among Spanish-language biographies, María Esther Vázquez's *Victoria Ocampo* (1991) and its expanded re-edition subtitled *El mundo como destino* (2002) are fundamental. Interest in Ocampo studies appears not to be diminishing but increasing. Two new biographies have been published in the last two years: María Soledad González, *Victoria Ocampo: Escritura, poder y representaciones* (2018) and María Celia Vázquez, *Victoria Ocampo, cronista outsider* (2019).

32 MRL is a researcher with CONICET (Argentina's National Scientific and Technical Research Council, which combines the functions of Canada's NSERC and SSHRC under one umbrella). She has directed two related collective research projects: 1) *Los hermanos Mansilla: edición y crítica de textos inéditos u olvidados* (Eduarda and Lucio Mansilla: edition and criticism of unpublished or forgotten texts) (2005–07); 2) *Eduarda Mansilla: la biografía. Redes familiares y amicales. Los epistolarios. Los escritos dispersos. Hacia un estudio crítico integral* (Eduarda Mansilla: biography. Family and friendship networks. Correspondence. Miscellaneous writings. Toward an integral critical study) (2010–12). The two

projects produced, among other texts, four different critical editions of Eduarda Mansilla's work. See below Select Bibliography of María Rosa Lojo.

33 See MRL, "Las escritoras del siglo XIX: Del silencio a la ficción biográfica" (forthcoming). Ocampo's personal library had no books by nineteenth-century Argentine women writers. Nor do their names figure in the complete index of *Sur*.

34 Echeverría, exiled in Montevideo, submitted his poem to the Uruguayan newspaper *Comercio del Plata* in January 1849, with a note announcing that his *Canto* commemorates "the most notable and glorious event in Argentine history since the *Revolución de Mayo* [the declaration of independence in May 1810]" (229).

CHAPTER ONE

1 "La mujer y su expresión," originally a radio broadcast (cf. 189n15), was then published together with "La mujer, sus derechos y sus responsabilidades" (Woman, her Rights and her Responsibilities) as the booklet *La mujer y su expresión* (1936). The courtroom metaphor is not accidental; the speech was part of a successful campaign by the Argentine Women's Union (Unión Argentina de Mujeres) to halt passage of a bill of law seeking to revert recent advances in women's civil rights (Cosse, 8–9; Meyer, 135–9).

2 Teresa de Ávila (1515–1582), canonical author of the Spanish *Siglo de Oro* (Golden Age), mystic, saint, and reformer of the Carmelite monastic order. Colloquially famous for her strict discipline and piety. But Bernini's sculpture *The Ecstasy of Santa Teresa* (1647–1652) inspired Jacques Lacan's comment: "vous n'avez qu'à aller regarder à Rome la statue de Bernin pour comprendre tout de suite qu'elle jouit, ça ne fait aucun doute" (*Livre XX: Encore*, 97). Lacan took mysticism seriously in his Seminar VI: "Dieu et la jouissance de la femme (83–98). VO met Lacan in 1930 (cf. 223nn41–2).

3 The *quinta* or country house belonged to Ricardo de Lafuente Machain, husband of a first cousin of Ocampo (Dyson, 80).

4 Zenobia Camprubí Aymar (1887–1956), a bilingual native of Puerto Rico, was Tagore's first and most important Spanish-language translator, publishing twenty-eight of his books in translation (González Ródenas, 240). Juan Ramón Jiménez (1881–1958), Spanish modernist poet and 1956 Nobel winner, helped "put the finishing touches" on her translations (Dyson, 64). María Rosa Lojo recounts that when her mother migrated from Spain to Argentina in 1948, she brought along her copy of *Obra escogida de Rabindranath Tagore* (trans. Camprubí, Madrid, 1943); Lojo consulted that copy, a treasured family heirloom, when writing this novel (email, 16 November 2018).

5 André Gide translated the *Gitanjali* as *L'Offrande lyrique* (Paris, NRF, 1913). Both Gide and Camprubí translated from Tagore's English version, which he himself translated from the original Bengali.

6 Enrique Rodríguez Larreta (1873–1961). Carmen refers to *La gloria de don Ramiro* (1908), well received throughout the Hispanic world.

7 Manuel Curros Enríquez (1851–1908). Important poet and journalist of the Rexurdimento (resurgence, renaissance) of Galician language and literature in the nineteenth century. Progressive and pro-republican, he ran afoul of the conservative religious authorities in Galicia. Like many Galicians, he emigrated to Havana in 1894, where he ran the newspaper *La Tierra Gallega* (The Land of Galicia).

8 Rosalía de Castro (1837–1885). Major poet and novelist who, like Curros Enríquez, wrote in both Galician and Castilian. That Carmen refers to her only by her first name indicates how familiar and well loved Rosalía de Castro was, especially for her *Cantares gallegos* (1863), often considered the first great modern work in the Galician language (cf. 216nn42–3).

9 Ricardo Güiraldes (1886–1927). Argentine novelist best known for *Don Segundo Sombra* (1926), a modernist-gauchesque novel. He was close to Valéry Larbaud, French critic and literary influence broker. Güiraldes married Adelina del Carril, who played an important (unsung) role as a literary translator; it may well have been her translation of Larbaud's famous 1922 article "James Joyce" that brought news of *Ulysses* to Buenos Aires (Cheadle, "Between Wandering Rocks," 60–1). Güiraldes befriended the younger avant-garde generation, published in their journals, and mentored Roberto Arlt.

10 *De imitatione Christi* (1444), by Thomas à Kempis. A classic of Catholic devotional literature.

11 The thirteenth poem of the *Gitanjali* (11).

12 In the long struggle between the Spanish and British empires, Ferrol was one of the few enclaves that, thanks to its geographical situation, was able to resist enemy occupation. With the Ferrol Expedition of 1800, the British did manage to land forces on the nearby beach of Doniños, but a small group of soldiers, helped by Ferrol's citizens, successfully repulsed them. Later, however, Napoleon invaded Spain in 1808 and occupied Ferrol in 1809.

13 The British Empire badly wanted to possess Argentina for strategic reasons. They unsuccessfully invaded Buenos Aires in 1806 and 1807.

14 Santiniketan was founded in 1901 with the help of agricultural expert Leonard Elmhirst, recruited by Tagore himself from Cornell University. Modelled on Tagore's unconventional ideas about education, the school emphasized creative self-expression (Dyson, 14–15; Young, 63–84).

15 From poem #15 in *The Gardener*. Bengali title: "Marichika" (Mirage). Dyson

translates the lines more literally: "What I want I want in error, what I get I do not want" (112). In the poem "A Victoria," Silvina Ocampo teased her elder sister by putting in her mouth a parody of the same verses: "What I don't have is mine if I want it. / What I have is not mine if I don't want it" (Dyson's translation from the Spanish, 112). In Dyson's summary: "The poem ... opens with the image of a musk-deer running amuck [sic] in the forests, intoxicated by its own perfume. The image would not be an inappropriate description of Victoria Ocampo in the decades before she had found herself an appropriate vocation" (112). The full poem in Tagore's English version reads:

> I run as a musk-deer runs in the shadow of the forest mad with his
> own perfume.
> The night is the night of mid-May, the breeze is the breeze of the south.
> I lose my way and I wander, I seek what I cannot get, I get what I do
> not seek. //
> From my heart comes out and dances the image of my own desire.
> The gleaming vision flits on.
> I try to clasp it firmly, it eludes me and leads me astray.
> I seek what I cannot get, I get what I do not seek. (*The Gardener*, 35)

16 William Henry Hudson (1841–1922) grew up in Argentina, then migrated to England when he was thirty-three. An ecological park, a museum, and a suburb of Buenos Aires have all memorialized him as "Guillermo Enrique Hudson." Hudson was "doubly canonized" in both English and Argentine literature (Reeder, 561). Borges considered his novel *The Purple Land* (1885) to be "the quintessential expression of gaucho culture" (qtd. in Reeder, 562). His *Argentine Ornithology* (1888) is one of several books he wrote on birds, also a salient theme in his childhood memoir *Far Away and Long Ago* (1918), perhaps the book Victoria was procuring that day. Tagore met Hudson personally in England in 1912 (Dyson, 321).

17 Spiritism was established by Allan Kardec, pen name of French author Hippolyte Léon Denizard (1804–1869), for whom the term denoted a science of the spirits and their relationship with the corporeal world. He was interested in exploring paranormal phenomena such as the channeling of voices of the dead through mediums, hypnotism, levitation, etc. The movement was strong in Buenos Aires in the latter decades of the nineteenth century, along with occultism, mesmerism, and theosophy, when mainstream scientists and important literary writers both took an interest in such matters, with varying attitudes. It still provided literary fodder to many writers in the first decades of the twentieth century, though few by the 1920s totally believed in such things. Tagore is being

somewhat ironic when he suggests that he and Carmen Brey will teach a little Spiritism.

18 The italicized passages are fragments from the draft of a letter written by Elmhirst, found by Dyson in the Elmhirst Records Office and reproduced in full (107–9). Dyson could not find a revised version of the letter in the Ocampo archives, and wonders if VO saw it at all. Unlike Carmen Brey, Dyson sympathizes with Elmhirst and his "penetrating insight" into VO's character (111).

19 Poem 17, *Gitanjali* (14).

20 Poem 35, *Gitanjali* (28–9).

21 Marguerite Moreno (1871–1948), French stage and film actress who adopted her mother's surname as her stage name. She spent seven years in Buenos Aires (1905–1912) directing the French branch of the Conservatorio Nacional de Arte Dramático, where she gave Ocampo lessons. When VO saw Moreno perform the role of Napoleon's son in Edmond Rostand's play *L'Aiglon* (1900), she experienced self-recognition: "that sick boy (his ravaging consumption seemed to me then an enviable illness) was as much a prisoner in Schoenbrunn as I was in [her parents'] house on Florida and Viamonte" (qtd. in Molloy, 60). Molloy reads this episode with great insight (59–60).

22 *La gran aldea* (1884), a novel by Lucio Vicente López that nostalgically depicts the tranquil life of the comfortable classes of Buenos Aires, before mass immigration altered the city.

23 The phrase, quoted ironically here, is attributed to the director of the (British-owned and financed) Argentine Railways, Guillermo Leguizamón (later knighted for service to the British Crown, henceforth Sir William Leguizamón). His detractors called him *el cata Leguizamón*: he was a native of Catamarca (in northwest Argentina), but *cata* can also mean *cotorra* ("parrot," "chatterbox"). In 1933 the Argentine vice-president, Julio A. Roca, Jr, negotiated the Roca-Runciman Pact, securing for Argentine ranchers their market for beef in Britain, in exchange for many commercial advantages for the British. The pact was denounced by Argentine nationalists on both the right and the left; the landowning oligarchy was accused of selling out the national interest for their own benefit. At the conclusion of the deal, Roca said: "Argentina, due to their reciprocal interdependence, is from the economic point of view an integral part of the British Empire." Leguizamón added the notorious sentence: "Argentina is one of the most precious jewels of His Gracious Majesty" (qtd. by Galasso, *Vida de Scalabrini Ortiz*, 150). Falcoff and Dolkart note that Argentina had long been considered an unofficial "sixth dominion" of the British Empire (after Canada, Australia, South Africa, New Zealand, and Newfoundland); "English economic primacy was still a fact of life for Argentine diplomacy during the 1930s" (*Prologue to Perón*, xv).

24 Argentina (< *argentum* "silver") was so called because the early explorers were
     seeking a route from the Atlantic to the silver mines of Peru. They never found
     silver or any other precious metal. Ezequiel Martínez Estrada opens his famous
     essay *Radiografía de la pampa* (1933) (X-Ray of the Pampa) with a chapter on
     "Trapalanda" (a fantastical place of fabulous wealth, like El Dorado): "We lived
     with [the fantasy] of those mines in our soul" (14).

25 Tagore later resigned his knighthood in protest against the Amritsar Massacre of
     1919 (Young, 77), in which British troops opened fire on a crowd of peaceful
     Indian protesters, killing 379 and wounding 1,200. For a concise summary, see
     Richard Cavendish, "The Amritsar Massacre," *History Today* 59, no. 4 (April
     2009), https://www.historytoday.com/archive/months-past/amritsar-massacre.

26 Señor Ocampo's worry was not baseless. The article entitled "Babel" appeared in
     La Nación in 1920; an expanded book version, *De Beatrice a Francesca*, was pub-
     lished in 1924. "This book was a substitute for a confession, for a confidence," VO
     wrote later (qtd. in Molloy, 67). Molloy comments: "Significantly, *De Francesca a
     Beatrice* is dedicated to Ocampo's lover in a coded inscription, a subversive ges-
     ture that effectively succeeds in calling attention to itself" (67). Beatriz Sarlo sur-
     mises that the affair must have been common knowledge among the porteño
     elite and that VO's family, "implausibly, pretended not to know" (*La máquina
     cultural*, 139).

27 Visva-Bharati ("where the world becomes one nest" [Dyson, 14]) was founded
     by Tagore in 1921 alongside the school at Santaniketan. The university invited
     scholars from both the West and the East and became "a significant centre of
     Buddhist studies and haven for artists and musicians" (Dyson, 14). It is still a
     prestigious national institution; see the Visva-Bharati website at http://www
     .visvabharati.ac.in/index.html (accessed 11 June 2021). The villages of Shilaidaha,
     Potisar, and Surul were all headquarters of the Tagore family estates. At Potisar,
     Tagore started an agricultural bank. At the village of Surul, renamed Sriniketan,
     he founded with Leonard Elmhirst's help an Institute of Rural Re-Construction.
     These projects became models "repeated and elaborated in many programmes
     of village self-development in India" (Dyson, 14–15).

28 Dyson (122) found this version of the poem in Tagore's notebook. Dyson reck-
     ons that VO would likely have read the following version, closer to the original
     Bengali: "And though thou speakest not my tongue, Woman, thou knowest from
     thy heart, / that the poet in me has ever been thine own guest on this earth, the
     guest of love" (qtd. in Dyson, 121).

29 Pedro Figari (1861–1938), Uruguayan painter but also writer of philosophical
     essays, poems, short stories, dramas, and criticism. In his book *Arte, Estética,
     Ideal* (1912), Figari expounds his ideas on art and its mission before taking up
     painting itself at the age of sixty, with a clear idea of what he wanted to do, as

Ángel Rama observes (10). His paintings evoke Uruguay and Argentina's common colonial past. He also took photos, several of VO, including the one where she sits at Tagore's feet. When Tagore left Miralrío, Figari and his family moved in (*Testimonios, series primera a quinta*, 117).

30 Opening lines of VO's letter to Tagore from San Isidro, 20–21 November 1924 (Dyson, 382–3).

31 Indirect rendering of Tagore's letter to VO, 14 (?) November 1924: "I am like an unfortunate country where on an inauspicious day a coal mine has been discovered with the result that its flowers are neglected, its forests cut down and it is laid bare to the pitiless gaze of a host of treasure-seekers." The letter continues as quoted in the novel: "My market price has risen high …" (Dyson, 374).

32 This paragraph signals a subtle shift in the status of the narration. That Carmen "felt like a novelist" is more than an arch, metafictional wink to the reader. Unlike the virtually direct quotations from existing documents (letters, etc.) indicated in this section by italics, the dialogue that ensues is composed from words and phrases spoken or written by both VO and Tagore which the novelist weaves into a conversation of hybrid status – a kind of documentary fiction. This change in the pact between author and reader is signalled by the change in punctuation, from the dash to quotation marks.

33 Tagore did use the phrase "your furniture poet" (Dyson 156–7). The poem by Baudelaire is "L'Invitation au voyage," poem 49 in *Les Fleurs du mal*. The lines that annoyed Tagore were "Des meubles luisants, / Polis par les ans, / Décoreraient notre chambre. / Les plus rares fleurs / Mêlant leurs odeurs / Aux vagues senteurs de l'ambre / Les riches plafonds / Les miroirs profonds / La splendeur orientale / Tout y parlerait / À l'âme en secret / Sa douce langue natale" (Baudelaire, 68).

34 Tagore wrote "A Skeleton" after a walk with VO on the pampa at Chapadmalal. Dyson (166) credits the literary critic Kshitis Roy for suggesting that "A Skeleton" was partly inspired by Baudelaire's "Une Charogne."

35 As Beatriz Sarlo observes, this episode points out the perils of cultural translation: "The lesson is unbearable not only for Victoria Ocampo, but probably for any intellectual from the periphery. Misunderstanding between languages is tolerable; the incommunicability of cultures is not, because the suspicion arises that the incommunicability is due to the culture towards which the transfer cannot be completed. Eight years later, Ocampo receives a similar lesson from Carl Jung, when she visits him in Zurich. Jung is ironic, uninterested, and rude (although VO hardly perceives it) … When she finally suggests an invitation to Argentina, Jung answers with cutting prejudice: 'What for? Who would be interested? Nobody would understand a thing I said'" (*La máquina cultural*, 116; Jung, 95).

36 From Tagore's poem "A Skeleton" (qtd. in Dyson 165).

37 The Orquesta Filarmónica de la Asociación del Profesorado Orquestal (APO). This Association of Professional Musicians, formally constituted in 1919 and dissolved in 1945, created its own orchestra in 1922 (Cuerda, 101, 109, 96). Ansermet was one of several internationally famous figures who conducted that Philharmonic Orchestra (cf. 206n32).

38 VO quotes Ansermet's letter in *Autobiografía, II* (181–2). Dyson brings critical nuance to this exchange, noting that Ansermet was taking a little too earnestly his friend Victoria's half-facetious accusation of Baudelaire's *rastacuerismo literario occidental* (Western-style nouveau-riche literary ostentation) (160–1). Jorge Luis Borges, in a review of Tagore's *Collected Poems and Plays* for the magazine *El Hogar* in 1937, steals the anecdote. With no mention of VO, he recounts a meeting with Tagore thirteen years earlier: "Baudelaire's poetry was talked about. Someone recited 'La mort des amants' ... Tagore listened with forbearance, but said at the end: *I don't like your furniture poet!*" Borges quotes the sentence in English, just as Ocampo reported it, and then translates "furniture poet" inaccurately (no doubt deliberately so) as *poeta amueblado* (literally, "furnished poet"). Borges then says with forked tongue that he sympathized deeply with Tagore. "Now, re-reading his works, I suspect that he was moved less by the horror for Romantic *bric-à-brac* than by his invincible love for vagueness" (*Obras completas, IV, 294*). In a move typical of the sly master of the "art of the insult," Borges turns his mockery of Baudelaire back upon Tagore.

39 VO's declarations of "friendship" could be rather extreme. After a quarrel with Elmhirst, VO writes him on 10 November 1924: "And let me say this: I was hurt, because I love you so much, so tenderly, that a slight injustice, coming from you, instead of rousing my anger (I have a bad temper) rouses my *pain!*" The letter ends: "Forgive all this foolishness. I love you and kiss your hands. I love you. – Victoria" (Dyson, 127; VO's emphasis).

40 Dyson (141–8) reproduces and discusses the "Fortress" document conserved at the Elmhirst Records Office.

41 The incident apparently took place on 14 November 1924. In the archives in Buenos Aires, Dyson found the passage in the unpublished French draft of VO's autobiography and translated it into English (103). Her nuanced interpretation of the incident is well worth reading (102–13).

42 Two paragraphs from Elmhirst's letter to Dorothy Whitney of 4 December 1924, reproduced in part by Dyson (171–2). In another paragraph between the two reproduced in the novel, Elmhirst asks his fiancée "to forgive and make allowances for the moodiness of these South American letters" (171).

43 "Our hostess is …": this paragraph is an adapted excerpt from Elmhirst's letter
    to Dorothy Whitney of 6 January 1925, sent from Río de Janeiro when Tagore
    and Elmhirst were on their way back to Europe from Buenos Aires (Dyson, 198).
    The triangulated drama had not ended with their departure. Elmhirst, exasper-
    ated, was still obliged to play go-between in the unresolved Tagore-Ocampo
    relationship.

44 The Casa Paquin was the Argentine branch of the Maison de Couture founded
    in 1891 by couturière Jeanne Beckers and her husband Isidore Jacob, known as
    Paquin. In 1896 they moved headquarters to London (the House of Paquin). To
    the London and Paris branches were added those in New York (1912) and, short-
    ly afterwards, Buenos Aires and Madrid. Jeanne Paquin (1869–1936) was the first
    major female couturière and a founding figure of the modern fashion industry.

45 This paragraph is a slightly adapted excerpt from the transcript of the speech
    Tagore made to Elmhirst at Miralrío on 25 December 1924, titled "My Idea of
    Christmas Day" conserved at the Ocampo archives in Buenos Aires, partially
    reproduced and glossed by Dyson (174–9). The two sentences beginning with "In
    this country" and ending with "*amritam*, immortality" are direct quotes (176).

46 The "river of death" refers to a myth recorded by Livy (Titus Livius). The
    Roman general Decimus Junius Brutus Albinus (85–81 BCE to 43 CE) "subdued
    Lusitania by capturing cities all the way to the ocean, and when his soldiers
    refused to cross the Oblivion river, he snatched the standard from the standard-
    bearer, carried it across himself, and thus persuaded them that they should
    cross" (Livy, 268). The Romans gave the name Lusitania to what is now Portugal
    and Galicia (the Latinate diminutive of "Gaul"). The soldiers feared that if they
    crossed the "Oblivion river" they would never return. MRL invokes this myth to
    great poetic effect at the end of her novel *Finisterre* (2005).

47 From "My Idea of Christmas Day" (qtd. in Dyson, 177).

48 *La laguna de los nenúfares* (1926). For an interesting analysis, see Unruh, "Walk-
    ing Backwards" in *Performing Women*.

49 From "My Idea of Christmas Day" (qtd. in Dyson, 178).

50 Rubén Darío (1867–1916), a major poet originally from Nicaragua, spent several
    crucial years in Buenos Aires, where two of his most important books, *Los raros*
    and *Prosas profanas y otros poemas*, were published in 1896. Darío was a leading
    figure of *modernismo*, a poetic movement antedating European Modernism that
    gave Spanish American literature international presence.

51 Unlike Julián Martínez, Jorge Luis Borges did mock Tagore: "Mais je trouve que
    Tagore est surtout un fumiste de bonne foi [an earnest charlatan] ou, si vous
    préférez, une invention suèdoise" (Milleret, 240). "Swedish invention" refers to
    Tagore's 1913 Nobel Prize in Literature. VO gets her revenge in "Fe de erratas

(*Entrevistas Borges-Milleret*)"; she not only protests Borges's injustice to Tagore, but also implicitly rebukes him for repaying her years of loyal defence of him (Borges) with disloyalty. She ends by quoting Amado Alonso's objections to Borges's negative review of a book by Américo Castro: "As an example of style, this passage by Borges is as excellent as others among his best writings; as information, it is erroneous; in its appraisal, unjust" (qtd. by Ocampo, *Testimonios quinta a décima*, 210). Alonso's sentence could arguably serve as an epitaph to the mischievous author of *El Aleph*.

52 Tagore's transcreation of "Ashanka" (Apprehension) written originally in Bengali at Miralrío, 17 November 1924. Tagore showed Victoria this English version on 20 November (Dyson, 123; Meyer, 70–1).

53 This is a condensed version of what Tagore told Victoria on 24 December 1924 when she asked him why he took on the burden of the children's school at Santiniketan. He insisted that all education be "peripatetic" (Tagore's word, qtd. by Dyson, 183–5).

54 The two children were Ruth (b. 1926) and William (b. 1929). The Elmhirsts renovated the old manor house of an estate at the village of Dartington, county Devon (Young, 103–29).

55 VO's *Tagore en las barrancas de San Isidro* (1961) (Tagore by the Ravines of San Isidro) is dedicated to her friend Leonard Elmhirst.

56 Dyson reproduces the entire article titled "Indians and Indians" (*The Standard*, 4 January 1925) and subjects it to a mordant critique (190–3). Whereas *La Nación* reported Tagore's regrets at not seeing the Inca civilization in Peru, writes Dyson, *The Standard*, "with superb Anglo-Saxon cunning, used Tagore's departure to take its revenge on the conquistador culture of Argentina and prove the superiority of British imperialism to its Spanish counterpart" by means of "slyly opportunistic, conveniently self-congratulatory, and arrogant humour" (190).

57 Cf. Tagore's letter to Victoria, 13 January 1925: "For me the spirit of Latin America will ever dwell in my memory incarnated in your person" (qtd. in Dyson 183, 390).

CHAPTER TWO

1 From Ortega's last public lecture (16 December 1916) of his first visit to Argentina. It is one of Ortega's few expressions of unqualified enthusiasm for Argentina and its people. However, he prefaced the remark by recalling an Indian legend about the Buddha as a young man "princely and beautiful" who, out of kindness, once turned himself into two hundred Buddhas so as to dance with as many young women dancers, each of whom believed she was dancing with the

one and only Buddha. Ortega glosses: "Enthusiasm is the power that multiplies us and leads us to intimacy with things, to be wholly with each one of them and to live for a while their peculiar life. Well, then, I tell you that this past winter my soul at some moment or other has danced that unreal dance with the soul of Argentina. I have been intimately concerned with your vicissitudes [*vuestros azares*] and have been an imaginary Argentine" (Ortega, *Meditaciones del pueblo joven*, 15–16; my translation). The poetic analogy seems to cast Ortega in the role of the infinitely kind and generous Buddha who deigns to intimacy with matters Argentine, the "vicissitudes" of her soul.

2 VO clearly alludes to Ortega's 1916 lecture (preceding note) in "Mi deuda con Ortega," a homage written on the occasion of Ortega's death in 1955. She uses the verb *poblar* approvingly: "Las ha poblado" (He has settled {populated, colonized} these lands) (*Testimonios, series primera a quinta*, 278).

3 Ramiro de Maeztu y Whitney (1874–1936), essayist, literary critic, and political theorist, member of the Generation of 1898, who spent long years (1905–19) working as a journalist in London. Influenced by G.K. Chesterton and G.B. Shaw, he was nevertheless ambivalent about English culture and ended up reaffirming traditional, Catholic Spain in his *Defensa de la Hispanidad* (1934). He was appointed ambassador to Argentina from 1928 to 1930 by the regime of General Miguel Primo de Rivera. As soon as Primo de Rivera fell in January 1930, Maeztu resigned and returned to Spain. Militantly anti-Republican, he was taken prisoner by the Republican government at the outbreak of the Spanish Civil War in 1936 and summarily shot (cf. 220n24).

4 Don Peregrino puns on the name of Miguel Primo de Rivera. In Spanish *primo* most commonly means "cousin," but it can also mean, colloquially, a person who is easily fooled or exploited (*DRAE*). The *rey 'bobón'* translates approximately as "the big dummy of a king"; *bobón* also plays on the name of the royal family, Borbón (Bourbon, in French and English).

5 The Institución Cultural Española was originally under the umbrella of the Asociación Patriótica Española, founded in 1896, with a dual mandate to promote the intellectual and moral influence of Spain and to help Spanish immigrants to Argentina in various ways. The two organizations eventually fused in 1990 under the name Asociación Patriótica y Cultural Española. See "Asociación Patriótica y Cultural Española," Cámara Española de Comercio de la República Argentina website, http://www.cecra.com.ar/pages/viewfull.asp?CodArt=114.

6 The Asociación Amigos del Arte (1924–42) was created to foster the work of local artists and played an important role in the cultural life of Argentina between the two world wars.

7 Founded in 1921 under the name Federación de Sociedades Gallegas, Agrarias y Culturales, its mission was to support the Galician farmer, foment the economic

and cultural development of Galicia, and promote liberty for the ensemble of Spanish peoples. The federation's official support for republicanism put them at odds with the government of Primo de Rivera and the Spanish right wing. The title of their fortnightly publication, *El Despertar Gallego* (The Galician Awakening), reflects their cultural nationalism. The Galician Federación in Buenos Aires is still very active to this day. See http://www.fsgallegas.org.ar/. Carmen Brey moves between the Spanish and Galician associations with no apparent sense of divided loyalties.

8 *Crítica*, established in 1921 by Natalio Botana, was Argentina's first sensationalist daily. Botana's biographer, Álvaro Abós, called him the Citizen Kane of Argentina, in reference to the Orson Welles movie based on U.S. newspaper tycoon William R. Hearst (Abós, *El tábano*, 11). Immensely successful, Botana had the daily's "palace for the people" built in 1926. It was the first Art Deco building in Buenos Aires, built by the architects Andrés and Jorge Kálnay. The decorative statues referred to by Carmen Brey can see seen in photos here: Alejandro Machado, "ARQ. JORGE KALNAY / C.A.B.A. / Av. de Mayo 1333 / Ex Edificio Crítica / Decoración de fachada Andrés Kálnay," *Andrés y Jorge Kálnay + Johannes Kronfuss – Catálogo on line de arquitectos húngaros en Argentina* (blog), 4 July 2008, http://andresyjorgekalnay.blogspot.com/2008/07/av-de-mayo-1333-ex-edificio-crtica.html. See also Wilson, *Buenos Aires* (78).

9 Victoria's witticism plays on the word *nena*, which means "little girl," often used as an infantilizing term for "young woman."

10 Alfonsina Storni (1892–1938), a poet of provincial petit-bourgeois background. Rebellious and romantic as a young woman, she had a child out of wedlock, becoming a social outcast. Nevertheless, she made her way in the world as a hard-working and quite popular poet and journalist. A smart dresser, she thematized fashion and clothing in her "Historia sintética de un traje tailleur" (Concise History of a Tailored Suit). (See "Alfonsina Storni's Misfits: A Critical Refashioning of *Poetisa* Aesthetics" in Unruh, *Performing Women*, 30.) Only two years younger than Victoria Ocampo, Storni lived in a totally different social world. VO recalls their single meeting in her *Testimonio* dedicated to Gabriela Mistral, who rebuked Ocampo for not having defended Storni (Meyer, 247).

11 The gold helmet of Mambrino had magical powers that rendered its bearer invulnerable; an invention of the chivalric novel *Orlando inamorato* (1486), by Matteo Maria Boiardo, whose adventures continued in Ariosto's *Orlando furioso*. Don Quixote thought he had found the magic helmet when he and Sancho Panza met a barber wearing his metal basin as a hat in Part I, Chapter XXI, "Which relates the high adventure and rich prize of the helmet of Mambrino, as well as other things that befell our invincible knight" (Grossman, 152).

12 Hermann von Keyserling, *The Travel Diary of a Philosopher*, first published in
    German in 1919. Manuel García Morente's Spanish translation was published by
    Espasa-Calpe, Madrid, 1928. VO wrote to María de Maeztu in December 1927
    urging her to follow up on her request – by telegram! – to Ortega that he
    immediately arrange for his disciple Morente to translate Keyserling's *Das spek-
    trum Europas*, scheduled for publication in January 1928, but delayed until 1931
    (*Autobiografía, II*, 206–7).

13 Letter from Ortega to VO, 17 July 1917 (Meyer, 53–4). I have mostly followed
    Meyer's translation, except for the numerous suspension points (it's not clear if
    these were in the original letter or if they are Meyer's ellipses). Where Meyer
    writes "understands me completely," I have translated literally the Spanish origi-
    nal *para siempre* as "forever." MRL has elided a passage that shows Ortega admir-
    ing himself in the mirror of his "Gioconda de las Pampas": "She *knows* me by
    heart … She likes my way of deforming the banality of things that life throws at
    our feet, my way of giving them a new life, dancing and rhythmic" (qtd. by
    Meyer, 54). MRL reserves for the poet Leopoldo Marechal this power to trans-
    form banal, quotidian things into poetry (page 107–8) – a nice irony, given that
    there was little love lost between Ortega and Marechal. The final sentence in
    Meyer's reproduction of Ortega's letter reads: "In my hotel room the whole
    night long, it seemed to me that a dream pearl was giving forth its pale,
    thoughtful brilliance" (54). Meyer comments: "A less implacable heart than Vic-
    toria's might have relented at these words" (53).

14 *De Francesca a Beatrice* (1924). Ortega's lengthy Epilogue for the book – more
    "like an open letter" to Victoria (Meyer, 55) – expounds his views on Woman;
    text reproduced in *Estudios sobre el amor* (11–40).

15 Argentina (*argentum*, "silver" in Latin) was thus wishfully named by the Spanish
    explorers seeking a route from the Atlantic to the silver mines of the Andes.
    Martín del Barco Centenera, Spanish priest, coined the name with his book-
    length poem *Argentina y Conquista del Río de la Plata* (1602) (Argentina and the
    Conquest of the River Plate).

16 In the original: Academia Argentina de la Lengua; Asociación de la Crítica; Cen-
    tro de Estudiantes de Filosofía y Letras; Ateneo Hispanoamericano; Club
    Español; Jockey Club; Club del Progreso (*Las libres*, 109). The Jockey Club,
    founded in 1882, became the cultural heart of the land-owning oligarchy of
    modern Argentina. Its original, luxurious building on the (once) fashionable
    Calle Florida is still a tourist attraction; see the Jockey Club website at http://www
    .jockeyclub.org.ar/JockeyNeWeb/ (accessed 11 June 2021). The Club del Progreso
    is even older, founded in 1852 after the defeat of Manuel de Rosas. The club
    stands for the values of classic nineteenth-century liberalism, as the Argentine

oligarchy understood it. Its membership includes many of the nation's past presidents. According to one social historian, the two clubs represent successive stages in the evolution of the sociability of the Buenos Aires bourgeoisie, the Jockey Club corresponding to that class's consolidation and its moment of greatest opulence (Sánchez, "Del *Club del Progreso* al *Jockey Club*").

17   *Nosotros* (1907–43), one of the most influential and long-lasting literary magazines of the twentieth century. *Myriam* (1915–19), an illustrated literary magazine that published, among many others, Alfonsina Storni (Lafleur-Provenzano-Alonso, 161).

18   Herbert Spencer (1820–1903), the English positivist thinker whose social Darwinism was very influential among the Generation of 1880 in Argentina.

19   Ricardo Rojas, *El país de la selva* (1907) (The Land of Jungle).

20   Leopoldo Lugones proposed that *Martín Fierro* and its sequel (1872; 1879) be considered Argentina's national epic, in a lecture series published as *El Payador* (1916) (The Gaucho Minstrel), coinciding with Ortega's first visit to Argentina (cf. 215n36).

21   See 200n1.

22   Tucumán Province. Its capital, San Miguel de Tucumán (founded 1565), is historically and symbolically important. In 1812 it was the site of a decisive battle in the South American Wars of Independence. The Congress of Tucumán consolidated the independence from Spain of the Provincias Unidas de Sudamérica on 9 July 1816; hence, the Avenida 9 de Julio in Buenos Aires, claimed to be the world's widest avenue. See Wilson (226–9).

23   El Escorial, a town in Castilia at the foot of the sere Guadarrama mountain range. In 1561, at the peak of the Spanish Empire, King Felipe II had an enormous monastery built there in honour of San Lorenzo (St Lawrence). In "Mi deuda con Ortega," VO evokes Ortega speaking of his "effervescent youth in the shadow of that mountain of stone domesticated by the edict of a king" amid the scent of white rockroses (*Testimonios, series primera a quinta*, 281).

24   Rosa Spottorno y Topete (1884–1980), wife of Ortega y Gasset.

25   Azorín, pseudonym of Juan Martínez Ruiz (1873–1967), writer of the Generation of 1898.

26   Gregorio Marañón (1887–1960), pioneer of endocrinology and humanist intellectual. Ramón Pérez de Ayala (1880–1962), writer and journalist. Both men, with Ortega, founded in 1931 the Agrupación al Servicio de la República, a group of Spanish intellectuals in defence of the newly declared Second Republic. (The First Republic [1873–1874] had been a short-lived experiment aborted by a military *pronunciamiento*, or coup.)

27   The Argentine version of Harrods, the first and only branch of the British department store, existed from 1914 to 1998. The elegant building on the Calle Florida is still maintained and serves as a venue for various cultural functions.

28 *Mundo Argentino* (founded in 1907), like its sister publication, *El Hogar*, was a very successful family-oriented, middle-class, middlebrow magazine.

29 Dame Rose Macaulay (1881–1958), English novelist, daughter of classical scholar George Campbell Macaulay. Dora Russell, née Black (1894–1986), English feminist, co-author with husband Bertrand Russell of *The Prospects of Industrial Civilisation* (1923). Charlotte Haldane, née Franken (1894–1969), English feminist author of the dystopian novel *Man's World* (1926), but also of *Motherhood and Its Enemies* (1927), later considered to be anti-feminist; her second husband was the famous biologist J.B.S. Haldane.

30 The novel *Inocencia trágica* did get coverage in *Mundo Argentino* (no. 925, October 1928), which MRL consulted (email 2 December 2019), and the novel's "evil" female protagonist appears to allude to Victoria Ocampo, or a woman corrupted by VO's example. Juan José de Soiza Reilly (1880–1959) was a popular journalist and novelist given to lurid sensationalism. His numerous novels, largely forgotten and out of print, include titles such as *No leas este libro … El amor, la mujer y otros venenos* (1926) (Don't Read This Book … Love, Women, and Other Poisons); *La muerte blanca. Amor y cocaína* (1926) (White Death: Love and Cocaine); *¡Criminales! Almas sucias de mujeres y hombres limpios* (1926) (Criminals! Women's Sullied Souls and Unsullied Men), whose prologue reads: "There are other criminals more savage even than thugs of knife and revolver. Others more fearful. Terrible. Horrible … They are delinquents whom no one yet dares to judge … Those criminals live in the most celestial impunity. Criminals!" (qtd. in Josefina Ludmer, *El cuerpo del delito* [Corpus Delicti], 321). A satirical epitaph in *Martín Fierro* 14–15 (25 January 1925) reads: "Soiza Reilly su diarrea / Literaria terminó. / Esta su lápida sea: / L.P.Q.L.P." (Soiza Reilly, his literary diarrhea's finished. Let his tombstone read: Son of goddam bitch.) Nevertheless, Ludmer convincingly argues that Roberto Arlt's novels, especially the now canonical *Los siete locos* (1929) (The Seven Madmen), owe much to Soiza Reilly's writings, in particular Soiza's *La ciudad de los locos* (1914) (The City of Madmen). See also Juan Terranova, "El escritor perdido." (Cf. Introduction, n13.)

31 Concepción Arenal Ponte (1820–1893), Galician writer, social-justice activist, and feminist. The occupation of kiosk-owner, as MRL clarified in an email (2 December 2019), alludes to the novel by Benito Pérez Galdós (often called the Charles Dickens of Spain) titled *La desheredada* (1881) (The Disinherited Woman), whose protagonist Isidora, of humble social origins, has an obsessive fantasy that she is of noble birth and has been unjustly disinherited. When she takes her fantasy to its ultimate consequences by appealing to a noble family, they offer to set her up with a kiosk so she can make a living. She refuses and ends up in prison, where she cries through the bars: "But I am noble! … Judges, lawyers, grandmother, all you people who have brought me here, I am noble! You shall

not take away my nobility, it is my essence and I cannot be without it" (Pérez Galdós, 440).

32 APM here stands for the Association of Professional Musicians, translation of the Asociación del Profesorado Orquestal (APO). In the original, Victoria uses the acronym APO. (Cf. 198n37.)

33 From Ortega's first lecture of his 1928 visit to Buenos Aires (*Meditación de nuestro tiempo*, 202).

34 Reference *Le Vicomte de Bragelonne* (1847–1850), third novel of Alexandre Dumas's trilogy beginning with *Les Trois Mousquetaires*. Vaux Philippe, twin brother of Louis XIV, is shut away in the Bastille. At one point Louis orders his face covered with an iron mask.

35 In her book *Mundo, mi casa. Recuerdos de infancia* (1965) (World, My House: Memories of Childhood) María Rosa Oliver gamely recounts how polio struck at the age of ten, concluding: "Although the consequences of the polio attack conditioned my daily life, strange as it may seem, I recall few things directly related to my paralysis. I installed myself in that condition without noticing any adaptive process. If in those days I suffered moments of anguish, they are not registered in my memory. On the other hand, I do remember asking myself, now and again, what would happen to a child from the nearby tenement buildings or the shacks near the family estate, if they were to fall ill; what kind of care they would receive if, like me, they could not walk on their own. The answers my imagination went on providing for those questions were indeed something I could never get used to" (183).

36 The Confitería del Gas (formerly, the Confitería del León) was located across the street from the Compañía del Gas, newly built in 1856. Taking advantage of the novelty, the confitería mounted two gas lamps outside its door, thus earning its popular moniker ("Confitería del Gas," *Historias inesperadas* [blog by *La Nación*], 20 August 2013, http://blogs.lanacion.com.ar/historia-argentina /arquitectura-2/confiteria-del-gas/). Another upscale café was the Confitería del Águila, established in 1852. When the president of Brazil came to Buenos Aires in 1900, the official reception was held at the Águila ("Confitería del Águila," *Café contado* [blog], https://cafecontado.com/tag/confiteria-del-aguila/, accessed 11 June 2021).

37 The original passage is worth quoting *in extenso*: "I knew that I would never walk on my own … that my body would not develop fully and harmoniously, and that in a house of short people I would be the shortest of all. I knew this but I cannot say that I resigned myself to it. I cannot say that for two reasons. First, because resignation implies a deliberate ignoring of a suffering which I, at least consciously, did not feel. Second, because it assumes a passive acceptance to a superior will which for me did not exist. There was no one to blame for my

misfortune. And since no one could be held to account for it, the best thing was to pay it no heed, as far as possible. There were other things in life to be answered for, and not by a supernatural will but rather by someone or something" (Oliver, *La vida cotidiana*, 39–40). Those "other things in life," as the continuation of the passage descriptively makes clear, were social and economic injustice.

38 Reference to the Basque sport played in an outdoor or indoor court with a hard rubber ball (*pelota*) which, as in the game of squash, is bounced off a solid wall or *frontón* using a curved wooden bat (alternatively, a racquet or even just the hand).

39 The Café Tortoni (Avenida de Mayo 835): "the most prestigious literary café still standing in Buenos Aires" (Wilson, 80) hosted many famous writers and celebrities, including Rubén Darío, Alfonsina Storni, Luigi Pirandello; even Ortega once spoke there (Wilson, 81). The Confitería Richmond (Calle Florida 468), another elegant downtown café and meeting-place for artists and intellectuals, was a favourite haunt in the 1920s of the *Martín Fierro* group (Borges, Marechal, and many others). The Richmond closed in 2011.

40 Algernon Charles Swinburne (1837–1909), Romantic English poet, playwright, and contributor to the famous eleventh edition of the *Encyclopædia Britannica*, known for his intense lyricism and unconventional behaviour; he frequented the Pre-Raphaelite group of painters and poets.

41 George Eliot (pen name of Mary Anne Evans), author of *Middlemarch* (1871–72). In that novel, the middle-aged Reverend Edward Casaubon, a pedantic and selfish clergyman, marries the idealistic nineteen-year-old Dorothea Brooke, who dreams of helping him write his book on Christian syncretism, *The Key to All Mythologies*. The marriage, for her, is a mistake.

42 The *jota* is the name for the letter "j" in Spanish, pronounced very differently from the English "jay."

43 Karl Christian Friedrich Krause (1781–1832), a post-Kantian German thinker, influential in the liberal circles of nineteenth-century Spain and Spanish America.

44 Hipólito Yrigoyen (1852–1933) was the first Argentine president to be elected, in 1916, under the new law of universal male suffrage and the secret ballot. For the first time, the burgeoning Argentine middle classes, with a large immigrant component, gained political representation. The reaction to Yrigoyen's reforms in favour of the working and middle classes came from within his own party, the Unión Cívica Radical. The conservative faction of the Radicals, under Marcel Torcuato de Alvear, held the presidency from 1922 to 1928. The more popular Yrigoyen was re-elected president in 1928 (cf. 224n47).

45 The Committee of Young Intellectuals for Yrigoyen did indeed exist as described in the novel. The members named here were all active in the literary

208 Notes to pages 79–80

avant-garde of contemporary Buenos Aires. Their political orientations varied: Nicolás Olivari, Roberto Arlt, and the brothers Raúl and Enrique González Tuñón were more left-wing than the others. Most participated to some degree in the journal *Martín Fierro* (1924–27), except for Nicolás Olivari and Roberto Arlt. The literary scene was riven by two different approaches to literature. The Florida group championed avant-garde aesthetics without political commitment; the Boedo group, aesthetically more conventional, believed in socially/politically committed literature. The two tendencies were real, the polemical fireworks intense, but the writers of both groups all knew each other. The composition of the Yrigoyen Committee shows that *martinfierristas* like Borges and Marechal inhabited the same social space as a Boedo writer like Olivari. The best fictional representation of that generation of writers and artists is Leopoldo Marechal's novel *Adán Buenosayres* (1948) (English translation *Adam Buenosayres*, 2014). Victoria Ocampo, in the 1920s, apparently had little or nothing to do with this effervescent literary scene.

46 Undated letter from Ortega to VO (Meyer, 63).

47 In the original: Ortega was leaving *con pena, con gloria* (*Las libres*, 145) (with heartache, with glory), an inversion of the expression *sin pena ni gloria*, an idiomatic phrase used to describe a mediocre performance by, for example, an athlete or artist: not a total failure, minimally acceptable, but unremarkable and uninspiring.

48 Ortega, "Epílogo al libro *De Francesca a Beatrice*" (cf. n96).

49 A veiled allusion to *La Trahison des clercs* (1927), a polemic by Julien Benda denouncing the betrayal by intellectuals of the higher interests of humanity in favour of nationalism and populism.

50 Ortega first expressed these ideas in his Fourth and Fifth Lectures in 1928 in Buenos Aires, respectively titled "Masas, dinero, política" (Masses, Money, Politics) and "El peligro de nuestro tiempo" (The Danger of Our Time). In the fourth lecture, he opposes the "masses" to the "select minorities." A "mass-man" feels he is just one more in the crowd; the "select man" is not to be confused with "the petulant man who thinks himself superior to others, but rather the man who demands more of himself than others do, even if he cannot personally achieve these superior demands" (*Meditación de nuestro tiempo*, 247). Ortega will develop these ideas further in his controversial *Rebelión de las masas* (1930), first translated into English in 1932 as *Revolt of the Masses*, retranslated by Anthony Kerrigan in 1985. That book became Ortega's most widely read work in Argentina (Earle, 483). His critique of "mass-man," according to Ortega's defenders, does not specifically refer to the lower, uneducated classes. For his critics, however, Ortega's apparent evasion of class conflict is a subterfuge dissimulating his essentially right-leaning politics. The novelized María Rosa Oliver alludes to this with her remark that he seeks those

"select minorities" among the upper classes. Peter Earle insinuates that during the Spanish Civil War (1936–39) Ortega was implicitly on the side of the Fascists: "He was not *independent* in his retreat to silence as his country tore itself apart. Rather, he deluded himself into thinking that he was neutral, despite the glaring [anti-left-ist] bias seen in his 'Epílogo para ingleses'" – an epilogue added to *Rebelión de las masas* in its 1938 edition (Earle, 481, 483). Ricardo Piglia likely had this book in mind when, in his classic *Respiración artificial* (1980) (*Artificial Respiration*, 1994), his character Tardewski, an alienated Polish intellectual, dubs Ortega the "Rey de los Asnos Españoles" (King of Spanish Jackasses) and his disciple (and Keyserling's Spanish-language translator), Manuel García Morente, as "Spanish Jackass Number Two" (*Respiración*, 171, 168).

51 These ideas of Ortega's come from "La Pampa ... promesas" (*Meditación del pueblo joven*, 105–15).

52 Roberto Arlt's popular *aguafuertes*, verbal sketches of *porteño* characters, appeared in the daily *El Mundo*. Collected since in many volumes, including his *Aguafuertes gallegas* (1997) (Galician Etchings). In his trip through Spain in 1935, Arlt would indeed appreciate Galician women in particular (Lojo, "Independizarse de España," 214–15).

53 El Molino (1915–1997), another famous *confitería* in downtown Buenos Aires (Avenida Rivadavia 1815), is an outstanding example of Art Nouveau architecture.

54 MRL quotes from the original version of the poem "Casi Juicio Final" (Almost Last Judgment): "Pobre de amor yo fui. / Sin embargo, las calles y la luna aún están a mi lado./ El agua sigue siendo dulce en mi boca y las estrofas no me niegan su gracia./ Siento el pavor de la belleza: ¿quién se atreverá a condenarme si esta gran luna de mi soledad me perdona?" (*Luna de enfrente*, 25). The English translation is mine, except for the title *Moon Across the Way* (see Borges, *Selected Poems*, 31ff). Later editions of the poem, in Borges's collected works, have significant variations.

CHAPTER THREE

1 Original: *Reise durch die Zeit* (1948). There is no English translation of the work, perhaps an indication of how far out of favour Keyserling had fallen, post–Second World War, in the English-speaking world. However, the Editorial Sudamericana published it in Buenos Aires in two volumes: *Viaje a través del tiempo. Origen y desarrollo* (1949); and *Viaje a través del tiempo. La aventura del alma* (1951) in J. Rovira Armengol's translation.

2 Keyserling's visits to all these places are recounted in the two volumes of *The Travel Diary of a Philosopher*, probably his best work.

3 VO-Keyserling correspondence in *Autobiografía, II* (219–33): "These letters

reached the culminating point of their exaltation *before* Versailles. Upon re-reading them, I was not surprised that K. got the wrong impression from the get-go" (211).

4 One of four major train stations in Buenos Aires. An unofficial neighbourhood in the barrio of Balvanera, the Once is the shortened form of Once de Septiembre (Eleventh of September) of the year 1852, when, after the Battle of Pavón, Buenos Aires and environs declared itself a separate state from the Argentine Confederation; the quasi-independence lasted until 1861. In the words of Germinal Nogués, "Saturday mornings in Buenos Aires the Plaza Once bursts into life, revealing the city's South American soul. There you find the same rhythm, the same noise, the same people, and the same colourful shop windows as you might find in Bogotá, or La Paz, or in Lima" (qtd. in Wilson, 262).

5 Carmen is thinking of the Spanish proverb: *Mejor solo que mal acompañado* ("Better to go on your own than in bad company").

6 The idiom means literally: "the poor fellow can't see three [persons] on a donkey." It is not peculiar to Galicia, as Marechal implies here, but is common throughout Spain. In popular Argentine usage, the term *gallego* (Galician) often extends (erroneously) to Spaniards in general.

7 La Perla del Once, a cafeteria that first became legendary thanks to the tertulias of Macedonio Fernández with the young avant-garde writers (Borges et al.). In the 1960s it became famous as a hang-out for the first generation of Buenos Aires rock musicians.

8 Macedonio Fernández (1874–1952). A legendary figure in Argentine literature; poet, metaphysician, humourist, brilliant conversationalist, he was the adopted mentor of the *martinfierristas*. He maintained an epistolary correspondence with the American philosopher William James. In 1928 the "illegible papers" mentioned in the novel were indeed gathered up by some of Macedonio's young "disciples" – Raúl Scalabrini Ortiz, Leopoldo Marechal, and Francisco Bernárdez – and published under the title *No toda es vigilia la de los ojos abiertos* (approximately: Not All Consciousness Is of the Waking Kind), a series of meditations on his doctrine of "absolute subjectivism or idealism." Being, writes Macedonio, is "*un almismo ayoico*" (25), literally: a non-selfish soul-ism or soulishness. The following year a miscellany of stories and humorous writings were collected under the title *Papeles de recienvenido* (Papers of a Newcomer). According to his biographer Álvaro Abós, he too participated in the above-mentioned Committee of Young Intellectuals for Irigoyen (Abós, *Macedonio*, 135–6).

9 *Luna de enfrente* (1925) (Moon Across the Way). Carmen recites from Borges's poem "Dulcia linquimus arva" (our country's sweet fields), a partial quote from Virgil's *Eclogues*: *nos patriae finis et dulcia linquimus arva*; "we are leaving our

country's bounds and sweet fields," says Melibœus to Tityrus at the beginning of the first Eclogue (Virgil, 25).

Borges's poem recalls the vocation of his military forebears who fought in the hinterland, then exploited it as *estancieros*. In contrast to them, the poet confesses: "Soy un pueblero y ya no sé de esas cosas, / soy hombre de ciudad, de barrio, de calle: / los tranvías lejanos me ayudan la tristeza / con esa queja larga que sueltan en las tardes" (*Obras completas*, vol. 1, 68). The translation by Thomas de Giovanni (with the help of Borges himself) reads: "As a town dweller I no longer know these things. / I come from a city, a neighborhood, a street: / distant streetcars enforce my nostalgia / with the wail they let loose in the night" (Borges, *Selected Poems 1923–1967*, 39). A more literal translation would be: "I am a townsman and no longer know these things. / *I'm a city man, a barrio man, a man of the street:* / distant streetcars swell my sadness / with their long plaintive wail in the late afternoon" (my translation; my emphasis). The Borges of the 1960s could never think of himself as "a man of the street"; with the English translation he is attempting to cast a veil over his youthful enthusiasm for popular culture, which the conservative elderly Borges came to abhor.

10 An allusion to a scene in Marechal's novel *Adán Buenosayres* (1948), where the quasi-autobiographical Adam recalls how the chambermaid Irma seduced him one spring morning: "he left off reading to look at what she wished him to see, even though he felt she didn't want him to look, not suspecting that she wanted him not to suspect that she wanted him to see, O Eve!" (Marechal, *Adam Buenosayres*, 17). Even though Adam, alluding to Schopenhauer, blames "Nature's famous trap," he still manages to tilt the burden of guilt toward Irma by implying her active collusion with "Nature" in contrast to his passive victimization.

11 Morón and Castelar, originally rural municipalities west of the city, have now been absorbed by the enormous Metropolitan Region of Buenos Aires. In the late nineteenth and early twentieth century, they had many *quintas*, or recreational country estates, for the upper-class families of Buenos Aires. María Rosa Lojo is a lifelong resident of Castelar.

12 In Spanish: Mar Océana (Latin *mare oceanus*, "ocean sea"). The term harks back to Homer's "ocean-stream" which, the ancients supposed, encompassed the disc of the earth.

13 A near-quote from Marechal's famous verse: "La Patria es un dolor que aún no sabe su nombre" (The Patria is a sorrow that knows not yet its name) in *Heptámeron* (1966) [Seven Days' Work]; several variants of this verse, in incantatory style, articulate the "Second Day: Discovery of the Patria" (*Obras completas*, vol. 1, 301). Cf. the *Canto de San Martín* (1950) (Song of San Martín): "¡La Patria es

un gran amor / que llora recién nacido!" (The Patria is a great love that cries like a newborn child!) (240).

14 The Patria figured as a *niña* or *muchacha* (little girl or girl) recurs throughout Marechal's poetic oeuvre; for example, in the poem "Niña de encabritado corazón" (Girl of Restive Heart) (*Obras completas*, vol. 1, 127–9); or in "De la adolescente" (On the Adolescent Girl): "La niña entre alabanzas amanece: / cantado es su verdor, / increíble su muerte" (The girl dawns amid praise: / her verdure is sung / her death unthinkable) (143). And again: "¡En las tierras australes … ríe tu Patria … con toda la frescura … de sus muchachas!" (In southern lands … your Patria laughs … with all the freshness … of its girls!) (242). In her article "La 'Patria Hija' de Leopoldo Marechal," MRL avows that Marechal's image of the "Nation as daughter" was important to her own development of a concept of the Argentine nation.

15 During the South American Wars of Independence (1810–24), the rebellious American-born criollos pejoratively called their Spanish-loyalist adversaries *godos* (Goths), alluding to the Christianized Visigoths who, in the wake of the demise of the Roman Empire, took over most of the Iberian Peninsula in the sixth century CE until they were challenged by the Islamic invasion of 711 CE. Spanish conservatism has traditionally identified itself with the medieval Christian culture established by the Visigothic regime.

16 The liberal Unitarian Party was for decades pitted against the conservative Federal Party during the civil wars that followed upon Argentine independence. The *unitarios* were porteño-based, friendly to northern European capitalism and to modern French, English, and North American cultural values, and hostile to Spain and the Catholic Church. The *federales* defended traditional Spanish culture and religion; their support base was rural and popular.

17 Juan José Catriel (1838–1910), one of a dynasty of chiefs of the indigenous Pampa nation. In the story "El Sur," Dalmann (Borges's fictional alter ego) recalls that his grandfather was killed by Catriel's men.

18 Borges will eventually turn the anecdote into his story "El otro duelo" (The Other Duel), collected in his book *El informe de Brodie* (1970).

19 The Humid Pampa (as opposed to the Dry Pampa) is an area of fertile grassland that covers most of Buenos Aires Province and large swathes of the adjoining provinces of Córdoba, Santa Fe, and La Pampa.

20 The Mapuche peoples have traditionally occupied the territory spanning the Andes in what is now Chile and Argentina. The Voroganos originated in Chile, then migrated into Argentina during the colonial period (Márquez Llano, 11).

21 "Mary Janes"; in Spanish, *zapatos guillermina*. A style of low-cut shoe with a strap across the instep, very popular with women in the 1920s. Also known as "bar shoes."

22 Lucio V. Mansilla (1831–1913), writer of the Generation of 1880, author of the
canonical *Una excursión a los indios ranqueles* (1870) (*A Visit to the Ranquel
Indians*). He is made a character in MRL's novel *La pasión de los nómades* (1994)
(*Passionate Nomads*).

23 Beginning with the detail of the Weil edition of *The Arabian Nights*, this whole
episode parodies Borges's widely anthologized short story "El Sur" (The South)
(in *Artificios*, 1944). The protagonist, Juan Dahlmann, travels south by train
from Buenos Aires. At a rustic *almacén* three rough gaucho-types tease him by
throwing nuggets of bread at his face. At the story's end, Dahlmann, knife in
hand, faces almost certain death in a duel.

24 *America Set Free* (New York: Harper, 1929). Keyserling wrote the book in English.

25 Keyserling praises the "institution of the Geishas" (*Travel Diary*, vol. 2, 189–205).
The Geishas' dance "produces the effect of angels in mediæval pictures of paradise" (189). The Japanese aestheticization of sex moves him to a polemic
against the Christian West: "This beautiful system is not applicable to us. Not
because we are better, but because we are too brutal on the one hand, and, on
the other, too biased by the ideas of Christian asceticism" (200).

26 Keyserling's theory of the three types of woman was apparently inspired by
the dancing at Udaipur, a legacy of that Indian city's medieval court and its
erotic culture. By contrast, the eroticism of the modern West, he wrote, was:
"threadbare and bad. In northern countries [it was] never good. There it
happens too rarely that a man is brought up and formed by women; without
training, his erotic faculties do not develop and as woman only exceptionally
satisfies higher demands than man makes upon her directly, no progress
takes place. Germanic men know, in matters of love, generally only two
things: vice and marriage. Both are equally bad means to erotic culture. Both
encourage laxity; both devitalise ... In the East to-day, and in the West during the period of classic antiquity, the corresponding feminine type was only
to be found amongst courtesans. From the Renaissance onwards this type has
separated itself more and more into a definite caste, and since the eighteenth
century it coincides with the ideal type of the lady of the great world. The
ancient courtesan and the modern Grande Dame are in reality of one spirit,
of one being; only the latter stands on a higher level because she is more universal. What men do not owe to intercourse with such women!" (180).
"[O]nly women of polygamous tendencies, possessing a wide emotional
horizon, women with varied sympathies and many-sided characters, are destined to the position of the queen, of the muse and the sibyl. The virtues of
the housewife preclude a wide and grand scale of effectiveness; the woman
who aspires to this scale thereby proves that she is not a type of motherhood" (181–2).

27 Teresa de Ávila (cf. 192n2). Mariana Alcoforado (1640–1723), Portuguese writer, nun of the Franciscan order of the Poor Clares. A series of passionate love letters, first published in Paris in 1669 as *Les Lettres Portugaises*, were attributed first to her, then by later scholarship to various French male writers. However, Myriam Cyr has recently argued for Mariana Alcoforado's authorship (*Letters of a Portuguese Nun*). See also Roxana Maria Popescu (105–11).

28 *Para Ti* (For You), a fashion magazine founded in Buenos Aires in 1922. At one time a weekly publication, it still exists as a monthly at https://www.parati .com.ar/. Isabella Cosse (3) suggests that *Para Ti* was somewhat liberal regarding feminine style and sexual education.

29 *El Hogar* (The Home), an illustrated family magazine, almost an institution of middle-class Argentine society. Founded in 1904 by Alberto M. Haynes, founder also of *Mundo Argentino*.

30 Eva María Duarte (1919–1952), later Juan Perón's wife. See Introduction.

31 The list alternates names of Argentine and Hollywood celebrities, with one exception. The Argentines are: Carlos Gardel (1890–1935), tango singer and movie star, first Latin American to record with RCA Victor. Olinda Bozán (1894–1977), actress in theatre and film. Tita Merello (1904–2002), tango singer and actress in popular theatre and film. Enrique Muiño (1881–1956), Galician-born actor who started out in the circus of the Brothers Podestá (a family of Genoan immigrants, pioneers of popular theatre in the River Plate region). Angelina Pagano (1888–1962), actress, famous especially for her work in children's theatre in 1920s and '30s Buenos Aires. The exception is Raquel Meller (1888–1962), Spanish actress who spent two years in Argentina during the Spanish Civil War.

32 "Mi dolor" (My Heart-Ache) (1930). Music by Carlos Marcucci. Lyrics by Manuel Meaños: "I'm back from distant lands / where in yesteryear I went seeking oblivion for my heart-ache [...] Heading for oblivion, which is a balm for suffering / I left taking my bitterness with me" ("Mi dolor," Todo Tango website, https://www.todotango.com/english/music/song/434/Mi-dolor/, accessed 11 June 2021; my translation).

33 Federico García Lorca's celebrated *Llanto por Ignacio Sánchez Mejías* (1935) is an elegy to a bullfighter gored to death in 1934. The first part, "The Goring and the Death," repeats on every other line the phrase "At five o'clock in the afternoon," marking the moment of death like the rhythmic tolling of a bell. See Sarah Arvio's bilingual edition, *Poet in Spain* (311–29).

34 In the original: *tortas fritas*, apparently similar to bannock bread.

35 La Virgen de Luján is an advocation of the Virgin Mary in Luján, a small town not far west of Buenos Aires. Emblematic of Argentine Catholicism, her cult dates from the seventeenth century. Since the nation's foundation, political and

military leaders have made a point of attending worship services in her honour. The lavish and imposing Basílica de Nuestra Señora de Luján was consecrated in 1930 during a period when the Argentine Church was pushing to regain protagonism in the public and political life of the nation.

36 His name combines the Christian name of Estanislao del Campo (1834–1880) and the surname of José Hernández (1834–1886), two key authors in the gauchesque tradition. Del Campo wrote *Fausto. Impresiones del gaucho Anastasio el Pollo en la representación en esta Ópera* (1866), in which the fictitious gaucho Anastasio the Chicken, after attending *Faust* at the Colón Theatre in Buenos Aires, tells in rustic gaucho language how he understood Gounod's opera. Hernández authored *El Gaucho Martín Fierro* (1872) and *La vuelta de Martín Fierro* (1879) (The Return of Martín Fierro), the quintessential gauchesque poem, later construed as the Argentine national epic (cf. 204n20).

37 Ignacio Coliqueo (1786–1871). Born in Chile, descendant of Caupolicán, Coliqueo was – like other great indigenous warriors – an important actor in the shifting military and political alliances of the civil wars following upon Argentine independence in 1810. In 1834 he became a lifelong friend of Manuel Baigorria, a Unitarian general in exile among the Ranquel Indians, who married Coliqueo's daughter. His relationship with Calfucurá (an ally of Manuel de Rosas for several decades), was fraught; mostly they were enemies, but after Rosas's downfall in 1852, Coliqueo became Calfucurá's second-in-command in the latter's campaign to unite all tribes under the watchword *La tierra india al indio* (Indian Land to the Indian People) (Figueiras, 39). Eventually, Coliqueo and Baigorria threw in their lot with Bartolomé Mitre; in return, the victorious Mitre granted lands in the zone of present-day Los Toldos to Coliqueo and his people. At his death in 1871, Ignacio Coliqueo was the last of his tribe to be buried according to the traditional funeral rites, in a Mapuche *curacahuin* (Figueiras, 98). By contrast, at his death in 1902 Simón Coliqueo was buried with full military honours, his coffin wrapped in the Argentine flag; no Mapuche customs were observed (Figueiras, 99). The Coliqueo line continues to this day. Doctor Haroldo A. Coliqueo, great-grandson of Ignacio Coliqueo, published in 1985 a basic dictionary of the Mapuche language (partially reproduced by Figueiras [85–94]).

38 The story of María Hortensia Roca (MHR), AKA *la santa María*, as told by Susana Dillon in her book *Las locas del camino* (Mad Women of the Road), illustrates not only intercultural conflict but also transcultural *exchange*. As Dillon remarks, "the rebel history of [women-]*machis* who were sanctified by *Indians and foreigners* continues to be ignored" (215; my emphasis). MHR's father was a white settler. Her mother, Rufina Morales, was daughter of Chief Antonio Namuncurá, the son of the great Chief Juan Calfucurá, aka "Lord of the Pampas." MHR's surname, however, came from her godfather, General Julio Argenti-

no Roca (1843–1914), chief architect of the so-called Conquista del Desierto, now usually considered a genocidal war on the indigenous peoples of Argentina. At the death of her husband, MHR began following *la reina Bibiana* (Queen Bibiana), an itinerant preacher of Spanish blood, wife of the son of Cipriano Catriel (an indigenous dynasty), and transculturated *machi*. MHR in turn became a *machi* with a multitudinous following of her own. They were not only Indians; gauchos, Spaniards, and Italians also flocked to her speaking events, which often became spontaneous celebrations and got out of hand. Such, it seems, was the incident referenced by the novel. There are at least two incompatible versions of the event, both of them incomplete and murky: one by Susana Dillon, another by white-settler amateur historians (Miguel Ángel Figueiras, following Padre Meinrado Hux). The latter narrative is one of "good Indians" (Simón Coliqueo) versus the "bad Indians" led by the Santa María, subversive insurrectionist. Dillon, by contrast, makes it sound like an a-political, out-of-control party, at worst a spontaneous mob action, brutally repressed by the police. The two versions coincide on a few basic facts: it happened in August 1900; Chief Simón Coliqueo called in the police from a nearby town; forty-six persons were arrested, including MHR; she died in 1943. Dillon adds that MHR was held in jail only briefly, "due to her family lineage" (215). Which lineage: her great-grandfather Calfucurá or her godfather General Julio Roca? Or both?

39 Pancho is the Spanish name Francisco.

40 *Carrera* or *corrida de sortija*: equestrian games dating back to the European and North African Middle Ages. The horseman goes at full gallop through a wooden frame two to three metres in height and must insert a *palillo* (small stick), carried between his teeth, through a ring suspended from the frame's transversal beam.

41 Francisco Brey's tale has historical verisimilitude. Figueiras reproduces a 1917 photo of a family reunion, forty-odd persons gathered in Tapera de Díaz: "in their physical traits and clothing one observes the fusion of customs and races: Spanish-Mapuche, Basque-Mapuche, and Italian-Mapuche" (115).

42 Carmen recalls, in the original Galician language, verses by Rosalía de Castro (1837–1885). The first is poem 15 of the *Cantares gallegos* (1863) (Songs of Galicia), written when the poet, living in Madrid, was lonely and homesick for Galicia (Carballo Calero, 12). Cf. 193n8.

43 Rosalía de Castro, *Follas novas* (1880) (New Leaves), from the final section, "As viudas d'os vivos e as viudas d'os mortos" (The Widows of the Living and the Widows of the Dead). Carmen recalls verses from the "¡Pra Habana!" (To Havana!); its fifth stanza reads: "This one leaves, that one leaves, / and all of them, all of them leave, / Galicia, you are left without men / who can work your soil. / You have instead orphaned girls and boys / and fields that are solitary, /

and mothers who have no sons / and sons who have no fathers. / And you have hearts that suffer / long absences without end, / widows of the living and the dead / whom no one can console" (translated by Havard, 44). The book is dedicated to the Galician Welfare Society in Havana, Cuba (Havard, 43).

44 The Banda Oriental refers to the east bank of the Uruguay River and the River Plate, the waterway forming the border between Argentina and Uruguay (República Oriental del Uruguay). Uruguay, until its independence in 1822, was one of the Provincias Unidas del Río de la Plata (United Provinces of the River Plate). With the term "Banda Oriental," Borges signals his romantic nostalgia for the times when Argentina and Uruguay were all one.

45 The term *gringo* in rural Argentina refers mainly to Italian farmers and small-business persons who, in the late nineteenth century, brought unwelcome competition to the established criollo landowners.

46 Marechal quotes from his "Poema del sol indio" (Poem of the Indian Sun): "Yo te anuncio una tierra donde cada mañana parirá un dios distinto" from the 1926 collection *Días como flechas* (Days like Arrows) (*Obras completas*, vol. 1, 114). Carmen again alludes to the poem a moment later with the sentence "burn your hands with the new sun."

47 Borges recounts the tale in his "Historia del guerrero y de la cautiva" (in *El Aleph*, 1949) (Story of the Warrior and the Captive) (*Labyrinths*, 127–31). María Rosa Lojo studies the theme of the white European woman taken captive by indigenes, a constant since colonial times, in the introduction to her edition of *Lucía Miranda* (1860), by Eduarda Mansilla.

CHAPTER FOUR

1 Conversation between Waldo Frank and María Rosa Oliver (*La vida cotidiana*, 258–9). Frank has invited her to lunch at a restaurant on the Calle Florida to recruit her for the project of a new inter-American journal. A moment later he tells her she must talk to Victoria Ocampo, "today if possible." But it was VO who called María Rosa that same day in the evening (259).

2 VO, "La mujer, sus derechos y sus responsabilidades" (1936). English translation in Meyer (228–34).

3 Napoleon's post-Revolutionary "Premier Empire" (1804–14).

4 Maurice Barrès (1862–1923), a major figure of right-wing French nationalism. Drieu compared his book *Un homme libre* (1889) to the great works of Montaigne and Pascal, and reread it every year, as did his personal friend and ideological antagonist, the Surrealist Louis Aragon (Desanti, 163).

5 *Le Jeune Européen* (1927). A political essay in which Drieu projects a new totalized Europe arising from the ruins of nationalism, its myths destroyed by the

First World War, but rejects "[n]arrow fascisms, babbling communisms, hysterical surrealisms ... feeble harbingers of a terrible weakness" (qtd. in Carroll, 133).

6 *L'Homme couvert de femmes* (1925). The protagonist Gilles, like his author, torments and is tormented in his relations with women. He even claims he is not the hunter but the prey (Desanti, 176). Gilles/Drieu dissimulated his psycho-sexual problems with cynical donjuanism; with this novel Drieu "fait éclater la convention don juanique" (explodes the Don Juan myth) (Desanti, 174).

7 *Blèche* (Weak) (1928). The protagonist Blanquans (another avatar of Drieu) is a conservative Catholic writer, a polemicist who lost his faith in God at the age of sixteen. Misanthropist and misogynist, he avoids his family and prefers the solitude of his room. VO did leaf through this book, as in the novel. She recalls a passage about the horror one feels for flesh one does not desire – surely a reminder of her Keyserling problem (*Autobiografía III*, 60–1).

8 *Genève ou Moscou* (1928), a book advocating for a strong, unified Europe and against nationalism and racism. Drieu will later abandon these ideas.

9 VO was a teetotaller (Meyer, 206). Ernesto Sábato recalls the long, abstemious meetings of *Sur*'s editorial committee: "one of her extravagances," he drolly observes, "Victoria was as ruthless as a Mormon or an Anabaptist" (qtd. in Liendo, 14).

10 "Saint Louis" was the French King Louis IX (1226–1270), canonized by the Church in 1297 and known as "le Prudhomme" (literally, a wise or sensible man; the "prudhomme" was a knightly ideal).

11 Letter from Drieu to VO, 28 June 1929 (Ocampo, *Autobiografía III*, 105). VO reproduces a portion of their correspondence from 1919 to 1942 in *Autobiografía III* (93–123).

12 Letter from Drieu to VO, 10 May 1929 (*Autobiografía III*, 97). In the same letter he writes that Keyserling is a charlatan.

13 Alejandro Bustillo (1889–1982), architect of many houses of Argentine aristocrats. A critic observed in *La Nación* in 1929 that "Señor Alejandro Bustillo ... a convinced classicist, was the one to design the house of Señora Victoria, following her instructions. He has done so against his convictions" (qtd. in Sarlo, *La máquina cultural*, 180–1). VO drew sketches in what she thought to be the style of Le Corbusier and had Bustillo execute the project. Beatriz Sarlo uses the episode as grist for her argument that VO was essentially a cultural translator, the house in Palermo being the first major "translation" of European modernist architecture to Buenos Aires (180). (Cf. 221n30.)

14 Alfonso Reyes (1889–1959), a great Mexican writer, scholar, and diplomat. He was in close touch with the avant-garde literary scene in Buenos Aires and elsewhere. His influential article "Jitanjáforas," a playful theorization of vanguard nominalism, appeared in the single 1929 issue of *Libra*, a journal originally projected by Leopoldo Marechal, Francisco Bernárdez, and Jorge Luis Borges (Borges withdrew beforehand; the journal died after one issue). See Rose Corral (*Libra*, 14–15).

15 Bernardino Rivadavia (1780–1845), first president of the United Provinces of Río de la Plata and promoter of Unitarian ideology: anti-clerical liberalism, Euro-friendly free trade, strong central government in Buenos Aires. His attempt to impose the Constitution of 1826, without the agreement of the provinces, resulted in civil war.

16 Juan Facundo Quiroga (1788–1835), leader and governor of the province of La Rioja, his influence extending over the neighbouring northwestern provinces. He sided with the Federalists during the Civil War. His spectacular murder in 1835 remains an unsolved mystery. Sarmiento mythified him as a figure of barbarity in *Facundo, o civilización y barbarie* (1845), nicknaming him the Tigre de los Llanos (Tiger of the Plains), whereas the great revisionist historian Vicente D. Sierra describes him as "un magnífico exponente del más puro señorío criollo" (Sierra, 510b) (a magnificent exponent of the purest criollo dignity).

17 "Quitilipe horse" means albino horse. The gauchos considered albino horses weak and unfit, because their bulging eyes reacted badly to bright sunlight.

18 Karl von Phorner (or Pforner or Pförtner) was a historical person. Departing from a footnote in David Peña's 1986 biography of *Juan Manuel de Rosas*, MRL elaborated his love story in *Amores insólitos de nuestra historia* (2001) (Incredible Love Stories in Argentine History) and retells it with new historical detail in "El improbable amor del alemán y la riojana" ("The Improbable Love of the German and the Riojana"), *La Nación* (22 September 2020, online). "The Mining Adventure of Rivadavia" (Sierra, 506–10) created a conflict in which two companies, both backed by British capital, were promised the same mining rights. Rivadavia was president of the Board of the River Plate Mining Company, a deal he personally arranged in London. Meanwhile, Argentine investors at home, including Quiroga, formed the Famatina Mining Company. The resulting imbroglio stymied both companies. Quiroga thwarted the plans of the River Plate Company; the outbreak of the civil war in 1827 aborted the operations of Famatina. Sierra mentions Carlos von Pforner, a captain of mines brought from Europe by the Famatina group (510b).

19 In his chapter on "Gana" in *South American Meditations* (1932), Keyserling recalls this incident of the golf course, changing it to a tennis court where the child was offered a peso an hour to pick up the balls. He construes the phrase *porque no me da la gana* as meaning "Gana does not urge me to so do" (158), artificially attributing agency to the "principle of GANA": "an unconscious elementary force which urges from within, over which consciousness has no control" (158). The chapter, and much of the book, is a thinly veiled exercise in pique and revenge against VO's rejection of his advances. Ocampo responded to his accusations, after his death, in *El viajero y una de sus sombras (Keyserling en mis memorias)* (The Traveller and One of his Shadows/Shades) (1951; cf. MRL, "El viajero"). His obsession with snakes comes from his own dreams and dark fantasies; he dubbed VO "the Anaconda of the Pampa." As Amy Kaminsky aptly observes in "Victoria Ocampo and the Keyserling Effect": "*South American Meditations* may well be the clearest example of the way foreigners find in Argentina a screen onto which to project their own desires, fears, and concerns" (Kaminsky, *Argentina*, 97).

20 The Torre de los Ingleses was built by the British residents of Buenos Aires in 1910 for the centenary of Argentine Independence. Its location in the small Plaza Fuerza Aérea (formerly, the Plaza Británica) is close to the stately Plaza San Martín. It has been officially renamed the Torre Monumental.

21 Carmen's thought hinges on the Spanish idiom *ahogarse en un vaso de agua* (to drown in a glass of water), approximately equivalent to the English "make a mountain out of molehill."

22 Señor Sovotnik may have read too much Soiza-Reilly-style pulp fiction (cf. nn8, 111); he assumes any well-dressed single woman to be in the sex trade. For discussion of the anxieties about sexual commerce in early-twentieth-century Argentina, see Donna Guy, *Sex and Danger in Buenos Aires* (1991).

23 *Los siete locos* (1929) (The Seven Madmen) and its sequel *Los lanzallamas* (1931) (The Flamethrowers), long rejected as substandard by *Sur*, are now canonical. In the prologue to *Los lanzallamas* Arlt snarls at the literary establishment and vows to write like "un *cross* a la mandíbula" (a cross straight to the jaw). In the 1950s and '60s Arlt was lionized by the literary counterculture as a writer of *porteño* noir. Ricardo Piglia's literary alter ego, Emilio Renzi, champions Arlt as the first "truly modern writer" of twentieth-century Argentine fiction (*Respiración artificial*, 133).

24 Frank's novels – among them, the experimental *City Block* (1922) – were noted but not successful, unlike his book-length essays, beginning with *Our America* (1919). *Salvos: An Informal Book about Books and Plays* (1924) is a collection of occasional pieces. *Virgin Spain: Scenes from the Spiritual Drama of a Great People* (1926) and later books were well received in the Hispanic world. Fluent in Spanish, Frank published in Madrid newspapers where he polemicized briefly with

Ramiro de Maeztu (cf. 201n3) (Chapman, "Waldo Frank in Spanish America," 510–12). Frank's *Primer mensaje a la América Hispana* (First Message to Hispanic America) (1930) was published only in Spanish.

25 Frank recounts this scene in *Memoirs* (173). Vicente López is a suburb of Buenos Aires, at that time about half an hour by train from the city centre.

26 The ideas of Spanish "verticality" and Argentine "horizontality" are developed in Frank's *America Hispana* (1931; rev. 1940): "Spain herself is a balance of wills – Celt, Semite, Latin, Goth – all scaled to the vertical Iberian. In the gaucho the perpendicular disappears, but the rigor which produced it persists, becoming horizontal" (96).

27 *The Re-Discovery of America* (281–2).

28 These ideas are expressed in Frank's *Our America* (1919) and again in *Re-Discovery of America* (1929). MRL discusses Frank in relation to Eduardo Mallea's essay "Historia de una pasión argentina" (1937); their texts "reflect one another like reciprocal mirrors," but Mallea "does not repeat or interpret the message of Frank. He reconstructs the experience of exaltation that message awoke in him" (Lojo, *Los viajeros intelectuales*, 78, 80). Frank is a model and hero for Mallea; by contrast, he bitterly rejects Keyserling (73).

29 Eduardo Mallea's first book, *Cuentos para una inglesa desesperada* (1926) (Stories for a Desperate Englishwoman). Unlike the fictional Frank, César Aira comments apropos of *Cuentos* that Mallea always came up with felicitous titles (*Diccionario de autores latinoamericanos*, 336).

30 This description of VO's house in Palermo Chico condenses that of Waldo Frank – the best ever, according to Beatriz Sarlo (*La máquina cultural*, 182). Frank writes: "the house emblem – coat-of-arms of its owner – is the *cactus*," and then: "Victoria Ocampo, woman of Argentina and America, in her cult of light, in her work of structure within the chaos of the pampa motion, has learned that she must clasp the bitter cactus in her hand, clasp it against her breast. She has prophesied for her country" (*America Hispana*, 126–8). (For A. Bustillo, see 218n13.)

31 María Rosa Oliver and Frank sustained a lasting friendship. Ideologically they were well matched; Oliver was a Communist, Frank a Communist sympathizer. Oliver translated *City Block*, retaining the original English title (Editorial Manuel Gleizer, 1937). Luis Saslavsky (Argentine filmmaker, 1903–1995) assured her that John Dos Passos's *Manhattan Transfer* was a pastiche of Frank's lesser-known *City Block* (Oliver, *La vida cotidiana*, 256, 258).

32 Pedro Henríquez Ureña (1884–1946), influential writer and intellectual from the Dominican Republic. His *Literary Currents in Hispanic America* (1945) was for decades a standard reference work in North America. For his legendary erudition, Borges called him "a precise museum of literatures" (Aira, *Diccionario*, 272).

33 Ricardo Rojas (1882–1957), author of the massive *La literatura argentina. Ensayo filosófico sobre la evolución de la cultura en el Plata* (1917–1922) (The Literature of Argentina: A Philosophical Essay on the Evolution of Culture in the River Plate). He coined the term *argentinidad* (Argentinity) in his historical essay thus titled (1910). Another neologism, *Eurindia* (1924), attempted a more inclusive renaming of Latin America, but never entered common usage. Rojas authored popular biographies of major historical figures; for example, General José de San Martín (1933) and Faustino Domingo Sarmiento (1945).

34 Jean Toomer (1894–1967), white American poet and novelist commonly associated (against his will) with the Harlem Renaissance. His novel *Cane* (1923) was written after working as a school principal in a black school in Sparta, rural Georgia.

35 Keyserling had written: "one may well violate a woman, but never force her to willing surrender, and only he really possesses her to whom she gave herself of her own free will" (*Travel Diary*, vol. 2, 354). Victoria seems deliberately to skewer Keyserling with his own words.

36 Reference to *Carmen*, the novel by Prosper Mérimée (1845) and the more famous opera by Georges Bizet (1875).

37 *Seven Arts* appeared monthly from November 1916 to October 1917. One of the "little magazines" rejecting the commercial model of the big American publications, its mandate was both literary and social. Van Wyck Brooks, participant in *Seven Arts* and Waldo Frank's biographer, stated that Frank was the magazine's "real creator" (qtd. by Carter, 31).

38 Allusion to "El jardín de los senderos que se bifurcan," the title story of Jorge Luis Borges's 1941 collection of short stories. English translation: "The Garden of the Forking Paths" (Borges, *Labyrinths*, 19–29). Borges dedicated this story to Victoria Ocampo.

39 After ignoring the *martinfierristas* in the '20s, VO recruited Borges for *Sur*; the two were ideological allies, their squabbles notwithstanding. Marechal, by contrast, by endorsing Peronism in the 1940s, broke ranks with the vehemently anti-Peronist *Sur* group. After a respectful 1939 article on VO and women's literature, Marechal, in *Adam Buenosayres* (1948), satirically caricatures Ocampo in the mock-inferno of Cacodelphia; in the circle of Lust she appears as Titania, one of the Ultras: "ultra-courtesans, ultra-poetesses, ultra-intellectuals" (493–6). Mocked are VO's feminism, her writing, her condition as an intellectual (Lojo, "Victoria Ocampo, personaje de novela," 180). This caricature, however, is just one among dozens in the novel, albeit the most offensive to our contemporary sensibilities. When Adam Buenosayres remarks on the "excessive theatricality" of the Ultras, he anticipates what Carmen Brey will see in VO (page 31). When Schultz accuses Titania of "troll[ing] the American continent" and abroad "to attract numerous male specimens, all of them

refined in the use and abuse of intelligence," he simply voices more brutally what many men of Ocampo's acquaintance thought privately. Her friend André Malraux, for example, openly teased vo about her "collection of great men" (Liendo, 23n53). Schultz's remark on Titania's "detestable mania for subordinating things of the spirit to the vague, exquisite, ineffable titillations of her 'sensibility'" strips away the courteous patina from Ortega's patronizing comments on vo's *De Francesca a Beatrice*, his epilogue qualified by Sarlo as "gallant, flattering, condescending, and full of devious criticisms [*reparos sibilinos*]" (*Una máquina cultural*, 124). As Guillermo de Torre found out in a "discreet survey" among friends, most women felt that Keyserling's representations of vo were a homage (*homenaje*) rather than an affront (*agravio*) (108); one man of the same intimate circle sympathized with Keyserling's sense of her betrayal (108–9). In Cacodelphia, "city of ugly brothers," Marechal comically exaggerates vices, failings, hypocrisies, bad attitudes – including common perceptions of the notorious vo-Keyserling affair. Aguilar and Siskind suggest that vo's response to Keyserling in *El viajero y una de sus sombras* (1951) (The Traveller and One of his Shades/Phantasms) was also a response to Marechal's satire (377n). See also Cheadle, "La 'Titania' de Marechal revisitada."

40 "Snobism and gender are conjoined in the misogyny shared by men [on both the right and the left] at the beginning of the twentieth century" (Liendo, 13). "One could almost say that the adjective 'snob' turns out to be quite handy to delegitimate a woman who wants to do 'things proper to men' such as read, write, or publish. // It is no surprise, then, given the time and her character, that Argentine society reduced Victoria Ocampo from the very beginning to the stereotype of 'the snob' ... The historian José Luis Romero seems to understand this phenomenon better than most of his contemporaries: 'Almost no one ever said it to her, perhaps because saying it outright is not the way of snobs; but she had nothing of the snob about her, except for the sin of being their model'" (qtd. by Liendo, 13). Romero seems very close to René Girard's theory of mimetic desire.

41 vo and Lacan argued over Cocteau's monodrama, *La Voix humaine* (1930), in which a young woman on stage talks on the telephone with her lover (offstage) who is about to marry another woman.

42 Josefina de Atucha and Adela "Tota" de Atucha, daughters of an aristocratic Argentine family. It was through Josefina that vo met Lacan. Tota de Atucha was at once vo's friend and competitor. A free-wheeling libertine, Tota was deep into the Surrealist scene and had an affair with Luis Buñuel. Through Tota vo met Le Corbusier, Mary McCarthy, Marie-Laure de Noailles, and *The Partisan Review* group (Liendo, 10–11).

43 The sea change in cultural politics, after the 1930 military coup, could not have helped vo's project to bring a Communist, Soviet filmmaker to Buenos Aires

(Neifert, 114–15). The VO-Eisenstein friendship was long-lived, despite their diametrically opposed politics. Thrilled by ¡*Viva México!* (1932), VO wished Eisenstein could film another "documentary poem" about Argentina (qtd. in Neifert,
115) – a great opportunity lost, as Neifert agrees (116).

44 The Panama canal episode condenses VO's account, which in turn seems to reference Waldo Frank's "Prelude: The Canal": "Like a dragon's back, the mountains bristle from Alaska to Tierra del Fuego ... At Panamá there is only mountain. The Atlantic and the Pacific have crept up until naught is left, neither to
east nor west, but the Andean backbone ... Up and down went [Columbus's]
blind ships, seeking the water passage through the mountain ... Panamá threw
Columbus back on Spain. Yet he was right ... He was off reckoning on time – a
few centuries too soon, a few eons too late – the way of mystics who with their
tragic lives bind past and future" (*America Hispana*, 3, 5). VO dimly echoes
Frank's poetic vision: "It had been necessary to cut the spine of America's back
(our old Cordillera), to open this road through, this communication ... Columbus must have set foot on this coast and left from here, discouraged, to go and
die an obscure death in Valladolid [Spain]" (*Autobiografía, III*, 202).

45 Antofagasta was one among several stops the *Santa Clara* made along the Pacific
coast. "Those desert-like places of the Peruvian and Chilean coast, inhabited by
mestizos in rags and malnourished Indians, drove me to neurasthenia" (*Autobiografía, III*, 203). The anecdote of the flower – in Spanish, *floripón* – is recounted
as well (203).

46 Cf. a contemporaneous letter (16 June 1930) from VO to Frank: "Waldo dear,
what has happened to the Spanish race? Panama and Peru fill me with dismay
just as our provinces and Uruguay do. In fact, to live in South America free from
dismay I need to remain within the tiny little circle I've made for myself" (qtd.
in the original French by Rostagno, 22; my translation).

47 Thomas McGann summarizes: "The career of Yrigoyen is a curious epitome or
parallel of the rise and decline of Argentine liberalism ... He was a criollo petit-
bourgeois who attained the summit of political power in 1916 as leader of the
middle class that emerged, especially after 1880, out of the favorable economic
conditions created by the classical liberalism of the oligarchy ... Many members
of the middle class found that they were not too uncomfortable sharing
political power with the conservatives ... Middle-class aspirations turned out
to be close to the accomplishments of the upper class" (37). The coup of 6 September 1930 re-established the political control of the oligarchy, now "a plutoc-
racy" of "neo-oligarchs [who] were heirs, literally and ideologically, of the conservatives of the generation of 1880, but ... no longer faithful to the liberalism
that had motivated the leaders of the previous era" (McGann, 39–40).
(Cf. 207n44.)

48 Reference to an insult proffered by Paul Groussac and quoted by Borges in his note "El arte de injuriar" (The Art of the Insult): without naming Rojas, Groussac refers to "that copious history of what organically never existed" (Borges, *Obras completas*, vol. 1, 421). Borges himself, in a review of Gilbert Waterhouse's *A Short History of German Literature*, refers in passing to the "paradoxical Doctor Rojas (whose history of Argentine literature is longer than Argentine literature)" (279). The poisoned barb embedded in a parenthesis is a stylistic trademark of Borges, which MRL pointedly reproduces in this passage.

49 A condensation of various statements made by Rojas (email from MRL, 15 January 2020). MRL defends Rojas's thought in her article "La condición humana en la obra de Ricardo Rojas" (The Human Condition in the Work of Ricardo Rojas).

50 The arrow logo on the cover of *Sur* graphically illustrates Ortega's influence, as though it had been shot by the archer of the logo marking a book series ("El Arquero") from Ortega's Editorial Revista de Occidente (the publishing arm of the journal). That *exlibris* shows an archer standing with bow drawn, the arrow pointing leftward, or westward, toward America. (Aristotle's metaphor of the archer who aims at ethical truth was one of Ortega's favourites). "The influence of the *Revista de Occidente* in Spain and Spanish America cannot be exaggerated … *Sur* was modelled on [its] universalist, multidisciplinary approach." Later issues of both *Revista de Occidente* (no. 37, 1984) and *Sur* (nos. 352–3, 1983) would document the parallels between the two journals (King, 39).

51 Norah Borges (1901–1998), plastic and graphic artist, intimate of the *Martín Fierro* group, illustrator of the famous children's book *Platero y yo*, by Juan Ramón Jiménez, and other books by Spanish emigrés in Argentina. Lino Enea Spilimbergo (1896–1964) and Héctor Basaldúa (1895–1976) were among the Grupo de París – Argentine plastic artists working in the French capital in the 1920s and '30s. Outside this group was Emilio Pettoruti (1892–1971); his 1924 vernissage at Friends of the Arts scandalized the local critics, but delighted *Martín Fierro* (10–11 September–9 October 1924).

52 These photos have circulated widely (see Google Images). Guillermo de Torre (1900–1971), author of the encyclopedic *Historia de las literaturas de vanguardia* (1925; updated and augmented 1962). Oliverio Girondo (1891–1967), a major poet to whom the original "Manifesto" of *Martín Fierro* is generally attributed. Canadian poet and translator Hugh Hazelton has recently published the first volume (the second is forthcoming) of *The Complete Works of Oliverio Girondo*.

53 Samuel Glusberg (1898–1987) brought Waldo Frank to Buenos Aires, having raised funds from the University of Buenos Aires and the Argentine-North American Institute of Culture (King, 40). Glusberg (pen name Enrique Espinoza) was also the publisher of successive journals: *Ediciones Selectas*

América (1919–22); *Babel* (1921–29); *La Vida Literaria* (1928–31). *Babel* had been non-polemical and open to writers of all orientations; *La Vida Literaria* "maintained the vitality of the Argentine intellectual scene at a difficult moment" (Lafleur, 138). "He was a self-made man, conscious of his modest social origins, and was not at home in the aristocratic milieu of much of Argentine cultural life" (King, 41). Glusberg's pan-Americanism made him Frank's natural interlocutor, and Frank initially had him and José Carlos Mariátegui in mind for his project of an inter-American journal to be called *Nuestra América*. The idea to involve Victoria Ocampo came later, after Frank met her in Buenos Aires at Friends of the Arts (King, 42). Frank acknowledges Samuel Glusberg in *America Hispana* (1931) as first among those "who helped me most" in accessing the necessary bibliographical material (xi). Glusberg's exclusion from *Sur* disappointed Frank: "Victoria founded *Sur*, and a very respectable display of culture it turned out to be. But Glusberg, the dynamic immigrant Jew with a Prophet's America in his heart [also Frank's own self-concept], and Victoria Ocampo, princess of good taste, separated almost as soon as they met. My cultural union remained a dream. My concept of the magazine as an organism meant nothing to Victoria for whom most of the American and Hispano-American authors, loved by Glusberg more for promise and intent than for complete achievement, also had no meaning. The elegant *Sur* published many a good piece, but it was remote from what I wanted and the hemisphere needed" (*Memoirs*, 171). He adds: "María Rosa Oliver wanted the magazine I wanted. Victoria could not work with her" (171). Here he overstates the case; María Rosa worked on *Sur*'s editorial board until 1958, the year her acceptance of the Lenin Prize alienated Ocampo. Frank concludes: "The ideational split of Victoria, Glusberg, and María Rosa was a symbol. The 'parts' of America were not yet ready to grow together" (171).

54 Jean Anthelme Brillat-Savarin was author of *Physiologie du goût* (1825), a famous book on gastronomy. Victoria's verbal slip was to write *alverjas* (peas), a form of the word widely used in southern Spain and Spanish America, instead of the "correct" form *arvejas* (also peas). Her error supposedly betrays a lack of sophistication; it would be roughly comparable to saying in English (à la George W. Bush) "noucular" for "nuclear," except that *alverja* is an old form and quite natural in Spanish, with its very numerous Arabic-derived words beginning with *al* (such as "alcohol"). In fact, the DRAE now lists *alverja* as a variant of *arveja* (< Latin "ervilia") with no comment on its (in)correctness.

55 The first issue of *Sur* carried a note by Borges on "El colonel Ascasubi," nineteenth-century author of a famous version of *Santos Vega*. But earlier, in his 1930 book *Evaristo Carriego*, he had written about "Las inscripciones de los carros." He was enthusiastic about the "poetry" of the old horse-drawn freight wagons, inscribed by their owners with a name, often a short pithy phrase, much as fish-

ermen name their boats. Apparently, some photographs of such wagon-inscriptions were included in *Sur*.

56 Letter from Waldo Frank to VO, 25 February 1931. This translation works with three different versions: 1) Meyer's English translation (114); 2) VO's 1967 Spanish version in "Posdata (Waldo Frank y *Sur*)" (*Testimonios, series sexta a décima* [98–9]); and 3) VO's Spanish 1980 version (*Autobiografía, III* [219–20]). Each version has significant variations. VO-1967 mentions not Glusberg but "Z." In VO-1980, "Z" becomes "G." After extensive interviews with VO, Meyer apparently felt authorized to name Samuel Glusberg. The parenthesis "(if it was him)" indicates that Frank was unsure, or incredulous, about the identity of the harsh critic, whose words VO paraphrased herself, as indicated when Frank writes: "Lo malo del artículo que me comenta es que está contaminado por una suerte de chauvinismo [*sic*] literario" (*Testimonios*, 99) (What's bad about the article you've told me about is that it is contaminated by a kind of *literary chauvinism*) (italics mine). In VO-1980, Frank's letter specifies "G." as the putative author of an article "marcado por una suerte de patrioterismo" (marked by a kind of *flag-waving patriotism*) (italics mine) – a definite uptick in rhetorical vehemence. VO-1967 speaks of Frank's "disappointment" with "Z"; VO-1980, of his "frustration" with "G." Leaving that sentence out of her translation, Meyer comments in her own words that "Frank was dismayed by Glusberg's criticism" (114). From the textual evidence one can infer that VO exaggerated Glusberg's criticism in her report to Waldo Frank, and then progressively exaggerated Frank's reaction to that same criticism. It is difficult to imagine the Americanist Glusberg as a "flag-waving chauvinist."

57 *Peregrino* means "pilgrim." Santiago de Compostela, in Galicia, is at end of the Camino de Santiago, goal of the pilgrimage established in the Middle Ages. The phrase "secular pilgrimage" points up the religious quality of Don Peregrino's socialism, which Carmen apparently shares.

Bibliography

MARÍA ROSA LOJO: SELECTED BIBLIOGRAPHY

(For complete bibliography, see http://www.mariarosalojo.com.ar/.)

Novelas and creative non-fiction

Lojo, María Rosa. *La pasión de los nómades*. Buenos Aires: Atlántida, 1994. Debolsillo, 2014. In English: *Passionate Nomads*. Translated by Brett Sanders. Minneapolis: Aliform, 2011.

– *Una mujer de fin de siglo*. Buenos Aires: Planeta, 1999. Debolsillo Random House, 2007.

– *Una mujer de fin de siglo*. Introduction and notes by Malva Filer. Stockcero, 2007.

– *Amores insólitos de nuestra historia*. Buenos Aires: Alfaguara, 2001 and 2019.

– *Las libres del Sur*. Buenos Aires: Sudamericana, 2004. Debolsillo, 2013.

– *Finisterre*. Buenos Aires: Sudamericana, 2005.

– *Todos éramos hijos*. Buenos Aires: Sudamericana, 2014.

– *Solo queda saltar*. Buenos Aires: Santillana, 2018.

Selected scholarly works

Lojo, María Rosa (ed.) et al. *Lucía Miranda* (1860, 1882), by Eduarda Mansilla. Frankfurt and Madrid: Editorial Vervuert-Iberoamericana, 2007.

Lojo, María Rosa (ed.), Marina Guidotti de Sánchez, and Ruy Farías. *Los "gallegos" en el imaginario argentino: literatura, sainete, prensa*. Vigo; La Coruña: Fundación Pedro Barrié de la Maza, 2008.

Lojo, María Rosa (ed.) and Enzo Cárcano (co-editor). *Leopoldo Marechal y el canon del siglo XXI*. Pamplona: EUNSA, 2017.

Lojo, María Rosa. "Buenos Aires en dos viajeros de Victoria Ocampo: Rabindranath Tagore y José Ortega y Gasset." In *La ciudad imaginaria*, edited by Javier de Navascués, 205–22. Madrid and Frankfurt: Iberoamericana-Ververt, 2007.

– "Eduarda Mansilla y Victoria Ocampo: escritoras y personajes de novela." *Revista de Literaturas Modernas* 41 (2011): 36–55.

– "Ernesto Sabato y Hermann von Keyserling: ¿afinidades electivas? Sudamérica, el continente ciego." *Inti. Revista de Literatura Hispánica* 71–2 (2010): 9–27.

– "Escritoras argentinas del siglo XIX y etnias aborígenes del Cono Sur." In *La mujer en la literatura del mundo hispánico*, edited by Juana Alcira Arancibia, 43–63. Westminster: Instituto Literario y Cultural Hispánico de California, 2009.

– "Escritoras y secretarias." *Telar. Revista del Instituto Interdisciplinario de Estudios Latinoamericana* 4 (2006): 17–30. http://www.filo.unt.edu.ar/rev/telar/revistas/telar4.pdf.

– "Genealogías femeninas en la tradición literaria. Entre la excepcionalidad y la representatividad." *Alba de América* 47–48.25 (2006): 467–85.

– "Género, nación y cosmopolitismo en Eduarda Mansilla y Victoria Ocampo." *Alba de América* 55–56.29 (2010): 137–49.

– "Independizarse de España: Avatares intelectuales de una relación bicentenaria." *Revista de Historia Americana y Argentina* 52.1 (2017): 199–232.

– "La condición humana en la obra de Ricardo Rojas." Pablo Guadarrama González, coord. *El pensamiento latinoamericano del siglo XX ante la condición humana.* 2004. www.ensayistas.org/critica/generales/CH/argentina/rojas.htm.

– "La 'Patria Hija' de Leopoldo Marechal." *Cuadernos del Hipogrifo. Revista de Literatura Hispanoamericana y Comparada* 14 (2020): 172–86.

– "Las escritoras del siglo XIX: Del silencio a la ficción biográfica." In *Historia feminista de la literatura argentina*, edited by Laura Arnés, Nora Domínguez, and María José Punte. Villa María: Eduvim, forthcoming.

– "María Rosa Oliver (1898–1977) y Victoria Ocampo (1890–1979): Dos maneras de narrar el Yo." *Mora* 23 (2017): 149–58.

– "Victoria Ocampo, personaje de novela. Un laboratorio de crítica y creación." In *Penelope e le altre*, edited by Rosa Maria Grillo, 179–87. Salerno: Centro Studi Americanistici, Circolo Amerindiano; Oédipus, 2012.

– "Victoria Ocampo: un duelo con la sombra del viajero." *Lectura y Signo* 2 (2007): 355–66.

VICTORIA OCAMPO: SELECTED BIBLIOGRAPHY

Ocampo, Victoria. *Autobiografía, I: El archipiélago – El imperio insular.* Buenos Aires: Ediciones Fundación Victoria Ocampo, 2005.

– *Autobiografía, II: La rama de Salzburgo – Viraje.* Buenos Aires: Ediciones Fundación Victoria Ocampo, 2005.

– *Autobiografía, III: Figuras simbólicas. Medida de Francia. Sur y Cía.* Buenos Aires: Ediciones Fundación Victoria Ocampo, 2006.

– *Testimonios, series primera a quinta.* Edición de Eduardo Paz Leston. Buenos Aires: Sudamericana, 1999.

– *Testimonios, series sexta a décima.* Edición de Eduardo Paz Leston. Buenos Aires: Sudamericana, 2000.

– *La mujer y su expresión.* Buenos Aires: Editorial Sur, 1936.

– *La laguna de los nenúfares.* Madrid: Revista de Occidente, 1926.

– *De Francesca a Beatrice.* Madrid: Revista de Occidente, 1924.

WORKS CITED: GENERAL

Abós, Álvaro. *El tábano.* Buenos Aires: Sudamericana, 2001.

– *Macedonio Fernández: la biografía imposible.* Buenos Aires: Plaza & Janés, 2002.

Aguilar, Gonzalo, and Mariano Siskind. "Los viajeros culturales en la Argentina (1928–1942)." In *El imperio realista,* edited by María Teresa Gramuglio, 367–91. Volume 6 of *Historia crítica de la literatura argentina,* edited by Noé Jitrik. Buenos Aires: Emecé, 2002.

Aira, César. *Diccionario de autores latinoamericanos.* Buenos Aires: Emecé, 2001.

Allison, Victoria. "White Evil: Peronist Argentina in the US Popular Imagination Since 1955." *American Studies International* 42.1 (2004): 4–48.

Arancibia, Juana A., Malva Filer, and Rosa Tezanos-Pinto, eds. *María Rosa Lojo: la reunión de lejanías.* Westminster: Instituto Literario y Cultural Hispánico de California, 2007.

Baudelaire, Charles. *Les Fleurs du mal.* Paris: Hatier, 2011.

Borges, Jorge Luis. *Obras completas,* vol. 1. Buenos Aires: Emecé, 1996.

– *Obras completas,* vol. 4. Buenos Aires: Emecé, 2005.

– *Selected Poems 1923–1967: A Bilingual Edition.* Edited by Norman Thomas di Giovanni. New York: Delacorte Press, 1972.

– *Labryrinths: Selected Stories and Other Writings.* Edited by Donald A. Yates and James E. Irby. New York: New Directions, 1964.

– *Texto recobrados (1931–1955)*. Buenos Aires: Emecé, 2001.

Bruno, Paula, coord. *Visitas culturales en la Argentina 1898–1936*. Buenos Aires: Biblos, 2014.

Cabello Hutt, Claudia. "Working to Pay for a Room of One's Own: Modern Women Writers in Latin America." *Tulsa Studies in Women's Literture*, 30.1 (spring 2019): 39–58.

Carter, Paul J. *Waldo Frank*. New York: Twayne Publishers, 1967.

Carroll, David. *French Literary Fascism: Nationalism, Anti-Semitism, and the Ideology of Culture*. Princeton, New Jersey: Princeton University Press, 1996.

Castro, Rosalía de. *Obra poética*. Ed. Benito Varel Jácome. Barcelona: Bruguera, 1972.

– *Cantares gallegos*. Ed. Ricardo Carballo Calero. Salamanca: Anaya, 1963.

Chapman, Arnold. "Waldo Frank in the Hispanic World: The First Phase." *Hispania* 44.4 (December 1961): 626–34.

– "Waldo Frank in Spanish America: Between Journeys, 1924–1929." *Hispania* 47.3 (September 1964): 510–21.

Cheadle, Norman. "Between Wandering Rocks: Joyce's *Ulysses* in the Argentine Culture Wars." In *TransLatin Joyce: Global Transmissions in Ibero-American Literature*, edited by Brian L. Price, César A. Salgado, and John Pedro Schwartz, 57–87. New York: Palgrave, 2014.

– "La «Titania» de Marechal revisitada." *Cuadernos del Hipogrifo. Revista de Literatura Hispanoamericana y Comparada* 14 (2020): 129–45.

Corral, Rose. Estudio introductorio. *Libra 1929: Edición facsimilar*. Mexico: Colegio de México, 2003. 13–37.

Cosse, Isabella. "La lucha por los derechos femeninos: Victoria Ocampo y la Unión Argentina de Mujeres (1936)." *Revista Humanitas* 26.34 (2008): 131–49.

Crespo Buiturón, Marcela. "Poéticas de exilio: María Rosa Lojo, un resquicio ontológico en la dimensión política." *A Contracorriente* 8.3 (2011): 116–39.

– *La memoria de la llanura. Los marginales de María Rosa Lojo usurpan el protagonismo de la Historia*. Lleida, Spain: Edicions Universitat de Lleida, 2013.

Crespo Buiturón, Marcela, ed. *Diálogo de voces. Nuevas lecturas sobre la obra de María Rosa Lojo*. Raleigh, North Carolina: Editorial A Contracorriente, 2018.

Cuerda, Cecilia G. "La orquesta sinfónica en las sociedades musicales de Buenos Aires: Asociación del profesorado orquestal." *Revista del Instituto de Investigación Musicológica "Carlos Vega"* 16.16 (2000): 91–112.

Cyr, Myriam. *Letters of a Portuguese Nun: Uncovering the Mystery Behind a 17th Century Forbidden Love*. New York: Hyperion, 2006.

Desanti, Dominique. *Drieu La Rochelle. Le séducteur mystifié*. Paris: Flammarion, 1978.

De Torre, Guillermo. "Victoria Ocampo, memorialista." In *Tres conceptos de la literatura hispanoamericana*, 96–114. Buenos Aires: Losada, 1963.

Dillon, Susana. *Las locas del camino*. Río Cuarto, Argentina: Universidad de Río Cuarto, 2005.

Dujovne Ortiz, Alicia. *Eva Perón: la biografía*. Buenos Aires: Aguilar, 1995.

Diz, Tania. "Del elogio a la injuria: la escritora como mito en el imaginario cultural de los años 20 y 30." *La Biblioteca: Mitologías* 12 (spring 2012): 310–30.

Dyson, Ketaki. *See* Kushari Dyson, Ketaki.

Earle, Peter G. "Ortega y Gasset in Argentina: The Exasperating Colony." *Hispania* 70.3 (1987): 475–86.

Echeverría, Esteban. *Insurrección del Sud. Obras completas*, vol. 1. Buenos Aires: Carlos Casavalle Editor, 1870. 226–72.

Esteves, Antonio R. "(Des)tejer lo ya tejido: la representación de escritoras." *Islas* 53 (2011): 98–120.

Falcoff, Mark, and Ronald H. Dolkart, eds. *Prologue to Perón: Argentina in Depression and War, 1930–1943*. Berkeley: University of California Press, 1975.

Fernández, Macedonio. *No toda es vigilia la de los ojos abiertos y otros escritos*. Buenos Aires: Centro Editor de América, 1967.

Fernández Bravo, Álvaro. Introduction to *Mi fe es el hombre* by María Rosa Oliver, 9–49. Buenos Aires: Biblioteca Nacional, 2008.

Figueiras, Miguel Ángel. *Cacique y coronel del ejército argentino. Y[gnacio] Coliqueo y su tribu*. [no publisher given], 1991.

Filer, Malva. "'Finisterre': Europeos e indígenas en María Rosa Lojo." *Hispamérica* 35.105 (2006): 119–24.

Fiorucci, Flavia. "El antiperonismo intelectual." In *Fascismo y antifascismo. Peronismo y antiperonismo: Conflictos políticos e ideológicos en la Argentina (1930–1955)*, edited by Marcela García Sebastiani, 161–93. Madrid: Iberoamericana/Vervuert, 2006.

Frank, Waldo. *The Re-Discovery of America: An Introduction to a Philosophy of American Life*. New York: Schribner's, 1929.

– *America Hispana. South of Us: The Characters of the Countries and the People of Central and South America*. New York: Garden City, 1940.

– *Memoirs of Waldo Frank*. Edited by Alan Trachtenberg. Introduction by Lewis Mumford. Amherst: University of Massachusetts Press, 1973.

Fraser, Nicholas, and Marysa Navarro. *Eva Perón*. London: Deutsch, 1980.

Galasso, Norberto. *Dos Argentinas: Arturo Jauretche, Victoria Ocampo. Correspondencia inédita: sus vidas, sus ideas*. Rosario: Homo Sapiens Ediciones, 1996.

– *Vida de Scalabrini Ortiz*. Buenos Aires: Ediciones del Mar Dulce, 1970.

Gallo, Edit Rosalía. *Las mujeres en el radicalismo argentino, 1890–1991*. Buenos Aires: Eudeba, 2001.

– *Nuestra Causa: Revista Mensual Feminista, 1919–1921. Estudio e índice general*. Buenos Aires: Instituto de Investigaciones Históricas Cruz del Sur, 2004.

García Lorca, Federico. *Poet in Spain*. Translation, selection, introduction, and notes by Sarah Arvio. New York: Knopf, 2017.

González, María Soledad. *Victoria Ocampo: Escritura, poder y representaciones*. Rosario, Argentina: Prohistoria Ediciones, 2018.

González Ródenas, Soledad. "Zenobia Camprubí, traductora." In *Zenobia Camprubí y la Edad de Plata de la cultura española*, edited by Emilia Cortés Ibáñez, 239–64. Seville: Universidad Internacional de Andalucía, 2010.

Greenberg, Janet. "A Question of Blood: The Conflict of Sex and Class in the Autobiography of Victoria Ocampo." Seminar on Feminism and Culture in Latin America. In *Women, Culture, and Politics in Latin America*, 130–50. Berkeley: University of California Press, 1990.

Grossman, Edith, trans. *Don Quixote*, by Miguel de Cervantes. New York: HarperCollins, 2003.

Guy, Donna. *Sex and Danger in Buenos Aires: Prostitution, Family, and Nation in Argentina*. Lincoln and London: University of Nebraska Press, 1991.

Havard, Robert G. *From Romanticism to Surrealism: Seven Spanish Poets*. Cardiff: University of Wales Press and Barnes & Noble, 1988.

Horan, Elizabeth, and Doris Meyer, eds. and trans. *This America of Ours: The Letters of Gabriela Mistral and Victoria Ocampo*. Austin: University of Texas Press, 2003.

Jung, Carl Gustav. *C.G. Jung Speaking: Interviews and Encounters*. Edited by William McGuire and R.F.C. Hull. London: Princeton University Press, 1977.

Keyserling, Hermann von. *The Travel Diary of a Philosopher*, 2 vols. Translated by J. Holroyd Reece. New York: Harcourt, Brace, 1925.

– *South American Meditations: On Hell and Heaven in the Soul of Man*. Translated by Theresa Duerr. New York and London: Harper, 1932. Facsimile printed by University Microfilms International, 1982.

King, John. Sur: *A Study of the Argentine Literary Journal and Its Role in the Development of a Culture, 1931–1970*. Cambridge University Press, 1986. https://www.cambridge.org/core/books/sur/B73C36AE8112FE99768EC4EC06 D43ECD.

Kushari Dyson, Ketaki. *In Your Blossoming Flower-Garden. Rabindranath Tagore and Victoria Ocampo*. 1988. New Delhi: Sahitya Akademi, 2017.

Lacan, Jacques. *Livre XX: Encore*. Texte établi par Jacques-Alain Miller. Paris: Seuil, 1975.

Laclau, Ernesto. *On Populist Reason*. London: Verso, 2005.

Lafleur, Héctor R., Sergio D. Provenzano, and Fernando P. Alonso. *Las revistas literarias argentinas (1893-1967)*. 1968. Prólogo de Marcela Croce. Buenos Aires: El Octavo Loco Ediciones, 2006.

Liendo, Victoria. "Victoria Ocampo: una esnob para el desierto argentino." *Cuadernos* LIRICO 16 (2017). http://journals.openedition.org/lirico/3761.

Livy. *Rome's Mediterranean Empire: Books 41–45 and the Periochae*. Edited by Jane D. Chaplin. Oxford University Press, 2007. ProQuest Ebook.

Lucie-Smith, Edward. *Latin American Art of the Twentieth Century*. London: Thames & Hudson, 2004.

Ludmer, Josefina. *El cuerpo del delito: un manual*. Buenos Aires: Perfil Libros, 1999.

Mansilla, Eduarda. *Lucía Miranda* (1860, 1882). Edition, introduction, and notes by María Rosa Lojo, with the collaboration of Marina Guidotti, Hebe Molina, Claudia Pelossi, María Laura Pérez Gras, and Silvia Vallejo. Frankfurt and Madrid: Editorial Vervuert-Iberoamericana, 2007.

– *Recuerdos de viaje* (1882). Edición de J.P. Spicer Escalante. Stockcero, 2006.

Mansilla, Lucio Victoriano. *Una excursión a los indios ranqueles* (1870). Edición y prólogo de C.A. Leumann. Buenos Aires: Espasa-Calpe, 1962. In English: *A Visit to the Ranquel Indians*. Translated by Eva Gillies. Lincoln and London: University of Nebraska Press, 1997.

Masiello, Francine. *Between Civilization and Barbarism: Women, Nation, and Literary Culture in Modern Argentina*. Lincoln: University of Nebraska Press, 1992.

McGann, Thomas F. *Argentina: The Divided Land*. Princeton, New Jersey: Van Nostrand, 1966.

Marechal, Leopoldo. *Adán Buenosayres*. 1948. Edición crítica de Javier de Navascués. Buenos Aires: Corregidor, 2013. In English: *Adam Buenosayres*. Translated by Norman Cheadle and Sheila Ethier. Introduction and notes by Norman Cheadle. Montreal: McGill-Queen's University Press, 2014.

– "Victoria Ocampo y la literatura femenina." *Obras completas*, vol. 5. Buenos Aires: Perfil, 1998293–297. [Original: *Sur* 52 (January 1939): 66–70.]

Martínez, Tomás Eloy. *Santa Evita*. Buenos Aires: Planeta, 1995. In English: *Santa Evita*. Translated by Helen Lane. New York: Knopf, 1996.

Martínez Estrada, Ezequiel. *Radiografía de la pampa*. 8th edition. Buenos Aires: Losada, 1976. English translation: *X-Ray of the Pampa*. Austin: University of Texas Press, 1971.

Márquez Llano, Eduardo. *Los mapuches voroganos en la historia bonaerense y en el partido de Bolívar*. Instituto de Investigaciones Históricas Juan Manuel de Rosas, 1991.

Meyer, Doris. *Victoria Ocampo: Against the Wind and the Tide*. With a selection of essays by Victoria Ocampo, translated by Doris Meyer. Austin: University of Texas Press, 1979.

Milleret, Jean de. *Entretiens avec Jorge Luis Borges*. Paris: Editions Pierre Belfond, 1967.

Molloy, Sylvia. "The Theatrics of Reading: Body and Book in Victoria Ocampo." In *At Face Value: Autobiographical Writing in Spanish America*, 55–75. Cambridge University Press, 1991.

– "Victoria viajera: crónica de un aprendizaje." In *La viajera y sus sombras* by Victoria Ocampo, selection and prologue by Sylvia Molly, 9–39. Mexico: Fondo de Cultura Económica, 2010.

Navarro, Marysa. "Of Sparrows and Condors: The Autobiography of Eva Perón." *The Female Autograph*. Edited by Domna C. Stanton. Chicago: University of Chicago Press, 1984.

Neifert, Agustín. "Eisenstein y Victoria Ocampo: amistad y un proyecto fallido." In *Diez escritores argentinos en el cine y otros temas*. Buenos Aires: Rosa Guarú, 2018. 107–17.

Oliver, María Rosa. *Mundo, mi casa. Recuerdos de infancia*. Buenos Aires: Falbo Librero Editor, 1965.

– *La vida cotidiana*. Buenos Aires: Sudamericana, 1969.

– *Mi fe es el hombre*. Introduction by Álvaro Fernández Bravo. Buenos Aires: Biblioteca Nacional, 2008.

Ortega y Gasset, José. *Meditación del pueblo joven y otros ensayos sobre América*. Madrid: Revista de Occidente; Alianza, 1981.

– *Meditación de nuestro tiempo. Las conferencias de Buenos Aires, 1916 y 1928*. Edited by José Luis Molinuevo. Mexico: Fondo de Cultura Económica, 1996.

– *Estudios sobre el amor*. 1964. 2nd ed. Madrid: Espasa-Calpe, 1966.

– *Revolt of the Masses*. Translation, annotation, and introduction by Anthony Kerrigan. Edited by Kenneth Moore. Foreword by Saul Bellow. Notre Dame, Indiana: University of Notre Dame Press, 1985.

Pérez Galdós, Benito. *La desheredada*. Madrid: Alianza, 1970.

Perón, Eva. *Evita: Evita Perón Tells Her Own Story*. London: Proteus, 1953. Original: *La razón de mi vida* (1951).

– *In My Own Words*. New York: New Press, 1996. Original: *Mi mensaje* (1952).

Piglia, Ricardo. *Respiración artificial*. 1980. Barcelona: Anagrama, 2001. In English: *Artificial Respiration*. Translated by Daniel Balderston. Durham, North Carolina: Duke University Press, 1994.

Popescu, Roxana Maria. *Overlooked: Representations of the Balcony in Print and*

Paint, from Boccaccio to Caillebotte. Cambridge, Massachusetts: Harvard University, ProQuest Dissertations Publishing, 2010. 3415266.

Rama, Ángel. *La aventura intelectual de Figari*. Montevideo: Ediciones Fábula, 1951.

Reeder, Jessie. "William Henry Hudson, Hybridity, and Storytelling in the Pampas." *Studies in English Literature* 56.3 (2016): 561–81.

Rein, Raanan. *Los muchachos peronistas judíos. Los argentinos judíos y el apoyo al Justicialismo*. Buenos Aires: Sudamericana, 2015. In English: *Populism and Ethnicity: Peronism and the Jews of Argentina*. Translated by Isis Sadek. Montreal: McGill-Queen's University Press, 2020.

Rostagno, Irene. "Waldo Frank's Crusade for Latin American Literature." In *Searching for Recognition: The Promotion of Latin American Literature in the United States*, 1–30. Westport, Connecticut: Greenwood Press, 1997.

Sánchez, Santiago Javier. "Del *Club del Progreso* al *Jockey Club*: transformación y refinamiento de los espacios de sociabilidad de la burguesía de Buenos Aires (1852–1882)." *Pasado y Memoria. Revista de Historia Contemporánea* 14 (2015): 151–78.

Sarlo, Beatriz. *La máquina cultural: Maestras, traductores y vanguardistas*. Buenos Aires: Ariel, 1998.

Sauter, Silvia (2005). "Tres escritoras proféticas: Ana María Fagundo, Olga Orozco y María Rosa Lojo." *Letras Femeninas* 31.2: 75–98.

Sierra, Vicente D. *Historia de la Argentina. Tomo 8: Época de Rosas. Primera parte (1829–1840)*. Buenos Aires: Editorial Científica Argentina, 1969.

Sitman, Rosalie. *Victoria Ocampo y Sur: Entre Europa y América*. Buenos Aires: Ediciones Lumière, 2003.

Tagore, Rabindranath. *Gitanjali and Fruit-Gathering*. Introduction by William Butler Yeats. New York: Macmillan, 1916.

– *The Gardener*. London: Macmillan, 1913.

Tarcus, Horacio, ed. *Diccionario biográfico de la izquierda argentina*. Buenos Aires: Emecé, 2007.

Terranova, Juan. "El escritor perdido (sobre Juan José de Soiza Reilly)." *El Interpretador* 28 (September 2006). https://revistaelinterpretador .wordpress.com/2016/12/01/el-escritor-perdido-sobre-juan-jose-de -soiza-reilly/.

Unruh, Vicky. *Performing Women and Modern Literary Culture in Latin America*. Austin: University of Texas Press, 2006.

Valenzuela, Luisa. "El juego de Carmen Brey." In Juan Alcira Arancibia et al., *María Rosa Lojo: reunión de lejanías*, 211–15.

Virgil. *Eclogues; Georgics; Aeneid I–VI*. With English translation by H. Rushton

Fairclough. Revised by G.P. Goold. Cambridge, Massachusetts: Harvard University Press, 1999.

Wilson, Jason. *Buenos Aires: A Cultural and Literary History*. Foreword by Alberto Manguel. Revised edition. Oxford: Signal Books, 2007.

Young, Michael. *The Elmhirsts of Dartington: The Creation of a Utopian Community*. London: Routledge & Kegan Paul, 1982.